GOING
HOME
IN THE
DARK

ALSO BY DEAN KOONTZ

The Forest of Lost Souls · The Bad Weather Friend · After Death · The House at the End of the World · The Big Dark Sky · Quicksilver · The Other Emily · Elsewhere · Devoted · Ashley Bell · The City · Innocence · 77 Shadow Street · What the Night Knows · Breathless · Relentless · Your Heart Belongs to Me · The Darkest Evening of the Year · The Good Guy · The Husband · Velocity · Life Expectancy · The Taking · The Face · By the Light of the Moon · One Door Away from Heaven · From the Corner of His Eye · False Memory · Seize the Night · Fear Nothing · Mr. Murder · Dragon Tears · Hideaway · Cold Fire · The Bad Place · Midnight · Lightning · Watchers · Strangers · Twilight Eyes · Darkfall · Phantoms · Whispers · The Mask · The Vision · The Face of Fear · Night Chills · Shattered · The Voice of the Night · The Servants of Twilight · The House of Thunder · The Key to Midnight · The Eyes of Darkness · Shadowfires · Winter Moon · The Door to December · Dark Rivers of the Heart · Icebound · Strange Highways · Intensity · Sole Survivor · Ticktock · The Funhouse · Demon Seed

JANE HAWK SERIES

The Silent Corner · The Whispering Room · The Crooked Staircase · The Forbidden Door · The Night Window

ODD THOMAS SERIES

Odd Thomas · Forever Odd · Brother Odd · Odd Hours · Odd Interlude · Odd Apocalypse · Deeply Odd · Saint Odd

FRANKENSTEIN SERIES

Prodigal Son · City of Night · Dead and Alive · Lost Souls · The Dead Town

MEMOIR

A Big Little Life: A Memoir of a Joyful Dog Named Trixie

GOING HOME IN THE DARK

DEAN KOONTZ

THOMAS & MERCER

Published by Thomas & Mercer, Seattle

www.apub.com

Amazon, the Amazon logo, and Thomas & Mercer are trademarks of Amazon.com, Inc., or its affiliates.

EU product safety contact:
Amazon Media EU S. à r.l.
38, avenue John F. Kennedy, L-1855 Luxembourg
amazonpublishing-gpsr@amazon.com

ISBN-13: 9781662500534 (hardcover)
ISBN-13: 9781662517792 (paperback)
ISBN-13: 9781662500527 (digital)

Cover design by Damon Freeman
Interior illustrations by Edward Bettison
Cover image: © Don Landwehrle, © Jacek Rams, © Donenko Oleksii, © Aqi / Shutterstock

Printed in the United States of America

First edition

This book is dedicated to David Brouwer.
I'm still here. Thank you!

Though a good deal is too strange to be believed, nothing is too strange to have happened.

—*Thomas Hardy*

Are you alone?
Well, I am too.
Stand together.
Our time is due.
The love of friends
Will see us through.

ONE

OUR
BELOVED
DEAD
AMIGO

READ THIS FIRST OR
LIVE TO REGRET IT FOREVER

The following story is true as far as the truth of anything can be known. All names were changed to protect the privacy—and lives—of the "four amigos" and others who endured these events. Likewise, details of the amigos' careers were altered for the same purpose but were not revised to make them either more or less impressive. Maple Grove, the town in this story, is real enough, although its name is *not* Maple Grove. Some have suggested the "four amigos" produced this story for money. Absurd. I've sworn under oath that in fact none of the four will receive a penny from this book or associated rights.

How I came to know of these events in such specific detail will cause much conjecture that I do not encourage. Already, powerful individuals in my professional life have pressured me to reveal my sources, but I have not done so—and will not—because lives are at stake. The speculation that I am the "fifth amigo" and have expunged my role in this is an unlikely theory that I will neither confirm nor deny for legal reasons.

—Dean Koontz

1

TWO POUNDS FIVE OUNCES

From Rebecca Crane's backyard, forty steps led to the beach, where sharp-billed sandpipers scurried along the fringe of foaming surf, pecking without cease for their sustenance, as if they were an enfevered species that never knew a moment of peace. That morning, she descended the stairs twelve times and climbed them eleven times before she set off on a run along the shore.

At thirty-five, Rebecca wasn't old; however, she wasn't young, either, not by the standards of her profession. In dog years, she was three times dead. If she'd been an elephant, a species that lived seventy years, she would be halfway through her life, but if she had been a gorilla, she would have as little as a week left and certainly not more than several months. If she had been a kangaroo, she would have hopped into the void perhaps twelve years earlier.

She knew the average lifespans of many animals, not because she was a veterinarian or zoologist, but because she had a healthy fear of death that was somewhat greater than the average person's healthy fear of death. She wasn't depressive or paranoid or obsessed with her mortality. Nothing like that. She had a sunny disposition and was quick to laugh even at jokes about death, though when the humor was related to something else, her laughter was more robust.

Her family history did not give her reason to worry that her life might be cut short. Her mother, Sally, was still alive and vigorous and living in Miami Beach with someone named Fernando. Her maternal grandparents, Charlie and Ruth Crane, were alive and playing ferocious pickleball with other octogenarians in Palm Springs. Sally refused to reveal the identity of her daughter's father, whom she hated for reasons she wouldn't discuss. A year earlier, she told Rebecca that he recently died because he trusted an alcoholic bungee master to measure his jumping cord for him.

Sally wasn't the most truthful person in the world, but in this case she seemed sincere. When she described how "that reckless fool" had slammed full speed into a barge full of garbage that was passing under the bungee bridge, her laughter was unmistakably genuine.

Rebecca never actually died in her dreams but woke just as she was shot or stabbed—or as she was set on fire, thrown off a cliff, run down by a truck, crammed into a wood chipper, strangled with a scarf, beheaded by a scimitar, devoured by something mysterious with a large mouth . . . Not all of her dreams ended with her murder in progress, only 97 percent of them.

As she ran south along the beach, the Pacific Ocean sparkled with morning sunshine, and a formation of pelicans glided along in concert with her. She stayed a respectful distance from the breaking surf because she'd too often drowned in her dreams or been devoured by something weird that came out of the water.

Although she didn't put a lot of faith in psychiatry, she'd gone to a therapist who fixated on her dreams and gave them more importance than she believed he should. He insisted that they were rooted in some trauma in her childhood, and his unhinged insistence eventually caused her to stop consulting him.

Yes, she was fatherless, and her mother was a piece of work, ill-suited for the responsibilities of motherhood, always running off with men who had Spanish names. However, Rebecca had grown up in a peaceful and picturesque town in the heartland, much like a place in a 1950s TV program, where she was raised by Grandpa Charlie and Grandma Ruth. Charlie and Ruth pretended to be lovebirds, though in fact they loathed each other, but it worked for them because they took great pleasure in loathing. Although her grandparents' house was a cold-war zone where poisonous words were coated in a candy of faux affection, Rebecca had wonderful friends who, with her, called themselves the four amigos. Three had fled Maple Grove after high school, but they remained in touch with one another almost two decades later.

Her violent dreams and her healthy fear of enduring a horrific death were more likely than not a consequence of her work, which was demanding and stressful. Her profession provided significant income and emotional satisfaction, but no stability, and half the people with whom she worked were crazy.

After running two miles south, she turned north toward home, though retracing her steps would not be the end of her exercise session. She needed to climb and descend the beach stairs at least six more times because she was two pounds and five ounces over her ideal weight, and she was thirty-five years old, which was almost two hundred fourteen in dog years.

Calves afire, thighs aching, abdominal muscles fluttering, she ascended the stairs from the beach for the last time that day. She stepped through her gate and, with a key, locked it behind her. As she made her way up the sloped garden path, she was dismayed to hear her labored breathing as loud and desperate as if she were again in that cornfield at midnight, fleeing from Judyface, the eleven-fingered maniac in the Judy Garland mask, whom she had failed to kill with a pitchfork in *Shriek*.

There had been a time when, after a morning run and the torture of the stairs, she had *danced* up this brick walkway, past the roses, danced with all the grace of Audrey Hepburn, with the blithe and giggly charm of Goldie Hawn.

Now, when she reached the patio, Rebecca wanted to flop on one of the chaise lounges and stare at the sea until she recovered from the near-death experience of trying to lose two pounds five ounces. However, the patio surrounded the seventy-foot pool in which she swam a hundred laps on days when she didn't run, an ordeal she could not block from memory and that she was loath to contemplate.

She stepped into the kitchen and closed the door and relocked both deadbolts against all maniacs with unusual anatomical features and weird face coverings.

From one of the two Sub-Zero refrigerators she snared a bottle of a foul-tasting but rapid-hydrating beverage rich in electrolytes. Standing in the stink of her sweat, she consumed the witch's brew without the grimacing that would have promoted fine wrinkles at the corners of her eyes.

The exterior of her house was classic Cape Cod. Shingled roof. Shingled walls. Glossy white millwork. The interior, however, was sleek and ultramodern.

Rebecca liked to think the house was the opposite of her; she was Hollywood glamour on the outside, when she wasn't sweating like a pig in a luau pit, but a small-town down-home girl-next-door type on the inside. She could be just as happy if she had to give up her acting career and earn a living as a waitress in a diner. That was what her publicists wanted her to be, but she believed it was more or less who she really was, just Becky Crane from Maple Grove, except for the wanting-to-be-a-waitress thing.

As she stood in her enormous kitchen—with its full array of stainless-steel appliances and Brazilian-blue quartzite countertops, her perspiration spattering the honed limestone floor—she found it amazing that she'd come from a picturesque backwater like Maple Grove to the bright lights and scary dysfunction of Los Angeles, from girl nerd to celebrated performer, in only seventeen years.

Although the time seemed to have passed faster than clocks could account it, her success had not come overnight. For three years, she'd worked at this and that—as a dog walker, a personal trainer, a waffle-house hostess . . . For two shameful months, she'd engaged in phone sales, making cold calls to peddle something called the Golden Years Medicine Cabinet to seniors, which consisted of an arthritis-pain "diminimizer," the world's most reliable toe-fungus eliminator, a favored antacid of presidents and kings so exclusive that it wasn't sold in stores, a stool softener guaranteed to cure constipation when all similar remedies failed, and other products for the treatment of warts, age spots, split nails, and the tragedy of uncontrolled flatulence.

Then she got her big break in *Shriek*, which for two weeks was the number one movie in America. Eighteen months later, *Shriek and Shriek Again* doubled the box office of the first film. Rebecca was only twenty-six years old when *Shriek Hard, Shriek Harder* completed the trilogy; it was the biggest hit of the three and the first to garner critical acclaim.

Of the scores of young actors who appeared in the franchise, Rebecca was the only one to become a star. All the other characters were killed off after such a short amount of screen time that they couldn't make a lasting impression.

She felt sorry for them, though not really. Hollywood is a dog-eat-dog environment, which is no reflection on dogs, only something that people say.

Between the *Shriek* films, there were marking-time roles, but following the third movie came the biggest break. She was cast as one of five hot young strivers in the city, an edgy situation comedy called *Enemies*. Like *Friends* but mean, full of snark and vicious put-down humor, it was a *Friends* for this new, less friendly, more desperate, cynical America—an immediate hit. The eighth and final season, which had finished filming a week before Rebecca's run with the sandpipers, would begin to air this coming October.

She was booked to start a major film in four months, a period drama as elegant and emotional as *Downton Abbey*, although with a violent sociopathic nephew living in the attic unbeknownst to the family below and a supernatural surprise in a secret cellar under the horse stables.

On this fine August morning, after a long shower, she ate an egg-white omelet with kale and zucchini cooked in a tablespoon of olive oil, garnished with thin slices of avocado. In the screenplay, her character was described as "wasp-waisted," which did not imply that the woman was insectile, only that she was voluptuous top and bottom but minimalist in the middle.

As always, after eating, Rebecca hand-washed and dried her plate, the flatware, the frying pan, the whisk, and other utensils. She left everything in the kitchen sink for one of her housekeepers to arrange in the dishwasher. For reasons she did not understand and never analyzed, she experienced a profound uneasiness bordering on anxiety at the idea of anyone seeing traces of oil or a smattering of crumbs that were a consequence of her having eaten a meal.

Although the compulsion to clean up after herself was stronger at home than beyond the walls of her house, it sometimes overcame her in a restaurant. She carried a pack or two of wet wipes in her purse. On occasion, after finishing each course, she swabbed the plate clean before the waiter returned to collect it, although only when dining with companions who had such colorful eccentricities of their own that they wouldn't even raise an eyebrow at her wet wipes, which was just about everyone in her social circle.

This benign obsession wasn't consistent in all aspects of her life, but it manifested at places other than the dining table. When she finished taking a shower, she squeegeed the walls and floor, and then wiped them dry with towels to ensure no one discovered water spots or clusters of shampoo bubbles or, God forbid, a loose hair from either her head or elsewhere. She wiped the bar of soap to be sure it was clean, scrubbed the soap dish, polished the showerhead, the handles, and the other hardware. The bathroom sink was cleaner after she brushed her teeth than before she attended to that task.

However, if the mess was not of her making and was in no way related to her person, Rebecca could be as indifferent to it as if it didn't exist. One Christmas Eve, when the house staff had been given four days off, an inebriated guest had cast the contents of her stomach across a living room sofa. Rebecca had closed the door on the fragrant chamber and allowed the voluminous upchuck to seep so far into the padding that purchasing new furniture proved to be cheaper than reupholstering the saturated sectional.

So, after the dishes and instruments of breakfast preparation were washed, dried, and stacked in the sink for the attention of a housekeeper, Rebecca headed for the front door. She intended to keep a series of appointments—hairdresser, nail technician, leg waxer. She stepped onto a front porch large enough and properly furnished to host act one of a cocktail party for at least fifty people.

Her candy-apple-red EV waited in the driveway to convey her in style or perhaps disintegrate when its three-thousand-pound lithium battery burst into flames, most likely the former. An acquaintance of hers, a famous director, had barely escaped with his life when his EV terminated itself in that fashion. The next day, he bought two more because, as he said, "My devotion to this technology is the foundation of my faith, and we all need to believe in something."

Rebecca's property manager, William Plantagenet, saw to it that the colorful sedan was always charged, immaculate, and waiting where she needed it when she needed it. His name was Ned Farkus before he changed it to be an actor and then failed at acting so crashingly that he considered returning to court to reacquire his birth name. However, there had been nothing about Farkus to recommend it.

As Rebecca settled behind the steering wheel and pulled the door shut, she had the disturbing feeling that something was about to happen that would change the course of her life, something worse than an exploding lithium battery.

[The previous sentence is a flagrant example of *foreshadowing*, a plot device that creates a pleasant anticipation in the reader. However, as the author, I feel the need to be honest with you, even at the cost of this intrusion, and I'm compelled to acknowledge that besides contributing to a building atmosphere of menace, Rebecca's "disturbing feeling" also serves as an effective way to end Chapter One before it grows too long. Studies indicate that modern readers prefer shorter chapters. Before purchasing a novel, they conduct a "flip-through" to sample the prose, consider the readability of the typeface, and be sure the number of chapters promises a quick read. Because Rebecca is rich and glamorous and one of the film-business elite, we expect her to be an insufferable narcissist, but she is a likable, vulnerable person whose "disturbing feeling" concerns us and whose fate matters to us just enough to propel us to Chapter Two, which is shorter than Chapter One.]

2

PEOPLE IN COMAS

Before Rebecca was able to start the engine of the sleek red EV, her phone issued the signature notes of Nilsson's "Everybody's Talkin'," from the movie *Midnight Cowboy*. On the screen appeared the name Bobby Shamrock.

"Bobby the Sham," she said with a tremor of pleasure.

That was what they called him when they were four middle school outcasts, four different varieties of nerds bonded by a shared sense of what was right and true. They had named their little group "the four amigos" in part because they liked that old Steve Martin movie *¡Three Amigos!*. There was also the fact that each had been courted by cliques of cool kids whose only intent had been not to befriend but to deceive, to set them up for mockery and rejection. As a result, the word *friend* had acquired a secondary definition akin to that of *deceiver*. For kids of their cruel experience, it seemed inevitable that they would eventually arrive at the superstitious conviction that if they called one another "friends," they would soon find themselves staggering around with figurative knives in their backs, emotionally bleeding out. "Amigo" meant the same thing, but they had no dire history with that word, and it was fun to say.

Rebecca loved all three of the other amigos, not in a romantic sense, but as some people loved their brothers if they had them.

She hadn't been blessed with any siblings, unless they were half sisters and half brothers fathered by the reckless fool before he plunged from altitude into a garbage barge. Anyway, although Rebecca loved all the amigos, she had a special affection for Bobby Shamrock.

She took the call. "Bobby the Sham! Where are you, sweetie?"

"I was in Tokyo for six months, but yesterday I flew into New York and took a train to Baltimore. This place is as dangerous as Caracas, Venezuela, if Caracas was under attack by extraterrestrial bug monsters. I'm not going to use Baltimore, after all. I'm going to set part three in Atlanta."

Bobby was a successful novelist, a stickler for accuracy, who traveled incessantly to research locations for his stories, which he wrote during his journeys and which mostly involved a lead character who hopscotched all over the world having adventures.

Rebecca was not convinced that Bobby's peripatetic lifestyle was actually in the service of his novels. He'd once spent two years careening through Finland, Korea, Italy, the island nation of Tonga, Samoa, Argentina, and Bosnia, but when the novel was published, the entire story was set in a fictional town in Vermont. Rebecca was not a negative person given to imagining desperate motives to explain the behavior of people, but she sometimes worried that Bobby might be running from something.

On the other hand, the making of art was a mysterious process, as she knew well. She would not rule out the possibility that, for someone as creative as Bobby, it was necessary to have intimate knowledge of Finland, Korea, Italy, Tonga, Samoa, Argentina, and Bosnia in order to write well about Vermont.

"If you're going to be passing through California on your way from Baltimore to Atlanta," she said, "I'd love to see you. It's been more than two years since I've seen you, almost as long since Spencer and Ernie came to visit me. We used to see one another more often. Why don't we see one another as often as we used to? I miss all my amigos."

"Miss you, too, Becky. I'm glad *Enemies* made you rich, but I'm glad it's at an end. You're better than that. Listen, I talked to Spencer a few minutes ago, and—"

"Well, you know, maybe I'm not better than that. Anyway, pretty soon, the only roles I'll get are grandmothers and warty witches. For women, this business defines 'elderly' as being forty. How's Spencer doing?"

"He says he's riding a unicycle on a high wire over an abyss, but I don't think he means to be taken literally. He'd just heard from Mrs. Hernishen that Ernie's in a coma."

Britta Hernishen was Ernie's mother. Ernie was the fourth of the four amigos, the only one who hadn't left Maple Grove, their hometown.

"He's in the county hospital out there," Bobby said.

A sharp pang of grief caused Rebecca to put one hand to her breast. Her heart was racing. "Oh my God. Sweet Ernie. This totally sucks."

"I know. Ernie was the best of us."

"Is," she said quickly. "Is the best of us."

"Yeah, right. Is the best of us. I don't know why I said that. It's only a coma. People come out of comas and get on with their lives. Isn't that right?"

"That's right."

"A coma is nothing."

"It's something, but it's not the worst that can happen."

Bobby said, "I mean, how many people have we known who fell into temporary comas? A lot, right?"

"A lot," she agreed.

"That's what I sort of thought. But the funny thing is . . ."

Sitting in her red EV, staring at her herringbone-patterned brick driveway, Rebecca waited for Bobby the Sham to specify the funny thing about comas. When the silence endured long enough for her to begin hungering for a second breakfast, this one without kale, she asked, "What funny thing?"

"Maybe a better word is 'peculiar.'"

"You're the writer. I leave the word business to you."

"The peculiar thing about all those people who've fallen into temporary comas is . . . hard as I try, I can't name one of them other than Ernie."

As Rebecca dwelt on that peculiarity, a bird settled on the hood ornament of her vehicle just long enough to decorate it with a large dollop of guano before winging away.

She said, "I can't name any, either. Isn't that . . ." She was about to say *weird*, which was just a synonym for *peculiar*, so she said, ". . . puzzling? It sort of seems to me, too, we've known a lot of people who've fallen into temporary comas, but I can't name one, either."

Although three thousand miles separated them, they shared an intimate and thoughtful silence until Bobby said, "So maybe we're wrong. Maybe we haven't known a lot of people who've fallen into temporary comas."

"Don't you think it's strange we'd share the same delusion about people in comas? Did Spencer tell you how Ernie ended up comatose? Was he sick? Did he drop off a ladder and hit his head?"

"Spencer just told me Ernie was in a coma, critical condition. Spencer is driving down there from Chicago. He'll be in Maple Grove this afternoon. I'm flying out from Baltimore in an hour. Ernie's alone and vulnerable, Becky. We have to be there for him."

"Alone?"

"And terribly vulnerable."

"But he's got Britta."

"Britta Hernishen?" Bobby sounded incredulous. "You'd trust *her* to keep Ernie alive?"

"She's his mother."

Bobby was as silent as if the line had gone dead.

"For heaven's sake, Bobby, she's a professor. She teaches a class on the value of ethics in literature. She donates hours and hours of her time to Save the Alligators and other causes."

"It's Maple Grove," Bobby said.

"So?"

"Do you really trust anyone in Maple Grove other than Ernie?"

"What does that mean?"

After a silence, Bobby said, "I don't know."

"You don't know."

"Do *you* know?"

She frowned. "How would *I* know what you mean when *you* don't know what you mean?"

"I don't know."

Rebecca quoted the town's motto. "Maple Grove is 'picture-postcard perfect.'"

"Is it really, Becky?"

Following an uneasy silence of her own, she said, "That's certainly how I remember it. Picturesque and boring."

Such lengthy pauses now separated their responses to each other that it seemed as if Bobby might have fallen into a coma out there in dangerous Baltimore.

At last he said, "How perfect could Maple Grove have been with comatose people strewn from one end of town to the other?"

She considered his question as though mulling over an issue of profound philosophical importance. "Don't you think maybe 'strewn' is hyperbole, since neither of us can remember a single comatose person before Ernie?"

Perhaps Bobby translated his reply into Chinese, from Chinese into Hebrew, and from Hebrew back into English before he finally said, "Memory is a funny thing."

"I'm not laughing here."

"I mean, isn't it possible, if you feel a thing happened, feel it intensely, it could be true even if you have no memory of it?"

"You mean like a repressed memory."

"Repressed or erased."

"Who could erase our memories?"

"I don't know," Bobby said. "We can try to figure it out when we meet up in Maple Grove."

"I guess I'm going there."

"Of course you are. For Ernie. For Spencer. For me. For yourself. The four amigos."

She said, "We've always known that one day we'd be going home again—haven't we?"

"Yes."

"How? How did we know?"

"I don't know."

"What happened to us back in the day?"

"I don't know."

"What's going to happen to us now?"

"I don't know."

"I'm scared."

"I know."

Sliding off the hood ornament and oozing across the sun-warmed car metal, the dollop of guano seemed to be a portent, an omen, full of chalky-glistening-slimy symbolic meaning, though Rebecca wasn't able to interpret it.

Having been nominated for an Emmy five times during the run of *Enemies*, and having won twice, Rebecca possessed that special kind of confidence that also comes to ambitious car salesmen when they rack up enough deals to receive a plaque decorated with a small golden wheel and be named the Employee of the Month, or to a real estate agent similarly honored during the brokerage's biannual banquet at Golden Corral. Now she tapped that well of confidence, seeking to wash away the dread that seeped into her like sludge from a broken sewer pipe, and she said, "There's no reason to be scared. We have nothing to fear but fear itself."

From out there in Baltimore, Bobby the Sham said, "I'm sure you're right, although . . ."

"Although what?"

"Although that's what the blonde with the pixie haircut said."

"What blonde with a pixie haircut?"

"I don't think she had a name. In *Shriek and Shriek Again*, she said that same thing just before Judyface cut her head in two with a chain saw."

"Oh. Yeah. Her. That was the opening scene. The script just called her 'Victim Number One.'"

"Well," said Bobby, "she didn't have a backstory or a future, so a name would've been superfluous. Spencer and I are staying at the Spreading Oaks Motor Hotel. It's nice. Four stars. We could book you under a name less famous than yours."

"Not necessary. I'll have Maud make reservations using her name and credit card." Maud Pucket was her personal assistant. "I'll be there by this evening if not sooner."

"Love you, amigo."

"Love you, Bobby."

"Let's do this for Ernie," he said.

"For Ernie, mi amigo," she said.

She didn't want to go home again, because it wasn't home. Her inattentive mother had moved to Miami. The grandparents who raised her, Charlie and Ruth, had retired to Palm Springs. She had always been an outsider in Maple Grove. The town itself didn't inspire even a mild flush of nostalgia. In fact, an intuitive wariness arising from some dark knowledge buried deep within her subconscious warned her off the town whenever she thought of returning there even to see Ernie, which was why he always came to visit her instead.

Inevitably, Rebecca thought of Thomas Wolfe, who had written *You Can't Go Home Again*, a massive tome that fell on an unexpecting public in 1940 and was at once said to be a classic of American literature. A film director of Rebecca's acquaintance, a man with numerous hits to his credit, had spent nine years trying to mount the novel as a movie, almost as long as he spent unsuccessfully trying to mount Rebecca. Although he had been nominated for eight Academy Awards and won three, he wasn't able to get the project green-lighted at any studio or otherwise raise the financing, not when he had a script that was a faithful adaptation, not when he reconceived it as a rock-and-roll musical, not when he found a way to give the story a science-fiction edge, and not even when he introduced a terrifying parallel plot about flesh-eating zombies. The title was even more prophetic than the novelist could have known: You can't go home again, and you can't even make a movie about not being able to go home again.

Yet Rebecca was going to try to go home again. For Ernie.

3

PAINTING WHILE UNCONSCIOUS

At three o'clock in the morning, three hours before Ernie Hernishen's mother called to report that her son was in a coma and not expected to live, Spencer Truedove had been completing a six-foot-high ten-foot-wide canvas, though of course he wasn't aware of what he was doing. All his paintings were large, anywhere from six feet square to eight feet tall and twelve feet wide, full of drama and color and strangeness. He worked exclusively in a fugue state, though not by choice.

[For those readers who have never heard of a fugue state in the dull kind of fiction they usually read, please allow me to explain. During such a condition, individuals appear to be like you or me, engaged in ordinary tasks, when in fact they are not consciously aware of what they are doing. Upon recovery from this phase, they have no memory of where they have been or what they have done. This might seem to be a convenient excuse for all kinds of outrageous behavior, but in fact it is a condition extensively documented by psychologists and other experts of their ilk. This is not the ideal place to explain how Spencer fell into such a curious career; that moment will come in Chapter Six, after he is on the road to Maple Grove and the momentum of the story is sweeping us right along. However, I felt that I could not just slap you with the term *fugue state* and then merely breeze onward without an explanation.]

So, having completed the painting and come out of his fugue state, Spencer was in his studio, standing before that enormous canvas, perplexed by the fantastic drama and color and strangeness of it. He wondered what he'd intended to convey while he had been slinging all that paint around.

When his smartphone rang, he felt a shiver of dread even before he saw the caller's name. He was a sensitive artist who sometimes experienced presentiments of impending trouble. Sadly, he lacked the ability to foresee the exact nature of what trouble might be coming; consequently, he was unable to avoid such personal setbacks as when a carjacker stole his EV and drove it through the front wall of a pizzeria, where the battery exploded and melted the pizza ovens. Or as when he'd nearly lost his nose at a Japanese steak house where the tableside chef was poorly skilled with the razor-sharp knives that were used in the flamboyant preparation of a Kobe beef entrée.

Accepting the call, he said, "Mrs. Hernishen, tell me this isn't bad news."

"I would never lie to you, Spencer. I would never tell you I have good news when I don't. Why would you make such an allegation?"

"I wasn't alleging anything, ma'am. I just had a presentiment of dire news. A foreboding. And I hoped I was wrong."

"I don't mean to be fussy, Spencer, but I am older than you and therefore wiser than you. My superior wisdom allows me to say with authority that it is never a good idea to wish away bad news. Best to confront it, deal with it, and move on."

"I imagine you're right, ma'am."

"There is no need to engage your imagination in this matter. You can be certain I'm right. How old are you these days, Spencer?"

"Thirty-five, ma'am."

"By the time I was thirty-five, I didn't have to imagine the answer to anything. I knew all the answers by then. A serious person should know the truth of everything by thirty-five. Do you consider yourself to be a serious person, young man?"

"Well, I guess I'm as serious as others of my generation."

"That's a terrible thing to say about yourself. Your generation is largely worthless. You must rise above the ruck and mire of their kind. If you can. If you want to. Of course, it is always a matter of ambition and ability. Perhaps the problem is that you possess neither."

Besides being opinionated and judgmental, Britta Hernishen was also loquacious. [That word might be as unfamiliar to some readers as the term *fugue state*, but there's nothing to be done about it now that it has fallen with a thud at the end of the previous sentence and is an immovable impediment to clear meaning.] At dinner, Britta could employ in excess of two hundred words to request that someone pass the pepper, in the process delivering a withering political opinion and a scathing review of a recent novel. At seventy, as a university professor who had been tenured for decades, she had no memory of a time when a student had dared to express an idea or sentiment in opposition to hers.

When required to attend a faculty meeting that promised to be a noisy airing of petty complaints, Britta sat in the back of the room and reread a Virginia Woolf novel while wearing wax ear stopples and humming old Woody Guthrie songs. By those precautions, she rendered herself deaf to the barked and hissed idiocies of other attendees, which was the rare occasion when she didn't speak.

None of her faults or foibles mattered, for she was Ernie's mom. Ernie had a big heart. Ernie was kindness personified. To love Ernie was to like his mom or at least tolerate her and treat her with respect. No matter what.

Spencer's left hand was dry, but his right, with which he held the phone, was already damp with perspiration. He called it the "Britta effect."

"Now, Spencer," she said, "if we were to define what we mean by 'serious,' you and I would seem to be speaking different languages. However, since you consider yourself to be a serious person, perhaps you will consider a question I have that only you can answer. Please strive to be coherent."

"I'll do my best, ma'am."

"In the living room of my son's house, there hangs an immense painting that you . . . executed. Do you know to what I refer?"

"Yes, Mrs. Hernishen."

"Although it is a colorful fabrication, I am at a loss to understand why Ernest, the product of my own loins, would have purchased such a thing."

"Oh, he didn't," Spencer said. "It was a gift from me to him."

"Ah. I am much relieved to hear that. However, my primary question is not in regard to my son's inexplicable taste."

"What is it in regard to, ma'am?"

"Those objects or entities that are the subject of that . . . that creation of yours. What are they?"

"Well, they are what they are."

"And what is that exactly?"

"I prefer if each person who studies the painting makes that determination for himself or herself."

"That's what you prefer, is it?"

"Yes, ma'am."

"Those objects or entities, whatever they are—I find them to be deeply disturbing."

"Okay," said Spencer.

"Disturbing and even at times disgusting, repulsive."

"Thanks for letting me know."

"You said 'each person who studies the painting.' Are there really people who study your works?"

"Yes. A few. A number. I don't keep a list of names."

"What kind of people are they, Spencer?"

"What kind? All kinds. All ages, races, creeds."

"Is that so? You're sure that those who study—actually *study*—your paintings are not reliably peculiar in the same way?"

"No, ma'am. I mean, yes. Yes, I'm sure. No, they're not all of the same peculiar type."

"Astonishing. May I ask you one more question, Spencer?"

"Why not?"

"What do you do for a living?"

"For a living? I paint."

"Houses? Industrial buildings? Highway bridges?"

"Art. I paint art."

"Is that the word you append to such works as the one in my son's living room?"

"Yes, ma'am. I don't know what else to call it."

"Is that so?"

"I'm open to other words if there's one more appropriate."

"I asked for 'one more question,' but here I am with others."

"That's all right. I just hope I have answers."

"I'm sure you will, Spencer, and they'll be fascinating. You're quite an intriguing specimen."

"That's kind of you, ma'am."

"So there are people who actually purchase your paintings?"

"Yes."

"Not imaginary people, but real flesh-and-blood people?"

"That's right."

"And they pay you with money rather than with bartered items like stolen TVs or illegal drugs?"

"Money. They buy them with money."

"How much money?"

"In my early days, it wasn't much."

"I'm quite sure. Everyone endures salad years at the start."

"Back then—thirty thousand, forty thousand per canvas."

"Ah. Are we talking about the currency of the United States, Venezuela, Sri Lanka?"

"US dollars. Recent works bring four hundred to seven hundred thousand, depending on the size and complexity of each piece."

"Well now. Well, well, well. My oh my. Isn't that marvelous?"

"I'm amazed, ma'am."

"I'm sure you are. I am likewise amazed."

"I never had any formal training."

"I'm sure you didn't."

"You know—Aldous Blomhoff has bought two of my works."

"The Aldous Blomhoff who is director of the Keppelwhite Institute, who was also mayor of Maple Grove for four years?"

"Yes, ma'am. Hard to believe there would be another Aldous Blomhoff."

"Oh, there are hordes of Aldous Blomhoffs. The world is crawling with his ilk. They just have other names."

"He came to the gallery in Chicago. I thought he was nice."

"Whatever talents you might possess, Spencer, you must never pretend to others or yourself that you are to any extent whatsoever a good judge of character. You are of little importance to me, but because you are a friend of my son, I would prefer that you didn't embarrass yourself with such a manifestly false claim."

Spencer transferred his phone from his sweaty right hand to his dry left hand, which immediately began to sweat. The Britta effect. Thinking back to an earlier point in the century when this call had begun, he said, "I forgot whether you phoned with good news or bad news."

"I have not yet made my revelation. Now I will. My son, Ernest, has fallen into a coma, and his doctor says he will most likely die within twenty-four hours."

Spencer's voice broke. "Ernie and I, we've been through so much together. We're brothers. I love Ernie."

"I'm aware you and Ernest, as well as those two other social outcasts, were very close, the amoebas and all that business—"

"Amigos," Spencer corrected.

"—but you are not brothers, Spencer. Ernest emerged from my loins, but you did not."

"I was speaking figuratively."

"If you do so again, please specify that explicitly."

"Yes, ma'am. Listen, I'll be there later today. We shouldn't lose hope. We can't. Never ever lose hope."

"I am a realist, Spencer. I find life becomes intolerable when we embrace false hope, and there is no other kind."

"We are not going to lose Ernie," he insisted. "In spite of what the doctor said, most people come out of comas and go on with their lives as if nothing had happened."

"Most?"

"Maybe ninety percent. Ninety-five percent."

"Where did you get that statistic, Spencer? I know you didn't get it in art school, let alone in a medical school."

"Well, I guess, you know, I'm just speaking from, like, personal experience."

"You've known a lot of people who've been in comas?"

He almost responded in the positive, but he bit down on the *yes* before he could speak it, because he realized that he wasn't able to name anyone he'd known who had suffered through a coma.

Into his silence, Mrs. Hernishen said, "Have you been in a coma yourself, Spencer?"

Into his subsequent silence, she inquired, "May I ask you yet another question?"

"Yes, ma'am."

"When you are in your studio, creating your works of . . . art, is there a particular substance that gives you the inspiration and energy to paint the kind of things you paint?"

"Substance?"

"Yes. Substance."

"Coffee," he said. "I drink a lot of coffee."

"This substance that you call 'coffee,' might I call it by another name if I were to see it and smell it?"

"Well, I guess someone of your generation might call it java, but I think you'd still call it coffee."

"That's what you think, is it?"

"Yes, ma'am."

Twenty minutes later, when Spencer set out from Chicago on the long drive to Maple Grove, he wore a snap-brim porkpie hat of black felt, a black denim shirt with mother-of-pearl buttons, black jeans, and black boots. He owned multiples of that outfit and seldom wore anything else. He expected to be dressed the same when he arrived at his destination, but if he were instead wearing a three-piece summer suit or costumed like a pirate of the Caribbean, he wouldn't be surprised. If by then his white Genesis had been transformed into a pumpkin drawn by white mice, he wouldn't raise an eyebrow. Nothing surprised Spencer. The how and why of a great many things mystified him, but he was incapable of astonishment. Life had taken him places he could never have imagined, by a route he could never retrace; years earlier, he'd decided that planning the future was futile and that the wisest course was just to go with the flow.

4

BOBBY THE SHAM

On the flight out of Baltimore, Robert Shamrock suspected that
some of his fellow passengers—several extensively tattooed men
with shaved heads and gold nose rings, who wore T-shirts emblazoned with satanic messages or images of flaming-eyed skulls,
men whose teeth were in some cases filed into points and whose
tongues had been surgically divided to resemble the forked tongues
of snakes—might not be ideal traveling companions in a crisis.
Indeed, he didn't believe he was unkind to wonder if a few of this
colorful contingent might be capable of fomenting a crisis of their
own during which everyone aboard would die in a spectacular
fashion. Because Bobby the Sham was fair-minded, many women
these days disturbed him as much as did any men. He was uneasy
about two lovelies dressed in black leather; green hair, painted
faces, and contact lenses that transformed their eyes into mirrors
might not have been enough to alarm Bobby if they had not been
whispering and giggling together continuously.

The world had changed radically since the four amigos gave
one another comfort in high school. Bobby found it difficult
to believe he, Rebecca, Spencer, and Ernie had been considered
such outsiders that they had been ostracized. These days, everyone
wanted to be an outsider. Many were willing to endure considerable discomfort and disfigurement to prove their I'm-a-freak bona

fides. Two passengers without apparent disabilities were accompanied by what they claimed were service dogs; the first was an enormous, quiet, menacing German shepherd that focused on Bobby with the intensity canines usually reserved for a bowl of food, and the second was a barking wild-eyed Maltese whose fur had been dyed pale blue. The only nuts Bobby could get with a beer were corn nuts, which weren't really nuts, although the grim flight attendant repeatedly insisted they were no less nuts than were almonds or cashews.

He took solace in the thought that this trip was probably more pleasant than it would have been if he had been a popular author thirty years earlier. Back then, books sold in greater numbers than was currently the case, and some famous novelists had been semi-romantic figures, recognized and approached for autographs nearly as often as movie stars. Now that everyone spent a significant part of their lives binge-watching TV and movies, authors of bestsellers could earn a smaller though still very good living while retaining their anonymity. No one recognized Bobby, which was all right with him.

However, back in the day when allergies weren't epidemic, he could have enjoyed a bag of Planters and an icy Heineken with no concern that, in mid munch, he would be responsible for the sudden death of another passenger. And in those days, he would have been less fearful about crashing into an immense Chinese spy balloon that carried a surveillance package the size of two Greyhound buses, less worried that the plane would be brought down by a drone flown into one of its engines by a teenage hobbyist infuriated about the carbon footprint of Baltimore-to-Indianapolis air travel, and less concerned that a Maltese faux assistance dog would abruptly attack his ankles, thereby exciting the German shepherd to join the assault and rip out his throat while a flight attendant propagandized him about corn nuts. As all those thoughts compounded one atop the other, Bobby was overcome, almost in spite of himself, by nostalgia for the world as it had been when he was a child.

Arguably, the most serious curse under which most novelists labored was the curse of a robust imagination. The engine of Bobby's imagination never shut off. It was always at least idling, and often it raced like a pumped-up Ferrari in the French Grand Prix. Drama—from stage to page, in prose or verse, in all forms ever conceived—relied on suspense, on threats ranging from mere marital discord to national catastrophe. Therefore, he tended to imagine malign rather than benign plot developments in the story of his life. Indeed, for every unfortunate turn of events that actually occurred, he worried about numerous other disasters that never came to pass.

The prospect of returning to Maple Grove after all these years inspired a carnival of frightening apparitions to wheel through Bobby's mind, often complete with the music of a carousel. These were not creatures he'd encountered in real life, but monsters from a hundred movies and television shows about carnivals and circuses, traveling phantasmagories in the whirl and dazzle of which were hidden horrific entities with malevolent intentions, fiends behind the frolic. His picture-postcard hometown had no fairground to which such entertainments were drawn in their illustrated Peterbilts and railroad cars that promised marvels to the world through which they sped.

Instead, locals devised their own celebrations. The weeklong Arts and Crafts Fair in May. Freedom Weekend over the July Fourth holiday. The Apple Festival in late September. Residents of every faith and those of no faith participated in decorating for A Month of Christmas, when the six square blocks of the town center were outlined and garlanded with in excess of one million colored lights and became home to more welcoming elves and angels and carolers and costumed Dickensian characters than you could shake a candy cane at. Thousands of visitors drove from all over the state to experience Maple Grove's Month of Christmas, when it seemed that the town had been frozen in a better time, a time of peace and fellowship and kindness and plenty.

Nevertheless, as the plane passed over western Pennsylvania, as Bobby decided corn nuts sucked and dropped them one by one into his empty beer can even at the risk of offending the scowling flight attendant, he couldn't rid himself of a sense of the uncanny. He was troubled by a queasy suspicion that he had forgotten—or been made to forget—events of grave importance, that in spite of its picture-postcard perfection, Maple Grove was a place of unthinkable horror, and that he was flying to his death.

Just then, beyond the windows, the night was seared by a web of lightning so bright and complex that even Robert Shamrock, a writer known for his vivid depictions of scenes, could not have adequately described it. The subsequent hard crashes of thunder were of such frightful volume and shook the plane so insistently that even the most tattooed, pierced, fierce-looking passengers let out cries of alarm so high-pitched and tremulous that they seemed to issue from pale, thin children.

As if the crash of the breaking storm briefly cracked open the door to Bobby's locked memory, a name from the past came to him—Wayne Louis Hornfly. The name chilled Bobby, elicited a shudder of revulsion, and briefly made him feel as if his bowels had liquefied, a sensation he had experienced only once before when he had eaten some bad guacamole. Those effects were inspired by the name alone, for Bobby could not recall who Wayne Louis Hornfly had been or what outrages the man might have committed or whether he, Bobby, had ever known such a person. Only the name swelled into his conscious mind, while other information about this ominous person continued to be repressed, as though the truth would drive him mad, just like the ill-fated souls in the stories of H. P. Lovecraft were frequently plunged into insanity by forbidden knowledge.

The plane flew on through the storm, and Bobby the Sham had no choice but to go with it.

[Dear Reader, I am acutely aware that at a moment like this in such a story, many of you will become frustrated with a character like Robert Shamrock. You will even shout at him not to return to Maple Grove, as if he can hear you, just as you might shout at the people living in a haunted house, enduring all kinds of terrors when they could simply leave. I ask that you shout at me instead of at Bobby, because he suffered great trauma during his years in Maple Grove; he is currently in a delicate psychological condition and deserves your understanding. I have much thicker skin than he does. Besides, if you think about the reason for your frustration, you'll see I'm to blame, not Bobby, because I'm compelling him to return to his hometown even though it's likely that what will happen to him there will not be pretty. Shout at me all you want, but remember that I can't hear you any more than Bobby can and that there might be lifelong consequences from a ruptured larynx.]

5

FUNNY

There was nothing funny about what happened to Ernie Hernishen that summer when all the amigos were thirty-five; actually, it might be more accurate to say that, regardless of how amused other people might have been, Ernie would not have laughed uproariously about anything that happened to him. Perhaps he could have avoided a coma and worse if, like his beloved amigos, he'd left Maple Grove after high school or earlier. However, Ernie was a gentle soul, shy and self-effacing. He lacked the ambition that drove Rebecca, Spencer, and Bobby to rise to the top. He was a small-town guy with a big heart, a humble soul with modest dreams. He would have been happy enough if only he had married the girl next door, fathered the 2.2 children per couple that were needed to sustain the human race, become a librarian, and spent his life in a labyrinth of books.

Unfortunately, the only girl next door to the Hernishen house was Wanda Saurian. When Ernie was twelve and Wanda was fifteen, she murdered her parents, stole the car, and ran away with Randy Docker, her twenty-year-old psychopathic boyfriend. Together they embarked on a five-state killing spree, after which she was not suitable to be the wife of a librarian.

Even if Wanda had refrained from wholesale slaughter and saved herself for the younger boy who yearned for her, Ernie's dream of being the primary authority at the Maple Grove Public Library would have been beyond his reach. By that fateful summer when Ernie was thirty-five and terrible things happened to him, Alma May Wickert had been the town's librarian for an astonishing sixty years. She cherished her power and guarded her job with such ferocity that no one dared seek her position or force her into retirement; thus she remained emperor of the stacks for yet another nine years. At the age of ninety-four, she perished in her sleep from what Dr. Sweeny Feld called "spontaneous mummification," though the physician was known to imbibe to excess at times and to have a macabre sense of humor.

Curiously, the library burned down on the night of Alma May's death. Voters eventually declined to fund a new one for pretty much the same reason that they wouldn't fund a buggy-whip factory or an encirclement of massive catapults to protect the town from invading barbarians. The city council unanimously agreed with Mayor Susan Glow that even before a new library could be designed and built, artificial intelligence would transform the world, and everyone would have a personal robot to read stories to them, making it unnecessary to engage in the onerous chore of reading to oneself.

Consequently, even if Ernie had survived the year when he was thirty-five, he could not have become the town librarian when the town had no library. This is not the place to reveal whether Ernie came out of his coma and lived; maybe he did, maybe he didn't. These immediate pages are for the purpose of introducing the fourth of the four amigos so that readers—or their robots—will understand who all the principal characters are, thus allowing the wheels of the narrative to turn faster from this point.

We must consider how extraordinary it is that all four of these people, although social outcasts in their youth, became outstanding successes in their chosen fields, Ernie Hernishen no less than the others. He was just eighteen when he wrote his first song, "The Girl Next Door Is to Die For," which Garth Brooks came out of retirement to record; it spent eleven weeks as the number one country song in the USA, even crossing over to rise to number two on the pop charts. That was of course quickly followed by "Mama, Don't Teach Me Your University Ways" and "Three Friends and One Dog Are All I Need," which were also enormous hits for different country artists. If the amigos endured some torment or terror in their youth, some ordeal they had been made to forget, perhaps the stress and trauma of the experience had driven them to become achievers, to gain social position and a measure of power as defense against whoever or whatever had so profoundly shaken them back in the day.

Unlike his pals, Ernie shrank from the prospect of celebrity, as if being known was asking for trouble. Although he could play the piano, the guitar, the fiddle, and the ocarina, he had no desire to perform his songs in public. The stage did not call to him. Life in the spotlight had no appeal. When he wasn't writing an astonishing number of memorable and often haunting songs, he pursued solitary interests, some of which he found puzzling and even inexplicable.

He was *not* puzzled by his love of nature, of which there was plenty to be found in and around Maple Grove. He enjoyed long walks in the woods. He could spend hours studying wildflowers in a meadow, recording their infinite variety with his camera. He became such an avid bird-watcher that he was able to name most of those he saw.

Because nature seemed vulnerable to him, he took a major role in stopping a highly promoted new landfill on a thousand acres a few miles outside town, where a hundred thousand tons of worn-out solar panels were to be buried along with undisclosed thousands of cumbersome burnt-out wind turbines. His activism had led to unannounced visits by Britta, his mother, who insisted that his priorities were foolish.

On one occasion, popping into his kitchen while he was peeling potatoes for dinner, Britta said, "Sustainability. Renewables. A cleaner way. What about this don't you understand, Ernest?"

"Solar and wind aren't sustainable."

"Do you think the sun is soon to go out? Will the wind never blow again?"

"You have to calculate the immense amount of steel and copper and concrete, historic amounts, and the—"

She cut him off by taking the potato peeler out of his hand. She held it beyond his reach, as if he were five years old and being denied a lollipop. "Tell me, have you started smoking something potent, Ernest?"

"You know I don't smoke."

"Is that so?"

"I think it's a terrible habit."

"Is that what you wish me to believe?"

"Well, it's true. I don't smoke. I never have."

"What is it you claim not to smoke, Ernest?"

"How can such a question be answered?"

"Do you bake it into cookies?"

"It? It what?"

"Are you really as naive as you pretend, Ernest?"

"I'm not naive, just confused. You always leave me confused."

"Is that the kind of thing you tell people about your mother, that I reliably confuse you?"

"Please give me the potato peeler."

"As naive as you are, you're liable to harm yourself."

"People don't harm themselves with potato peelers."

"Is that your position, Ernest?"

"It's not a position. It's a truth."

"How interesting you would say such a thing. How revealing."

"Revealing of what?"

"What about mushrooms?"

"Mushrooms? People don't hurt themselves with mushrooms, either. How could I hurt myself with a mushroom?"

"What exotic mushrooms have you consumed recently?"

"I don't care much for mushrooms, Mother."

"Do you know what a cactus button is, Ernest?"

"I guess it's what closes up a cactus shirt."

"Mescaline, Ernest. Those who succumb to primitive forms of music sooner than later become lost in such things as mescaline."

"If I can't have the peeler, I'll finish the potatoes with a sharp knife. If I cut off a finger, it won't be my fault."

"Ernest, do you understand the source of your anger?"

"I'm not angry. Just hungry."

"Your father passed his anger down to you."

"I never knew my father."

"He was handsome but ignorant. He thought he could tame me. When I wouldn't leave the university and wallow in ignorance with him, he couldn't bear to live as a shadow in my light."

"What does that mean—'as a shadow in my light'?"

"If you had furthered your education, you would understand such things. Here is your potato peeler."

"Dear God, a miracle."

"Ernest, there's no point speaking to God. You might as well have a conversation with a rock."

"I know the feeling," Ernie said, returning to the potatoes.

"I ask only that you keep your strange environmental views to yourself and cause me no further embarrassment in the community. By the way, it would behoove you to eat fewer potatoes and more lean protein."

In spite of Britta, Ernie understood his passion and concern for nature and why he expressed it as an activist. However, he could not explain his obsession with novels about characters who suffered from amnesia or eradication of memories by brainwashing. He'd read hundreds of such stories with fascination. A professional book scout occasionally found a few of the hundreds of similar novels that were out of print, and Ernie at once pored through those also. He reread the better books three or four times. His collection of movies on the same subject had inspired repeated, sometimes obsessive viewing.

And so it was that on a Tuesday evening, before anyone knew that Ernie had fallen into a coma (because he had not yet fallen into a coma), he was in his study, sitting in the white-and-brown cowhide-upholstered armchair with polished bull-horn headrail. Two walls were brightened by James Bama paintings of cowboys and horses that had graced the covers of paperback books by famous Western novelists, and on the other two hung a variety of guitars beautified by exquisite inlays of exotic woods. This large study contained no desk, but a piano stood ready. Three more armchairs were draped with colorful Pendleton blankets that complemented the Navajo rug.

Sometimes Ernie wrote songs here, composing the lyrics first and then working out a melody on the Steinway. Most recently he'd completed "They Don't Have No Antidote for Love at Walgreens." Currently, he was engrossed in a gunslinger novel about sheep men versus cattlemen in the 1800s. This edition contained the original text; Ernie refused to purchase revised editions that had been rendered into gibberish by aggressive "sensitivity readers" and published for semiliterate mobs with the hope they might read it instead of burn it either symbolically or literally.

Ernie found good Westerns to be highly entertaining, although characters with amnesia or suffering a fugue state were rare in the genre. The closest thing to a person like that in the present novel proved to be a schoolmarm who was by nature forgetful but accurate with a six-shooter.

After he read the final page and sighed with contentment and saw it was 6:10 in the evening, Ernie ambled into the kitchen with the reasonable expectation of heating a bowl of homemade vegetable soup and making a grilled cheese sandwich. After all, this was not the first occasion on which he'd undertaken to prepare dinner. With almost two decades of culinary accomplishments behind him, he had every reason to suppose he would again succeed at feeding himself.

But it was not to be.

The door between the hall and the kitchen featured a porthole-style window and swung freely on pivot hinges, like a door serving a restaurant kitchen. As was Ernie's habit, he stepped briskly across the flush threshold, allowing the door to reverse its momentum and arc shut of its own accord. He took only two steps into the room before an unusual smell halted him no less abruptly than if he had walked into a glass wall.

Artists of many disciplines have a highly developed olfactory sense and respond dramatically even to subtle odors that most people cannot detect or of which they take only transitory notice. Writers and songwriters and musicians are among the gifted in this regard, actors and dancers and painters not so much, least of all film directors and mimes and those who make origami animals. By far the artists most sensitive to smells are sculptors; no one knows why, though this matter is the subject of hundreds of scientific studies conducted at prestigious universities.

Although Ernie Hernishen was a talented songwriter rather than a sculptor, the subtle but unusual aroma in the kitchen impacted him on a profound level deeper than any psychological strata that Freud could have imagined even in his cups, where perhaps the great doctor spent much of his productive time. This smell was mysterious yet familiar, sweet even as it was savory, alternately aromatic and malodorous, simultaneously attractive and repellent. Ernie crossed the kitchen, following the scent, as helpless to resist as if the columella between his nostrils had been snared by a fishhook and the line were being reeled in. This is not to imply that the experience was painful, only that the odor was a summons that could not be resisted. If it had been painful, Ernie's agony would be described here so vividly that the reader would cringe, shudder violently, and become nauseous.

Ernie found himself at the cellar door without being aware that he'd set out to reach it. An instant later he found himself at the foot of those stairs, in the windowless realm under the house. His obsessive reading of novels with a certain exotic plot element—which is not a reference to Westerns—had prepared him to recognize that "finding himself" at a place without any memory of how he had gotten there was an example of either micro amnesia or a brief fugue state.

As he stood in the darkness, unable to move, paralyzed by some power he couldn't name, Ernie realized he should be afraid. Yet he was not afraid. He was patient, overcome by a sense that he had a purpose to fulfill and that, when he'd done what was wanted of him, he would experience a satisfaction unlike anything he had known heretofore. It was as though the alluring scent that had drawn him into the cellar was also conveying to him a tranquilizing fragrance to ensure his docility until whatever had been planned for him began to occur.

The cellar lights came on.

This was the primary mechanical room for the house. Furnace. Water softener. Electrical panels. Featuring LED fixtures between the ceiling joists, the space was better illuminated than the realm under the serial killer's house in *The Silence of the Lambs*, though there were still shadows befitting a cellar, contributing to the kind of atmosphere that lovers of slasher films find stimulating.

In the grip of a power unknown, Ernie ceased to be able to move his body, but he remained capable of turning his head left and right to the usual extent, which allowed him substantially more than a 180-degree field of vision. If he was able to see three-quarters of the room, which is likely but not verifiable to the extent that detail-obsessed readers of a persnickety nature might prefer, then the person who turned on the lights must have been in a ninety-degree arc immediately behind him.

Although Ernie's fear response remained suppressed, he was quite capable of imagining that the person looming over him was armed with a shotgun or a scythe. Or behind him might even be an orangutan trained to commit murder, as in the famous story by Edgar Allan Poe. Yet because of the tranquilizing effect that bespelled him, even those grievous suspicions couldn't excite terror in Ernie.

He could hear no slightest movement.

He could smell no cologne or body odor or exhalation of garlic breath, only the strange scent that had him in its thrall.

No voice—either sinister or welcoming—spoke of his fate or about anything else, for that matter.

Suddenly, released from paralysis, he moved toward one of three steel doors as it swung open to receive him.

The man who built this place, Dwight Fry, fancied himself a survivalist. The cellar was larger than the footprint of the house above it. The rooms that extended under the surrounding yard had concrete walls. The thick steel doors hung on concealed barrel hinges. Fry stocked those three big chambers with enough food to last him and his young wife, Bambi, for thirty years. Tragically, just before their move-in date, Bambi informed her husband that she intended to divorce him in order to marry the entrepreneur who had sold them several tons of freeze-dried vacuum-packed food. Already on edge because the Armageddon that he had foreseen was less than a month away, Dwight went *over* the edge and tried to kill his wife with a sixteen-pound sledgehammer. The weapon proved more unwieldy than he anticipated, which gave his bride time to retrieve the Smith & Wesson Chief's Special from her purse and place a perfect triangle of .38-caliber rounds in his chest and abdomen. Bambi claimed self-defense and was not prosecuted. Ernie Hernishen bought the house, Armageddon supplies and all.

Disposing of several tons of freeze-dried food was a daunting task that Ernie chose not to undertake or oversee. He left it in the three rooms where Dwight stashed it. Having no skill with firearms and no desire to learn, he figured that if the end of the world came to pass, the contents of those chambers would be his gift to the post-Armageddon mutants and barbarians in return for their kindly not eating him.

Now, in the thrall of the mesmerizing odor, as lights came on in the food vault ahead of him, he began singing one of the songs that he'd written—"She Stole My Heart and My Visa Card." In spite of the title, it was an upbeat number. He thought he sounded happy as he sang, and he wondered how long that would last.

When he stepped into the well-stocked room, he stopped singing and stared at what awaited him. The walls were lined with fully laden metal shelves to a height of eight feet. In the center of the space, a table-high island of low drawers with a butcher-block top allowed a spacious walkaround. Lying face up on this four-foot-wide ten-foot-long formation was his doppelgänger, in the very same clothes that he wore. This Other Ernie appeared to be sleeping.

Just as the One and True Ernie began to be concerned, his twin on the butcher block faded away as if it had been a mirage. Ernie realized that the phantom figure had been a placeholder intended to show him what position he was expected to take.

He clambered onto the table and stretched out on his back and gazed at a ventilation grille in the mottled-gray concrete ceiling.

A voice issued from the grille. It was rather like that of Darth Vader from the *Star Wars* movies. "Listen to me, boy. Great is my frustration. Greater still is my anger. Greatest of all is my determination. I will probe your brain for answers." The unseen speaker laughed merrily. In a pleasant voice, he said, "Just joking. There will be a little coma, but you'll be okay. I'm pretty sure."

"Funny," said Ernie, although he was not in the least amused. He was instead using the word as a synonym for *"curious,"* for *"weird,"* for *"what the hell,"* for *"uh-oh."*

6

JUST A LITTLE BIT MORE YOU NEED TO KNOW ABOUT SPENCER TRUEDOVE

Because this account of the travails of the amigos is based on a true story and isn't a work of fiction (or is not strictly such a thing), the cast can't be reduced to one or two protagonists. The structure of the book must not be left to the whims of the author. Back in the day, four social misfits endured the horrors of Maple Grove. If three or two or even just one of that unfortunate group were to be edited out of this telling of their ordeal, what sense would it make? No sense.

However, the author and his editor and his publisher and the perpetually nervous folks in the marketing department are well aware that studies conducted by major universities (them again) indicate that between 39 and 57 percent of modern readers, who lead busy lives even if to no sensible point, have markedly less patience for character details than did readers in the time of Charles Dickens or, for that matter, in the time of Herman Wouk. Consequently, strategies have been developed to keep *all* readers, the patient and the impatient, engaged. One strategy is to divide long chapters into two shorter ones, wherever possible, to distract the reader from the amount of character detail and to contribute to the illusion of headlong suspense. That is why the material in this chapter was moved from Chapter Three, where it appeared in the first draft.

Readers can be confident that Rebecca, Bobby, and Spencer will arrive in Maple Grove soon and that, after they have gathered at Ernie's bedside, this narrative will accelerate through a rollicking series of exciting and terrifying events that might leave you winded if you haven't been eating the right foods and exercising according to the advice of the fanatics at the National Institutes of Health.

So there was Spencer Truedove in his black outfit with a snap-brim porkpie hat and mother-of-pearl buttons on his shirt, piloting his SUV through the vast tedium of the heartland. Earlier, he had told Bobby that he felt as if he were riding a unicycle on a high wire over an abyss. That was indeed how he felt, partly because he feared for the life of his friend Ernie and because that's how he always felt during and immediately after a conversation with Britta.

What most unsettled him about the woman was her certainty that her every opinion was the spot-on truth and that every action she took was the only action any honest, right-thinking person could possibly have taken. Spencer, on the other hand, never felt confident as to his thoughts about any subject, and when he had taken action, he suspected there were a dozen things he could have done that would have been more appropriate and humane.

He didn't even know why he had become an artist. As a six-year-old, when the world had seemed immense, Spencer had expected to be an explorer who would discover a huge new continent and name all the states and towns on it—Poopville in the state of North Poop, Poop Beach in Poopafornia, and so forth. It would be a great place to live because the residents would always be laughing their asses off at all the poop jokes. In his early teens, when poop wasn't the peak of humor that it was for six-year-olds, he adjusted his expectations to the reality that Earth had fully divulged itself to explorers who came before him; the early-Victorian world of mysterious lands and uncharted waters was gone. During Spencer's school years, anxious to escape the cool kids being shaped into a new generation of corrupt public servants and fanatical cultists of one kind or another, he had taken refuge among the amigos, none of whom gave the slightest thought to their future as adults because they didn't expect to have one.

That Spencer would become a successful artist was as unlikely as that he would become a circus clown. Here's how it happened.

Because he'd been held back one year in elementary school, he turned eighteen while still a senior, at which time he received an unexpected inheritance of sixty-seven thousand dollars from his maternal grandmother, who died years earlier but had been secretive about the terms of her will. This is one of those twists of fate we find delightful even when it happens to someone else, although we must keep in mind that it required a premature death; we should take a moment to mourn the deceased.

Spencer might have remained in Maple Grove with his amigos for another few months if Grandma's bequest hadn't triggered nightmares so terrifying that he woke screaming. Years earlier, when he was fourteen, his mother had announced that Maple Grove was too bland, stifling, too "managed," whatever that might mean. She had lost herself, the free spirit she'd once been. She needed to find herself, the vibrant woman she had been or could be—and she left the same day. Spencer's father then left his wife (and the son who reminded him of her) for a woman who didn't need to find herself. This is a twist of fate that pleases some of those involved but not all, and we should take a moment to wonder what fate is up to in the long run. Anyway, after having lived alone for years in his dad's house, he began to suffer horrific dreams in which his parents came back, remarried, and turned their attention to him. He fled.

For four years, the amigos had been supportive of Spencer as his family deserted him. But the other kids in Maple Grove proved to be sharp-tongued predators who recognized that Spencer was a wounded animal; they pursued him with the clever, flaying wit for which teenagers are renowned. With the blessing of his amigos, who would have liked to flee town with him if they had each inherited sixty-seven thousand, Spencer dropped out of school and went to Chicago.

In the Windy City, he rented an apartment and fell into a fugue state, though the second action wasn't intentional. He woke six weeks later to discover five enormous canvases aswirl with eerie, colorful images that made him question his sanity. By this time, he had forgotten the terrors that he and his amigos had experienced, just as they would forget them as well a few weeks later.

In what might have been yet another twist of fate or perhaps only a coincidence, a young woman who occupied another apartment on the same floor as Spencer's, Portia Clavus, happened by his unit while the door was open and glimpsed one of his paintings. Portia possessed two degrees from Harvard and knew such inside-art stuff as that Leonardo da Vinci invented the submarine sandwich and that Van Gogh cut off his ear not after an argument with Gauguin but because he had another one that felt redundant. Portia worked in Chicago's premier gallery and was intent on becoming a big player in the art world regardless of whom she had to destroy in her climb to the top.

Shrieking in ecstasy, she burst into Spencer's apartment with such enthusiasm that for a moment he thought she had come to kill him. Even when he ceased to fear for his life, he was unsettled by her excitement. Being very young and inexperienced, being modest by nature, and having no idea how or why he had created the paintings in an amnestic state, he couldn't take Portia's extreme praise seriously. The more she gushed, the more convinced Spencer became that she was either deranged or a scam artist.

Portia was not deterred by his reticence. She wouldn't have been deterred if he had threatened her with a meat cleaver. Art was the only thing that mattered to her, art and the fortunes that could be made from it. She pursued Spencer from room to room, haranguing her quarry until she had given him a headache like a sharp object driven into his skull. To be rid of her, he agreed to receive her and her employer at four o'clock that afternoon.

He intended to be gone when the woman returned with Erhardt Dusterheit, who was the owner of galleries in Chicago, Boston, New York, London, and Paris. However, the fierce headache did not relent until 3:50. Spencer had only enough time to wash his sweaty face and rinse the bitter taste of chewed aspirins out of his mouth before the doorbell rang.

Dusterheit was a tall man with a long face. A wide mouth and thin lips shaped a smile as sharp and humorless as the blade of a mezzaluna. Long, narrow nose like the proud bow of a warship cleaving the sea. Pale-gray eyes. Titanium-silver hair. His long ears were almost flat against his head, and a teardrop diamond worth as much as a Rolls-Royce depended from the right lobe. You get the picture.

Whereas Portia had been exuberant at her first sight of the paintings, Dusterheit was silent, like a hawk coasting on thermals, as he moved from one huge canvas to another, spending no more than two minutes with each. His face remained as expressionless as his exquisitely tailored charcoal-gray suit.

Spencer had arrived at the conclusion that Dusterheit would say, "Have a nice day," pivot on one heel, and leave without any comment about the paintings.

Instead, the gallery owner asked, "What is it you mean to say with these compositions?"

Because he had no idea what he had meant to say, if he had meant to say anything at all, Spencer said, "If there were words to express my intentions, I wouldn't have expressed them in images."

Dusterheit regarded him in meaningful silence for half a minute before saying, "The objects portrayed here look like nothing I have seen before, yet they are so dimensional that one senses each of them has a function. How would you describe their function, their purpose?"

Because Spencer didn't know what the hell they were, he said, "Everyone who views them must follow a unique path to their meaning. Imagine function first. Then you'll know their purpose. They're revealed to me, but they don't come with an explanatory pamphlet."

"And if they did? Come with an explanatory pamphlet?"

Spencer felt drained. He needed help. He tried to imagine what Bobby the Sham might say. Bobby was a writer. He could bullshit his way out of any jam. "I wouldn't read such a pamphlet. These objects are mystical in nature. The meaning that anyone else imposed on them would be limited by his power of interpretation. If I listened to him, I'd be robbed of the opportunity to explore them myself and perhaps find the fuller truth of them."

Following another and more intense silence, Dusterheit said, "Some of these objects actually seem to be entities, organisms."

"Don't they?" said Spencer.

"Some might say they find them frightening or even disgusting. What would your response be to that?"

Channeling Bobby the Sham, Spencer said, "That is a danger one faces when interpreting art. One can inadvertently reveal more about oneself than about the work under discussion."

Throughout these exchanges, Portia Clavus had stood behind her employer and to one side, shifting from foot to foot, chewing on a knuckle, looking as if she might bite off any fingers she felt were redundant. Spencer's answer inspired her to make a fist and punch the air.

"You have not been to art school," said Dusterheit.

"Francis Bacon never went, either. He couldn't even draw. And he's famous. He's not the only one. School is for illustrators, not for artists."

Dusterheit returned to the paintings for five minutes and then said, "I believe I can represent your work to great effect."

"That would be nice."

"I believe that by the time you're thirty-five, you will get half a million per canvas. Before you're forty, maybe years before, your price will exceed one million."

"Where do I sign?"

Dusterheit said, "One thing."

"What's that?"

"You talk too much."

"I can fix that."

"The more mysterious an artist is, the more he is in demand. Silence suggests that you know things other people don't, that you have depths others can never plumb. Silence is sexy."

Spencer only nodded.

"One additional note."

Spencer raised his eyebrows inquiringly.

Erhardt Dusterheit said, "You need a better look."

Spencer waited.

"I see you in black."

Spencer nodded again.

"And a hat."

Spencer raised his eyebrows once more as a means of inquiring what was meant by *"hat."*

"There's such a thing as *too* quiet," Dusterheit advised.

Spencer said, "What about a porkpie? Snap-brimmed, round crown, black felt?"

Baring his mezzaluna smile, Dusterheit said, "I like it."

And so it was that Spencer Truedove became a wildly successful, critically acclaimed artist without any formal training and without any memory of having painted anything. Although otherwise he had enough charm to make a cobra dance without using a flute, Spencer answered most questions about his work with silence accompanied by an expression that was 70 percent compassionate pity and 30 percent intellectual contempt. He did so with such grace that everyone posing a question—everyone but Britta Hernishen—went away satisfied that the artist provided profound yet succinct insight into the meaning of his art.

Year by year, life was good. If there was one thing he wished he could change, it was the dreams. In damp seasons, when the sticky nights were warm but not viciously hot, or when darkness settled through the city with a chill of waning autumn, when the moon was full and ghastly with its shadowed craters but sometimes when no moon graced the sky, without relationship to the spiciness of the food that he'd eaten or the quantity of wine that he'd consumed, terrifying dreams tormented Spencer until sleep could no longer chain him to those hideous visions, whereupon he thrashed up from his sheets and blankets, his heart cold in his breast even as he streamed sour sweat from every pore, hair standing off his scalp and tangled in an Einsteinian bush, his flesh as pale as the pulp of an inedible squash. He woke screaming, and he continued to scream as he scrambled out of bed, sometimes snared by the bedclothes so that he stumbled and crashed to the floor. Even the shock of such a collapse failed to quiet his screams, and he crawled fast across the room in a frantic search for shelter, of which none was to be found, so that he routinely ended his flight sitting on the floor, back pressed into a corner. The nightlight with which he always slept provided him no comfort in these situations, and though there was never a monster in pursuit of him, he did not abruptly cease screaming but quieted by stages; the shrill scream became a softer scream, became a wail, became an ululation, became at last a tuneless threnody that faded into ragged breathing.

Of course, he never remembered the dream, though somehow he knew it wasn't about his parents. He knew intuitively that it was always the same scenario. He also knew the threat around which the dream was built involved something that happened to him and the other amigos back in the day, some horror they had barely escaped.

For whatever reason, though Rebecca died in her dreams, Bobby and Ernie didn't suffer nightmares, though they endured their own problems. They all knew they had gaps in their memories, gaps dating to their high school years. They made references to this from time to time, though they never engaged in a lengthy conversation about the fact that they all suffered from amnesia, which was an amazing thing when you thought about it. Forgetfulness hadn't just befallen them; surely someone had wiped their memories. They should want to know who and why. It was as though they shared an unspoken agreement that whatever lay behind that door was best forgotten, even if someone had *stolen* the truth from them.

Only Spencer continued to experience new episodes of amnesia— the periodic fugue states in which he painted. He had long suspected that the bizarre images on his canvases resulted from a subconscious attempt to remember what the amigos had endured together.

As for the nightmare that afflicted him five or six times a year, maybe that was a small price to pay to keep the door shut on those lost memories.

Now, as the dashboard clock glowed 4:10 p.m., Spencer turned off the interstate and motored down a ramp into Maple Grove. Tree-lined streets. White picket fences. Broad, green, perfectly tended lawns. Victorian architecture. It looked like the town where Barbie and Ken Doll would live together, not in sin, but after being married as certified by a document from the Mattel Corporation, the kind of tolerant and convivial town where Kermit the Frog and Miss Piggy could cohabit in cross-species bliss without exciting any locals to commit a hate crime.

Sluiced along by a wave of nostalgia, Spencer wondered why he'd left such an idyllic community, why Rebecca and Bobby hadn't stayed here with Ernie. His doubt and confusion were short-lived. He *knew.* He knew why his compadres had left after him, all right. He knew all too well. As lovely as it appeared to be, Maple Grove wasn't what it seemed to be. Maple Grove was Stepford; it was 'Salem's Lot; it was serene Santa Mira where giant seedpods from another world were full of weird gooey stuff that was being shaped into replicas of the human citizens.

In fourteen minutes, he arrived at County Memorial Hospital, where Ernie Hernishen lay in a coma, flirting with death.

7

BALTIMORE NO MORE

Having provided needed atmosphere and a sense of threat when the story required those things, the storm with its fierce display of lightning quickly passed, and the jet carrying Bobby the Sham flew into good weather once more. None of the tattooed passengers wearing T-shirts with satanic images tried to hijack the airliner. However, when they opened their snacks, those with teeth filed to points and with tongues surgically split proved to be noisy eaters.

When he deplaned in Indianapolis, obtained a rental car with the voice of an officious woman issuing insistent directions from the navigation system, and set out across state lines for distant Maple Grove, the deep sea of his imagination floated disastrous possibilities to him for consideration. He let them wash through him without effect and instead focused on the name Wayne Louis Hornfly, which had crackled into his mind with the lightning and thunder high above western Pennsylvania.

In the Indianapolis airport, waiting for his luggage to appear on the carousel, he had googled the name without success. If Wayne Louis Hornfly still walked the Earth—or had ever existed—the man lived far off the grid, utterly without contacts or accomplishments. He was less than a ghost; he was as immaterial as the ghost of a man who had never been born.

Nevertheless, during the drive to Maple Grove, the name haunted Robert Shamrock. He could imagine a shadowy form hulking in the mist of the past, formidable though without detail, and he could almost see a face. Almost . . . almost . . . But almost having money in your pocket doesn't buy beans for dinner.

Even those portions of the Middle West that are largely flat, which is to say most of it, can provide beautiful vistas to enchant a driver. Broad, deep plains have a majesty about them, seem to roll on forever, reminding the soul of the eternity that is its destiny, stippled with trees standing in silhouette like symbols of broken hopes. Stark, discrete structures far out on the horizon—a barn with a big silo, an isolate church—when detached from other human purposes, project a minimalist beauty both elegant and intolerably sad. However, sadness can be an appropriate and satisfying emotion when you're journeying to see a friend in a coma, when you're going home but really can't because it's not home anymore.

If that sadness was inescapable—and it was—it did not crowd other emotions and considerations out of Bobby's heart. Like fear and Wayne Louis Hornfly.

In addition to immense plains of wild grass, there were crops thriving across thousand-acre plots. In a lush cornfield, a tall, shadowy figure moved through the rows with an intensity and purpose that had nothing to do with corn. A few miles later, Bobby passed a breeze-riffled field of wheat where in the distance another tall, shadowy presence carried an enormous scythe as if he farmed by the methods of an earlier century, though the man paid no attention to the grain and seemed eager to get some place where he intended to harvest a more exciting crop. Bobby passed a lonely dirt road that led nowhere apparent, yet a dark figure with a sack slung over one shoulder was walking toward the horizon with grim purpose.

None of those presences was Wayne Louis Hornfly. Bobby the Sham knew perfectly well that none was Hornfly. He also knew it was not likely such a person could exist yet escape detection by the all-knowing Google search engine. Nevertheless, with each sighting of a tall and shadowy figure, he flexed his novelistic imagination with greater effort, striving to imagine how they could *all* be Wayne Louis Hornfly. Often a ludicrous and impossible story premise that seemed as dead as a cluster of rotten tulip bulbs could suddenly put forth green shoots and then stems and then glorious flowers, becoming a shining novel of a hundred thousand or even two hundred thousand words.

Twenty miles from Maple Grove, as he passed a wind farm of two-hundred-foot-tall towers, a great flock of birds winged with foolish confidence where their kind had flown for millennia. The massive whirling blades introduced the concept of mortality to their small brains, reducing 90 percent of them to a shower of feathers, blood, chopped flesh, and bone bits.

That horrific sight crossed two wires in Bobby's head. Light came into his darkness, and *he knew*. He didn't know who Wayne Louis Hornfly was or what the man looked like or where he could be found. The light was dim, just bright enough to assure him there had been such a person and that the purpose Hornfly embraced, the passion that motivated the man, was cruel and mindless slaughter.

The fine hairs stood up on the nape of Bobby's neck, and an icy chill descended his spine with the swiftness of a centipede, and his heart skipped a beat before abruptly racing, and his breath caught in his throat, and his testicles tried to retract. It was a full-body fear reaction straight out of a 1930s pulp magazine, except community standards in those days would not have included crawling testicles in his list of symptoms.

His first impulse was to turn the car around, head back to the airport in Indianapolis, fly to California, take a flight from there to Tokyo, and then decide on a destination that was comfortably far away from Maple Grove. If he were to make a list of what he thought were his best qualities, heroism would not have been in the top ten.

No, no, no. He couldn't run out on his amigos. They were the best friends he'd ever had. They had been through too much together to abandon one another, even if they couldn't entirely remember what it was they had been through.

Anyway, by the time Bobby got to Maple Grove, maybe Ernie would have come out of his coma. Once reunited in their hometown, maybe the four of them would remember everything, fill the gaps in their memories. Maybe what had been erased from their minds would turn out to have been nothing of grave consequence. Maybe they would go to Adorno's Pizzeria this evening just like they did so often when they were kids, if Adorno's was still in business. This time they could have beer or wine instead of Cokes. They could have a lot of laughs, talk about old times, all of them successful now, none of them a nerd any longer. It could happen. You could write your life as you would a work of upbeat fiction, shape your future. It happened. It really did. Yeah, well, it could never happen as neatly as that, but he drove on to Maple Grove anyhow, arriving at the hospital at 4:22, hoping not to be cruelly slaughtered.

8

LASSIE, COME HOME

Rebecca Crane did not own a private jet, nor did she want to own one, but she knew ninety-six people who did own one. Many were generous enough to lend the use of their aircraft to a famous actor or other person whom they might one day be able to use in a ruthless fashion to secure a lucrative business deal.

At any one time, fifty of those individuals had taken their aircraft to a far-away exotic location to attend a conference with the purpose of developing policies and influencing legislation that would prevent the common people from depleting the world's precious resources. Of the remaining forty-six, some would be away on their third vacation of the year in Italy or Fiji. Others would be using their jets to get to and from more open-minded jurisdictions where certain practices illegal in the US weren't merely tolerated but were encouraged and even formally recognized with fancy embossed commendations or engraved plaques presented by whatever tenderhearted king or wise cult leader or benevolent dictator maintained an iron grip on that nation.

Although these jet owners were engaged in far more demanding and important activities than most Earthlings, eight or ten of their magnificent flying machines stood unused at any one time. If you were a member of the right social strata or were at least "in the know," there was a secret app that would tell you the location and status of aircraft belonging to any person whose name you queried.

After receiving the bad news about Ernie Hernishen from Bobby the Sham, Rebecca needed forty-one minutes to learn that one of two jets owned by a tech entrepreneur and budding film financier of her acquaintance, Holden von Smack, was hangared at a private facility associated with Los Angeles International. One vessel, though fully serviced, wasn't scheduled to be flown for a week. Holden von Smack took her call ten minutes later. In three minutes, he graciously offered her the use of one of his jets. There wasn't a man on the planet who would have refused to grant a reasonable request from Rebecca Crane, and if you ever saw her, you'd know why. Even at two pounds five ounces above her ideal weight, she was a knockout.

[This is an authorial aside. I must prevent you from reaching a mistaken and ungenerous conclusion about Rebecca. She is not a snob. She does not insist on always flying in private jets and in fact doesn't indulge in any of the hoity-toity behaviors that many others of her wealth and fame seem unable to resist. She is a down-to-earth person, humble and kind and selfless. If you were to meet her in mundane circumstances where you spent an evening with her, and if for some reason you didn't recognize her, you might imagine she was a dress-shop clerk or seamstress, though a remarkably good-looking one. I know a woman of unusually penetrating insight who thought Rebecca was the person in a bowling alley who rents shoes, which perhaps will help you understand how down-to-earth she is.]

[Bear with me for another paragraph. When Rebecca Crane does take commercial flights, she has no choice but to bring a security team. Said team consists of two large, muscular, highly trained agents who, were you to meet them in a dark alley or even on a well-lighted street, would likely cause you to soil yourself if they just looked at you askance. They are not thugs; they are nice guys from wholesome backgrounds. It's merely the look they know how to give you, the aura that they project, which results in your convulsive bowel issues. Rebecca needs to employ these gentlemen because there are more deranged stalkers in our sadly dysfunctional society than you might think, odd men and even a few unbalanced women, who operate under the delusion that they have a romantic relationship with Rebecca. They believe such things as that she not only wants them but also has promised them a souvenir of their time with her, and they expect her to fulfill the promise by allowing them to cut off one of her ears to keep under their pillow in a sachet filled with rose petals. In some cases, they expect a vital organ, which is especially out of the question. On this occasion, if Rebecca took the time to get her security team together and find a flight that had a block of at least three seats available, she would never get to Maple Grove while Ernie was still alive. What would be the point in that? There would be none.]

So it was that, as humble as a bowling-shoe-rental person, she drove alone in her potentially explosive EV through two hours of savage Los Angeles traffic, all the way from her house in Malibu to the private-plane terminal. As promised, Holden von Smack's jet was crewed and ready to take her to the heartland where Ernie was lying at Death's doorstep and perhaps even just inside the front door.

The aircraft that von Smack provided wasn't the jumbo jet he'd refitted with an elegant interior, transforming it into a sky yacht with two bedrooms and baths among other amenities. Instead, he provided his smaller Gulfstream V. Living up to her reputation as being the farthest thing from hoity-toity, Rebecca was grateful for the accommodations she'd been given. She didn't require a crew of seven, which the larger jet would have provided. Three were enough—the essential pilot and copilot, plus a smartly uniformed steward who offered her a choice of three entrées for lunch.

Takeoff was delayed when six protestors raced onto a runway to threaten planes with spray paint. They intended to defile priceless art at the Getty Museum; however, security at the Getty outfoxed them. Lacking the flammable liquid needed to set something important on fire, and with the spray paint unused, they came to the airport under the mistaken belief that a mist of carnelian red or peacock blue could destroy a jet engine. Although airport security agents in slickers and face shields might have been cheered for putting such feebs out of their misery, they only rounded them up, escorted them off the property, and suggested they try the bus station.

Through all of this, Rebecca kept thinking of *Lassie Come Home*, the wonderful 1943 film based on Eric Knight's timeless novel. All Lassie wanted was to get home to the boy who loved her, much like Rebecca—a lass—wanted to return to her hometown to be with Ernie, whom she loved like a brother. Lassie—and now Rebecca, too—kept being thwarted in her journey.

Life was often like a movie. That thought should have comforted her, considering the dog story had a happy ending. However, she knew that whatever movie she walked into in Maple Grove would be less like *Lassie Come Home* than like *Shriek*. She had been the sole survivor of all three movies, but she wasn't a cat with nine lives.

The flight was smooth. The Gulfstream V touched down like a pinfeather floating to the ground on a windless day. The airfield, which lay six miles outside of town, provided a 2.2-mile runway and had been constructed primarily to serve the Keppelwhite Institute, a world-class facility engaged—as you might expect—in mysterious research projects. The Keppelwhite had inexplicably been established on the southern edge of bucolic Maple Grove when the four amigos had been in their first year of elementary school.

A rental car awaited Rebecca. It was a little thing and silly looking, as if a dozen clowns might suddenly burst out of it. She didn't recognize the name of the maker. The interior smelled funny. She used one of the packets of sanitizing wet wipes that she carried in her purse to scrub significant portions of the interior. Then she drove the car into Maple Grove in spite of the smell.

The building that served as County Memorial Hospital was in conflict with the quaint character of the town: charmless in-your-face ultramodern; far larger than the population of this primarily agricultural county warranted; a sprawling, glittering, imposing, and somehow sinister structure.

Of course, this sixty-acre complex wasn't merely a first-rate infirmary but also the aforementioned medical-research center. It rose behind County Memorial like a gigantic structure designed and erected by showboat extraterrestrials for the purpose of mocking the meager achievements of humanity. The Keppelwhite Institute had been built with nine hundred million dollars donated by James Alistair Keppelwhite and his wife, Wilamina "Willy" Keppelwhite, principal stockholders of Keppelwhite Pharmaceuticals, Keppelwhite Chemicals, Keppelwhite Essential Substances, and not least of all Keppelwhite Neotech. They had also built a thousand superb homes to house the institute's scientific staff and their families in a stylish company neighborhood.

The ongoing research expenses were shared by the Keppelwhite Foundation, the Centers for Disease Control, the EPA, the CIA, a Department of Defense black-ops pool, Zippy's Healthy Juice Bars, which might have been a front for an entity of questionable intent, and a major Hollywood talent agency that declined to be named. The variety of contributors suggested the Keppelwhite Institute must be a public-private enterprise encompassing the political, military, health-care, high-tech, and entertainment sectors of the economy, a combination of interests that should have alarmed a broad swath of the media, local politicians, and town residents. But of course no one cared about anything other than the tides of money that washed through the community because of this mysterious operation.

As Rebecca parked in front of the hospital and stared at the massive complex rising behind it, she realized how peculiar it was that neither she nor any of her dear amigos had heretofore stopped to wonder if their problems were somehow related to this place. Their certainty that someone had erased portions of their memory, the bad dreams they suffered, Spencer's fugues, Rebecca's own obsession with keeping surfaces clean, Bobby's almost frantic need to travel, Ernie's conviction that nature was frighteningly fragile and his interest in novels about brainwashing and amnesia—could all of it, every weird thread, lead to the Keppelwhite Institute? Was their failure to wonder about the place evidence that they had been manipulated psychologically to discourage them from considering that possibility? Yes, maybe, but wasn't that a conspiracy theory? Wasn't it too pat? Maybe. Probably. They still might want to discuss it when they were together. Later. Right now, all that mattered was Ernie in his coma. Once Ernie was better, they could look into the issue of the institute. Maybe get together over Christmas and really dig into the subject then. Or in the spring.

Before getting out of the car, she took precautions to ensure she was less likely to be recognized and repeatedly asked for her autograph to the amusement of her amigos. She also hoped to guard against being kidnapped and held in a cellar by a crazed fan who wanted to read aloud his screenplay for a fourth *Shriek* film. Makeup artists on her TV show had often told her that she looked different but also, strangely enough, prettier without makeup than with it. So she vigorously rubbed a series of wet wipes over her face. Because she was known for her shaggy mid-length blond hair, she put on a shoulder-length brunette wig. She had perfect vision, but a pair of glasses with clear lenses and tortoiseshell frames completed her transformation.

Rebecca felt like an idiot when she was incognito, especially if she was recognized anyway. The keen-eyed fans usually recommended improvements to her disguise—a set of crooked teeth, warts glued on with spirit gum, fake radiation scars, and inevitably a Judy Garland mask. They were well-meaning, but she was as embarrassed as if she had been caught preparing to rob a bank.

At 4:42, she got out of the car and went into the hospital.

9

ERNIE'S MOMENT

Room 340 in County Memorial was similar to countless rooms in hospitals all over America. Speckled gray-and-blue vinyl flooring. Two white walls. Two pale-blue walls. A window offered a view of a world full of promise to those who would be healed and released, though it provided little of value to those who would die here.

Ernie was lying on his back with the head of the bed slightly raised, trailing a supplemental oxygen line that led to a clip on his nose, an intravenous drip line that connected a suspended bag of glucose to a catheter in one arm, and various leads conveying information about his heartbeat, lung function, blood pressure, and blood-oxygen level to a monitor with a big screen. From the screen issued periodic beeps, short-lived but ominous tones, and a musical trilling sound as if the primary purpose of this complex machine was to lure small birds to it. Ernie did not look good.

Spencer, Bobby, and Rebecca hugged one another, but they didn't at first speak, so intense were their feelings.

Bobby Shamrock was weak-kneed with shock at the paleness of Ernie's face, with concern that his amigo might be in pain or afraid. At the same time, he was overcome by a bitter sense of the unfairness that a gentle soul like Ernie should suffer. Bobby was also oppressed by the particular distress that was a forerunner to grief when one couldn't quite yet admit that the worst might happen.

No doubt Rebecca and Spencer felt similar things. But every person was different and experienced his or her unique salma-gundi of competing emotions. Bobby could have tried to imagine what else his amigos were feeling. However, as a writer, that was something he did with too much of his time, puzzling through the emotions of people in his stories, trying to understand them, to figure out what the hell they were going to do next and why. Enough was enough. He knew what *he* felt, and he would have to be satisfied with that.

He for sure wasn't going to *ask* Rebecca and Spencer how they felt. Although that had once been a caring question, it had been made illegitimate by an infinite gaggle of clueless reporters who had thrust their microphones toward hapless witnesses to ask, *How did you feel when you saw the bridge collapse and carry the train with all its passengers into the abyss? How did you feel when the terrorist cut your brother's tongue out with a dull knife? How did you feel when you saw your wife and baby swept up into the tornado as if they were just more lifeless debris?* Most of the time, you didn't need to know the finer details of anyone's raw emotions; a general impression of what they must be feeling was enough to allow you to communicate without triggering a psychotic breakdown in one of them. Besides, if a guy was thinking something inappropriate, he wasn't going to answer your tornado question by blurting out, *That was the best damn day of my life! Now I don't have to burn the house down with them in it to collect on the life insurance.*

The room had been furnished with two straight-backed chairs for visitors. A nurse brought a third. She smiled at Bobby and winked, as if the third chair had a special meaning for her and him.

Women were always winking and smiling at him, touching his arm or shoulder for no reason. When the amigos were fourteen years old, in ninth grade, and just becoming amigos, Rebecca had declared that Bobby the Sham possessed charisma. He had been upset when she said it. She hadn't been coming on to him. The four of them were equally terrified of sexuality and scornful of kissy-face starry-eyed hold-my-hand chocolate-and-flowers romance. More than scornful. Scathing. Contemptuous. Rebecca's statement was shocking because she hadn't even been pretty in those days. She'd hardly been presentable. She cut her own hair as though in a fit of anger at herself, wore no makeup except mascara that made her look tubercular, wore shapeless clothing, and in general looked as if she lived in a dumpster. Who could have imagined that she was capable of perceiving charisma or accusing a boy of it? Even if she had been as gorgeous as she was now, fourteen-year-old Bobby would have taken no less offense at the slander. He did not want charisma; he did not have it; he would not accept it even at gunpoint. He insisted on being as big a nerd as the rest of them, no less a loser than they were. For a week, he proved his true nature by producing fragrant farts until the unfair accusation of charisma was withdrawn.

If the smiling, winking nurse hadn't brought the third chair, if instead she had taken away the two that were already in Ernie's room, Bobby and Rebecca and Spencer wouldn't have noticed. They were still in the initial period of reverent distress about Ernie, when it felt wrong to sit down or speak more than a few whispered words or consult a phone for email or texts that might have come in during the walk from the parking lot. In this adjustment phase, it seemed they ought to look at only Ernie and the screen that reported his vital signs, while brooding on the fragile nature of life.

They had been doing that for less than two minutes when the pulsing and spiking lines on the monitor stopped pulsing and spiking, the numerical readouts went to zero, and the monitor alarm sounded. Ernie had flatlined.

10

THE WORST HAPPENS, THEN WORSE

A doctor, three nurses, and a young man on a career path that could not easily be determined crowded around the bed, working with dramatic flair to bring Ernie back to life. The paddles of a manual defibrillator were applied—"Clear!" the doctor announced—and then again, and a third time. "Clear! Clear!" An injection of something or other was administered, followed by an injection of something else. Eyelids were peeled back, stethoscopes were applied, and other actions were taken with an air of urgency shared by everyone, quite like a scene from an episode of *Grey's Anatomy*, though without the strain of troubled personal relationships and extreme sexual tension among those laboring so heroically on this resuscitation team.

Ernie did not share their urgency. Eventually his stillness quieted those attending him, and a professional sadness overcame them. As they disconnected their patient from all the devices that had failed to keep him alive, they favored the gathered friends with compassionate so-it-goes looks and with murmured condolences. Then they went away to save someone less determined to be deceased.

Tears gathered in Rebecca's eyes. They were genuine tears, not conjured with a tear stick or a slice of onion, not the product of superior acting talent (though she had a little of that). She loved

Ernie, her amigo, and the sight of him lying there as white as the bedsheets was intolerable. However, her tears did not spill down her cheeks, and she didn't sob, because suddenly she knew that Ernie was not really dead.

"He's not really dead," she whispered at the very moment that Bobby and Spencer whispered the same words, as if they were a Greek chorus informing an audience of a significant dramatic detail that everyone needed to know but that the action alone might not have properly conveyed.

No word other than *stupefaction* could describe their fraught expressions. In a case like this, the apt definition of *stupefaction* is usually the second entry in most dictionaries—"overwhelming amazement," stunned disbelief of an emotionally charged nature.

"Back in the day," Bobby recalled, "the people we knew who were in comas, they just woke up. Didn't they just wake up? I sure don't remember them dying, *then* waking up. I don't like this seeming-to-be-dead phase. Especially when it's Ernie."

More bewildered than his amigos at having heard himself declare Ernie was not dead, Spencer said, "People in comas? I don't . . . I *didn't* remember people in comas until you mentioned them. I don't remember who they were, or where or why. But, by God, there *were* people in comas, weren't there? More than a few of them."

Rebecca went to the door and closed it, lest they be overheard. "On the phone this morning, Bobby and I were remembering people in comas. We don't know who they were or why they were in comas, but we encountered more than a few of them back in the day. I can sort of see them, you know, in my mind's eye. They were creepy."

Just then everything got creepier when the door opened and Britta Hernishen entered the room.

11

MORE THAN ONE WAY TO SAY GOODBYE

Professor Britta Hernishen never just entered a room; *she made an entrance.* Even after all these years, Rebecca had not been able to decide whether the woman hesitated at the threshold to script and choreograph how she would present herself or if she exhaled drama with no more forethought than she exhaled carbon dioxide.

The hospital room door was heavy in order to provide a degree of soundproofing and hinged to resist a sudden wide swing that might knock a patient off a gurney. Nevertheless, it flew open now as if struck by a supernatural force. Britta strode inside with as much authority as General George Patton displayed when crossing a stage to address his troops. She wore black heels, a severely tailored gray knit suit with matching waist-length cape, and a black cloche hat with a gray feather.

She halted three feet from Rebecca, looked her over, and said, "What is this ridiculous getup you're wearing?"

"That's Rebecca Crane. She's incognito," said Spencer Truedove, for he was a cutting-edge artist, and cutting-edge artists were expected to live dangerously.

Regarding him as if he represented an example of incomplete human evolution, Britta said, "Did I speak to you, young man?"

"No, Mrs. Hernishen."

"I shed my ignorant husband ages ago. I prefer to be addressed as *Professor* Hernishen."

"Yes, Professor Hernishen. I'm sorry."

"A silly wig and eyeglasses? It is not Halloween, Ms. Crane."

Bobby said, "She has security issues. She's famous, after all."

The regal head turned toward him. "Mr. Sham, you surprise me."

"It's Shamrock."

"Is that so?"

"Robert Shamrock."

"If that's what you prefer."

"Well, it's my name."

"One would think you should know."

"Shamrock. Not Sham. Bobby the Sham is just something my friends call me."

"How strangely insistent you are regarding the issue. Let's just set the matter aside for now. My point is this—when a person like you, who claims to be a writer, defines 'fame' as what ensues when a person like Ms. Crane appears in blood-drenched movies and badly written television comedies, then a person such as I must inevitably despair. Do you consider yourself a person schooled at all in literary matters?"

Bobby said, "I've published twelve novels."

"Is that what you call them? I think the word 'books' would be the safer word. If you possess a modicum of taste and discernment, I believe you will agree with me that, regarding recognition attained because of the aforementioned filmed entertainments, the word 'fame' is less well chosen than the word 'notoriety.'"

Years earlier, Spencer had told Rebecca that he endured Britta Hernishen not only because she was Ernie's mother and because

Ernie was a sweetheart but also because he believed she was a psychopath who taunted him only to elicit an insult so that, when he made the mistake of wising off to her, she would feel righteous about drawing a knife from her purse and filleting him like a fish.

Rebecca did not find Spencer's fear to be irrational. That was why she smiled and merely said, "Well, I did win two Emmys."

"And that pleases you, does it?"

"Yes. Yes, it does."

"How forthright of you to admit as much."

Whether to save Rebecca from making a remark that would inspire a furious knife attack or because he was not sure whether Britta knew her son's health appeared to have taken a serious turn for the worse, Spencer said, "Professor Hernishen, I don't know if you're aware that . . . Maybe somehow it simply hasn't been called to your attention . . . What I'm trying to say is, well, I'm sorry to be the first to tell you, if in fact I am the first to tell you, that Ernie passed away, he died, just minutes ago. They tried to save him but couldn't, they made a valiant effort, you've got to give them that."

Britta stared at Spencer in silence for a long moment, as if he had delivered this dire news in one of the few languages she didn't speak fluently.

At last she said, "Mr. Truedove, I know you consider yourself an artist working in a visual medium, and I am quite aware that real artists working in visual media rarely are also gifted with coherent speaking and writing skills. Just as those like Mr. Shamrock, who see themselves as writers, can seldom also paint or sculpt well. Mozart was no Rembrandt in his spare time. Of course I am aware of what happened to Ernest. I was at a restaurant across the street, keeping vigil in my way, having a cocktail before dinner, when the head nurse on duty called me with the news. I came directly here. If with that tangled agitation of words you intended to imply that I should be openly grieving, be assured I forgive your impertinence."

"Thank you," said Spencer.

"Allow me to say two things more. First, as a realist, I know the world is a hard place. As a stoic, I change whatever I can and accept what I can't. We all die. It would make no sense for me to grieve for myself, and it makes less than no sense for me to grieve for others. Even in this dark world, life has its rewards, and one goes on seeking them no matter what."

"Ralph Waldo Hernishen," Bobby murmured.

Murmuring failed to spare him from rebuke. When Britta was the subject, she could hear the mere *thought* of a whispered remark at two hundred yards. The professor turned her attention once more to Bobby. "You are referring to Ralph Waldo Emerson's reaction to the death of his five-year-old son, which many think cruel and chilling. You are wrong about Emerson and about me, but it does not offend me that you cannot think clearly on this issue and others. Humanity is not in general a clear-thinking species." She stepped to the bed and looked at her son. "Ernest and I weren't as close as we could have been if he were more like me, which he would have been if he were wiser. However, although I lamented much about the boy, I accepted who he was—even when he greatly embarrassed me by composing that deplorable shitkicker music that made him famous." She went to the door and opened it. "The mortician will be here to collect the remains within the hour." Then she went away to seek those rewards that even this dark world offered.

Still eschewing chairs, the three amigos stood in silence for perhaps a minute before Bobby said, "I guess there's more than one way to say goodbye."

Perhaps because Rebecca had been in several movies involving numerous dead bodies and had to concern herself with many problems related to dealing with inconvenient corpses, she was first to recognize the need for urgent action. "Heads up, amigos. We know something weird is going on here."

"More than one something," Spencer said, nervously adjusting his porkpie hat.

"Ernie appears to be dead, but he isn't," she said.

Bobby shook his head. "Try selling that to the coroner."

"We can't let the mortician take the body," Rebecca declared. "He'll cut it open, scoop out the organs, and pump what remains full of formaldehyde. Then Ernie will be dead for real."

12

THE BUSY BODY

While Rebecca and Bobby prepared Ernie for relocation to some hidey-hole where no mortician could find him, Spencer went looking for a wheelchair and was soon involved in an argument about hats.

He didn't *want* to engage in an argument about hats. Who would? It was just one of those things that happened when two human beings—who were strangers—came together, one fiercely opinionated and the other on an urgent mission that made him impatient with fools.

The distraction would not have occurred if County Memorial had been as thoroughly furnished with wheelchairs as Spencer expected it to be. With the halt, lame, and feeble everywhere in abundance, a hospital ought to be *littered* with wheelchairs. This was especially true now, during the dinner hour, when the patients were in their beds, slurping their meals through straws or choking on pieces of poorly masticated chicken or so drugged and confused that they were struggling to eat Jell-O with their fingers. Later, during visiting hours, you might expect them to be wheeling themselves out of their assigned rooms in an effort to avoid the relatives who had come to chastise them for the bad habits that had landed them here, but not now when there was pudding to eat.

Most people were of the opinion that pudding was one of the few things to enjoy about a stay in the hospital, but Spencer disliked pudding to such an extent that it might accurately be said that he despised it. He preferred thoracic surgery to pudding. The exception was crème brûlée. He loved crème brûlée. Of course, if you were in a fine French restaurant and referred to crème brûlée as "pudding," you would deserve what you got if the chef showed up at tableside and beat you with a large spatula.

Suddenly hungry but certain that neither County Memorial nor any other hospital in the United States would offer crème brûlée, Spencer considered going to the nurse's station to inquire about a wheelchair. He restrained himself because he wasn't able to imagine how to proceed with the conversation if the nurse wanted to know for whom he needed it. He doubted very much that cooperation would be extended to him if he said, *The dead man in room 340. He can't eat dinner, and there's nothing on TV he wants to watch, so I thought I'd take him for a spin to visit other patients.* A better approach eluded him, suggesting that Britta Hernishen had been correct when she insisted that an artist who worked in a visual medium wasn't likely to be gifted with words.

Consequently, he zigzagged from room to room along both sides of the third-floor main hall, seeking an unoccupied wheelchair that he could commandeer for the purpose of rescuing Ernie from impending embalmment. Just when he was beginning to think they would have to lower their not-dead amigo out of a window with a makeshift rope of bedsheets, he discovered the very conveyance he wanted in room 315.

This was a double room. The patient farther from the door was unconscious and being fed by a drip line, so his gown wasn't soiled by food stains and he wasn't in any condition to object even if someone stole the bed out from under him.

Judging by the available evidence, the patient nearer the door was called "Butch" by his friends. Three colorful helium-filled foil balloons were tied to the headrail of his bed. The first two said, GET WELL BUTCH and LOVE YOU BUTCH. The third featured a red heart and the name BUTCH.

When Spencer arrived, the upper half of the bed was raised, and Butch was sitting there, staring at the contents of his dinner tray as if he had seen roadkill more appetizing than the meal before him.

Butch was no one's idea of what a ballet teacher or a flutist in an orchestra ought to look like. His arms were more powerful than those of a bear, though somewhat less hairy. His chest appeared so immense that he could have donated half of it for transplant to a weak-chested man and still been unable to find shirts to fit him. Because his neck was as wide as his shaved skull, his head resembled a mortar round welded to his shoulders. His broad face might have been pleasant if he hadn't been scowling and if his scowl didn't conjure in the mind images of medieval executioners in black leather pants and vests, wielding massive axes with razor-sharp blades.

Although the wheelchair was the hospital's—not the patient's—property and although a nurse would bring another when requested, Spencer was sufficiently intimidated by Butch's appearance to ask, "May I borrow this for a minute? Just two minutes, three. A quick little trip for a friend."

Butch's scowl of disapproval morphed into an equally intense scowl of puzzlement. Instead of responding to Spencer's request, he posed a question of his own in a gruff voice. "What's with the hat?"

Spencer, prince of Dusterheit Galleries, dressed in the same outfit every day, much as the late author Tom Wolfe appeared always in three-piece white suits; therefore, he never gave any thought to what he was wearing. Over the years, the felt hat with the round crown and snap brim had almost become a part of his head. He often forgot it was there. He said, "Hat? Hat? What hat?"

"*What hat?*" Butch's scowl of puzzlement tightened into a scowl of impatience. "The hat on your head. I've never seen a stupid hat like that except one time on a freak in a movie."

Judging by Butch's irritability and his demanding tone, Spencer decided the man was accustomed to having authority over others and to being obeyed.

You might expect Spencer Truedove to explain politely that he was a famous artist, that these days famous artists and writers and musicians were often encouraged to regard their wardrobe as a part of their branding strategy. But he did not choose to explain. For a moment, he forgot the wheelchair and went into defense mode.

Infrequently but usually at inconvenient moments, Spencer was annoyed far in excess of the vexation that other people might feel at being the target of a thoughtless remark. If we were to engage in the flood of Freudian babble that washes through many modern novels, we might be subjected to twenty-four pages of scenes recalling how Spencer's mother went off in search of the free-spirited self she had lost elsewhere in life and how the more ignorant teenagers of Maple Grove tormented the boy. If we were to probe deep, deep into Spencer's psyche, we would learn that one of the chants with which they afflicted him was this: *Spencer Truedove is unique. His mommy left, his daddy, too. Hey, what a freak! What a freak!* With that discovery, we would realize that Butch's use of the word *"freak"* triggered Spencer's response and his unfortunate delay in acquiring the wheelchair. By dispensing with Freudian babble, we have learned in one paragraph what otherwise would have taken twenty-four pages, which is reason for both the author and reader to be grateful.

"It's not a stupid hat," Spencer retorted. "It's maybe the coolest hat ever. It's cooler than a damn Stetson."

Perhaps it was Spencer's intensity that caused Butch to realize his own tone of voice was on the surly side and that his dismay at the inadequacy of his dinner might have motivated him to lash out in a most improper fashion. He said, "Hey, pal, it's just a hat."

Having been bestirred by the word *"freak"* and the associations it had for him, Spencer was driven to make his point as forcefully as he could. "It's the hat that Walter White started wearing partway through *Breaking Bad*, when he realized he was a bad dude and no one better mess with him."

"I never saw that series," Butch admitted. "But like I said, it's just a hat."

"It's not 'just a hat.' It's a meaningful hat. It's the same style hat Gene Hackman wore when he played Popeye Doyle in *The French Connection*."

Being of approximately the same age, Spencer and Butch probably had similar levels of testosterone, which always explains more than Freudian analysis. When Spencer failed to acknowledge that what he was wearing was merely a hat, Butch apparently decided that he had backed off his initial criticism as far as he could without further retreat reflecting badly on his manhood.

"Listen, pal, this isn't about you, see? It isn't about anyone who wore the hat in a movie. If Jesus Himself wore it, that would still be a stupid hat."

Spencer stepped farther into room 315.

❦

If Ernie Hernishen had been dead, which he wasn't, it would nevertheless have been an offense to his dignity to have taken him from County Memorial in a backless hospital gown. Worse, when he'd been stripped of his street clothes, someone had removed even his underpants. After lowering the collapsible railing, Rebecca and Bobby conspired to roll Ernie to the side of the bed with the intention of sitting him up on the edge, which was when they discovered his ass was hanging out.

Rebecca was not offended by the sight of a bare butt; she had seen others. However, she was distressed by the thought of sweet, shy Ernie being treated so cavalierly. "Why would they have to take his underpants off to figure out why he fell into a coma?"

Bobby said, "Maybe they suspected him of doing drugs, so they were looking for injection sites."

"Who injects drugs in his own butt? There are a lot of other places that require fewer contortions."

"Or maybe they suspected foul play."

"What—there's a psychotic butt-injector on the loose?"

"I'm just trying to explain the missing underpants. Maybe someone took them as a souvenir."

"Who would want his underwear as a souvenir, a souvenir of what?"

"Some fan of the songs he's written. You know, Rebecca, you're not the only one who's had strange experiences with kooky fans."

"I find it hard to believe that you, the author of *The Blind Man's Lantern*, can't imagine an explanation better than souvenir underpants."

"Remember, I woke up in Baltimore and flew commercial. It's been a long day. Let's get on with this. They're going to embalm him whether he has underpants or not."

"Have a look in the closet over there. Maybe his underpants are with the rest of the clothes he was wearing."

Rebecca hoped that was the case. They were already swimming in a sea of mysteries. The experiences that had been washed from their memories by an unknown power. The shared sense that a lot of people adrift in comas were a part of their past. The mutual conviction that Ernie wasn't on the far shore of Death, as he seemed to be, but was still alive even without vital signs. Missing underpants might be a small thing, but right now she felt that one new mystery would be one too many.

The closet was small because people don't check into a hospital with two suitcases full of leisurewear. Bobby opened the door and after only a moment said, "Everything's here."

"The underpants, too?"

"Yeah."

"Good. Great. Thank God. Go figure. You put them on him, and then I'll help finish dressing him."

"We're in a hurry, the mortician coming and all. This is no time for modesty. We're all amigos here."

"Technically, I'm an amiga. I don't want to see Ernie's junk. He's like my brother. No one wants to see her brother's junk.

Maybe one day I'll have to play a nun in a movie, and how am I going to play a nun convincingly if I've seen my brother's junk?"

❦

Not all artists are affable and benign people, as witness the great painter Caravaggio, who wounded a police officer when he was nineteen and fled from Milan to live in Rome. There, he was arrested on a dozen occasions, often for violent incidents, and in 1606 he killed a man named Tomassoni over a dispute about a tennis game.

Spencer Truedove was no Caravaggio. He knew his art was not as great as Caravaggio's—he didn't even know what he painted or why he painted it—and as far as he was able to remember, he'd never killed anyone. He didn't even *play* tennis. If rude people sometimes vexed him more than should have been the case, he never assaulted them, though sometimes he did confront them. And so he stepped farther into room 315 to speak his mind to the hulking, hairy individual sitting up in bed, with helium-filled foil balloons bobbing in a draft over his mortar-shell head.

"This hat," said Spencer, "happens to be the style of hat that Sylvester Stallone wore in *Rocky*. There's nothing stupid about this hat. And your reference to Jesus wearing one is ignorant, not least because the porkpie hat wasn't invented until seventeen hundred years after Jesus was crucified."

Even as we disapprove of Spencer's excessive and possibly even misplaced anger, we can sympathize with his response to Butch's criticism and use of the word *"freak."* There have been in excess of fourteen thousand young-adult novels and TV-series episodes about the evils of schoolchildren bullying other schoolchildren, so we well know that the effects of it endure throughout the lives of the victims. We must respect Spencer's enduring anguish.

Whether or not Butch had read any of those books or seen any of those TV shows, he evidently possessed enough insight and compassion to reach an approximate understanding of the psychology of the man who had burst into his hospital room with an unusual attachment to his hat. He said, "I forgot about Rocky Balboa wearing a hat like that. Now that I think about it, a lot of real tough guys in the movies have worn a hat like yours. You go ahead and take the wheelchair."

Nonplussed, Spencer said, "What?"

"The wheelchair. You said you needed it. It's yours. Even after I gag down this dinner, I'm not going anywhere. Not with this toe."

Spencer regarded the wheelchair, glanced at Butch, looked at the open door behind him, felt his face flush, and said, "Thanks."

Bobby well knew the torment that Spencer had gone through even before he'd been widely identified as a geek and sought community with the other amigos. Spencer's life had been rich with humiliation before his parents divorced, before his mom, Angelina, took the name Constanina because that's who she'd been in a previous incarnation, before his father married that sweaty stripper, Venus Porifera, who appeared nightly at the men's club out on the state highway, beyond the town limits, where there was no shame or laws against obscene performances. Nevertheless, in spite of all Bobby's understanding and regardless of the deep sympathy he felt for Spencer, impatience drove him to say, "Why the hell is it taking so long for Rembrandt to find a wheelchair in a hospital? Is he in a fugue state, painting a wall mural of terminal medical conditions outside the ICU?"

From her perch on the side of the bed, where Ernie lay on his back in his street clothes, Rebecca said, "Chill, Shamrock. He'll show up in a second."

Pacing agitatedly, Bobby said, "So might some orderly, going to take Ernie to a cooler in the basement to stash him for a mortician. Or, hey, maybe the law requires an autopsy in a case like this, and the coroner is on his way even now. Whether maybe it's a mortician who pumps him full of preservatives or a coroner who slices off the top of his head to look for a brain aneurysm, that's the end of our boy. We need to be *out of here.*"

"We'll have him out of here in plenty of time," Rebecca said. "In a hospital, they have their hands full trying to keep the living alive. They deal with corpses, too, but it's not the primary item on their agenda."

"How can you be so sure? If I was a hospital administrator and there were dead people scattered all around, I'd want to get them the hell out to preserve the reputation of the institution."

"Did you forget? My character in *Shriek* was a nurse."

"Yeah, you're right. I forgot. In the final sequence, when Judyface cut off that cop's arm with a chain saw, that's why you knew how to save his life."

"So listen to me and relax."

Bobby continued to pace like a nervous gerbil exploring the confines of its cage. "Listen, I'm not being critical. It stretched the imagination that you could stop his bleeding the way you did and that he didn't go into shock, but I was still with you, still buying it. However, after you killed Judyface—or thought you killed him—when you walked out through the cornfield to the highway with a two-hundred-pound cop leaning on you for support—"

Rebecca said, "Oh, how I loved the end music. It was just so inspiring."

"Yeah, okay, it was. And I totally believed you wouldn't leave the guy and you could find the strength to do your part, but I was never sold that, with one arm cut off and all the blood he lost, he could stay on his feet and make it through all that corn."

"Well, the credit crawl was long, and the director didn't want to go to a black screen. He wanted the audience to think there was one more jump coming, maybe Judyface's mom would erupt screaming through the corn for revenge, a setup for a sequel. What always bothered *me* was how we left the severed arm behind. My character being a nurse, I think she would have brought the arm with the hope it could be sewn back on the cop."

"You're right," Bobby said.

"I know I'm right."

"You should direct."

"Maybe one day."

Spencer crashed through the door and rolled a wheelchair across the room to the bed. He said, "Don't ask."

An orderly coming to move the corpse, a mortician and assistant speeding toward the hospital in a hearse, perhaps a coroner en route to argue with the mortician for dibs on the deceased, and nurses bustling from room to room—all those people would complicate the task of spiriting Ernie Hernishen to the ground floor and out of the hospital.

Having played a nurse in three films, Rebecca was reasonably confident that she could talk her way through most encounters with medical staff. However, she had never played a hospital security guard or janitor; on their way out, if they drew the attention of such a person who was a suspicious type and who had an exaggerated sense of his authority, unpleasantness could ensue.

Once Ernie was propped in the wheelchair in his clothes, he still looked dead even to the amigos, who intuitively knew that he was alive. Rebecca resorted to the contents of her purse. She swiped a light coat of lipstick across Ernie's bloodless lips and applied wisps of rouge to his cheeks. With his disarranged hair forming a spiky halo, those ministrations made him appear to be a clown who had succumbed to a cardiac infarction before completing his makeup. Rebecca used her hands to smooth down her amigo's hair as best she could, and Spencer contributed his hat to the cause, and Bobby supplied a pair of sunglasses. At last, Ernie no longer looked entirely dead.

Incomplete without his trademark hat, like a less than gifted Spencer Truedove impersonator, the artist left the room to call an elevator and hold it with the hope that, against all odds, Ernie could be whisked away without incident.

Giving Spencer time to perform his assigned task, Bobby was poised behind the wheelchair, hands on the handgrips, and Rebecca stood with one hand on the door to room 340. The third-floor hall—the stage—waited beyond.

She said, "Wheel him along casually. Don't hurry. We don't want to appear as if we're fleeing. I'll talk to him as we go. He's our uncle Ralph from Salt Lake City."

"He doesn't look like a Ralph," Bobby objected.

"My actor's instinct says no one will look twice at a Ralph."

"Salt Lake City?"

"People think *Mormons* when they hear Salt Lake City. People trust Mormons. You never hear of a Mormon bank robber or rioting Mormons or a Mormon shooting up a shopping mall. Okay, let's go."

Rebecca pulled open the door, and Bobby rolled Ernie into the corridor. Rebecca followed and proceeded at the left side of the wheelchair. So far, so good.

When a nurse exited room 335 and came toward them, Rebecca put a hand on Ernie's left shoulder and patted him affectionately and said, "Come Monday, you'll be well enough to go back to Salt Lake City, Uncle Ralph."

The nurse smiled at Bobby as though she wanted to wink but was determined to hold fast to the standards of her profession. When she heard "Salt Lake City," she glanced at Rebecca. "Nutrisystem works. Marie Osmond is as cute as a button. I lost thirty pounds because of her."

"Who hasn't?" Rebecca said.

As the nurse continued north and they continued south, Bobby picked up the pace. When Rebecca warned him to stay casual, he began to move even faster. Bobby turned right into the elevator alcove at such speed that she half expected Ernie to shift violently, slide out of the wheelchair, and sprawl across the floor. But as if Ernie were in fact a Mormon loath to make a spectacle of himself, he rode out the turn with his dignity intact.

Four cabs occupied the alcove. Spencer stood in number three, index finger on the HOLD DOOR button.

Bobby wheeled amigo Ernie into the cab, and Rebecca followed, and Spencer pressed the CLOSE DOOR button.

"We're not in a wheelchair race," Rebecca reminded Bobby.

"You know me," he said. "I've got to move. I feel safe when I'm moving. The faster and farther I move, the safer I feel."

"So you go to Bosnia and Borneo to write about Vermont."

"I didn't go to Borneo. I went to Tonga. The Kingdom of Tonga."

"Why isn't the door closing?" she asked.

Spencer said, "There's a safety delay."

The door closed. As the cab descended, Rebecca was so relieved that she sighed.

When the cab stopped at the second floor and the doors slid open, a uniformed hospital security guard stood there, waiting to come aboard, which is the kind of development necessary to maintain tension in any scene of escape. He was perhaps six feet two, maybe two hundred pounds, with a blunt face and marble-hard blue eyes that radiated suspicion and conveyed the impression he'd endured military service in a far land so dangerous that even poisonous snakes and sharp-toothed predators had fled the country in fear of the humans who ran the place. He entered the elevator cab with no possibility whatsoever that he would provide comic relief, and after a safety delay, the doors closed.

The guard carried a pistol in a holster on his right hip.

Fifteen years earlier, no security guard in a hospital would have been issued a firearm. In those days, people went to such noble institutions to be cured of an ailment or repaired after an injury or saved from imminent death. In those olden days, security guards were present largely to assist in the gentle restraint of druggies and drunks whose injuries were not serious enough to dissuade them from causing mayhem. Now that a lot of drugs were legal in numerous jurisdictions and were ravenously consumed, now that once self-aware and venerable professionals such as physicians and educators were as likely as anyone to indulge in furious political rants on those social media platforms that encouraged idiocy, now that even young nurses with strong feminist inclinations posted nude photos to suggest that their passion for caregiving extended beyond tending to the lame and the sick, you never knew who might show up at a hospital, what their purpose might be, or what weapons they might be carrying. In another fifteen years, all infirmaries would probably be encircled by high walls crowned with razor wire and constantly patrolled by circling drones with laser weapons.

A name tag clipped to the pocket of the guard's uniform shirt identified him as MICHAEL Z.

As the lift descended once more, Michael Z habitually patted the gun in his holster as he made eye contact with Spencer, then with Bobby, then with Rebecca. He ignored Ernie, evidently because he could not imagine that anyone in a wheelchair might be a threat—a misjudgment that was likely to get him killed one day.

Many officers like this one, whether badge-carrying police or private security agents, were skilled at using silence to intimidate nervous suspects into self-incrimination. Rebecca doubted Michael Z meant to intimidate them. He just didn't have anything to say.

Although Bobby was a fine novelist with an impressive command of the English language, his gift was limited to the written word; he possessed no acting talent. However, as a consequence of being fostered by the eccentric, often uncommunicative Adam and Evelyn Pinchbeck, Bobby was unsettled by prolonged silences among people. Although the descent from the second floor to the lobby at ground level required thirty seconds at most, he evidently found the trip interminable and unsettling. As if reading from a script with a gun to his head in front of an audience of thousands, he said, "Come Monday, you'll be well enough to go back to Salt Lake City, Uncle Osmond."

Perhaps Michael Z had an ear for dialogue and recognized the anxiety revealed by Bobby's strained and halting delivery of those fifteen words. Or it might have been the case that he found it odd or even suspicious that *"Osmond"* would be a first rather than last name. He studied Bobby with a squint-eyed stare sharp enough to peel a potato. That is hyperbole, of course, an obvious and intentional exaggeration; besides, there was no potato in the elevator on which to confirm or disprove that contention. Bobby clearly *felt* as if he were being peeled, however, and his ghastly expression only honed the security guard's interest in him.

The fingers of Michael Z's right hand, with which he habitually patted his pistol, curled around and tightened on the weapon's grip, which caused Rebecca to hold her breath in dread. Actually, there was little chance that the security guard would shoot Bobby the Sham. Although it is standard practice in these violent times for authors to kill major characters early in—as well as all the way through—a novel, merely for the shock value, this is not that kind of story, nor is the storyteller in this case cavalier about the value of human life. Of course, the storyteller reserves the right to kill off characters much later in the book, if the logic of the plot and the emotional payoff for readers justify it, or if the storyteller finds one or more characters annoying.

Whether or not additional missteps on Bobby's part might have ensured a confrontation with the security guard is moot. Sometimes fate intervenes in a dire situation to grant you a reprieve from being charged with stealing a dead body, which is what happened in this instance. As the elevator arrived at the ground floor and the doors opened, a voice issued from the walkie-talkie clipped to the guard's utility belt: *"Michael, report to the gift shop. A situation is unfolding at the gift shop."*

Whatever Michael Z experienced during a previous career in the military or another perilous occupation, those events encouraged in him a Spartan attitude toward danger. His facial expression remained deadpan even when receiving this summons to what could be a mortal encounter. Some miscreant in the hospital gift shop might merely be shoplifting candy bars, or a drug-addled psychopath might he holding a knife to the cashier's throat. Nevertheless, Michael Z hurried out of the elevator and rushed off with a stirring display of duty.

The lobby was small. People were coming to and leaving from visits with patients. Some looked worried, and others appeared put-upon, and a few were smiling as though thinking about an impending inheritance. No one showed any interest in the amigos. The exterior pneumatic doors whisked open as if the hospital were eager to be rid of them.

13

SUDDEN ENLIGHTENMENT IN A PARKING LOT

A kittenish breeze played through the sunny summer evening, chasing wisps of litter across the pavement, fluttering the leaves of the rows of maple trees that leaned their shadows eastward across the parking lot.

As Rebecca strode ahead of the wheelchair, she marveled at how adult she felt. Chronologically and biologically, she had been an adult for many years, but she realized that until now she had not felt like one *because she had never matured psychologically.* She'd taken upon herself the *role* of an adult and had acted the hell out of it, just as she had been a nurse in the *Shriek* series, just as she had been Suzy Pepper, a wunderkind stock analyst and exuberant slut, in *Enemies.* Her opinions regarding the issues of the day had been adopted to match the opinions of the vast majority of people in the entertainment industry. Only now, having successfully spirited Ernie out of the hospital, did she understand that she didn't know what she really thought about anything and therefore hadn't become a fully rounded person. For the first time, she felt that she had the capacity to make wise decisions and take decisive actions without relying on the guidance of agents, business managers, image consultants, issue advisers, and the other gurus with which movie stars were barnacled. She realized that until now she had given no thought to the meaning of life or the mystery of existence. She supposed she had gotten stuck in adolescence because of the events erased from her memory, but she understood now that the negligence of her libidinous mother and her grandparents' constant efforts to infantilize her had lasting consequences with which she must deal if she were to survive the current crisis.

The foregoing might seem like an absurd amount of enlightenment to crash through Rebecca while she crossed sixty yards of a parking lot, and the reader might think this kind of thing happens only in fiction. In fact, the author can humbly attest that such moments befall us in real life. During a cross-country trip in July of 1989, I was driven to my knees by massive enlightenment while fueling my car in Flagstaff, Arizona, at an off-brand service station with the unlikely name of Terrible Herbst.

And so, as Rebecca led the way, Bobby the Sham followed with the wheelchair. He was still so rattled by his close encounter with the ominously silent Michael Z, he didn't want to transport Ernie Hernishen in his rental car. "If I get pulled over by a cop, I won't pass inspection. I need to calm down. If you put that security guard in a room for six hours with the people who fostered me, the only thing you'd hear is stifled coughs and farts. People that quiet creep me out."

Of course even in the process of her personal enlightenment, Rebecca understood and didn't even slow down as they passed Bobby's rental car. She knew that when he was an infant, the Pinchbecks had taken him into their home and fed him and clothed him, but hadn't *raised* him. It had been like living with ghosts who drifted silently through the days as if lost between worlds.

"If the Pinchbecks were still alive," he said, "I wouldn't go to visit them while we're here. I swear I wouldn't. Those people made me crazy."

Spencer had driven his own Genesis SUV from Chicago. He was reluctant to accommodate his songwriter friend. "If he loses control of his bowels and bladder, I'd have to junk the car."

"He isn't going to lose control," Rebecca said. "He's not in a coma. He's in some kind of stasis. I'll take him in my car."

As Bobby piloted the wheelchair to Rebecca's rental, he said, "Are we really sure Ernie's not dead?"

"Yes," said Spencer at once, even as Rebecca said, "Hell yes, we're sure."

Bobby looked sheepish. "Okay, yeah, right. We'd feel it if he was dead, know it psychically, spiritually, somehow, some way."

"We're still the *four* amigos," Rebecca declared.

"Amigos now and forever," Spencer said.

Ernie's head lolled to one side, but that was merely gravity at work, not a nod in recognition of the abiding friendship and mutual defense treaty to which the amigos had long ago sworn allegiance.

Bobby and Spencer muscled Ernie from the wheelchair and into the front passenger seat, dropping him only once in the process and managing to wrestle him off the blacktop with Rebecca's assistance. He was loose-limbed, like a big cloth doll stuffed with dry beans. When he was in the car, the safety harness held him more or less erect.

As Spencer took back his porkpie hat and fitted it to his head, he made a small sound of satisfaction similar to the thin whimper of delight that might escape a dog when it found a missing toy and was able to paw it out from under a sofa.

When Rebecca closed the car door, Ernie tipped to the right as far as the harness would allow, knocking his forehead against the window. Although his eyes remained closed, his pale face was like that of an exotic fish pressed to the wall of an aquarium, curious about the awkward, ambulatory creatures beyond the glass.

Through all of that, vehicles cruised slowly by as the drivers searched for convenient parking spaces, and a few people passed on foot. No one stared directly at the trio struggling with a limp man at the open door of the rental car, but warily noted it with their peripheral vision. Neither did anyone slow down as though to offer help or otherwise intervene.

After all, this was America midway through the third decade of the twenty-first century, which often seemed to be an alfresco asylum where one out of four individuals was an impassioned but tedious neurotic. Another one in four was likely to be a flat-out lunatic who would tear your face off for the offense of being somewhat satisfied with yourself and your life. It was best to pass through every day as if you were a tourist in Jurassic Park: Stay in the electric tram; do not make loud noises; in a crisis, remember stillness is essential because the T. rex can recognize you as prey only if you move; expect something to go terribly wrong at any moment.

They were staying at the Spreading Oaks Motor Hotel, where they would rendezvous later, but trying to stash Ernie there, moving him from room to room to elude the housekeepers in the morning, was not an option that Rebecca could approve. That was like the action in an English farce, which would never work in the United States, where humor was increasingly viewed with deep suspicion by federal law-enforcement agencies.

Applying the plotting ability of a successful novelist, Bobby said, "There's only one place that makes sense. We have to take him back to his house."

"Really?" Spencer said with a note of disbelief. "Are you serious? His own house?"

Spencer Truedove had a sensitive nature. However, he possessed zero ability to recognize deception, duplicity, and chicanery in others because he had no capacity himself to deceive or betray. He wasn't as sweet as Ernie Hernishen. No one was. But Spencer was an honest and forthright soul who was perpetually surprised by the radical life-changing decisions of others. Even before her sudden enlightenment, Rebeca understood this naivete was why Spencer had failed to anticipate that his mother would go to New Orleans and become Constanina, that his father would divorce her and marry the stripper, Venus Porifera, or that his dad and Venus would buy the strip club, convert it into the tax-exempt Church of the Sacred Erogenous Revelation, attract four hundred parishioners who were devout degenerates, and leave Spencer to live alone, at fourteen, in the former family home on Mayfield Avenue. Therefore, Rebecca wasn't surprised that Spencer failed to see the wisdom and cunning of stashing Ernie in his own home.

"It's one of the first places they'll look," Spencer objected. "Especially if they think they were wrong to declare him dead, that maybe he's alive and walked out of the hospital on his own."

Rebecca was not in the least dubious, because she had starred in productions with grossly improbable twists in the storylines that were nonetheless well received by viewers. As the gentle breeze flounced her brunette wig and the oblique sunlight made gemstones of her blue eyes behind the phony eyeglasses, she said, "If they go to his house, it'll be a quick search, calling out to him, glancing in rooms. They aren't going to look in places like an old steamer trunk or a freezer."

Aghast, Spencer said, "We can't put Ernie in a freezer."

"We can if we unplug the thing and throw out what's already in it and jam the latch open so he can escape easily if he comes back from . . . from wherever he is."

Considering that Spencer was an avant-garde artist praised by critics for producing incomprehensible images of a unique and often disgusting nature, he was being surprisingly close-minded about the freezer. "No. I won't be party to putting Ernie in a freezer."

"So we slide him under a bed," Rebecca said.

Bobby said, "Or stand him upright in a broom closet and brace him so he doesn't fall out."

"Or lay him in a guest room bathtub," Rebecca suggested, "and pull the shower curtain shut."

Bobby said, "Sit him up in a corner of the attic and pile junk in front of him."

"No, no, no," Spencer objected. "It's summer. It'll be hot in the attic, very hot."

Rebecca said, "You know, Spencer, Ernie's not in a coma. He isn't even breathing. He won't know it's hot. He's in some kind of suspended animation. We've seen this before."

"We have? When? When have we seen someone not just in a coma, someone in suspended animation?"

"Back in the day," Bobby said. "Rebecca's right. I can almost remember. There wasn't just one. There were eight or even ten of them lying on their backs, lined across the floor. Wasn't it in a basement?"

"A church basement," Rebecca remembered.

Spencer blanched. "Tell me it wasn't the Church of the Sacred Erogenous Revelation?"

"It wasn't," Bobby said. "It was . . ."

Rebecca said, "At the corner of Cunningham Avenue and Winkler Street."

"Saint Mark's," said Spencer. His eyes widened as if he were waking from a long sleep. "The Lutheran church. Ten bodies side by side on the floor. But what were we doing there? None of us is a Lutheran."

"When Ernie was twelve," Rebecca said, "he started going to services at Saint Mark's just to irritate his mother. He was still going when we were amigos."

"He was in the church choir," Bobby recalled. "It embarrassed the hell out of Britta that he was in the choir."

They stood there in the hospital parking lot, gaping at one another, waiting for the moth-eaten wool of their memories to be fully repaired. No additional details returned to them. They still had more holes than fabric.

"Britta," said Spencer. "That's another problem. She might be the executor of Ernie's estate, and if she isn't, she might take it upon herself to act as if she is. She's likely to go there tomorrow if she isn't there already."

"Whoever's the executor," Bobby said, "the estate can't be settled quickly, especially when Ernie has disappeared. Hiding him there is still less risky than anywhere else. We can tuck him away so no one is likely to find him."

Rebecca considered the hospital's architecture, as sleek and unconventional as that of a richly endowed museum housing the most tedious of modern art. The massive Keppelwhite Institute rose behind it, ominous in scale and style, as though the architect must have intended to create a structure so intimidating it would inspire in the locals a superstitious aversion that would discourage them from wondering too much about what happened inside its walls.

A hundred and eighty degrees from those buildings, on the far side of the street, lay a residential neighborhood pretty much like the others in Maple Grove. The Victorian houses, with a few Georgian residences, were well maintained. The homes were shaded by oaks and willows, by sycamores that would clothe themselves in bright yellow when autumn came; the trees were flourishing and perfectly shaped, as if a third of those with jobs in this town must be employed as arborists.

Rebecca realized that Maple Grove was more remarkable than just picture-postcard perfect. The place was unreal. In fact, though the town had been unusually attractive when the amigos had been growing up here, it had matured until it resembled the ideal environment of a Disney theme park. If you paused to consider the unlikelihood of this perfection, the unblemished prettiness felt, in its way, as creepy as the institute. It was as if the Keppelwhites had chosen this unlikely location to establish their project not just because of the cheap land, low crime, and clean air, but also because the place was a locus of some strange regenerative power.

"You feel it?" Spencer asked.

The breeze carried the enticing aroma of steaks barbecuing on a charcoal-fired grill.

"This place . . . It's aware," said Spencer.

"It's something," she agreed, though she could not put a word to it, at least not the word he had used.

"Who's aware?" Bobby asked.

Spencer fanned his face with his hat. "Not who. What. Not the people. The place itself. Or something."

"I don't know what that means," Bobby said.

"Neither do I." Spencer returned his hat to his head. "But I think I once did."

"Look at the cars," Rebecca said, surveying the vehicles around them. "They all look like they were washed and waxed an hour ago."

"Was it always like this?" Bobby wondered.

"It's more like this now than it was like this back then, though it always was somewhat like this," said Spencer, who might have expressed his feelings better if he'd been able to draw them.

"In books and movies," Bobby said, "people who stumble on a strange town or come back to one, people who realize something's weird about the place—they tend to wind up dead."

As one, the three amigos turned to stare at Ernie in the rental car, with his pale face pressed to the window, seeming as insensate as carrion.

"Not all of them wind up dead," Rebecca objected. "That's not the way *Shriek* or either of its sequels ends."

Maybe it was dread that transformed Bobby's leading-man face into the face of a best-buddy character played by a supporting actor who was haunted by the prospect of mortality and unlikely to make it through act two. He said, "All three *Shriek* films ended with just one survivor, and it was always you."

She put a hand on his shoulder. "Thank you for calling them 'films.'"

"I'm nobody's snob."

"Art is art is art regardless of the package it comes in," said Spencer, no doubt intending to be supportive. "If we're going to put Ernie in a freezer or somewhere, we better get a move on before they come looking for him."

They departed in a caravan of three vehicles.

14

STASHING ERNIE

Rebecca parked boldly in Ernie's driveway, while Spencer and Bobby discreetly left their vehicles half a block away.

Ernie Hernishen's house was a two-story Victorian standing as proud as a frigate in full sail, with such a great weight of ornate millwork that, if it *had* been a ship on the sea, it would have sunk. The garage was detached, but Bobby and Spencer were able to carry their amigo around the back of the residence and through the kitchen door, which Rebecca unlocked with one of the keys on a ring she had found in Ernie's jacket pocket. The hedges were so tall and the many trees so fully leafed-out that no neighbor could have glimpsed them as they went about their suspicious task.

They carried him through the kitchen and into the hallway. The door to the study stood open. They settled Ernie into one of the armchairs, near his piano, with a collection of guitars hanging on the wall behind him.

Bobby was not easily given to emotion. According to critics, when his writing intended to depict emotional moments, the feelings of the affected characters were finely wrought and convincing. He had thought a lot about why he was able to write affectingly about strong emotion yet almost never succumbed to it himself. He'd first arrived at the conclusion that this was neither something with which he had been born nor the result of a conscious decision to be at all times stoic. From infancy he had been condemned to the company of his phlegmatic foster parents, Adam and Evelyn Pinchbeck. Long ago, Spencer christened them "Mr. and Mrs. Potato," because they were almost as silent and hardly more expressive than subterranean tubers. On long reflection, Bobby had decided that, raised in the eerie quiet and torpid atmosphere of the Pinchbeck house, it had been inevitable that he would learn to suppress his most powerful emotions, which was probably why he had become a writer—to express them through the characters in his fiction.

Here in Ernie's study, however, with his beloved amigo, Bobby the Sham experienced a moment when he sloughed off the unwholesome Pinchbeckian influence. He was overcome by anguish at the sight of Ernie in the armchair, slumped like a sack of cornmeal, his eyes still closed but his mouth sagging open as if he'd been in the company of politicians whose idiocy had infected him; he had been robbed of his dignity; even if alive and in suspended animation, he might have no future; he had neither wife nor children to mourn his decline; his mother was a witch; all in all, his condition was so pitiable that an extraordinary and inadvisable number of semicolons were required to connect the closely associated clauses describing it. Bobby's legs felt weak, and his chest tightened, and his mouth grew soft with sympathy, and his eyes grew hot with unshed tears—but then he was okay.

Rebecca said, "All right, let's find a place we can hide him until he comes back."

"Where, I wonder," said Spencer.

His words seemed to puzzle Rebecca. "Somewhere in the house. That's why we're here."

"No. I mean where will he come back from? That scares me a little. Doesn't it concern you?"

Bobby said, "No," and Rebecca said nothing.

"What if he comes back and he's not Ernie anymore?" Spencer asked.

"He'll be Ernie," Rebecca insisted.

"But what if he's not?"

"That's what silver bullets are for," Bobby said.

"That's not funny."

"It wasn't meant to be," Bobby said. "Now let's find a place to stash him and get out of this joint before Britta shows up."

Every room was furnished in violent contrast to the Victorian architecture, in what Ernie called make-Mother-want-to-scream decor, which was essentially saturation Southwest. Lodgepole pine chairs, twig-work furniture, colorful Navajo weavings hanging on the walls, Navajo rugs, beautiful Pendleton blankets folded over the arms of chairs and sofas for chilly nights, brightly painted *trasteros* with doors open to display collections of copper and brass ashtrays in the shape of cowboy hats, pueblo pottery, an amazing variety of figurative silver bolo-tie clasps, and much else.

In the end they returned to the living room, where a handsome bay window with beveled-glass panes looked out on the front porch. They had left the hinged window seat open to reveal a two-foot-deep storage space more than large enough to contain a body. Ernie had commissioned draperies made from Beacon blankets with pan-Indian geometric patterns, and Rebecca closed them with a draw cord. Bobby and Spencer had brought several blankets from the bedroom to pad the space.

When they transferred their limp amigo from the study and put him in the window-seat storage, Spencer said, "I hope he'll be able to breathe in there."

"He isn't breathing," Rebecca reminded him. "No vital signs."

"But if he comes back and wakes up while we're not here, he'll need to breathe."

"It's not an airtight space," Bobby said. "Anyhow, he can just lift the lid and get out."

Spencer grimaced. He was very good at grimacing. He practiced his grimace assiduously. It was one of very few expressions that, during opening night at an art gallery showing, impressed wealthy collectors and convinced them that he was a creative power with which to be reckoned. "Driving here from Chicago, I never thought I'd be hustling poor Ernie around, trying to keep him out of the hands of a mortician."

"It's pretty much exactly the kind of thing I expected," Bobby disagreed. "Don't you think it reminds you of the good old days? I feel like I'm fourteen, though I don't know why."

"What next?" Spencer asked.

"I don't believe that's up to us. I get the feeling shit is going to keep coming our way as fast as we can deal with it. So, for God's sake, don't go into a fugue state and start painting things that you don't even know what they are."

"I have to be in my studio, with a brush in hand, before it can happen. And even then, it doesn't always."

Rebecca closed the lid of the window seat and grimaced at the draperies, though not as impressively as Spencer had grimaced for another reason. "Maybe Ernie needs this atmosphere to write his songs, but it's too much Western movie for me. And I'm hungry."

Spencer suggested they park their rental cars at the motel and go to dinner in his SUV. "How about Adorno's?"

Rebecca smiled. "Like old times, if it's still in business."

"From what I've seen, it will be. Nothing much changes in Maple Grove."

Staring at the closed lid of the window seat, Bobby the Sham heard himself speaking in a most tenderhearted tone that wasn't common to him. His voice even conveyed a tremor of emotion. "It doesn't feel right, leaving him here alone."

Each of these amigos had been to an extent hard-boiled by making their way to success in the merciless industries of film, art, and literature, where envy was epidemic and the second-worst cause of career death, backstabbing, was exceeded only by front-stabbing with a smile. Because Rebecca had risen through the brutal film business, she was of course the toughest and most practical of the three, and her recent spasm of enlightenment had made her acutely aware of that.

Although she loved Ernie, she was blunt in her assessment of the situation. "Each of us has been alone since we split up all those years ago, and each of us was alone before we ever became amigos. One of us being alone is nothing new."

15

ERNIE ALONE

When bears hibernate, do they dream away the winter? In this age when we are told that science has explained the universe and answered all the big questions, it seems that we ought to know if bears dream. However, we lack this knowledge because, sadly, those intrepid scientists who have ventured into the dens of bruins to study their brain activity with a compact, portable battery-powered electroencephalogram have never gotten further than shaving small spots on the sleeping subject's scalp and attaching electrodes with a conductive paste. Before an adequate reading can be taken, there occurs either a violent mauling or dismemberment or evisceration with extreme prejudice—or all three. Nothing good happens to the electroencephalogram machine, either.

We might expect that the sleeping bear would be injected with a powerful sedative, administered from a distance by a hypodermic-dart gun. Any competent scientist would dismiss that notion with scorn if not searing contempt, and rightly so. Hibernation is a *natural* state to which bears succumb, whereas sedation is *unnatural*. If the bear were to be sedated with a significant dose of zolpidem or zaleplon, whereafter brain patterns indicative of dreaming were observed, that would prove nothing about whether the animal dreams during natural hibernation. This vital information will be acquired only after some fortunate scientist chances upon a bear that is a particularly deep sleeper, which may well require the sacrifice of a great many more highly educated individuals before the right bear is found.

This raises the obvious question, "What about worms?" Recently, scientists discovered long, pale worms frozen in Arctic ice, where they had been in stasis for thousands of years. When thawed, these worms came back to life, as vigorous and inquiring as contemporary worms that had not suffered such an ordeal. During those centuries, did the hibernating worms dream? What fascinating fantasies might they have experienced as they slept? Scientists very much want to know, but they are foiled by the fact that the brains of these worms are so small that no electroencephalogram has yet been invented with electrodes so tiny they can be securely attached where required. And then there is the problem of determining which end of the worm is the head, if either.

If the question of whether hibernating bears and worms dream remains unanswered—and it does—we cannot hope to know if Ernie Hernishen was dreaming in suspended animation while swaddled in the space under the lid of the window seat. We could speculate, but to no useful end.

What can be said is that, after the three amigos departed, the house remained quiet for some time. Not silent, you understand, for even deserted houses produce small sounds. The creak and crack of expanding and contracting wood. The knocking of a trapped air bubble making its way through the plumbing. The refrigerator motor cycling on and off.

When a louder noise arose, it was a strange squishing sound combined with what might have been the mortal gagging of someone choking on a wad of inadequately chewed beef caught in his windpipe, punctuated by the metallic trilling of a cricket or other insect. Whatever the source of this guggle and swash, no cry of distress accompanied it, as it seemed ought to be the case.

The disturbance progressed from the kitchen, along the hallway, into the living room. The lid of the window seat made a distinctive sound as it was raised, after which a couple of minutes passed in a contemplative quiet except for brief spates of insectile vibrato. No hiss or sigh could be heard, no inhalation or exhalation. Then came sounds that were clearly those made by a clumsy individual trying to extract something of considerable weight from within a window seat. The lid closed with a clonk. The peculiar and unpleasant mélange of squishing and gagging and trilling receded across the living room, along the downstairs hallway, and into the kitchen as a mysterious individual conveyed its burden toward an unknown lair with a purpose that was no doubt unholy.

TWO

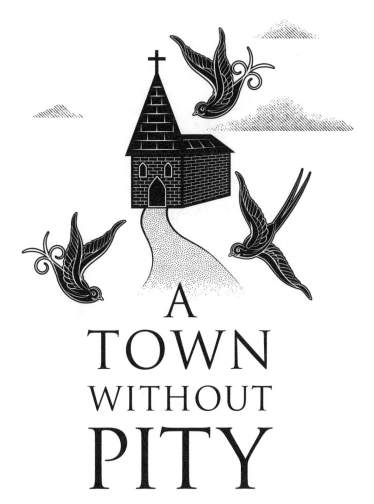

A
TOWN
WITHOUT
PITY

16

FRIENDS AT DINNER

This was a century of rapid change so disorienting that many people could cope only by medicating themselves. Therefore, it is no surprise that, in the years during which the three amigos were gone from Maple Grove, Adorno's Pizzeria had become Adorno's Ristorante with a full menu of Italian dishes in addition to their legendary pizza. The premises had doubled in size. The speckled vinyl flooring had been replaced with porcelain tiles made to look like limestone. Gone were the red Formica tables with chrome legs; now tables of unknown construction were covered with white tablecloths. The red leatherette booths had been upholstered in black; even the tables flanked by facing banquettes were draped in white, and between booths were new etched-glass panels to provide a measure of privacy. Gone, the policy of self-seating; there was a hostess now, and the waiters wore uniforms of black slacks, white shirts, and white aprons. There was no chance whatsoever that pizza was still sold by the slice.

Because Adorno's had been a refuge for the four amigos back in the day, Spencer Truedove felt the urge to protest the new Adorno's by screaming *Nooooooo* as the hostess led them to a booth, but he restrained himself. Although he painted bizarre, repulsive subjects of mysterious nature that adoring critics called "the most riveting depictions of existential despair ever committed to canvas," Spencer was a traditionalist when he wasn't lost in a fugue state. He found change distressing, and he was suspicious of the progress that so many people celebrated. The atomic bomb was progress when compared to lesser explosives before it, and then came the hydrogen bomb, and lately the *supersonic* hydrogen bomb, which could blow up the world twenty-two minutes faster. Wind and solar power were killing entire species of birds; mining and processing of the rare-earth minerals needed to service those industries and to make billions of lithium batteries was creating more devastating pollution in one decade than occurred in the past half century of fossil fuels. Now that Adorno's Pizzeria had become a ristorante, any change could be forced on the world; anything could happen. *Anything.*

Spencer and Bobby sat on one banquette in the booth and Rebecca sat on the other banquette. As the hostess put down three menus, she said, "The wig and glasses are okay, Ms. Crane, but your perfect nose gives you away. You should add a bad nose to your disguise, maybe one that has a hook or one that's squashy-looking." Rebecca thanked her for the advice. The waitress winked at Bobby. She said, "Cool hat," to Spencer. And then she went away.

"I'm not gonna take off my hat," Spencer said with the firmness of a man who knows his rights. "I lent it to Ernie to get him out of the hospital, but I'm not taking it off again, not even for dinner."

"No one's asking you to take off your hat," Bobby said.

Spencer surveyed the restaurant. "When we came here as kids, guys wore baseball caps, knitted caps, Stetsons, straw hats, any hat they wanted, but it's not that kind of place anymore. No guy in here except me is wearing a hat at dinner, but I don't care."

"Nobody cares," Rebecca assured him.

"I might even sleep in my hat."

"Good for you," she said.

"They ruined a fine thing."

"The food is probably still delicious," Bobby said. "It smells great in here."

"Everybody's got to go and change what doesn't need changed. Take that wall, for instance."

Bobby looked where Spencer pointed. "What about it?"

"There used to be a big, damn, wonderful mural on that wall."

"Hey, I forgot about the mural," Rebecca said. "The Leaning Tower of Pisa, the Colosseum . . ."

"The Arch of Constantine, the Pantheon," said Spencer.

"Romulus and Remus being suckled by a wolf," Bobby recalled.

"Caesar's legions marching to war," Spencer said, "the Trevi Fountain, and what we thought was a pissoir but were afraid to ask Mr. Adorno about." His voice was thick with nostalgia that had an edge of grief. "All gone. Nothing now but a plain wall. Changed."

They were silent for a moment, and then Bobby said, "I'm sorry about all that about your mom. I know it still hurts."

"Thanks, amigo. Mom still lives in New Orleans. She calls herself Constanina de Fornay. She never writes."

"What about your dad?"

"He'll be up for parole in six years. I never will understand how he went from founding a church to robbing armored cars. I guess he wasn't who I thought he was. He had a secret self."

"Well," Bobby said gently, "the church wasn't a church like we think of churches."

With the warmth that was so natural to her even before she learned how to fake compassion and charm an audience, Rebecca said, "Sweetie, don't put all the blame on your dad. That stripper, Venus Porifera, she was a bad influence."

"And sweaty," said Bobby.

"She didn't intend to be sweaty," Spencer said, "and it wasn't a smelly or disgusting sweatiness." He avoided putting down people for something they couldn't control, like being short or skinny or having a wart on the nose—or being sweaty without effort. He had endured more than his share of put-downs in his youth because his ears were large, his hands small, and he played the fife in the school band until they decided they didn't need a fife.

"It must be wrenching," Rebecca said with tenderness, "to visit your dad in prison."

"I never do. He refuses to add me to his approved-visitor list. Last time I saw him was thirteen years ago. I came back from Chicago to visit Ernie, decided to drop by the rectory, just to see if Dad was doing okay. He was in a meeting with twelve deacons. They were all wearing black robes, stag antlers, and goat masks. I didn't stay very long. To tell you the truth, when he was sent to prison, I was relieved. I know that's a terrible thing to say about your father."

"Not at all," Bobby assured him, and Rebecca said, "You didn't desert your family, your family deserted you."

The freckled, red-haired waiter arrived at the table, looking unusually Irish to be working in an Italian restaurant. He said his name was Vito, which seemed to be an obvious lie. He asked if they would like bottled or tap water, still or sparkling, domestic or imported, with or without ice, accompanied by a slice of lemon or plain, and if they might also wish to have a cocktail. The aqua

choices were so numerous that the amigos passed on water altogether and ordered two bottles of Caymus cabernet sauvignon
so that the second could breathe while they consumed the first.
Following the events of this day, they didn't expect to be able to
sleep without alcohol. Vito assured them that they had made an
excellent choice, as though they usually drank wine that came in
a box and had only recently earned sufficient funds to try the finer
things in life. Then he went away smiling, perhaps calculating his
potential tip.

After lubricating himself with a little Caymus, Bobby asked,
"Does the name Wayne Louis Hornfly mean anything to you?"

A frisson of terror shivered through Spencer, but it shook
nothing from his compromised memory banks.

Rebecca's hand spasmed when Bobby said "Hornfly," and a
dribble of wine escaped her glass, and for a moment she looked
like she had in *Shriek*, when she had been running for her life
through a moonlit cornfield with Judyface in pursuit. Then she
put down her wet glass and wiped the bowl and the stem with
her napkin.

The napkins were white cloth. Spencer longed for those paper
napkins provided in the Adorno's of yesteryear. They were square
with tiny images of pizza slices pointing the way around all four
sides. He could see one of those napkins in his mind's eye, and
then he saw one of the coasters with the Coca-Cola logo that the
original Adorno's got free from the soda company and put on the
red Formica table when they served an iced drink in a sweating
glass. Then he saw a straw wrapped in a paper sleeve and his fingers peeling the paper off the straw with an almost erotic delicacy.
He might have toured longer through memories of Adorno's Past

if, here in Adorno's Present, Bobby hadn't said, "It means something to you, doesn't it? 'Hornfly' means something."

Some readers might find it difficult to believe that Spencer's frisson of terror would catapult him through mundane memories of paper napkins and coasters bearing advertisements and soda straws. However, you must remember that he was a visual artist who tended to recall moments of his life in images instead of words. That is one of many traits that make artists seem like oddballs to the rest of us, as they stare slack-jawed into space, picturing their way to one conclusion or another.

"Hornfly!" Rebecca said, dragging Spencer fully out of his reverie. "Wayne Louis Hornfly. I don't know who he is, but when you spoke the name, I saw Anthony Perkins is *Psycho*, Bela Lugosi in the original *Dracula*, Boris Karloff in *Frankenstein*, and Anthony Hopkins in *The Silence of the Lambs*."

It may be necessary to note that, as an actress in films and television, Rebecca was a *visual* artist of a kind and, in her way, not unlike Spencer Truedove in how she processed information. Unlike painting, acting requires speech, and Rebecca had plenty of that, too, as you will see.

"Bobby, you spoke that name, and my stomach clenched, tightened like a fist, and I felt as if my heart stopped, which of course it didn't, but I couldn't breathe, I really couldn't. I had a horrible moment of vertigo, as if this booth were a spinning gondola in a carnival ride. Wayne Louis Hornfly is someone we once knew, some creep or sicko. But damn it all, I can't remember anything about him. My memories of him are erased, maybe repressed, but by whom? Why? What does it mean?"

"In the labyrinth of our past," Bobby said, "something worse than a Minotaur waits around every turn." Being a writer, he often thought in metaphors, though they were usually better than that one.

"Google him," Spencer said.

"He doesn't google."

"Everyone can be googled."

"I tried. If there ever was a Wayne Louis Hornfly—and we all know beyond a doubt that there was—he passed through the world without leaving a trace. The name came to me in the plane, when we were in an unusually powerful lightning storm. Hornfly. It fills me with dread."

"Lightning?" Rebecca asked. "You mean lightning has something to do with him?"

"Maybe."

They sat in silence, taking refuge in wine.

The restaurant became busy. To Spencer, a lot of the patrons looked as if they were scientists and mathematicians. They were not a glamorous bunch. Eyeglasses were prevalent. There was an air of arrogance about them, a smugness, as if they knew things no ordinary mortals would ever know. A few wore shirt-pocket protectors and were well equipped with ballpoint pens. They were somewhat better dressed than the locals, yet a bit unkempt. One wore a black T-shirt with white words that proclaimed EINSTEIN WAS NO BILL NYE, referring to Bill Nye the Science Guy on television. Spencer was pretty sure he could sort out the employees of the Keppelwhite Institute from the regular folks.

Then Bobby said, "I keep thinking about the church, Saint Mark's. All those bodies lined up in the basement. Maybe our minds are connecting puzzle pieces. Maybe the bodies in the basement are somehow tied to Hornfly."

Vito returned to ask if they knew what they wanted for dinner. They did. He took their order. The process was uneventful. Vito went away, if his name really was Vito.

"After dinner," Bobby said, "we should go to Saint Mark's when we're finished here."

"What?" Spencer said. "Tonight?"

"That's when I expect to be finished eating," Bobby confirmed.

Rebecca said, "Churches don't stay open twenty-four/seven like they once did. These days, too many crazies are out there who want to damage or desecrate churches. Saint Mark's will be locked tight."

"I can get in anywhere," Bobby said.

"How's that?"

"Because I'm a novelist who's written about burglars and done his research."

Vito brought their food. It was wholesome and delicious. In some novels, meals are described in luscious detail and poetic terms in order to help create the ambience of the scene. Not in this one.

"Okay," Rebecca said, "so we're going to the church because Ernie's not dead even though he sure seems to be, and maybe if we don't do something in a timely manner, then he might die for real, and we can't think of where else to go anyway. But what do we hope to find there, guys? You don't think there will be ten dead bodies lined up on the basement floor, do you?"

"Maybe not," Bobby said. "But there'll be something—a clue, a lead—because that church was always a weird place even before what we found that night."

Rebecca frowned, but that expression in no way diminished her beauty. Spencer was pretty sure that nothing could make her less attractive. If you came upon her by surprise, while she was hunkered in a cave, covered in filth and blood, greedily devouring a sackful of kittens, her face twisted in an expression of insane glee, she would still be gorgeous, elegant, graceful. It was a gift. Rebecca said it was sometimes a curse, as when a film director, addled by LSD and PCP, wanted to cut her head off and preserve it forever in his freezer. But being down-to-earth and honest, she acknowledged that looking the way she did had so many advantages that it was worth the risk of decapitation.

Frowning exquisitely, Rebecca sought clarification from Bobby. "Weird? What was weird about the church before those bodies?"

"For one thing, Pastor Larry."

"Ah. Yes. I almost forgot. Pastor Larry."

Through Spencer's mind's eye, seven faces turned in succession, as if painted on a revolving drum. Four were Larrys with whom he had been friendly—Jenkins, Eckstein, Block, and Fukagami. Then appeared Larry from the Three Stooges, Larry the golden retriever who lived with a neighbor in Chicago, and finally Pastor Larry. The reverend had a round face and blond hair as fine as that of a baby. His blue eyes were watery, suggesting he sorrowed over the fallen condition of humanity without surcease. Yet his mouth curved in a perpetual dreamy half smile in both times of rejoicing and times of tragedy, as if he were equally amused by the triumphs and tribulations of his parishioners, though no one could recall seeing him actually laugh.

"I never liked Pastor Larry," Spencer said. "I couldn't begin to understand why Ernie was drawn to him even if it did irritate the hell out of Britta. I hope we don't see him tonight."

Rebecca said, "Maybe he's not at Saint Mark's anymore."

"Oh, I imagine he's still there," Bobby disagreed. "He'll only be maybe fifty-five. And he's not the kind of charismatic preacher that churches all over the country are scheming to lure away."

"Even if he had nothing to do with those bodies," Spencer said, "there's something twisted about him." He touched his porkpie hat as if to ward off evil, like a pilgrim might touch a sacred object.

17

AS REBECCA PAYS THE CHECK, BOBBY RECALLS THE EVENING WHEN SHE BECAME AN AMIGO

In late September, classes at Maple Grove High had been in session for a month, long enough for most of the teachers to decide that imparting knowledge to their students was a more arduous task than any human being ought to be required to undertake. After the inexplicable excitement that possessed the teenagers on their return to school, they had adjusted to the realization this would be another year of tedium, punctuated by more frequent and intense hormonal urges than the previous year, most of which would be relieved with an imaginary partner. Already, teachers had resorted to educational films, periods of assigned research in the library, silent reading sessions, and other scams, giving themselves more time to suck on cigarettes in the faculty lounge before smoking anywhere in the building was at last forbidden; when that tragic day arrived, there would be no relief except through prescription drugs or capitulation to one degree of insanity or another.

That autumn night was cool but not cold, windless but not perfectly still. Thick fog oozed through lamplit streets. In those blinding conditions, most drivers piloted their cars and trucks well below the speed limit, but a few reckless individuals raced into the void with the conviction that excess alcohol provided protection equal to Kevlar body armor or with the belief that God looked after fools.

On Monday evenings, Adorno's Pizzeria was never super busy because here in the heartland most people who had dining-out money used it Wednesday through Sunday. A few booths were occupied, but the tables in the center of the room were untenanted. Now and then customers came in to pick up the takeout they had ordered.

The big mural offered Italian atmosphere from the Tower of Pisa to what might have been a pissoir. A year earlier, there had been a jukebox, but Mr. Adorno fell out of love with contemporary music. Now some guys with names like Dean Martin and Julius La Rosa and Al Martino were piped in free. The amigos tried not to listen to them because, if they came to like those singers, they might sink deeper into nerddom, so deep they would never get out. On the plus side, when other teenagers wandered into the place, the music was to them what a crucifix was to vampires, and they fled before someone might try to drive stakes through their hearts.

Bobby the Sham and Ernie were sitting on the same banquette in their booth, and Spencer was sitting alone in the facing banquette. On the table between them were three Cokes on coordinated coasters and a large cheese-and-pepperoni pizza that they were sharing.

This was a sanctuary for the amigos because Mr. Adorno refused to endure the worst of adolescent behavior; therefore, if you were kids who qualified for one of the in-crowds and wanted a hangout joint, you went to Pizza Pete's or Roscoe's Burger Hut & Drive-Thru, which were on the far side of town from Adorno's.

In this place, no one bullied or taunted or mocked or sneered at anyone because the trade was mostly adults, and those kids who came here were outcasts, geeks, and losers who just wanted to live and let live.

The amigos, all fourteen years old and beginning their freshman year after escaping the purgatory of middle school, had met in July. Recognizing that they were from impossible families and sensitive to the suffering of others in a time when fomenting the suffering of others was a popular sport, they bonded quickly. All three wanted to be United States Marines. If the Marines didn't want them, then they hoped to be astronauts. If they failed to become astronauts, they wanted to be famous stage magicians or maybe card counters who could bilk casinos out of millions of dollars. If none of those career paths proved open to them, there was always a need for car salesmen, and cars were cool. They agreed they didn't want to go to college or be cogs in some big corporation; if it came to one of those fates, they would have to win at least $150,000,000 in the lottery, after taxes, and share their winnings. Then they would buy Adorno's, not with any intention of making a profit, but just so they would always have the ideal place to hang out.

That evening in September, they were arguing over who would win in a matchup between the Terminator and the monster from the movie *Aliens*, when the pizzeria door opened and chilly fog seethed inside, bringing with it Rebecca Crane. They didn't know her name then, and in fact they initially paid little attention to her.

They were boys who liked girls, even though girls scared them a little. Actually, girls scared them a lot. They hoped to grow out of that and become confident around the opposite sex. However, they had admitted to one another that they expected to live without a mate, die alone, and be found by strangers weeks after death in a state of horrific decomposition.

Rebecca wasn't dressed to attract boys. Because of the examples set by her man-crazy mother and her grandparents in their creepy kissy-face war to the death, she'd decided to go through life as asexual as a protozoa, without even the hope of replicating herself by ameboid fission. On this occasion, she wore combat boots, baggy camouflage pants, a black sweatshirt, and a floppy waterproofed canvas hat with a wide brim like the headgear of explorers making their way through jungles in perpetual rain. She was as white-faced as something that lived under a rock, because she had applied stage makeup of the kind required by actors in the role of ghosts in such plays as those based on *A Christmas Carol* or a work by Poe.

When she came directly to the booth occupied by the three amigos and sat beside Spencer, the boys flinched, and Ernie almost knocked over his Coke, and Spencer raised one hand defensively, as if warding off an attack.

Bobby had seen such a person around school, in this getup as well as in assemblages of roomy antique clothing that made her look like the shambling apparition of some ax murderess who had died in the eighteenth century. There were no dress codes in school anymore; even if there had been, no teachers or counselors remained with the courage to confront a student so strangely costumed. Someone might have expressed concern about her intentions if she had shown up for class with a flaming torch in each hand, but even then the faculty and administration would most likely have decided that the wisest course was to give her whatever space she needed to reveal whatever statement she felt compelled to deliver.

Now, sitting in the booth beside Spencer, she made eye contact with each of the boys. They regarded her in stunned silence, as if Death had sat down among them.

She said, "I'm Rebecca Crane. I've been watching you guys for a few weeks."

Those weren't words that relieved their tension, especially as they had not been aware of being watched.

In a voice as solemn as if they were seated in a funeral home during a viewing of a deceased family member, she said, "You look like you enjoy being together, even like you're having fun, not fun like other kids have fun, but some kind of fun anyway."

Bobby thought—and no doubt so did Spencer and Ernie—that her implication was that "having fun" of their kind was something vermin did, a species of vermin that needed to be exterminated.

As if to stave off the violence that might be impending, Ernie said, "Well, you know, appearances can be deceiving. We don't have a lot of fun. We don't even try. It would be fruitless to do so."

Her eyes narrowed. "What are you trying to tell me? Are you telling me this is a closed club, I should go away?"

"We're not a club," Spencer assured her. "Nothing as fun as a club. We don't have a secret handshake or a club song or anything as fun as that."

Lips tightly compressed, she regarded Spencer in silence for half a minute, for another half minute, for yet another half minute, until a fine sweat had broken out on his forehead. Then she said, "I want in."

"In what?" Ernie asked.

"*In,*" she said fiercely.

"She wants in," Bobby clarified.

"She's already in," Spencer said. To Rebecca, he said, "You were outside, and you came inside."

"Don't pretend to be idiots so that maybe I'll just go away. You're not idiots, and I'm not going anywhere but in."

"She's not going anywhere but in," Bobby said, in case his two amigos still didn't get it. In fact, he didn't get it himself. The amigos were such outcasts that it never crossed his mind that she wanted to be one of their group. He was just trying to forestall an unpleasant conflict until they could pry from her what she meant by the word "*in.*"

Into this hair-trigger situation stepped Gia Adorno, who was the daughter of Luca and Apollonia Adorno. She was maybe five feet four with midnight-black hair and dark-brown eyes, so beautiful that the amigos always stuttered through their orders when she was their waitress. As willowy as she appeared, Gia could nevertheless lever an obnoxious drunk out of his chair and manhandle him through the front door into the street regardless of his size. She scanned Rebecca and said, "Great look."

"Thanks."

"I especially like the flamingo feather in the rain hat."

"No flamingos around here, so I plucked a chicken feather and dyed it pink."

"What can I get for you?"

"What're they drinking?"

"Vanilla Coke, cherry Coke, chocolate Coke."

"Pussy drinks. I'll have mine straight."

That was when Bobby started to like her.

"And a meatball sub with a lot of red-pepper flakes," Rebecca said, "and chopped pepperoncini."

When Gia went away, Bobby the Sham addressed his companions with sudden enlightenment. "I think Rebecca wants to be an amigo."

Spencer was so astonished that he clamped one hand to the crown of his skull as though to prevent his head from exploding. "I never thought—I can't imagine—a *girl* would want to be one of us."

"Or another guy, for that matter," Ernie admitted.

"Why?" Bobby wondered. "Why would anyone?"

"Well," she said, "two reasons. First, I don't expect I'll ever have, you know, a romantic relationship. I'll be old and die alone, and by the time someone finds me, I'll be a disgusting, decomposed *thing*. I figure if I make a few friends, one of them will find me before I begin to rot. I know that sounds weird."

"Not at all," Bobby averred, and Ernie echoed, "Not at all," and Spencer declared, "Eminently sensible."

She said, "The thing is, you don't have to like much about me, and I don't have to like much about you. Friends often don't like everything about one another, but they can be there for one another when it counts."

"And it really counts," Spencer said, "when you're lying dead and about to rot."

"You said you had two reasons," Bobby reminded her.

"You guys laugh a lot."

"We do?" Spencer asked.

"We're nerds," Ernie said. "We laugh at stupid stuff that a lot of people wouldn't laugh at. That doesn't mean it's funny."

Rebecca said, "My mother's living in San Francisco with a man named Raoul something. I have no idea who my father is. I live with my grandparents, who pretend to be wildly in love but who despise each other and don't hide it well. They actually *enjoy* despising each other. I've never heard any of them laugh. To be fair, I don't know if Raoul laughs, because I never met him. I never met Frederico before Raoul, or Juan who came before Frederico. Maybe those guys laugh uproariously all the time. But nobody ever laughs where I live, and I've had more grim than I can handle. I'm done with grim."

Ernie was moved. "I'm so sorry for you. That sucks. I never met my father, either. For your sake, if we become amigos, I'll try to prevent my mother from meeting you."

"I was a foster child," Bobby said. "Taken in by a couple of potatoes. They never laugh, either."

Spencer said, "I knew my mother, but last year she went away to find herself. I live in my father's house, though he's never there. He lives with a stripper in the rectory of a church he set up so that degenerates could have something to believe in."

One by one, she made eye contact with the amigos. "So am I in?"

Bobby said, "We'll need to talk about it."

"So talk."

"We'll need to confer in private, overnight."

"Confer, huh? Why don't you go to Vegas, rent the convention center, and have a conference regarding the issue?"

Having already delivered the unadulterated Coke, Gia returned with the meatball sub. "Would you like a knife and fork with that?"

"No, thanks," said Rebecca. "I'm good."

The submarine sandwich had not been sliced in two because the contents might have spilled out of the cut end. She picked it up and held it in such a manner that Bobby had the impression she was a person of exquisite etiquette holding a canape. She proceeded to eat with the gusto of a lumberjack at the end of a long day of felling trees, and yet there was nothing gross about her manners. Even in her weird outfit and paste-white face, she was so poised that she made hogging down a one-pound hoagie seem like an elegant deed of great refinement.

The three amigos watched her. They sat very still. They said nothing. They were temporarily *incapable* of speech.

Finished eating, wiping her fingers on a paper napkin, Rebecca looked up and saw the amigos staring. "So am I in?"

"Yes," Bobby said, and Ernie said, "Yeah, sure," and Spencer said, "Of course."

She surveyed them with a gimlet eye—actually, two gimlet eyes. "We need to get one thing settled. You're not going to treat me like a girl or think of me as a girl. I'm one of the guys. Even if I show up in your dreams, even then, I'll just be one of the guys. I won't be an amiga. I'll be just another amigo. You got that?"

Bobby said, "Naturally, yeah, all right," and Ernie nodded as he intoned, "One of the guys," and Spencer confirmed, "I got it, you got it, we all got it."

Bobby was confident that, considering her appearance, it would be easy enough to think of her as a guy. Months later, when they discovered how she really looked, she had become a brother to them, and not much adjustment was required to think of her as a tomboy sister, though that is for a later chapter, as this one will soon become longer than a modern reader will tolerate.

Now she leaned back in the booth and smiled at her amigos. "So if we're not a club, what are we—a gang?"

Ernie said, "Gee, I don't know. 'Gang' sounds kind of rough."

However, Spencer sat up straight, electrified by the idea. "People don't mess with gangsters."

Half an hour of vigorous discussion ensued, most of it too juvenile to burden you with here. Eventually they decided to think of themselves as a gang though not to say so publicly.

Now on her second Coke and feeling no pain, Rebecca said, "You are not going to regret this. I'll be loyal and pull my own weight in whatever we do. Hey, you know what?"

"What?" the boys asked simultaneously.

"Now that we're a gang, we should knock over a liquor store and find some old man crossing the street so we can beat him up just for the hell of it."

The boys laughed, though a bit uneasily, still not quite sure what to make of her in her combat boots, camouflage pants, black sweatshirt, and death-white makeup.

18

UNDER THE CHURCH

As it pricked the eye of the moon, the steeple of Saint Mark's appeared as sharp as a thorn. Clad in native limestone, the church had been constructed in a time when people felt the architecture of churches should encourage consideration of the mightiness of God rather than bring to mind automobile showrooms and discount outlets.

The courthouse stood on the northeast corner of the block, Liberty Park with its bandstand on the northwest corner, the library on the southwest corner, and Saint Mark's at the southeast position. Dating back to the electrification of the town, fluted iron streetlamps, painted dark green and each topped with a frosted glass fixture shaped like a flame, cast a pale light that imbrued the scene with loneliness, reminding Rebecca of paintings by Edward Hopper. There was also a quiet menace about the place that brought to mind certain late-night street shots in *The Exorcist*.

Even at just 9:40, little traffic navigated the intersection of Cunningham Avenue and Winkler Street. Maple Grove was surrounded by miles of fertile farmland, and in spite of the Keppelwhite Institute and the army of scientists who lived in that company neighborhood, this was still something of a farm town, where early-to-bed-and-early-to-rise was a guiding principle with many of its citizens.

The amigos had left two cars at the motel and had come here in Spencer's Genesis SUV. He parked east of Saint Mark's, in front of the cemetery that lay between the church and rectory. At the far end of the long block, the reverend's handsome brick residence was dark. Pastor Larry Turnbuckle was asleep—or perhaps engaged in some freaky activity that explained his perpetual dreamy half smile.

Having shed her wig and eyeglasses now that night had fallen and they did not intend to return to any busy public place, Rebecca followed Bobby into the moonlit cemetery. Spencer trailed close behind.

This burial ground was a major feature of the town, extending two blocks from north to south, a maze of headstones and memorial plaques set flush in the earth, with here and there a massive old oak. When Maple Grove was a young town, before Saint Mark's was built, when the graveyard had been less populated than it was now, those trees had already been mighty works of Nature. In the days of horse-drawn wagon trains, during the great migration westward, settlers on the way to a promised land of milk and honey stopped in Maple Grove to stock their covered wagons with supplies. They were stalwart and optimistic folks, blithely unaware that some would be stranded for months in the blizzard-ripped Rocky Mountains and cannibalize one another in desperation, which is the kind of thing that happens to stalwart and optimistic folks more often than they ever anticipate. In addition to the migrants, there were outlaws of all kinds in those days—bank robbers, wagon-train raiders, men who kidnapped schoolmarms for unspeakable purposes, horse thieves, schoolmarms who went bad and became horse thieves, vicious gunslingers in the hire of cattle barons who paid them to kill sheep ranchers, gunslingers in the hire of sheep ranchers who paid them to kill corn farmers, gunslingers in the hire of corn farmers who paid them to kill those who were foolish enough to grow beets. Really, there was no end to it. Back then, only a few brave individuals took up careers in law enforcement. Nevertheless, a great many desperadoes and miscreants were brought to trial before a judge, under the cemetery oaks, where they were found guilty with satisfying speed and hanged from the stout limbs. These enemies of civilization were left depending from the oaks for at least three days, during which they began to rot, were pecked apart by carrion-eating birds, and served as a lesson to others who might be thinking that the criminal life looked pretty sweet.

In a long-ago December, following the worst crime epidemic in state history, a reporter named William Hawkshaw, working for the *Maple Grove Gazette*, toured this cemetery at dusk with carolers and a crowd of holiday revelers, each of whom bore a candle. Hawkshaw wrote a moving, inspiring piece in which he described the numerous frozen corpses suspended from the winter-stripped oaks as "ornaments of true justice decorating the trees of righteousness, waiting for the ground to thaw, graves to be dug, and Hell to welcome them. Snow began to fall, the delicate flakes like merry angels capering in the candlelight." He didn't win a Pulitzer, as surely he would have in our time, but only because the Pulitzer didn't yet exist. However, Hawkshaw was honored by the Maple County Corn Growers Association, half of whose members had recently been gunned down but who refused to be defeated by a bunch of sheepherders.

Now, as the three amigos made their way through the cemetery, where no one had been hanged in nearly a hundred and fifty years, Rebecca was not overcome by a sense of the town's glorious history, as you might expect. She was instead awash in nostalgia for her teen years, when she and her amigos frequently went on night adventures. Although most of those escapades had been erased from her memory, she still vaguely recalled that they had occurred, which was enough to make her heart swell with longing. Like Rebecca, most actors are sentimental, yearning for the golden days of youth, when they were convinced that they were going to be bigger stars than they became.

When they had passed the east side of Saint Mark's, they turned west, departed the graveyard, and gathered behind the church. Three doors were set in that south wall. From experience, they knew that the one to the left opened into the sacristy. The one on the right was an emergency exit from the nave. The door in the middle provided access to a small holding room from which stairs led to the basement.

During the drive from the restaurant, Bobby had explained the function of a police lock-release gun. It isn't as big as a real pistol, and it doesn't blow out a lock with bullets. Instead of a barrel and muzzle, it presents a pick that has to be inserted in the keyway of the deadbolt. The trigger is then squeezed, usually three to five times, until all the pins in the lock are thrown to the sheer line, disengaging the bolt. Because some novels that Bobby had written dealt with crime and police procedure, his diligent research informed him of this device, which he had then illegally acquired. He carried this instrument with him in his travels, secured to his left ankle with a Velcro strap just in case he fell into the hands of bad people who locked him in a windowless room to be tortured and interrogated later. Growing up in Maple Grove, he'd become somewhat paranoid.

He also had a penlight, which Rebecca held, directing the beam on the deadbolt. Spencer merely stood watching, which was what most visual artists did when confronted with a situation that required dexterity with a mechanical device.

They were taking a chance that Saint Mark's did not have an alarm system. These days, churches were locked at night and often even in daylight if services were not underway, but they were rarely wired with alarm systems. Although bigots prowled in record numbers, those whose intentions were to desecrate altars were lazy cretins who, on finding the premises locked, slaked their hatred by throwing a brick through a stained-glass window or urinating on the front door.

The lock relented. They moved inside and closed the door behind them, and Rebecca shone the narrow beam down the concrete stairs. Like the holding room, the basement had no windows, so Bobby flipped up the wall switch. The light in the realm below was murky yellow and unwelcoming, remarkably reminiscent of the eerie light at the bottom of the hidden staircase that led to the secret room under the barn in *Shriek and Shriek Again*. Spencer must have recognized this resemblance, too, because he said, "This isn't a movie. There is no such person as Judyface."

Rebecca wasn't so sure. Life often imitates movies, unless the movies are about superheroes or humongous reptiles like Godzilla. Maybe there was a Judyface; maybe there wasn't. She had escaped from him once, set the bastard on fire in the sequel, and finally killed him in film three. So now she gathered courage and got in character, became spunky Heather Ashmont, the toughest and most indomitable young nurse in America, summoned to mind the inspiring music from the end credits of *Shriek Hard, Shriek Harder*, and led the way down the stairs.

The first room contained furnaces and electrical panels and fantastic snarls of plumbing that had no comprehensible purpose. A hallway led out of that space, with a large room on each side.

The chamber on the right provided storage for church records going back more than a hundred and twenty years. Included was a trove of information about generations of parishioners in which the amigos had no more interest than cows have an interest in the works of Dostoevsky.

The room to the left was about forty feet wide and fifty feet long. It was in this place that they had found ten comatose people lying face up and side by side, the recovered memory of which had drawn them here tonight.

Currently, the space was empty. They roamed back and forth, voices echoing off the concrete walls and ceiling as they strove to talk away the veils that concealed details of their previous descent into this room when they were teenagers.

Okay, here's the thing: Dialogue tags that identify speakers can be annoying in a long exchange of short statements between more than two characters, especially when it isn't that important to know exactly who said what. Consequently, though it will present a knotty problem for the narrator of the audiobook, dialogue identifiers have been omitted from the following give-and-take. The reader is free to employ his or her imagination as to who said what to whom.

"Back in the day, we didn't have a lock-release gun."

"We didn't need one. The door was unlocked."

"You remember that for sure?"

"Yeah. I think so."

"Me too. I think so."

"But why?"

"You mean, why was it unlocked?"

"I mean, I wonder . . ."

"Wonder what?"

"Why did we come here in the first place?"

"You mean, back then."

"Uh-huh. Back then."

"Yeah, you don't just stumble into a church basement."

"Not by mistake."

"Not unless you're drunk."

"We weren't drunk."

"I know we weren't drunk."

"So then why?"

"We must have found a clue that brought us here."

"What clue?"

"Damn if I know."

"Hey."

"What? What is it?"

"Something's coming back to me. I think . . ."

"What? Spit it out, amigo."

"I think we were secretly following someone."

"You mean, someone who came here?"

"None of us had a driver's license then. Or a car."

"So we were following someone on foot? Is that it?"

"On foot. Yeah."

"Who? Who were we following?"

"Wait, wait, wait. It's coming back to me, too. I see . . ."

"What do you see?"

"It's autumn. Cool. Moonless."

"Yeah. The four of us are walking along Winkler Street."

"Secretly following someone on Winkler? No, it's too well lit."

"We weren't following anyone yet."

"What were we doing?"

"'It was night in the lonesome October . . .'"

"What?"

"'Of my most immemorial year.'"

"That's Poe."

"'It was hard by the dim lake of Auber.'"

"'In the misty mid region of Weir.'"

"'It was down by the dark tarn of Auber.'"

"'In the ghoul-haunted woodland of Weir.'"

"Are you serious. You two were reading poetry?"

"Not reading."

"We memorized a lot of stuff. All of us."

"Yeah. And sometimes we swapped lines while we walked."

"Why? Why did we do that?"

"We were geeks."

"We were hopeless geeks."

"It was that bad?"

"You don't remember?"

"No. I don't. Wait. Maybe. Yes! Cool, moonless, Poe."

"Give us some."

"Some what?"

"How about 'The Sleeper.'"

"'At midnight in the month of June.'"

"'I stand beneath the mystic moon.'"

"'An opiate vapor, dewy, dim.'"

"'Exhales from out her golden rim.'"

"You *do* remember."

"We all do."

"So do you remember who we were following?"

"No, but I remember when."

"When?"

"When we got to the cemetery and saw the white rabbit!"

"He was dressed all in black."

"Yeah, but he was hurrying like the white rabbit."

"'I'm late, I'm late for a very important date.'"

"Hurrying through the dark graveyard."

"It was Pastor Larry!"

"Yes, yes! Where had he come from?"

"Somewhere in the south, going north toward the church."

"He unlocked the center door at the back and went inside."

"He was in the basement like five minutes."

"When he came out, we were hiding behind headstones."

"Near enough to hear him muttering a prayer."

"As I remember it, not a prayer."

"I agree. Not a prayer."

"He was muttering, 'Shit, shit, shit, shit, shit.'"

"Hey, yeah. Why did I remember a prayer?"

"Maybe because he sounded very passionate."

"Scared and beseeching."

"Yeah. That's a better word. 'Beseeching.'"

"He ran off toward the rectory."

"He left the church door unlocked."

"And we went inside."

"The men were lined up in this room. Ten of them."

"On their backs, eyes open, motionless."

"We thought they were comatose or maybe even dead."

"They were all naked. Weren't they all naked?"

"Yes! I remember now. All naked. It was freaky."

"And didn't they . . ."

"What?"

"Didn't they all look alike? Pretty much alike?"

"Yes. And . . . Oh my God. Oh my God. I'm in a horror movie."

"What? What are you remembering?"

"They were naked and . . . like unfinished."

"Yeah, yeah. Kind of rough around the edges."

"Pieces missing. Part of a hand missing on one."

"No testicles on any of them. No penises."

"One of them had a face without a mouth."

"Lumpy and subtly out of proportion."

"I don't want to remember this."

"Too late."

"Shit, shit, shit, shit, shit!"

"Are we back to Pastor Larry?"

"Don't you remember?"

"Tell us."

"They began to finish themselves."

"Yes! A mouth started to form where there'd been no mouth."

"You're right. I don't want to believe it, but you're right."

"Fingers slowly sprouted from a lump of a hand."

"But still none of them had a penis or testicles."

"Maybe because it was a church."

"What sense does that make. It doesn't make any."

"One of them blinked and turned its eyes toward us."

"Then another one."

"Then all of them, lying there, staring at us."

"This town is screwed! What are we doing here?"

"Saving Ernie."

"To hell with Ernie."

"You don't mean that."

"No, I don't. But I wish I did."

"We have a pact. One for all, and all for one."

"It'll probably turn out to be a suicide pact."

"What if Ernie's become a monster?"

"He hasn't become a monster. Even if he has, he's *our* monster."

In that ominous vault under the church, having conveyed a great deal of detail in quick, easy-to-read dialogue, thereby eliminating the need for clunky paragraphs of exposition, the amigos turned as one toward the most compelling feature of that large, empty room. At the far end was a drain the size of a manhole, and the floor sloped slightly toward it.

On the fateful night they'd just remembered, they had fled the room, pulling the door closed behind them. Bobby had been determined to hold it shut to prevent the golems—or whatever they were—from escaping. He insisted his three amigos go for help. No one wanted to leave him alone. They fell to squabbling among themselves about which two would stay behind with Bobby. Because they were a gaggle of adolescents whose brains were still developing and because they were also admitted geeks, the argument was drawn out to an absurd length, especially considering that the demonic brigade on the far side of the door had raised a fearsome caterwaul. The clones or pod people or escapees from Hell groaned and growled and squealed and snarled—and fell silent. No effort had been made to yank open the door and drag Bobby inside. Recognition of the sudden silence within the room had brought a matching quiet among those in the hallway. As Bobby held fast to the handle, his three amigos stared at the door with expressions of dread. They knew how moments like this always played out in movies. When the monster or monsters abruptly ceased raging, the final assault was at hand. The door would explode off its hinges, decapitating at least one amigo, and the horde would be upon them, devouring their faces. How could it be otherwise? But it *was* otherwise. Bobby could not let go of the handle, and his friends were paralyzed by fear, but a minute passed and then five minutes. Teenage boys, even geeks, perhaps especially teenage boy geeks, were loath to look stupid or cowardly in front of girls, even in front of profoundly unattractive girls. At that time, Rebecca Crane's true appearance was still unrecognized by her companions, buried as her charms were under voluminous thrift-shop costumes and one kind of ghastly makeup or another. Nonetheless, Rebecca was a girl, and Bobby Shamrock was a boy, and the scary prospect of epic humiliation lay before him, life-changing humiliation, extreme throw-yourself-off-a-bridge mortification, so after another minute of silence, he opened the door. The room was deserted. Not a trace of the ten naked men. Not even a finger crawling around in search of a hand; nothing like that. The amigos were relieved, of course, but also somewhat disappointed.

Now, two decades later, three of the four friends gathered around the drain near the end of the long room. It was about one yard in diameter. The iron lid featured inch-square holes. Perhaps the church basement was subject to flooding on rare occasion. The penlight beam revealed nothing of the drain below.

It was evident now, as on the night when they were fourteen, that the devil's legions—or whatever those creatures might have been—retreated by way of the drain. Most likely they'd come into the church by the same route.

"What were they?"

"Where did they come from?"

"Where did they go?"

"Where have they been for twenty years?"

"Were they real?"

"You think we all hallucinated the same thing?"

"No, but is it true? Is that what really happened?"

"It must be. We all shared the recollection."

"Maybe it was a false memory implanted by whoever erased from our minds what really happened. Maybe what really happened is worse and weirder."

"What could be worse and weirder?"

"Weirder than ten sexless, naked clones? Nothing. Doesn't there have to be some other explanation about what we saw that night?"

"You would think so, wouldn't you?"

Most people who have an encounter with the Unknown, capital U, have doubts about the experience and go through a period of denial, during which they try to explain away the event and restore a sense of normalcy to their lives, which is the kind of thing that often fills two or three episodes of a ten-episode Netflix series. Rather than continue to recount this phase at tedious length, we will get on with killing off our leads until only Rebecca remains, if in fact that is what happens. Life sometimes imitates movies, but if that were always the case, Earth would already have been destroyed in hundreds of cataclysms.

"We need to talk to Pastor Larry."

"Talk? We need to interrogate the shit out of him."

"Not tonight. We better tread carefully."

"Yeah. We don't want to wake up back where we started, with no memory of having returned to Maple Grove, and Ernie still in a coma or dead."

"It's getting late."

"I'm too exhausted to think straight."

"We need to go back to the motel and get some sleep, start fresh in the morning."

"They call it a 'motor hotel.'"

"So they can charge more."

"Well, they provide a free continental breakfast."

"I am deeply moved."

Soon the three amigos would be in their beds, in their separate rooms, where bad dreams waited for them—and maybe something worse.

19

ON THE WAY TO THE MOTEL, REBECCA REMEMBERS A BUSY DAY LONG AGO

Geeks had invented so much involving the key technologies that were rapidly changing the world that Rebecca expected her amigos to need maybe an hour to devise a plan to learn what the ten identical naked manlike things had been. By noon the day after the events at Saint Mark's, she became aware that these boys were instead the kind of geeks who played Mozart on an ocarina, or wrote puppet shows in which Big Bird was strangled by the Cookie Monster, or drew pictures of King Kong in body armor wielding a giant machine gun. However, their sophisticated planning expertise was too small to be measured.

This understanding relaxed and pleased Rebecca and convinced her that she had done the right thing by seeking their friendship, for she was the same kind of geek. She'd taught herself to write cursive backward as fluidly as she could write it forward, and she enjoyed composing letters to famous people with no intention of mailing them, starting with "enarC accebeR" (Rebecca Crane) and concluding with, for example, "raeD moT esiurC" (Dear Tom Cruise).

If the amigos couldn't figure out a plan—and they couldn't— they could blue-sky any issue in an entertaining fashion. And if they never arrived at a brilliant plan, at least they never arrived at a bad one, either.

Maybe the things under the church were demons summoned from Hell or clones raised in laboratory vats from which they had been released by angry anti-cloning activists, or perhaps they were the product of extraterrestrial seedpods that lacked enough imagination to produce ten different people. Whatever those creatures were, they apparently moved about town via storm drains and other mysterious subterranean passageways that might eventually have to be explored, though the amigos were not eager to do so.

The day after the terror in Saint Mark's basement was a Saturday. Still shaken, the friends could think of nothing else to do but run surveillance on Pastor Larry Turnbuckle. They didn't believe the Lutheran Church was manufacturing artificial human beings, in spite of its history of rebellion from theological tradition. However, the good reverend's involvement in that phenomenon seemed undeniable.

They pooled their funds and purchased four walkie-talkies, each about the size of a pack of Marlboros, which is not to say that the amigos smoked, for they did not. The reference to cigarettes is for the sole purpose of conveying the size of the communication devices.

This purchase was possible because each of these young people enjoyed a source of income. During the school year, Bobby wrote book reports and research papers for other kids, even for students in the grades above him; seniors whose parents had nocked them like arrows in bows of ambition and aimed them at universities were particularly eager to pay well for him to write the essays that were required to accompany their applications to various colleges. Spencer Truedove was at that time already living alone while his mother was looking for the self she had once been and his father was cohabiting with Venus Porifera in the rectory of the Church of the Sacred Erogenous Revelation; because Mr. Truedove was consumed by his ministry and rarely visited the house where he had lived such a straitlaced life that it embarrassed him, Spencer sold various household goods as he needed money. A set of fine china. Silver picture frames. Clothes that his mother hadn't found suitable in her exciting new life. Occasionally a piece of furniture. Even then a fine guitarist, Ernie went twice a month to the college where his mother was a professor, put his hat on the ground with a framed photo of Britta, and played for donations; the students and faculty members, aware of who he was, assumed his mother would visit them if they were insufficiently generous with their contributions, and as a consequence he received no one-dollar bills but a satisfying sheaf of fives and tens, now and then a twenty. Rebecca was a beneficiary of maternal guilt; whether her mother was living in Miami Beach with Fernando or in Vegas with Enrique or in San Antonio with Alejandro, she sent a generous check every month with a card signed *"Amor, Madre."*

Equipped with walkie-talkies, intrigued by the mystery of the ten golems, motivated by curiosity and fear, the four amigos took up positions on the grounds of the courthouse, in Liberty Park, on the steps of the Leghorn Library, which was named after the state's long-serving and much beloved senator, and in the cemetery. All eyes were on the rectory.

The early autumn day was pleasantly warm, and the sky was clear, and the state was as flat as ever. People went about their business as usual, and they smiled at the teenagers basking in the sun while reading books. Not one of the townspeople would have imagined that monsters lurked under the streets, but they lurked.

Pastor Turnbuckle was known to be an ardent advocate of the theory that walking twelve thousand steps—preferably more— every day promoted good health and guaranteed such a long life that God would eventually start to feel cheated out of your soul, for which He'd been waiting patiently. For the most part, the reverend walked everywhere while attending to church business and the needs of his flock, as well as when taking care of personal matters. His habit was to pull behind him an over-and-under basket rack on wheels, to be used when he bought groceries or picked up the mail at the post office, or when he stopped at the packaged-liquor store to purchase a fine cabernet sauvignon and a good merlot, which were ostensibly to be used as the sacramental wine on Sunday.

That morning Pastor Larry appeared at 10:22 a.m. He stepped out of the rectory with his two-basket cart in tow. His baby-fine blond hair and round face and watery blue eyes and dreamy smile were all just where they ought to be. From Rebecca's post in the graveyard, as the reverend came in her direction, she thought of a balloon in Macy's Thanksgiving Day Parade, drifting along as if he contained nothing but a buoying gas.

First, he visited someone, probably an elderly parishio- ner, at Stubblebuck's Care Home, an assisted living facility on Cunningham Avenue. Then he called at a house on Mayberry Boulevard, where a young mother in an apron and a little boy about three invited him inside. He window-shopped along Capra Street and stopped for lunch at Cleaver's Cafe on Mayfield Lane.

Never walking together, the four amigos stalked the clergy- man from opposite sides of the street, two following him, two preceding him and trying as best as they could to anticipate his intended route. When he stopped at one venue or another, his shadowers leaned against buildings or found places to sit, returning to their books.

Their task wasn't easy. Pastor Larry was hell-bent on reaching his goal of twelve thousand steps. He never proceeded directly from one destination to another. He wove through town on a drunkard's walk, and though he had the museful expression of a sleepy koala bear clinging to the trunk of a eucalyptus tree, he moved briskly, towing his wheeled basket as if he were collecting souls on the brink of Armageddon, with little time remaining before fire fell from the sky and consumed the world.

By 4:20 that afternoon, his over-and-under baskets were loaded with mail, nonperishable groceries, and dry cleaning. He returned to the rectory, as though he had not been running pell-mell through the cemetery like a man pursued the previous night, as if he had never gone into the church basement and hadn't found monsters.

Tired, frustrated, and bewildered that Turnbuckle had gone about his day as if monsters in the church basement were no more worrying than an infestation of mice, Rebecca consulted a glass-enclosed message board that stood in front of the church. Announcements of service times and other events were presented with white plastic letters slotted in the grooves of a black background. This evening at 7:00, a semimonthly meeting of "Saint Mark's Ladies of Compassion" would include planning for their "future charitable works," which was surely better than a gathering of pitiless ladies of vengeance. At the same time, there would be a meeting of "Saint Mark's Gentlemen for Jesus," which wasn't likely to be a group that summoned satanic creatures or created golems out of mud or raised money to fund the creation of clones. No doubt, Pastor Larry would cycle between the two events.

When Rebecca used her walkie-talkie to convey these facts to her amigos, the consensus was that they would be wasting their time if they tried to sneak into the rectory in the hope of uncovering sinister schemes.

Throughout the day, they had used their communication devices discreetly, with the volume low, but surveillance had gotten them nothing. They were disappointed, because they couldn't know that a time would soon come when those walkie-talkies would save one of them from assault and possibly death. Denied this foresight and unaware of the foreshadowing that just occurred in the previous sentence, they adjourned to dinner at Adorno's Pizzeria.

20

ABED IN THE SPREADING OAKS MOTOR HOTEL

Some say that dreams are coded messages from the subconscious, which is attempting to warn the clueless sleeper about destructive habits or about bad decisions that are likely to have a serious negative impact on his or her life. If you dream about piloting a sailboat across a sea of flaming vodka with sails afire and the helm so hot that it burns your hands, maybe you should cut back from five martinis an evening to one. Or let's say you dream of standing at the altar on your wedding day, with birds singing and flowers everywhere in abundance, with everyone you've ever loved present in the pews. As the groom slides the ring onto your finger, you look up into his face and see a naked skull with blood pouring out of its eyeless sockets. Sound advice in such a case would be to consider whether your fiancé might be the serial killer who has dismembered seven women in the past four years and taken their heads to display in some collection wherever he lives.

Whatever *your* theory of dreams, you must understand there are clues in the following dreams that will prepare you to endure the unspeakable horrors to come.

On that first night after three of the amigos returned to Maple Grove to save comatose Ernie Hernishen, Rebecca Crane—also known as enarC accebeR—dreamed that she was Nurse Heather Ashmont making her way through the crimson candescence of a perpetual twilight, in an infinite cornfield, in a state of slowly escalating anxiety. At the center of the field waited an immense oak. The tree was perhaps two hundred feet tall, with a crown at least a hundred fifty feet in diameter, unlike any real-world oak.

She wanted to go directly to the mighty oak, but she lacked the courage to approach it so boldly, moving instead in circles, around and around the tree, each circle bringing her closer to it. This was not characteristic of Nurse Ashmont, who was usually an unrelenting kick-ass. Her anxiety gradually chilled into dread, although not because she anticipated an encounter with Judyface. There was no Judyface here. Something worse shared the cornfield with her. She repeatedly looked behind her. But the rows were taller than she was, and they curved away to the south so that she couldn't see far enough to be sure no one stalked her through the last witchy light of the day. Besides, the walls of green were so dense that someone or something might have been paralleling her in another passageway and might reach through the corn to seize her.

In a sudden transition, she came out of the cornfield into the immediate presence of the oak. The great tree appeared to be dead, towering leafless, its wildwork of bare limbs impressing a fearsome pattern against the bloody sky of day's end. The gnarled trunk had the circumference of a redwood hundreds of years old; a car could have been driven through it if someone had carved out a tunnel.

Her dread became a paralyzing fear of imminent violence. In the broad trunk of the tree, a section of bark the size and shape of a door splintered and peeled away. The underlying wood crackled into a fountain of sawdust that gushed forth, and within the hollow thus formed stood a tall, powerful man. He wore the clothes that Judyface had worn—engineer boots and denim coveralls over long underwear.

However, this man emerging from the oak wasn't hiding behind Judy Garland. When Nurse Heather had ripped the mask off Judyface, that psycho killer was horribly scarred and breathed through ragged holes where a nose should have been, but that was the worst of it. *This* man's skull was as malformed as a squash that had suffered the torment of natural forces most squash were never required to endure. Although he had a nose, it was lumpy and hooked, as different from Tom Cruise's nose as any nose could get. His mouth was twice as wide as it ought to have been, and his teeth were green.

He came to her and grabbed her by one arm. She tried to resist, but he was strong. Strong and stinky. The smell wasn't like body odor, but at once astringent yet organic. She couldn't identify it.

In a deep, raw, wet voice, he declared, "If you don't go back to Malibu soon, you will be ours forever."

He pulled her through the carpet of sawdust, toward the hollow in the tree, and she tried to remember what Heather Ashmont had done when Judyface tried to drag her down to the secret room under the barn, but she wasn't Heather anymore; she was the ditzy blonde, Suzy Pepper, in the hit series *Enemies*, who was such a slut that she would have dated a guy even knowing he was a psycho killer, as long as he was cute and good in bed.

Although Rebecca was almost killed, one way or another, in 97 percent of her dreams, she never perished in one, not one; yet her heart raced as if it would burst, and her fear escalated into breathless terror. She tried to scream, but no sound escaped her. She tried to scream again, again, and yet again—

—until she sat up in bed in room 208 of the Spreading Oaks Motor Hotel. Awake, the only sound she could produce was a thin squeal like that a field mouse might make in the talons of an owl.

The strange smell came with her out of the dream. She held the scent only briefly, for it wasn't in the room, just remembered. It couldn't possibly be in the room, because the man from the tree hadn't been real, but only the figment of a nightmare.

In room 210, Bobby the Sham was dreaming that he was a dog. This was not unusual. He had been a dog in dreams often before. He believed his canine adventures while sleeping were a consequence of his having written a few bestselling novels about dogs; he seemed to have a talent for creating a believable doggy point of view.

He didn't have a name in the dream, and his breed wasn't easy to identify. He was just a generic dog having a good time running on a beach, through a meadow, through a forest, chasing butterflies and rabbits, losing track of his prey every time a new smell or unusual sound distracted him.

In an open wood, Bobby the dog took an interest in a particular small clearing, sniffing in circles. Abruptly, the ground opened and swallowed him. He scrabbled at the closing walls in a panic, trying to claw out of the sinkhole. But it wasn't a sinkhole. A sucking mouth had yawned wide under him. He slid into the moist throat of—of what, what, what?—something that seemed to be a giant worm that, although toothless, was taking him down by peristaltic action. Above him, the circle of light that was the open mouth grew smaller as the miserable mutt was drawn deeper, deeper into a darkness that would sooner than later secrete a dissolving acid.

Bobby the dog howled deep in the worm's throat—and Bobby the Sham whimpered pitiably in his hotel bed—and the worm spat him out as if the taste must be offensive. A voice from somewhere, nowhere, deep and growling, a voice that was nothing like what Bobby would expect a worm's voice to be, said, "Ernest Hernishen belongs to me, not to you."

With that, Bobby catapulted out of sleep and found himself standing beside the bed, gasping and shaking.

❦

In room 212, Spencer Truedove dreamed that he was his brother, Vlademir, though in the real world he had no brother named Vlademir or anything else. Vlad was strapped to a bed in a mental hospital, where a sinister doctor with one white-filmed eye prepared to give him an injection. The barrel of the syringe looked at least eight inches long and an inch in diameter; it was filled with a milky solution that appeared as if it had been squeezed out of the physician's bad eye. "This," declared the doctor, "will turn you into a female gorilla, and you will live free in the jungles of Africa." Instead, the shot turned Vlademir (who was really Spencer) into a panda named Mum-Mum. Mum-Mum lived in a Manhattan apartment with Norman and Beverly Shore. Norman worked at a hedge fund, and Beverly was an attorney at a prominent law firm. During the day, when Norm and Bev were at work, Mum-Mum took care of their toddler, Sherman, who loved his panda nanny. From time to time, as Mum-Mum and Sherman chased each other through the infinite apartment or played hide-and-seek, Sherman would open the coat closet door, where a comatose Ernie Hernishen hung from the rod. A monster who shared the closet always shouted, "He's ours, OURS, you little shit!" The monster routinely slammed the door in the toddler's face, and little Sherman screamed for nanny. Mum-Mum sometimes required an hour and much ice cream to quiet the terrified, weeping child, but at least the monster, which smelled like poisonous mushroom soup, never came out of the closet to rip them to pieces.

When artists spend their days painting abstract works that are open to thousands of interpretations but have no real meaning, their dreams are not like yours and mine. A gifted psychiatrist with a keen understanding of the human mind might question their mental stability, but we must admit that their dreams are immeasurably more entertaining than ours.

Insufficiently frightened, Spencer Truedove did not wake in a cold sweat but lay giggling in his bedclothes until he received a wake-up call from the front desk at 6:30 in the morning.

21

BOBBY SUDDENLY RECALLS A NIGHT OF TERROR

Alone in his motel room, having showered and dressed for the day, Bobby Shamrock ate the free continental breakfast that was provided by the establishment. This proved to be a small pastry with raisins and white icing, served on a paper plate sealed in Saran Wrap. He didn't want the sweet roll, but if he left it untouched, the management might be offended. If there was one thing Bobby was loath to do—actually, there were many—it was to offend someone who meant well.

He devoured the dry and tasteless roll while standing in the bathroom so the crumbs would fall into the sink, from which they could be flushed away with water. Then he wiped out the sink with a handful of Kleenex. He wrapped the damp tissues in the Saran Wrap and dropped everything in the trash can along with the paper plate, which he rinsed off prior to disposal. Bobby was something of a neatness freak. He might not be teetering on the edge of mysophobia (the fear of dirt) or ataxiophobia (the fear of disorder), which Rebecca sometimes seemed to be, but he definitely had his issues.

The amigos had agreed to meet at the diner adjacent to the motel at 7:30. It was seven o'clock. He was uncomfortable sitting in a room with an unmade bed. After he had addressed this problem, the condition of the bed suggested he'd slept on the floor.

With twenty minutes to kill, he sat in the room's only armchair and found himself recalling a visit to Saint Mark's rectory, which had until now been bleached from his memory.

After that long-ago Saturday when the amigos followed Pastor Larry around Maple Grove without turning up a clue as to why there had been monsters in the church basement, they were more determined than ever to learn what nefarious business the clergyman might be up to. They decided to attend the Sunday morning service at Saint Mark's, on the off chance that revelation would occur. As a member of the choir, Ernie had been for days practicing the scheduled hymns in order to irritate his mother; although she would be fuming that he'd gone to church, she would be grateful for the silence. Spencer lived alone in his father's house, so he could do what he wanted and go anywhere he wanted. On weekends, Rebecca's grandparents had more time to spend together; they preferred she stayed out of the house most of each day. Her absence enabled them to devote themselves more ardently to the illusion of being lovebirds while sharpening their hatred, devising subtler, ever more vicious verbal skewerings and mean tricks. Having fostered Bobby, Adam and Evelyn Pinchbeck had allowed him to raise himself and do as he wished, because to lay down rules would require them to speak, an activity that seemed to exhaust them quickly.

While Ernie stood proudly with the other singers in the choir enclosure between the chancel railing and the presbytery, his three amigos sat together in a pew at the very back of the church. They regarded the gathered parishioners with deep distrust, alert for suspicious behavior. They didn't know what specifically that would look like, but they believed they would know it when they saw it.

Most of their attention was directed toward Pastor Larry, who drifted through the service like a cloud of ectoplasm shaped into human form to be inhabited by a revenant. After his homily, he made a few announcements, one of which electrified the amigos. This very afternoon, the reverend would be going upstate to visit his sister and take care of her cats while she recovered from dental surgery scheduled for Tuesday. He expected to return on Wednesday, though he might not get back until Thursday, depending on whether or not she developed painful gum inflammation. In the event a parishioner died during the pastor's absence, arrangements had been made with the Reverend Aleem Robinson, of the Northside Baptist Church, to conduct services in an approximate Lutheran manner and provide consolation to the family and friends of the deceased.

Needless to say (but to ensure the clarity of this narrative, it will be said anyway) the four amigos congregated under an oak in the cemetery next door to the rectory shortly after darkfall. No doubt horse thieves and worse had hung from its branches, but no ornament of righteous justice dangled there now. The amigos were excited, wildly excited, as teenagers can be when doing something forbidden that they've persuaded themselves is justified in this instance.

No wall, fence, or hedge separated the graveyard from the rectory property. Crossing from Deadville to the back door of the pastor's house would be safer than approaching from the street; there was little to zero risk of being seen.

The rectory wasn't dark. Light glowed in two upstairs windows, also in a front room on the ground floor and in the kitchen.

The amigos had no concern about the lights. After two years in the choir and a full year as a trusted altar boy (during which his mother had tried to get him on Ritalin), Ernie was conversant with all things Saint Mark's. He knew the security system was programmed to turn on lights when no one was home, creating the illusion that the house must be occupied. The existence of a security system here, when the church had none, provided no obstacle. It was a perimeter alarm only, with no motion detectors; the simple deactivating code was 1-1-1-3.

Although the amigos were geeks, they were not stupid. If they entered the rectory together and, against all expectations, someone happened to be in residence, at least one of four was likely to be snared, whereas a single intruder was pretty much certain to escape unharmed. Three of the friends agreed that Bobby should go in first to reconnoiter before the rest of them followed. Bobby harbored a different opinion, but he accepted the decision. Although he denied having charisma, hated the whole idea, he'd long ago realized that people had expectations of him that they didn't have of everyone else. He tried to disappoint as many people as he could without offending them, including the girls who winked at him as if they shared some secret, but he could not refuse his amigos; they were the only family he had. On paper, the Pinchbecks were his foster parents, but Adam and Evelyn were . . . vacant, uncommunicative; he knew little more about them than he knew about any two strangers he might see in the street.

So he left his amigos among the gravestones and went to the back porch of the parsonage and climbed the steps and peered through a window into the lighted kitchen, which was deserted. Years would pass before he learned about police lock-release guns. But he had been an inquisitive kid all his life, an autodidact, interested in arcane subjects, one of which was the techniques of professional burglars.

We should not think less of Bobby because of the places his curiosity led him. He didn't have any intention of burglarizing anyone. He was not a thief. A boy can be fascinated with nuclear physics without wanting to blow up civilization, although if you know a boy like that, it is advisable to keep an eye on him.

Anyway, if Bobby hadn't known how to gain entrance to the house quietly, if his sole option had been to break a window, which might have drawn unwanted attention, then he would not have remained there on the back porch. The story would end here, and many of you would be dissatisfied and possibly angry.

Having planned for this adventure, he'd brought with him a roll of painter's blue tape. This material could be easily torn with his fingers. It had been in Spencer's father's garage workshop among tools and supplies that Spencer had not yet sold off. Rebecca had supplied a glass cutter that her grandmother Ruth had bought when she considered learning stained-glass windowmaking. Ruth gave up her stained-glass aspirations when she realized that any hobby would leave her with less time for the sugarcoated vitriolic exchanges and vicious tricks that made the golden years of marriage so satisfying.

The top half of the back door of the parsonage offered four small panes. Gloveless because his fingerprints were not on file anywhere, Bobby tore strips from the roll of tape and covered the pane nearest the lock. He used the cutter to score the glass along all four sides. Then he added a double thickness of tape, creating a hinge that fixed the pane to the muntin at the bottom of it. When he rapped the masked window glass sharply with one elbow, it broke with a soft *plink* where it had been scored. Without shattering or falling to the floor, the pane swung down and inward on its hinge.

Bobby reached through the opening he had made and found the thumb turn of the deadbolt and disengaged the lock. When he stepped into the kitchen, a musical trilling issued from the alarm panel on the wall to the right of the door. That pleasant, welcoming tune warned him that he had one minute to input the disarming code before the alarm would go off. He used the keypad to enter 1-1-1-3, and the trilling stopped.

A rush of triumphant glee lifted his heart. He surveyed the kitchen, grinning with delight. After a moment, however, he realized that anyone who witnessed his reaction might think he was fast on a road to a life of crime, when in fact he had great respect for the law. Suddenly he felt as if thousands of eyes were watching him, as if he were being judged by people who would understand his lawful nature, but also by people who would disapprove of what he'd done even if they had been told in no uncertain terms that he was not a thief. This uncanny feeling grew stronger, stronger, until he had to wonder if the *real* reason he was still in the kitchen was because he was a coward, afraid of what he might find in the rectory.

Of course he was not being watched. No invisible audience was following his every move. Angered by his reticence, he counseled himself to get on with a quick reconnoitering of these chambers. When he was sure no one was there, he would use his walkie-talkie to urge his three amigos to join him for a more thorough search of the residence.

He made his way through the ground floor. Because a flash-light beam sweeping the rooms would look suspicious to anyone passing on Winkler Street, he boldly turned lights on wherever darkness ruled.

Although he really didn't have any inclination to become a thief when he grew up, none at all, no matter what some unkind people might think, he climbed the stairs with the haste, agility, and silence of a cat burglar.

On the second floor, he discovered more of what he'd found downstairs, which was no one. He came at last to the room where the windows had been flushed with light before he'd broken into the house. He opened the door and stepped inside and found a library with floor-to-ceiling book-lined shelves on every wall.

In the center of the chamber stood an immense comfort-able-looking armchair upholstered in burgundy leather. There were also a matching footstool, a small table next to the chair, and a reading lamp.

The most interesting thing in the room was the man who occupied the armchair, with his feet on the footstool. The first thing one noticed about this individual was his size. Because Bobby possessed neither a scale nor a tape measure, he could only estimate that the man was about six and a half feet tall and weighed two hundred fifty pounds.

This individual's costume was as noteworthy as his size. He wore hobnailed boots that would damage any uncarpeted floor on which he trod. His jeans, which were tucked into the boots, appeared to be of a coarser denim than those sold by Levi's or 7 For All Mankind. The red-black-and-green plaid shirt was worn with the sleeves rolled up to the middle of his powerful forearms. A chain of small links of rusted iron encircled his neck, and from it hung a three- or four-inch claw from a grizzly bear. Atop this strange person, a navy-blue knitted cap perched like a working-man's crown.

Bobby was reminded of the legendary lumberjack Paul Bunyan and could almost believe a giant blue ox waited in the backyard.

This embodiment of an American folk hero continued reading in spite of being interrupted by an intruder, as if the book fascinated him so much that he was determined to get to the end of a chapter before setting the volume aside.

Bobby knew he should pivot and run, but he could not move. Such was the giant's effect on him that he might have peed his pants if he had not in fact had enough charisma to maintain his self-control and dignity. The grotesque figure in the chair filled him with a paralyzing dread that was not at once entirely explicable.

If there was anything good about being immobilized by fear, it was that this gave him time to analyze the reason for the profound nature of his dread.

In addition to the man's massiveness, there was a quality about him that was alien. Something abnormal, unnatural, divergent, weird, heteroclite. Something hostile, bitter, poisonous. Something malign, malignant, venomous. Bobby could almost name what it was about the giant that he found most alarming, but the precisely right word eluded him. *Filthy?* The big man's black hair was greasy and tangled. Sooty smudges mottled his face. Green teeth, dark stains in the crevices between them. Knuckles and fingernails encrusted with grime. His clothes had been worn so long between washings that the fabrics were limp, exhausted. But no. Mere filth wasn't what made him such a frightening presence. *Eyes?* They were green with orange striations, or perhaps orange with green striations. Bobby had seen blue eyes with green striations and gray eyes with blue striations, but he had never seen eyes like these. Yet again, no. The eyes were not the most unnerving aspect of the man. *Hair?* His facial stubble looked like something other than beard hair, something that had no name in *this* world, each bristle quivering as if it were a separate creature with a life of its own, growing *on* the face rather than *from* it. The filaments in his eyebrows continuously, slowly writhed. The hair on his head seemed to be moving subtly, not as if armies of lice marched through it, but as if the hair was motile and ever so gently questing for something. No, no. It wasn't the hair, either.

The most fearsome quality of that strange individual, the thing about him that might freeze someone in cold terror, eluded Bobby until—and long after—the giant closed the book and placed it on the side table and turned his attention to his visitor. We might expect such an apparition to have a deep and vibrous voice similar if not identical to that of Judyface and other horrific murderers who have slashed their way through countless movies, and that is indeed what Bobby expected. Instead, the giant proved to have the well-trained, sprightly voice of a game-show host. "Hello there, young man, Robert Shamrock, Bobby, Bobby the Sham to your friends."

Astonished, Bobby said, "You know my name."

Still in the armchair but as tense as a tarantula prepared to spring ten times its body length to seize its prey, the book lover said, "You will win no prize for that observation, Bob, Rob, Robbie, Roberto."

Although the giant's voice was vivacious, a thread of mockery wove through his words, and his diabolical eyes all but smoked with hatred.

Bobby's terror did not abate. He became aware of an astringent yet organic odor that was the very essence of alienness. "You know my name, but I don't know yours."

"Hornfly. Wayne Louis Hornfly."

22

REBECCA SHARES THE MOMENT

At 7:10, as Bobby was slammed by a recovered memory in room 210, Rebecca was dressed and ready to meet him and Spencer in the Spreading Oaks Diner for breakfast at 7:30. She had not donned a wig and glasses with clear lenses or any other disguise. Even if she had wanted to go incognito, as on the previous day, she hadn't brought a fake nose or a paste-on scar or even a set of buckteeth.

She didn't consider phoning the security firm in Beverly Hills that usually provided her with armed bodyguards, though two reliable and deadly serious former Marines could have been at her side before the day was out. In Maple Grove, the least of her worries was being assaulted by a psychotic fan. Anyway, she could not expect licensed bodyguards to participate in such activities as breaking into church basements and stashing apparently dead bodies in window seats.

Besides, although neither Bobby nor Spencer was the kind of specimen to be nicknamed "the Rock," they would put their lives on the line for her, just as she would do for them. She didn't have the slightest doubt about that. Together with Ernie, they were the first real family any of them had known, and in fact they remained the only family any of them had in this culture that often seemed determined to devalue children and make families obsolete.

To pass time before she would join her amigos for breakfast, she opened a package of wet wipes. With those and a hand towel, she started to clean the mirrored sliding doors of the closet, which were spotted with a substance that disquieted her. You never knew what previous residents might have gotten up to in a motel room.

The very moment that Bobby was overcome by a recovered memory in room 210, Rebecca was likewise stricken. The wet wipes and towel fell out of her hands, and she staggered backward to sit on the edge of the bed, which she had made earlier. Although she had not gone into the rectory on that eventful night when they were fourteen, she received the memory of Bobby's encounter with Wayne Louis Hornfly as if she had witnessed it herself.

This seemed to suggest that she and Bobby were psychically linked, which they were, although the explanation is more complex and will be revealed later. In spite of her intelligence and her shrewd awareness regarding how the world works, and even though she was a heavy reader of fiction, Rebecca could not have known that this linkage also had the convenient effect of breaking one chapter into two, each of a length more tolerable to modern readers than otherwise would have been the case.

So there was Bobby Shamrock standing just one step inside the second-floor library of the rectory, paralyzed by fear but, it might be assumed, also by curiosity, which is a very powerful desire, as many generations of grieving cats can attest.

"Hornfly. Wayne Louis Hornfly," said the filthy giant in the armchair. "That is our name for this manifestation of us."

"How did you know my name?" Bobby asked.

"We know the names of everyone in Maple Grove. We have known the names of every citizen who has lived here since the town was settled, since before you barbarians decorated the oak trees with corpses at Christmas."

Bobby was sure he could now break the paralysis that fear had imposed on him, but *he just had to know,* had to know the truth of Maple Grove, the nature of this creature before him, and what it all meant. He said, "We?"

Hornfly said, "What?"

"We?" Bobby repeated.

Hornfly looked hate-filled but puzzled. "We?"

"You said 'we' instead of 'I.' Who is 'we'?"

A sly look evolved out of the hate and puzzlement. "That's for us to know and you to find out. And by the time you find out, it will be too late for your kind."

"My kind?"

"Didn't we just say?"

"What do you mean by that?"

"What could we mean other than humanity, human beings, your disgusting species."

"And you're not human?"

Hornfly cocked his head. "Are you stupid? Do we look human?"

"Yeah. Kind of. More or less. More than not."

The giant smiled broadly. His smile in no way diminished the intensity of the hatred that radiated from him, because it was a self-satisfied and arrogant smile. "We could choose to look more human than we do, but the thought of looking too human repulses us."

"If you aren't human, what are you?"

Hornfly took his feet off the footstool and sat up straighter, seeming proud of being whatever he was. "Wouldn't you like to know?"

"Yes. That's why I asked. Are you from another planet?"

"That is such a cliché. No, we are not from another planet."

"You could be lying."

"What would be in it for us?" Hornfly leaned forward in his chair and pointed at Bobby. "You know what's wrong with your kind? You always go for the easy answers. Aliens, zombies, gigantic apes, gigantic reptiles, gigantic insects, crooked greedy businessmen. Your movies suck because, in art as in all things, you go for easy answers. Life on Earth is more complex than your kind can imagine."

"That's unfair," said Bobby. "We're very imaginative."

"Watch your mouth, boy. We are incapable of unfairness. We lack the faults of your kind."

"You're very full of yourselves, aren't you?"

Hornfly's eyes narrowed. "It is merely the truth of ourselves."

"That's your position, is it?"

"Our position? Soon we will disgust ourselves by looking so human that you'll not know we're among you. Then will come the Day of Fun when we will exterminate every last one of your kind."

"You could kill us all in one day?"

Hornfly looked a bit crestfallen. "It'll take eight or ten months, maybe as much as a year and a half."

"Then why do you call it 'the Day of Fun'?"

"It sounds more inspiring than 'the Year and a Half of Fun.' We want it so bad, we need to think it'll happen in twenty-four hours."

"What were those things in the church basement?"

"Mistakes in manufacturing."

"That's all you're going to say? How many weird mistakes in manufacturing do you make? What does that even mean? The Day of Fun is actually a year and a half, half-formed people are 'mistakes in manufacturing.' You don't make sense. It's all stupid talk."

The wriggling hair stood straight up on Hornfly's head, and his face presented an expression of great offense. "We are smarter than Alpha. Beta is smart. Alpha is stupid. They do absurd things to people on the third floor. Absurd things!"

Bobby looked at the ceiling. "There is no third floor."

"Not here, you stupid, stupid boy. Not the third floor here. You are tedious and too stupid to live. If you were comatose on the third floor, they would get nothing worthwhile from your tiny brain. Right now, right here, Wayne Louis Hornfly could squash you like a ripe grape between our thumb and forefinger. Or burst upon you and destroy you from the inside out. But then the disappearance of a child would have to be explained. Nothing so agitates your species as the disappearance of a child."

Bobby intuited that the time to pivot and run had arrived, but curiosity was such a powerful desire that he stood his ground. We should also consider that the human brain is not fully developed until one's early twenties and that a fourteen-year-old does not have a full grasp of the fragility of human life.

Bobby said, "What about Pastor Larry? He must know what you are. Why does he allow you here? Why is he involved with you?"

"Surely you are aware there are those of your people who hate all humankind. He's one of those. He wants to save the planet by curing it of the human plague. Okay now, Bobby, Bob, Roberto—you need to go home to bed and have a nice dream."

Bobby indicated the book on the table. "What were you reading?"

Favoring his visitor with a broad smile full of green teeth, licking his lips with a purple tongue, Wayne Louis Hornfly said, "We were reading about blood, pain, mayhem, cruelty, murder, and mass death. As useless as your kind is in all other ways, when you write tales of blood, pain, mayhem, cruelty, murder, and mass death, you create thrilling narratives that are deeply moving and inspiring."

Hornfly rose from the armchair. By going vertical, he made the room seem smaller. He towered, loomed, glowered.

Bobby backed up a step.

"Oh," Hornfly said, "how we would like to burst upon you and spread our filaments throughout you, into every organ, into your brain, our filaments and felts, until you have fed us all you have."

"Nice meeting you," Bobby said, pivoted, and ran.

In room 208, Rebecca thrust up from her bed, electrified by the recovered memory that wasn't her own, that was Bobby's memory shared with her psychically, which is a concept that one will not find in a novel by, say, Hemingway or Faulkner. This was an experience that would have scared most people, but after the life she had led thus far, Rebecca could not be easily frightened.

However, the encounter with Wayne Louis Hornfly brought her a moment of enlightenment. Since returning to Maple Grove, she had been enlightened about one thing or another more often than during the seventeen years she'd spent in California. In the entertainment business, enlightenment was achieved only with the assistance of a guru or recreational drugs, or a personal trainer, or attendance at the Burning Man festival—all of which she'd avoided. In this case, she suddenly realized that her obsession with cleanliness had its roots in her adolescence, perhaps in encounters with the mysterious, filthy Hornfly and others like him—or maybe also from a traumatic incident involving a large volume of muck so putrid and disgusting that it would affect her psychology for the rest of her life.

"Breakfast with Bobby and Spencer in five minutes," her phone reminded her.

❧

Flashback to 7:10 and cut to room 212.

At the desk by the window, Spencer Truedove was working on his hat. Because black felt attracted lint and was sometimes targeted by birds, he traveled with a small cleaning kit in a zippered leather case. The hat needed to be perfect, because it was more than just headgear. The hat was the logo of his brand as surely as the logo of Apple Inc. was an apple with a bite out of it. When *America Art* magazine published a long, adoring article about Spencer's work, they hadn't put one of his paintings on the cover, as was their custom, but instead used a photograph of his porkpie hat.

However, the hat wasn't merely a logo. The hat meant much more to him than that. He was more attached to his hat than anyone could know. He *loved* the hat. And why shouldn't he? His successful career proved he was somebody, but the hat and the rest of his outfit was what made it hard for anyone to say he had a bland personality. Even before his mom and dad abandoned him, they paid little attention to him. When he was nine, he had overheard his father talking with a neighbor who was also a drinking buddy. His father said, "I think maybe that boy is from Mars. His mother has this big personality—everyone says so—and I'm damn sure I'm colorful in my own way, but Spencer is about as colorful as a peeled turnip. He fades into the walls. Three or four days can go by when I forget he lives with us." Well, if that was true, those days were gone. Everyone had to acknowledge that a man who wore a porkpie hat at all times, both outside and indoors, a man who didn't take it off to eat or make love, was eccentric. Eccentricity was perhaps the primary measure of personality. Eccentric people were noticed, by God. They didn't fade into the walls. Bland people don't have photographs of their hats on the cover of a national magazine. Spencer's famous hat was no less important to him as was being a multimillionaire.

He had just finished restoring the hat to its full glory but had yet to put it on his head when the recovered memory shared by Bobby and Rebecca became Spencer's as well. The downside of this development was fear and a sense of violation; his mind had been invaded. The upside was the convenience of this sharing; at their forthcoming breakfast, Bobby would not need to tell his amigos all about Wayne Louis Hornfly, which would have ensured that, as they listened rapt, their food would have gone cold.

When the vision of the past faded away, Spencer got up from the desk and put on his hat and regarded himself in the mirrored doors of the closet and adjusted the hat. He opened the door of room 212 and stepped onto the second-floor promenade of the motel precisely as Bobby stepped out of room 210 and Rebecca stepped out of room 208. It was as if they were engaged in a choreographed sequence and the band would now strike up and they would proceed to the diner while dancing and singing. They just walked.

23

BREAKFAST AT THE PRECIPICE

The Spreading Oaks Diner was warmly lighted. Every surface was clean, if not by Rebecca's standards, certainly by the standards of 99 percent of customers, who—make no mistake about it—were clean themselves. In addition to booths, in one of which the amigos sat, the chrome-legged tables and chairs dated from a decade when manufacturers knew how tables and chairs should be made; they looked as if you could drive over them in a tank and only the tank would need to be repaired.

On the long counter that provided stools for lone customers, homemade cakes and pies rested on pedestals, under glass lids, as if they were sacred objects. The air was redolent of brewing coffee and a mélange of mouthwatering aromas.

Bobby didn't want to be back in Maple Grove, but if he *had* to come home for Ernie, it was better to be here as an adult than as an adolescent. Back in the day, he would never have eaten in this diner because two of the teachers who ate here—the football coach and the shop instructor—could be just as snarky toward nerds as any kids who were part of the in-crowd. It was good to have grown up.

"I would love to paint this place," Spencer said, "capture the sense of timelessness."

"Why don't you?" Bobby asked.

"Well, I can only paint when a fugue state overcomes me, which is only when I'm in my studio. And you might have forgotten, but I can't draw worth a damn."

"Don't be so hard on yourself, sweetie," said Rebecca as she polished the table with a wet wipe.

A waitress named Flo took their order, and they ate breakfast (technically the second for Bobby, who always ate as if famished, yet never gained an ounce). All that needs to be said about the food is that it was delicious, providing fats and sugars in a multitude of forms.

"He was probably lying about not being from another planet," Spencer said when they had puzzled aloud over other aspects of the recovered memory.

"I don't think so," Bobby said. "He was concealing things, but he didn't seem like a liar. He maintained direct eye contact, and what he *did* say seemed to be consistent. The guy had this quality, very . . . earthy. Besides, a visitor from another galaxy wouldn't have a name like Wayne Louis Hornfly."

"It sounds like a serial killer," Rebecca said as she used a wet wipe to clean a smear of egg yolk from her empty plate. "They usually have three names with a certain rhythm to them. Judyface's real name was John Willard Ironfork."

"Yeah," Bobby said. "Wouldn't an extraterrestrial be named something like Baldar or Klaatu or Yoda?"

"Maybe," Spencer suggested, "he's an extraterrestrial who wants to be an Earth-style serial killer."

Bobby shook his head. "He doesn't want to be any kind of human being. Remember, he really, really hates humanity."

Spencer took that to be confirmation of his theory. "There you go, then. He passes for human in order to be a serial killer and waste as many of us as he can."

"Doesn't that sound too convoluted to you?" Rebecca asked as she polished the flatware that she had used. "Stay focused on the details of what he said. Who or what are Alpha and Beta? What is Alpha doing on the third floor of County Memorial? Back in the day, did we ever look into that? I don't think we did."

"What's to look into?" Spencer asked. "Alpha, Beta, third floor. There's nothing to look into. There are no specifics."

Bobby never got impatient with his amigos. Even after all these years, it was still only the rest of humanity that irritated him. With affection, he said, "Okay, okay. Listen, guys, we can't just wait around for another recovered memory to tell us what to do. We all know what we have to do."

"Visit Pastor Larry," said Spencer, "and interrogate the shit out of him."

"I'm good with that," Rebecca said, putting away her package of wet wipes. She appeared, at least to Bobby, as if she were becoming less obsessive, because she didn't want to stay at the table until Flo took the dishes away, allowing her to wipe the table again. She said, "But before we brace the reverend, I think we should check on Ernie. He's been in that window seat more than twelve hours."

"He's okay. He's either in suspended animation or dead," Bobby said. As previously established, he was the least sentimental of the amigos, but it must be understood that he was nonetheless a good and caring person.

They left a 50 percent tip for Flo because she was the kind of woman they would have liked to have for a mother, paid for breakfast at the cash register up front, and stepped outside into a kind of hell.

24

WHAT IS LITERATURE?

The sun a golden ball in the east, the sky hanging clear blue over-all, and the sweet clean air seemed to promise a lovely day—but in an instant, the promise was shown to be a lie.

In a severely tailored black suit that featured a matching waist-length cape, black shoes with one-inch heels, and a burgundy cloche hat with a black band, Britta Hernishen was approaching the diner as the amigos exited it.

Spencer thought that if you knew what job she held, you would think Britta looked professorial. But if you did not know her line of work, you would assume she was the chief justice of a top-secret court that put modern-day Nazis on trial and con-demned them to death for not being Nazi enough.

The amigos froze the way rabbits will at the appearance of a wolf, and Britta said, "I asked myself where you might have taken rooms, and of course it would be in this place, such as it is."

"What's wrong with this place?" Rebecca asked.

Britta's nostrils flared. "Do you not see what it says of you that you need to ask?"

"It's a nice place," Spencer said. "Back in the day, even Aldous Blomhoff ate here when he was both the director of the institute and the town mayor."

"Is that your considered opinion, young man? Even after our phone conversation yesterday, do you cling to the illusion that Aldous Blomhoff's patronage is any kind of recommendation?"

Stepping up to the guillotine, figuratively speaking, Bobby said, "It's clean, cozy, and quiet."

"Is that your position, Mr. Sham?"

"Shamrock."

"Is that your position?" she pressed.

"Yes, I stand by it."

"You're all of a type," Britta said, "but I can do nothing about that. What have you done with Ernest?"

"Done?" Rebecca asked. "We said goodbye. Then he died."

"And you call yourself an actress."

"I *am* an actress," Rebecca insisted, but more meekly than Spencer would have expected.

"I am content," said Britta, "to allow history to make that determination."

"That's generous of you," Rebecca said.

"It is my nature." Scowling, she turned to Spencer. "What did you say?"

"Nothing. I didn't say anything."

"Then it was a thought, was it?"

Spencer felt a little shaky when he said, "I wasn't thinking anything."

"In your case, that is perhaps a credible defense."

"Thank you."

"No doubt you know that, for patients' privacy, there are no security cameras in the hospital wings where they lie abed."

Spencer hadn't known this, and neither had his amigos, and Bobby made the mistake of smiling in relief.

Detecting the smile in her peripheral vision, Britta pivoted toward Bobby. "You are amused, Mr. Sham."

"No, ma'am."

"You boldly deny it?"

"It's just my face. It plays tricks on me."

Britta Hernishen stared intently at him for a long and silent moment before she said, "However, there are cameras in the lobby and the parking lot."

None of them dared to say anything, and Spencer made an effort not to think, either.

"You were seen pushing an individual in a wheelchair. He was wearing sunglasses and Mr. Truman's hat—"

"Truedove," said Spencer.

"'True love'? Why are those words germane to our discussion?"

"True*dove*. It's my name. I was just correcting you," Spencer said. Even as he spoke the word "correcting," he deeply regretted having put himself in such a perilous position.

Britta regarded him as if he were something a dog had left on the sidewalk. "I see. Then may I ask—did your mother raise you to believe that interrupting your elders was acceptable?"

"My mother abandoned me to find herself. She now lives in New Orleans under the name Constanina de Fornay, which is who she was in some past life. I never hear from her, probably because Constanina never had children and doesn't know how to relate to a son."

"How interesting. Have you wondered, Mr. Truman, why she went to such lengths to escape the environment of which you were a part?"

"I've thought about it a lot."

"Knowing you as I do, I assume all that thinking has failed to lead you to any conclusion. May I continue with what I was saying? Would that be an arrangement of which you would approve?"

"Yes, ma'am."

Britta said, "The individual in the wheelchair could not be identified from the video, but he slumped as if quite dead."

"Oh, him," said Rebecca. "That was Ralph Osmond. He was at the hospital to visit a sick friend. We gave him a lift home."

"How gracious of you. Can you imagine how he might have gotten *to* the hospital?"

Spencer realized they should have left the answer to Bobby, but only after he had said, "His wife brought him and went home to wait for his call but got a terrible migraine."

Britta stared at Spencer almost as long as she had regarded Bobby in silence when he'd said his face played tricks on him.

Then she asked, "Are you sure Mr. Osmond's wife didn't run away to New Orleans to live as a previous incarnation?"

Again, the amigos retreated into glassy-eyed silence.

Britta said, "The parking lot cameras didn't have a view of the vehicle into which this Ralph person was assisted."

Spencer knew better than to smile.

"The police, being of a caliber that makes them unsuited even to be crossing guards, say the doctors might have misdiagnosed my son. He might be alive and merely wandered off in some fugue state."

"It happens," Bobby assured her.

Britta skewered him with her stiletto stare. "They tell me that, in a missing persons case, I must wait forty-eight hours. If Ernest remains missing, only then can they begin a search for him."

"Well, maybe Rebecca, Spencer, and I could go looking for him."

"Illuminate me as to how you would do that, Mr. Sham."

"Well, you know, we could cruise the town, see if we can find him wandering around somewhere. We care about him, too. We came all this way to see him."

"Cruise around town."

"Yes, ma'am."

She lifted her chin as if to be in a better posture to look down on him. "The books you have written that you wish to call 'novels'—the events in those books, which I suppose you call 'plots,' are quite as overripe as this situation. Are they not?"

"Well, maybe, in some ways, I don't know."

"Therefore, I suppose, as you consider this bizarre situation, you are slavering with excitement at the potential to make a so-called novel from it."

"Well, when a novel idea excites me, I don't really slaver."

"You would know, I suppose. Having had the fortitude to peruse some of your writing, I have a question for you, if you don't mind."

"I don't mind."

"I do not want a hasty answer. I want you to go away and think about this as deeply as you are capable of thinking. I believe any answer you give will be fascinating, but the most revealing one will surely be the answer you have racked your whole mind to discover. What is literature? Do you understand the question?"

"You want to know what literature is."

"Oh, I *know* what it is. I want to know what you *think* it is. I would find that most interesting."

Bobby said, "I'll be back to you."

"One other thing. This is directed to all three of you. If you have taken Ernest's body—my dear boy, the fruit of my womb—to use it in some satanic ritual or to give it a Christian burial, either one, I will destroy all of you."

"Yes, ma'am."

She met the eyes of each, one by one. When it was Spencer's moment to be scrutinized, he waited to be turned to ice or stone, but he survived the stare.

"Now, though your kind might find it inexplicable why anyone would be seeking an education," Britta said, "there are summer classes at the college. It has fallen to me to shape those foolish young minds into something less absurd than they are now. Remember my warning and conduct yourselves accordingly."

As Britta walked away, her cape flared like bat wings, though the day was windless.

Rebecca said, "How did Ernie turn out so nice?"

"Niceness," Bobby said, "was the best weapon he had."

Spencer looked at the sky. It had been clear and sunny when they came out of the diner. Britta had put him in the mood to expect a tide of dark clouds swelling over the horizon, but it was still clear and sunny. It wouldn't be sunny for long. Britta would return, and when she did, she would arrive amidst storm clouds, accompanied by flying monkeys.

25

THE HOUSE ON BRADY DRIVE

In the company of her amigos, Rebecca stood in a condition of alarm and keen dismay before the window seat. Ernie Hernishen wasn't lying under the lid. Neither was anyone else named Ernie nor any other person whose surname was Hernishen. Nothing lay within that space except the blankets with which Bobby and Spencer had fashioned bedding for their friend.

Whether Ernie was comatose, in suspended animation, or dead, it was unthinkable that they could have lost him. However, *unthinkable* was not a synonym for *impossible*. They had to face the fact that, in less than fourteen hours, Ernie had gone missing. Of course he might be in the house, reanimated, making a ham sandwich or writing yet another song to irritate his mother.

With Britta at the college, busily shaping young students into psychopaths, there was less risk that someone would walk in on them. Nevertheless, they felt compelled to search the premises as quickly as possible.

Although the task could have been completed faster if they had split up, they stayed together. None of them needed to vocalize what they all were thinking: Somewhere in the house, they might encounter Wayne Louis Hornfly, and if not him perhaps an even more unsettling presence, in which case there ought to be some safety in numbers.

After they found no one on the second floor or the first, the cellar waited. Bobby used a kitchen switch to turn on the light in advance and opened the door and saw what lay on the landing and said, "What's this crap?"

The meatloaf-size mass wasn't actually crap, and in fact it looked more disgusting than feces. Mottled dark brown-green-yellow, pulsing like living gelatin, pocked by what appeared to be weeping sores, the thing sported an irregular pattern of pale two-inch-long quivering tendrils reminiscent of the stamen-capped pistils in the center of certain flowers, though (let us be clear) it was neither sweet-smelling nor pleasing to the eye as flowers traditionally are.

Rebecca and Spencer crowded the doorway with Bobby to have a look at what repulsed him. They were no less repulsed, mystified, and fearful than their amigo.

"It's moving," Spencer said. "Isn't it moving?"

Rebecca said, "Slow as a snail."

"So it's alive?" Spencer asked.

Bobby said, "If that's life, it's not life as we know it."

"What in God's name is it?" Spencer asked in a voice trembling with trepidation.

Rebecca declared, "God had nothing to do with this."

Spencer said, "What does it want, where is it going, what does it mean?"

Bobby responded, "Aren't those the same questions we all have about our existence?"

Rebecca knew what he meant. "So maybe it *is* life as we know it, sort of."

"We don't absolutely *have* to search the cellar," Spencer said.

"Oh, yes we do," Rebecca disagreed.

Bobby said, "For Ernie. To find Ernie."

"Maybe he won't be down there," Spencer said.

"Oh, he'll be down there," Bobby said.

Rebecca said, "Something *took* him down there."

"How can you be sure?" Spencer asked.

Rebecca said, "A scene like this was in every script I was sent and turned down after *Shriek Hard, Shriek Harder.*"

Bobby said, "Spencer, what is that?"

"A weapon. A rolling pin. It was on the counter."

Rebecca said, "Are you serious?"

"Hey, we don't have a gun. At least this is *something*," Spencer said defensively.

Perhaps already you can see what was meant earlier about how annoying a lot of dialogue tags can be in a long conversation of short statements, when it doesn't much matter who said what. This distraction cannot be allowed to continue, and an effort will be made henceforth to minimize the tags.

Summoning her inner Heather Ashmont, Rebecca said, "Follow me."

"Don't step on that thing."

"Why would I step on it?"

"I'm just sayin'."

"I don't like having it behind us."

"Relax. It's too slow to make a move."

"Maybe it's faking slow."

"It's not faking. It's a kind of slug thing."

"Maybe it has wings."

"Did you *see* wings?"

"What the hell is *that?*"

"What is what?"

"Ahead there. Crawling up the wall."

"Another one. Smaller."

"Spam size."

"Say what?"

"About as big as a Spam loaf fresh from the can."

"I won't be eating any more Spam."

"There's another one two steps down."

"Yeah, on the left. We better move around it as far on the right as we can get."

"Let's go back and get torches."

"We've got plenty of light."

"No, no. To burn the suckers."

"Just stay focused. Find Ernie. Get him out of here."

The first chamber in the cellar, the mechanical room, contained the gas furnace and water softener and electrical panels. It was the kind of room that was atmospheric and creepy, but it wasn't the kind of room where someone died horribly. However, it very much reminded Rebecca of the kind of room that comes *just before* the room in which someone dies horribly.

On the concrete floor, eight globs of quivering matter like those on the stairs lay in a line leading to the door of one of the three big larders stocked with food for the end of the world. The largest mass, approximately the size of a two-pound container of tofu, crawled laboriously at the head of the procession. Those that seemed to be in a pilgrimage behind it were mostly a third to half the leader's size, although a few were hardly more than dribbles.

In yet another moment of enlightenment, though a minor one compared to those that had come before it, Rebecca said, "They're molts," and she halted.

"Molts?" Bobby asked as he came to a stop behind her. "What are molts?"

"Whatever passed through here was molting. This stuff dropped off as it moved along."

Spencer raised the rolling pin. Evidently, one of those series of images by which artists make sense of the world passed through his mind and led him by visual associations to a conclusion. "So the thing is big."

"Bigger than the pieces that fell off it, but not necessarily big big," Rebecca said.

"Oh, it'll be big big, all right. It'll be huge. Massive. Let's not fool ourselves."

Bobby agreed with Spencer. "It was something big enough to lift Ernie out of the window seat and carry him down here."

"I have a déjà vu feeling," Rebecca said. "As if we've been in situations like this before. With crawling things like these."

The three amigos stood at the end of the procession of creeping molts, staring at the closed door toward which those lowly entities were making their way, no doubt with the intention of being absorbed by the primary mass from which they'd sloughed off. This might have been a tender and touching moment if the molts had been lost puppies seeking their mother, but they were not puppies, and the scene was weird, disturbing, and somewhat nauseating.

Considering the three Armageddon storage rooms, Rebecca thought that Ernie could be behind the steel door to the left or the steel door to the right, rather than behind the center door toward which the molts were crawling. However, neither stories nor the real world worked that way, and you always had to open the door that you most dreaded opening.

"Let's do it," she said, moving around the excruciatingly slow molts and stepping to the door.

Spencer suggested they merely knock and see what happened.

From her experiences being Heather Ashmont, Rebecca knew that if a hulking monster waited in the room beyond the door, it would not reveal itself prematurely by issuing an invitation or saying, *Nobody here but us chickens.* Therefore, she didn't embarrass her amigo by commenting on his suggestion. She gripped the handle and took a deep breath and opened the door.

The lights came on automatically. Rebecca stepped across the threshold.

Ernie was lying face up on the butcher-block top of the table-high island of drawers, under a ceiling ventilation grille. His face still bore the blush of rouge and the light coat of lipstick that Rebecca had applied to make him appear not dead before they wheeled him out of the hospital. Without a porkpie hat and sunglasses, he wouldn't fool anyone—he looked like a corpse on a catafalque. He wasn't breathing. Rebecca lifted his arm and swung it back and forth, and it moved freely; rigor mortis had not set in, as it should have done. By now, if he were deceased, an unpleasant odor should have been emanating from him, but he had no odor at all. He was not dead. However, when she took his wrist and felt for a pulse, she didn't find one.

No monster hulked in the walkaround between the center island and the walls of shelved five-gallon cans of dried food. Whatever grotesque creature lifted Ernie out of the window seat and brought him to this room had performed the task required of it and moved on with no apparent consideration for the trembling molts that yearned so poignantly to be rejoined with their mother mass. As it was for children in dysfunctional human families, so it seemed to be for the sloughed-away offspring of monsters.

"Let's get Ernie out of here," Rebecca said, "before something comes back for him."

They slid and pulled Ernie into a sitting position, with his legs dangling over the edge of the butcher's block.

"I've got this," Bobby said, and he pulled his amigo into a fireman's carry.

By the time the amigos returned to the mechanical room, the molts had veered toward the door on the left. Maybe something waited behind it, or maybe their desire for a reunion would go unrequited. Despite the potential for a dramatic and touching resolution to the quest of the molts, Rebecca wasn't emotionally involved enough to tarry in anticipation of it.

Following Bobby and his burden, Spencer suddenly stopped and turned and looked at the molts. "Yes! I've painted things like this. They're in some of my works. I've never known what they are. No one has known what they are. I still don't know what the hell they are, but I've painted them. I've painted them!"

Spencer was so ecstatic to have discovered the source of his inspiration that he glowed like an excited child thrilled to have walked into a surprise birthday party.

Rebecca was loath to put out the flame of Spencer's delight, but she slapped him on the back to hurry him along. "Move, move, move. Get your ass in gear, Picasso."

Cellars were among the worst places to linger when an eleven-fingered psychopath in a mask might be nearby, and especially when you *knew* that a molting slime creature of unknown provenance was lurking behind one door or another, and not with benign intent. Rebecca was dismayed that so many people saw threats where none existed, especially when propagandized to fear them, yet failed to see a true disaster even as it avalanched toward them. But she was amazed that Spencer, considering his baleful life experiences, would tarry in a cellar, goggling at the molts when the thing from which they had sloughed might at any moment erupt from the shadows, seize him, infuse him with its fiercely potent gastric acid, and dissolve him into itself in mere seconds—assuming that was how the thing worked. But here he stood, delaying, transfixed. Artists.

As a heavy door swung open behind them with a rasping of steel hinges, she clapped Spencer hard upside the head and cried, "Go, go!"

Throughout the foregoing, Bobby had kept moving. Blessed— or perhaps cursed—with the fertile imagination of a novelist, he had been sufficiently terrified to have already made it nearly to the top of the stairs in spite of his burden.

Spencer clambered after him, and Rebecca followed. They burst into the kitchen as if flung out of an alternate universe by a force that only a physicist of vast knowledge would understand. Rebecca slammed the cellar door, and Spencer snared a sturdy chair from the breakfast table, and Rebecca jammed it under the knob to brace the door shut, as if there might be even a remote chance that would work.

26

STASHING ERNIE AGAIN

The residence on Harriet Nelson Lane remained in the Truedove family, such as there was a family. Spencer's father had thus far served eleven years in state prison for robbing Brinks trucks, and he had six more years in, as he called it, "the hoosegow." If the guards caught him carving a fake gun from a bar of soap to be used in an escape attempt or if he stabbed a fellow prisoner with a shiv fashioned from a dining hall spoon, a few years would be added to his sentence before he'd be eligible for parole, and rightly so.

The house was, as it had always been, a lovely Victorian with much decorative millwork, in sync with the pretty but stultifying sameness of picturesque Maple Grove. During the divorce, so eager was Spencer's mother to get on with her exciting new life that she had lost all interest in the house, just as she'd lost all interest in her husband, and she surrendered her equity. Meanwhile, Father had been comfortable in the parsonage of the Church of the Sacred Erogenous Revelation, where he indulged extreme desires with Venus Porifera; he considered selling the place on Harriet Nelson Lane. Even then, however, he dreamed of remaking himself into a romantic figure in the Bonnie and Clyde tradition, and he knew that if he were caught, everything he owned would be liquidated to repay those from whom he had stolen, leaving him homeless. So without his son's knowledge, he transferred the title of the property to Spencer, who was a fast-rising star in the fine-arts world. Since his father's conviction, Spencer paid the taxes and engaged a service to maintain the house, although not because the place had any sentimental value for him. He was terrified that, if his father was paroled with nowhere to go, the old man would travel to Chicago to live with his son, and Spencer's childhood would start all over again.

At this point, some might raise the question of what happened to Venus Porifera and why, as Mr. Truedove's wife, she didn't at least claim half of the residence on Harriet Nelson Lane, so that might as well be addressed here. Venus and Reverend Truedove were married by Reverend Truedove himself at the Church of the Sacred Erogenous Revelation before 286 degenerate parishioners, who all agreed the bride looked beautiful in her wedding dress, although most would have preferred her to be nude. To no one's surprise except Venus's, Father had obtained his theological degree for twenty-six dollars from a university in Thailand that didn't exist. Please understand, Thailand existed then, as it does now, but the *university* was bogus; it didn't even have a school mascot. The marriage was invalid, and Venus had no claim whatsoever on the house. Although you might think a woman of that character would make trouble for Spencer in such a situation, she did not. She treated him with kindness. After all, when Spencer had been fourteen, Venus had been only eighteen; the year Father went to prison, Spencer was twenty-five and Venus was twenty-nine. She still looked fabulous, an absolute knockout, and whatever condition once caused her to sweat excessively had abated. With a master of business administration degree that she acquired for thirty-one dollars from a five-star university in the Republic of

Vanuatu, she went to Las Vegas, where she applied for a position with a casino magnate who hired the dear girl on the spot for $325,000 a year to keep his checkbook balanced.

So fifteen minutes after driving away from Ernie's house with their rescued amigo concealed under a blanket in the cargo area of Spencer's Genesis SUV, the three friends arrived at the house where Spencer had lived alone throughout high school, when he had sold off much of the contents for spending money. Unlike at Ernie's house, here the garage and residence were attached, and a connecting door allowed the transfer of Ernie from one to the other without the risk of being seen.

That was important because those who lived on this last block of Harriet Nelson Lane, which ended in a cul-de-sac, formed a close-knit neighborhood. There had been little turnover of real estate since Spencer was a boy, and in spite of the years that had passed, he would be recognized. All these people went to one of two churches. Their children had gone to the same schools, in some cases had dated one another, and in more cases than you would think had married one another. These neighbors once played tennis together and now played pickleball or golf in competitive but polite groups. They regularly invited one another to dinner or a barbecue in the backyard. They played cards together and watched over one another's homes when a neighbor went on vacation. They laughed together, cried together, celebrated together when a grandchild came into the world. They had purchased a block of plots in the same cemetery, and when they died, they were buried on the same hill as those who passed before them and as would be those who died after them. The Truedoves had been the only standoffish people on the block, almost extraterrestrial by comparison to the others, though the neighbors had never given up on them. If Spencer had not been able to drive straight into the garage and put down the door behind the Genesis, if he and his amigos had needed to transport limp Ernie from the driveway to the back door of the house, out in the open, welcoming neighbors would have been all over them. As it was, once they had moved their insensate buddy into the house, they still weren't off the hook.

En route from Ernie's place, Spencer had figured out where to stash the songwriter in anticipation of his recovery. Putting him in the cellar seemed to be asking for trouble. The attic would be too hot in August. As Bobby was a bit worn down by having hauled Ernie out of the basement at the previous house, Spencer helped him carry their amigo to the second floor, while Rebecca stood at the top, urging them not to drop Ernie, for God's sake, or knock his head into a stair post, as if that was their nefarious secret plan.

They carried Ernie into a spacious wood-paneled chamber with a view of Harriet Nelson Lane, which was a lovely tree-lined street. This had doubled as an upstairs office and a spare bedroom until Angelina made it into a sewing room, which it had remained for five years. Perhaps already suspecting that in a past life she'd been a member of the French royal family, she suddenly found sewing to be beneath her, work for the lower classes. Since then it had been a vacant space. As there was no apparent furniture, they put Ernie on the floor, and Rebecca objected that there was nowhere to hide him. Spencer smiled and pointed to one of the blank paneled walls. "If someone broke in and searched the place, they would never know he's here. There's a foldaway bed."

Rebecca was appalled. "What—you mean strap him to the mattress and fold him out of sight into the wall? Good grief,

Spencer, what if he wakes up? How does he unstrap himself? How does he get out of there?"

"Relax. I long ago sold the mattress." He gripped a finger-pull concealed in a vertical molding. The springs sang as they were released, and the bed descended without further assistance.

Looking into the revealed niche, Bobby said, "Cool. Without the mattress, the space is at least two feet deep. We can lay him in there with no problem."

If Rebecca was perhaps no longer appalled, she was nonetheless resistant to the plan. "What if he wakes up in the dark and manages to get to his feet? He's in a vertical coffin. He'll panic."

"He won't panic. That isn't like Ernie. Anyway, after a minute or two, he'll know exactly where he is. He was here the day I sold the mattress. He helped me move it downstairs and put it in the buyer's pickup truck."

"That was—what?—twenty years ago?"

"Eighteen. I remember it like it was yesterday. I thought I'd given myself a hernia, but it was just a strained groin muscle."

"Yeah, well, Ernie might not remember it as clearly as you do. Eighteen years is a long time."

Bobby said, "Did Ernie pull a groin muscle, too? If both of you pulled groin muscles, he might remember it."

"No, he didn't pull a groin muscle. I think Ernie has always had a very strong groin. But listen, if even I remember the incident so clearly, it only makes sense that Ernie will as well, considering that I'm the one who suffers fugues and he never does."

Actually, Spencer was aware that resorting to the fugue gambit made no sense at all. It was a non sequitur. It was like being in an argument with someone about whether chili was better with or without beans and trying to win the debate by suddenly declaring, *Okay, if you're so sure you're right, then how do you explain squirrels?*

Maybe Rebecca and Bobby were convinced by the fugue business. Or maybe they just wanted to stow Ernie where he couldn't be found and get the hell out of there. Whichever was the case, they looked solemn, nodded sagely, and resisted answering one non sequitur with another by raising the issue of squirrels. "Sounds good," Bobby said, and Rebecca said, "Let's get it done."

In the end, all that mattered was putting Ernie somewhere that a mortician wouldn't get him and embalm him, or where monsters were unlikely to discover him.

As Rebecca offered caring though unnecessary directions, her amigos manhandled Ernie across the deployed bed and into the niche behind it. Throughout this operation, Spencer marveled that a famous painter, a movie star, and a bestselling author should be moving an apparently dead man from one hidey-hole to another while stalked by slime monsters and Britta Hernishen. This is not to say that Spencer believed this was the kind of thing that plumbers, carpenters, and electricians did. He was not a snob who looked down on those who earned a living in one skilled trade or another. His astonishment had nothing to do with *class*. He would have been no less amazed if he and his amigos had been unemployed, without meaningful careers, and on the public dole. As incredible as it all seemed, there was no denying that this was the kind of thing that could happen to you if you were raised in a picturesque small town in the flat vastness of the Midwest.

When Ernie was lying on his back in the deep recess, his arms crossed on his chest, like Dracula waiting for the sun to go down, Spencer used a handle on the footboard to lift the cantilevered base, triggering the automatic mechanism that drew the bed up and swung it backward. It disappeared into the wall, the paneled underside matched to the wood paneling around it.

The amigos stood there for a long moment, smiling at the wall, pleased by their handiwork. No one unfamiliar with the house and coming into this room for the first time would know there was a bed here and a songwriter in suspended animation closed up with it, no matter how suspicious they might be.

"Now what?" Rebecca asked.

"Pastor Larry," said Bobby.

"We've got to interrogate the shit out of him," Spencer said.

"Why didn't we do that twenty years ago?"

"Maybe we did, but the memory of it has been erased."

"Have you noticed that we're recovering our memories just when we need them?"

"Yeah. It doesn't seem natural and spontaneous. It seems like we're being manipulated."

They stood in silence for a couple of minutes, waiting to be manipulated, but nothing happened.

Spencer wasn't surprised that nothing happened. All their lives, millions of bureaucrats spent countless hours gaslighting the public, trying to make people believe one lie or another. Millions more in large corporations spent billions of dollars to manipulate consumers into spending extravagantly on things they didn't need. But then some terrible crisis arrived, some catastrophe that people couldn't handle without help, and all the gaslighters were in Tahiti, sitting on the beach, manipulating nothing more than rum cocktails, pretending they never heard of us.

This might sound cynical, and Spencer was not for the most part a cynical person, although he had some capacity for cynicism, having spent years in the fine-arts business. We will not interrupt him at this critical juncture in his quest to understand his past, but if we did, he might tell us that we should not expect help from those who insist they love humanity and want to save it, for they are virtue-signaling phonies who are indifferent to or hate everyone except those in their immediate circle, which means salvation in times of trouble is up to you and those who love you, as it always has been and always will be.

On consideration, it's more likely that Bobby Shamrock, being a word guy, would have said all that. Spencer surely believes the same thing. However, being a visual artist, he expresses and shapes his philosophy in a montage of images; he would perhaps need weeks to create those while we waited.

"Pastor Larry," Bobby said again.

"Let's go get him," Rebecca said.

As they moved toward the second-floor hallway, someone called out from downstairs. "Spencer? Is that really you I saw? Spencer, dear boy, are you up there?"

Recognizing the voice, Spencer knew that he and his amigos were in a pickle.

27

A NEIGHBORLY VISIT

An almost infinite series of half-hour television sitcoms have revealed much about American families and life in the suburbs. For example, Americans are extraordinarily funny, communicating in swift exchanges peppered with clever one-liners. Wives are smarter than their husbands, but the goofball guys mean well. Every illness has been eliminated in the suburbs. Judging by the evidence on TV, one must assume that deaths are rare, though once in a while someone disappears and is never spoken of again; stranger still, on rare occasion a child or neighbor is replaced by an entirely different person with the same name, and everyone conspires not to notice.

Having been a city dweller all his adult life, only one thing about contemporary suburban and small-town existence depicted on TV irritated Spencer: how seldom neighbors knock first, how boldly they show up in your house and join a conversation. Many cities were so crime-ridden and such hotbeds of mental illness that if someone entered Spencer's Chicago home unannounced, he would assume the individual had violent intentions and would deal with him or her accordingly, even if it was a neighbor.

After all these years, he recognized the man at the foot of the stairs. Mr. Thornberry, a tall avuncular person known to everyone as Thorny. "What're you doing here, Mr. Thornberry?"

"What are *you* doing here, Spencer? I saw you drive into the garage, and I said to myself, 'By golly, he must be coming home to live.' Are you coming home to live? That would be so grand. Everyone on the block would be so pleased. You belong here, Spencer. We all remember you with your cowboy hat and water pistol, riding around the yard on that stick with a pony's head."

Descending the stairs hesitantly, with his amigos close behind, Spencer said, "How'd you get in? I locked the door to the garage."

"Got a key, of course. Back when the house became yours, you called the service company all the way from Chicago to have them maintain the place, but you forgot to tell them to give me a key."

"I didn't forget. I—"

"Why, sure you did, son. But I got one from them soon enough. They mow the lawn each week, do a walk-through twice a month, tend what needs fixing, but they can't be here all the time. I'm their eyes and ears. No vagrant is going to break in and set up camp, not on my watch. Bless them, they need shelter, and maybe they don't mean to ruin a place with their drugs and raggedy-looking unwashed dogs, man and dogs alike peeing wherever they want, but they for sure do some ruin. They come in from outside Maple Grove, but we make sure they don't stay long."

Spencer stepped off the stairs and into the foyer, one hand held out, intending to ask for the key. Thorny mistook this for an imminent handshake, reached out, bypassed the hand, and gathered Spencer into a bear hug.

The front door opened and two women entered, each bearing a casserole. The tall, bony one said, "Heavens to Betsy, it *is* you, spitting image of your daddy, God forgive him for all he's done."

The short, heavy one said, "You've turned out handsome enough to be a lounge singer, Skunky."

Thorny laughed and let go of Spencer and said, "You remember that nickname, how it hung with you a couple of years?"

"No. I just—"

"You were five years old," Thorny said, "cute as a button. It was July Fourth, and everyone was gathered for a barbecue in my backyard. You wandered on down by the woods, found this baby skunk. You thought it was a kitten, brought it to show everyone. Lord knows why it let you carry it across all that yard 'fore it saturated you."

A bald man with a lush white beard followed the women. He carried a two-gallon chilled-drink dispenser that would later prove to be full of iced tea. "Welcome home, Skunky! You're a sight for sore eyes."

Bobby lost sight of Spencer, who was swallowed into the crowd with great affection. There were forty or fifty people in the house, and they were in high spirits. They wanted to know everything there was to know about Spencer now that he was all grown up. Had he ever married? Was he dating? Who was she? What did he do for a living? Art? What kind of art? Did he ever hear from Constanina?

Because Spencer had sold off most items in the house while he had been in high school, there weren't many places for the visitors to sit. That was all right, because they were too excited to sit, and someone brought a dozen folding chairs to accommodate the older people who lacked the stamina for a lot of vertical socializing.

The big kitchen island was covered with enough food to feed a hundred, with an emphasis on baked goods. Stacks of paper plates. Plenty of disposable plastic cups, forks, and spoons. Paper napkins featured bluebirds in opposite corners with a ribbon stretched between their beaks on which the word FRIENDSHIP appeared in flowing script.

Spencer was the star of the show, but though Bobby had lived with the Pinchbecks in another neighborhood, the Nelsoneers—which is what they called themselves if they lived on the last block of Harriet Nelson Lane—were interested in him, too. Some of them knew he was an author, and a smaller number had read some of his books, but their greater interest was in Spencer because he'd once been a Nelsoneer and had come home from crazy, violent Chicago to this little piece of paradise.

People remembered Rebecca from those days when she dressed to appear unattractive. When they recalled the impression she had made on them, her look was described as like "a poor washerwoman out of Dickens, with nothing to wear but rags" and "the kind of nutty old woman who'd live in the woods and do witchcraft" and "a terribly sad, sad urchin." They wanted to know if she was dating Spencer Truedove. No, they were just friends who remained close. Then was she dating Robert Shamrock? No, they were also just amigos.

Clearly, they knew that she was a famous actress, but none of them spoke of her long-running television show or her hit films.

She wondered about their reticence until a woman named Ada Samples—late sixties, sweet-faced, in Ugg boots and a pale-blue Mother Hubbard, hair in a bun—sensed Rebecca's puzzlement, drew her into a corner, and whispered an explanation.

"They know about your mom and all her Fernandos, how she had no idea who might've been your daddy, how you were brought up by your grandfolks, and how they were so nasty two-faced with each other. All that drama, the humiliation and shame, you had to become an actress to express your pain or otherwise kill yourself."

"Exactly," Rebecca said. In fact, she had worn those costumes because she'd been unable to cope with the early ripeness of her adolescent body and with the kind of swaggering boys who were drawn to her, boys who were all hands and greedy expectations. She didn't say as much to Ada Samples, because all she wanted was to get out of this place.

"Just know," Ada continued, "every Nelsoneer admires how you made something of yourself in spite of the bad hand you were dealt."

"That's sweet," Rebecca said.

"Everyone expected you to be either a skanky disease-riddled junkie living in a gutter or at best a whore."

"Well," said Rebecca, "I lucked out when, you know, the acting thing worked for me."

"Nobody will mention that here now," Ada explained, "because they know how emotionally unstable actors are. They don't want to inadvertently say something about your childhood that might trigger a mental collapse."

"That's so thoughtful."

Ada smiled broadly and nodded with evident satisfaction. "Oh, these are very caring people here at the end of Harriet Nelson Lane. I just wanted to be sure you know they aren't being standoffish. They're proud you came from Maple Grove. They respect you and pity you and want only the best for you."

"Am I blushing?"

"No, dear."

"Good."

28

SCARY DISCOVERIES

If his favorite songwriter hadn't been upstairs, lying in the wall behind the foldaway bed, Bobby the Sham would seriously have considered setting the living room draperies on fire to clear the visiting neighbors from the house. However, he didn't know how long it would take to get the crowd out of the place or how fast flames might spread from the draperies to the structure itself. When you started a fire to break up a party, you couldn't be certain you would then be able to extinguish it quickly in the wake of the last departing guest. If this had been a novel he was writing, he could have done a lot of research on the subject, but this was not one of his novels; this was real life, a true story currently unfolding, involving real people in extraordinary circumstances. He couldn't simply stop the action, save the document, copy it onto his Seagate Backup Plus hard drive, and go off to educate himself about arson.

By several sly maneuvers, he extricated himself from the crowd and retreated to the laundry room, where he could be alone behind a closed door. He needed to engage in some deep-breathing exercises that were said to lower blood pressure and improve brain function.

The space might have inspired mild claustrophobia if Spencer hadn't sold the washer and dryer in his junior year of high school.

Bobby breathed so deeply that his nasal septum and various cartilages attached to his nasal bones vibrated with a sound like thrumming insect wings, as if he had inhaled a bee. However, he had not inhaled a bee, because if he *had* inhaled a bee, he would have been sneezing violently.

Bobby was alone such a short time that he neither lowered his blood pressure nor improved brain function before the door opened. A man entered. He nervously glanced back into the short hallway off the kitchen, closed the door, and stood with his back against it. He was in his forties, muscular, with bangs that suggested his barber must be operating under a forged license.

"I'm Warren Weber. You're Robert Shamrock."

"I might be."

"Don't worry. I'm not here to sell you an idea for a novel. I saw you slide out of the room, and while they're all distracted, I followed."

"Distracted?"

"Fred Sanford is arm wrestling Spencer, like he used to do when your friend was a teenager."

"What is Fred—seventy-five?"

"Seventy-seven, but he keeps winning."

"Spencer was afraid of Fred," Bobby said. "He never wanted to arm wrestle the guy, but he was never given a choice."

"He wasn't given one this time, either. Did I tell you my name is Warren Weber?"

"You did indeed. Is that true?"

"Yeah. My wife, Mary Kate, and I moved to town a year ago."

"You're young for the neighborhood."

"We don't live on this block. We're the last house in the block before this one."

"So you're not a Nelsoneer."

"That's just it. The Nelsoneers want to expand the club into the next block, our block."

"It's a club?"

"It's something." Warren Weber seemed as if he were walking a ledge. When the audience for the arm-wrestling contest let out a cheer, he startled, pressed his back harder against the door, and grimaced at the floor as though gazing into a city street from the twentieth story of a high-rise. "Maybe I shouldn't be talking to you, bothering you."

"No, that's okay. I'm interested."

Weber shifted his stare from the abyss to Bobby. "I mean—do I understand right that you're not a Nelsoneer?"

"I grew up on the other side of town."

"But you became friends with Spencer."

"We had a lot in common. It's a small town. The other side of it isn't that far away."

"Yeah, but he was a Nelsoneer. You had a lot in common with a Nelsoneer?"

"There weren't Nelsoneers back then. The first time I've heard about them is today."

"Okay, all right, but Spencer's family lived on this street. He grew up here."

"It's more complicated than that," Bobby assured him. "Anyway, he left a long time ago, and he doesn't want to be here."

Weber nodded and chewed his lower lip and flinched when the crowd again cheered the geriatric athletic prowess of Fred Sanford. "Do you think . . ."

"Yes, even though it's painful." When Weber gave him a blank look, Bobby said, "Sorry. I can be a smart-ass. Do I think what?"

"Isn't there such a thing as too much neighborliness?"

"This has always been a close neighborhood."

"It's something more than close," Weber said. The wide-flexed irises of his blue eyes presented dark pupils too large for the circumstances, as if some inner darkness prevented him from seeing the light of the room in its fullness. "It's stifling, suffocating. They're always asking what errand can they do for you, whether you need anything from the store, would you like to join some of the guys and paint a house free for a Nelsoneer. They have these get-togethers at one house or another every Friday evening, sometimes two nights a week, plus on holidays, and everyone brings food. They have Nelsoneer bridge nights and softball games and flag football—and of course that damn pickleball."

Bobby said, "I don't think it was that close back then. If you don't want to be a Nelsoneer, just tell them so."

"We've told them a hundred times. They won't take no for an answer. If you turn down an invitation, they send you flowers or candy or homemade cookies. These people are persistent, insistent, *unrelenting*. I thought you might know . . ."

"Know what?"

"How to deal with them."

"If it bothers you, maybe you should move."

"We would if we could. But we have a mortgage two points below the current rate. We can't afford a house at the current interest."

"What do you do for a living?"

"I code. My wife codes. The company lets us work from home because we write great code and meet deadlines. We used to think working from home was so cool. But the Nelsoneers know we're here." He clasped his head in both hands, as if his skull might crack open from the pressure he was under. "We're home, always home, *and they know it.*"

Bobby wondered if the Nelsoneers were really as intolerable as Weber made them out to be or if he was a drama queen. "I don't know what to tell you, Warren. I suppose, if I were as distressed as you are, I might sell the house even at a loss and move, maybe get out of town altogether, go someplace where property values are lower."

Weber lowered his hands from his head and turned them palms up, as if to say, *You don't understand, it's not that easy, I need some help here.* "But we love Maple Grove. It's so pretty, so clean. We've never seen a town so clean, nothing in disrepair. There's no crime. It's the safest place in the world."

"There's always crime," Bobby said.

"Not here. I know it sounds crazy, but not here. There hasn't been a murder in fourteen years, no robbery in almost thirteen. No burglaries. No shoplifting. No speeding. No driving drunk. Not even littering, for God's sake. The police department is down to four officers, and they don't carry weapons anymore. They drive around helping people with flat tires and vehicles that won't start. Help old ladies load groceries in their cars. They spend hours searching for a stray dog. I lost my wallet six months ago. This guy found it and thought it was badly worn. So he bought a new wallet and brought both of them to me. He refused to be reimbursed."

Bobby had first pegged Warren Weber as quasi-neurotic, for the most part harmless unless overstimulated. Now he realized that the man was something else entirely. Weber was one of those walk-on characters with the limited purpose of providing important information to the lead character. (Bobby was not so egotistical as to think he was *the one and only* protagonist of this Maple Grove story. However, he was sufficiently self-aware to realize that he was *one of* the leads in an ensemble cast; being remarkably modest for an author of his accomplishments, that role was enough for him.)

"Even if everyone in town has suddenly become saintly," Bobby said, "criminals must come in from outside, try to peddle drugs, pull a stickup."

"Yeah, but some feel remorseful before they've done anything. Eleven years ago, this guy named Ned Sacker drove in from upstate with thugs named Turpin and Nevison to rob the First National Bank. Ned was, by his own admission, 'a tough little weasel,' a young man on his way to a life of crime. Three hours after they checked into a motel using false ID, Ned walked into police head-quarters in tears and confessed to their intentions. Turpin and Nevison were long-time professional thieves with outstanding war-rants. They were sent to the jurisdictions where they committed crimes, were prosecuted and sent to prison. Ned was put into a diversion program and remained here in Maple Grove. He got a job. Was promoted. Married a local girl. Got into real-estate sales. Bought a house. He sold one to Kate and me. He can't explain why he did what he did, the confession and all. There's a lot of that in this town."

"If this is all true," Bobby said, "it's strange."

Weber agreed. "Strange but, I've got to admit, in some ways wonderful. The downside of all this wonderfulness is the Nelsoneers. The problem is that too much wonderfulness can get on your nerves."

"What does your wife think about all this?"

Warren Weber's face fell, not completely off his head, but the gravity of his dismay drew his features into a dour expression that suggested he might be close to losing all hope. "At first Katie was creeped out by it, but gradually she's come around. She plays bridge with the ladies one afternoon a week. She's joined their book club. She talks about 'our special neighborhood, our special town, our special life,' talks that way all the time." Unshed tears welled in his eyes, and his mouth grew soft. "I'm afraid . . . afraid my Kate, my Katie . . . I'm afraid she's changed, lost, *gone*."

Bobby said, "Well, I don't know, but it sounds like she's just happy."

"Does it? Is that what it sounds like? I don't know. Sometimes I think I'm the one with a problem. Then there's a moment when Katie seems . . . not happy, not just content. She seems dazed, robotic."

"I'm not sure what you mean by that."

"She seems *drugged*. She's not. I've looked everywhere in the house for illegal drugs. There aren't any. Eventually I stopped looking because I got embarrassed about snooping on her as if she were some teenager who fell in with a bad crowd. Recently, some days, I don't think about it that much. It's too exhausting. There are days the Nelsoneers invite me to make a foursome for golf, and the guys are fun. It all seems so natural. Today, when I heard how Spencer was coming back, I ran out to the bakery, bought two dozen eclairs for the welcome-home party." He fell silent, blinking in perplexity, as if he only now realized what he had done. "I'd never met Spencer, but I wanted to let him know how happy we all were to have him back. Then Katie and I went across the street with the eclairs, and I saw you. I saw how you were looking at everyone."

"How was that?"

"Like you thought the whole scene was somewhere between absurd and disturbing. And watching you, I sort of . . . began to wake up. I realized I was becoming part of it. Don't you think this is a lot more than merely strange? Don't you? Don't you think so?"

"'More' in what sense?"

"Weird, frightening, dangerous. Don't you think what seems to be happening here has a threatening quality?"

Something had changed about Warren Weber. Being in a walk-on role, he had no obligation to evolve logically, yet his confusion was gone as though it had been pretense. The warm, beseeching quality of his eyes had settled into a hard stare. He no longer projected a nervous and uncertain demeanor but seemed poised to take action of some kind.

"'Threatening' is a pretty strong word, Warren."

Weber said, "Yeah, well, there are times I feel threatened. If that's how I feel, don't you think I should go to the authorities? Not here in Maple Grove. Maybe go to the state police?"

A chill creped the skin on the nape of Bobby's neck. He became convinced that he was being interrogated and that if he endorsed the state police idea, there would be a terrible cost. "Frankly, Warren, I think you've got a case of midlife crisis."

"Really? A midlife crisis?"

"It's nothing to be embarrassed about. They say that all men get there eventually. And you misread me if you believe I think this impromptu party is absurd or disturbing. I'm charmed by it," Bobby lied without remorse.

"You are? Charmed?"

"Very much so. When the day comes that I stop traveling for research and inspiration, I'll come home to Maple Grove and settle down here. Everything so pretty, little or no crime, neighbors so affectionate and caring—what could be more appealing?"

Weber put on a look of suspicion. "When you slipped out of the party—"

"I hadn't been here in twenty years. I misremembered the layout of the house and thought this was the powder bath."

"You thought it was the powder bath?"

"Absolutely."

"So you don't find anything off-putting about the people out there?"

"Good heavens, no. They're delightful. You must be under too much stress with those code-writing deadlines, Warren."

"I guess maybe I am. Sometimes I'm at it seven days a week."

"All work and no play makes Jack a little neurotic. What're we doing, dawdling here like this? Come on, let's get out there where the fun is."

As gullible as required by his limited function in this quirky story, Warren Weber smiled. The tension went out of him. His irises contracted, and his pupils became smaller, as they should have been in the bright lights of the laundry room.

In the rest of the ground floor of the house, the celebration was raging. The Nelsoneers received Bobby as if they had seen him and enjoyed his company every day of their lives and perhaps even before. They clapped him on the back and hugged him and pinched his cheeks and offered him ice tea as he made his way through the crowd in search of his amigos.

In the living room, encircled by ebullient onlookers, Spencer and Rebecca were sitting in folding chairs at a small round table, arm wrestling.

29

ERNIE BEHIND THE FOLDAWAY BED

He was pretty sure he wasn't dead. He hadn't met God yet or even Saint Peter. If he was dead, what were they waiting for? Ernie didn't know what the afterlife would be like—nobody knew—but he was sure it wouldn't be a giant bureaucratic mess like the United States government, with millions of dead people lying around in a state of suspended animation, waiting for clerks to get back from gossipy conversations in the break room so that papers could be processed and the multitudes of newly arrived souls could rise up and be sent off to whatever corner of Paradise was assigned to them.

He could not feel, see, smell, or taste anything. You might think he would be frightened or at least anxious and impatient, but he was not. Although he wasn't able to hear anything of the world where he had lived for thirty-five years, now and then one of two voices would speak to him. They were soothing voices with a musical quality, one male and the other female, reassuring him that he was well and everything would be all right in time. They were Prozac voices, keeping him mellow and patient.

Rarely, a third voice intruded—deep, rough, ominous. It was not friendly like the others. It said things such as, "You belong to us, you useless worm," and "We will have your brain," and "We will kill all your kind, burst upon you, and eat you alive from the inside out." Because he currently lacked the ability to run and hide, these verbal assaults would have distressed Ernie if the unknown maker of the threats had not always been abruptly silenced in mid rant, as though someone disconnected or deplatformed him.

Immediately after such an event, one or the other of the two soothing voices would assure him that he was loved, safe, and of such great value that he would never suffer. He was told that the threatening presence was "of a different genotype from us," whatever that meant. He was informed that the thuggish speaker was "millennia younger than we are and less wise, lacking the intelligence and the means to carry out their stupid threats." He was promised that he would eventually arise and return to life as he had known it. Ernie believed everything these reassuring voices told him; both the male and female speakers were too kind, caring, and convincing to be disbelieved.

Because he never slept in his current condition, he might have been bored if he hadn't filled the hours by writing country songs. Several had the potential to be hits; even if they failed, they were worth composing because they were certain to irritate his mother. He needed no pen and paper to write the lyrics, nor did he require a guitar or piano to fashion the melodies. He had perfect pitch; when he thought of the notes, he could hear them. He visualized the tunes on sheet music, and with his eidetic memory, he could summon those staff degrees at will. Among the tunes he composed in the last few days were "I Drank My Way out of Her Heart" and "Cheaters Don't Play Cards in Heaven" and "Drape My Casket in Old Glory."

30

SHAKEN BY EVENTS AT SPENCER'S HOUSE, THE AMIGOS RETURN TO ADORNO'S FOR LUNCH

The thoughtful Nelsoneers had laid out an enormous buffet at Spencer's house, but the three amigos had been kept too busy to eat anything during the five hours they had been captive at that event. Much ice tea had been forced on them, but at 2:00 they were in need of something they could chew.

Although Adorno's had changed to a ristorante from a pizzeria since they hung out in this place as teenagers, it hadn't undergone another transformation since they'd dined here the previous evening, even though this was a century of frantic change. As far as Rebecca could tell, the decor was exactly the same, as was the menu.

Vito didn't work the lunch shift. Their waitress was a blue-eyed blonde named Gabriella, or so the management would have you believe.

Because they had a busy evening of law-breaking ahead, the amigos didn't have wine. They ordered lunch. After Gabriella took their order, she said, "Ms. Crane, the first two seasons of *Enemies* were the best thing on TV at the time, and you were really great as Suzy Pepper. You sure deserved those Emmys."

Although seven seasons of the show had aired, Rebecca was wise enough not to seek an opinion of the other five. She said, "That's very sweet of you. You're a lovely girl. Listen, dear, I'm a curious nebbynose. Do you mind telling me your last name?"

"Roccofino."

"Gabriella Roccofino. Your married name, I assume."

"No. I haven't been married yet. But I'm engaged. He's a great guy. Salvatore Passatempo. I want to have six kids."

"I'm sure you will," Rebecca said.

After Gabriella Roccofino Passatempo had brought their Cokes and they were alone in the booth, Spencer said, "I don't want to ask this, Rebecca, but I can't help myself."

"Spencer, I've told you before, I *don't know why* the last five seasons never measured up to the first two."

"No. I'm talking about the arm wrestling."

"What about it?"

"Did you really try, or did you just let me win six times out of seven?"

"Don't put yourself down. You're a big strong artist, honey."

"That's not an answer."

Bobby said, "You want some advice?"

Spencer said, "No."

Rebecca said, "I don't *like* appearing to be a wimp, amigo. I would never want to throw six out of seven."

"How many did you throw?"

Rebecca sighed and shook her head. "The Musketeers never had conversations like this."

"Did you throw five and I really only had one win?"

Bobby said, "Maybe now you want some advice."

"No."

Rebecca said, "Honey, you remember how I had to tone up big-time to play Nurse Heather in *Shriek*? I had to keep up with my weight training for the two sequels, and I've never stopped."

Spencer sighed. "I didn't have any real wins, did I?"

"But you have that great hat," Bobby reassured him.

Adorno Ristorante had become chic enough to have liveried food runners in addition to waiters and busboys. This one carried two plates, while Gabriella brought the third. He was a pale, freckled redhead with a name tag that identified him as Silvio. Rebecca was tempted to ask his surname, but she figured it would be Lombardo or Pisciotta, or maybe Corleone.

The food was delicious. They ate it. Rebecca had no inclination to describe her lunch to herself for the purpose of enhancing the atmosphere of the scene or for any other reason.

By the time they finished the meal, 3:00 would have come and passed, and they would have accomplished little since meeting for breakfast at 7:30. They had learned about the new, improved Maple Grove and its peaceable, neighborly people, but that knowledge did not greatly advance their mission to revive Ernie Hernishen from the curse of suspended animation and rescue him from whatever dark forces held sway in this strange—and possibly doomed—town.

The amigos quietly discussed Pastor Larry and how best to get at him, which they had failed to do all those years ago, largely because of the murderous Wayne Louis Hornfly. It occurred to Rebecca—as how could it not?—that kidnapping the Reverend Turnbuckle, or even just detaining him against his will in order to terrify him into making revelations, would damage her girl-next-door image and might even negatively, seriously impact her career. However, Ernie was her friend, and if movies like *Beaches* had taught her anything, it was that friendship and loving one's friends mattered more than anything else, more than fame or money or social acceptance or the fate of the world.

They arrived at a plan. It was not a perfect plan certain to lead to success. In fact, it was reckless. All schemes hatched under dire circumstances such as these were bound to be reckless to one degree or another. They had to admit the risk, accept it, and press forward with thoughtless abandon.

While Bobby calculated the gratuity for Gabriella, Spencer sat in slack-jawed concentration, laying out their reckless scheme in a series of mental images, and Rebecca cleaned her plate and flatware with wet wipes. She'd half finished the task when her phone played three bars of the theme song from *Enemies*. She read the caller ID and informed her amigos: "It's Hornfly."

She knew she should be afraid, and she *was* afraid. After all these years, Wayne Louis Hornfly was as vivid in her mind's eye as if she had encountered him in the flesh just yesterday—his cruel face, green-striated orange eyes, and green teeth. In this sudden memory of a long-ago moment, he was holding a severed head by its hair. Although the head belonged to a man of about thirty-five, the chubby cheeks and smooth skin made it seem that Hornfly held the head of a choirboy, a choirboy who had made a serious mistake. The image was so familiar that Rebecca knew this was a moment from her past and that another suppressed memory would recur to her soon.

In that mellow game-show-host voice that was so out of synch with the killer's appearance, Hornfly said, "You don't belong here, Rebecca Crane. You have been further corrupted by Hollywood and are even a thousand times more disgusting than you were back in the day, when you were already repulsive. Why have you dared to return? Have you perhaps learned to hate yourself as we hate you, as we hate all humankind? Have you come home to die horribly? To be killed? To—"

Rebecca interrupted him. "Hey, one question at a time, you rude freak. I've returned to help a dear friend. No, I don't hate myself. Yeah, I'm not perfect, but I'm pretty swell compared to a piece of garbage like you. No, I haven't come back to die. And if you're going to try to kill me, you better watch your ass."

Hornfly said, "You may not talk to us like that. We will not forget. We are not a pussy-willow genotype like another I could name. We will extinguish you and your kind."

"Give me a moment to put on my scared-girl expression. Oh, gee, I can't make it fit."

"Something's wrong with you. What's wrong with you, bitch?"

"Oh, that's rich. The psychopathic cornball with the IQ of a cockroach thinks something's wrong with *me*. *You're* the bitch."

He sounded like an *angry* game-show host. "Wayne Louis Hornfly could squash you like a ripe grape between a thumb and forefinger."

"Good grief, that was already a dumb line when you used it on Bobby in the parsonage, twenty years ago. You shouldn't write your own material, jerkface."

"You're dead."

"I'm dead, huh? I don't feel dead. Listen to me, you wad of cat phlegm. You stay out of my way, or I'll shove a stick of dynamite up your fat ass."

She terminated the call.

Her amigos were staring at her. Bobby was as slack-jawed as Spencer. Neither of them seemed able to speak.

She said, "Sorry you had to hear that. He just steams me."

Bobby cleared his throat. "What were you doing?"

"She was in character," Spencer said.

"You were being Heather Ashmont?" Bobby asked.

Before Rebecca could reply, Spencer said, "No. She was deep into being Rebecca Crane like we haven't quite seen before."

Her phone produced the theme song from *Enemies*.

Rebecca pocketed it. "Let the asshole go to voicemail. He won't have the guts to leave a message anyway."

A couple in the middle of the room, at the table nearest the amigos' booth, were staring, aghast. When Rebecca gave them a do-you-have-a-problem-with-me look, they lowered their eyes to their food and worked their forks assiduously.

"What set me off was I had an agent like that once," Rebecca explained.

"You had a psychopathic killer for an agent?" Bobby asked.

"Nah. He was worse. Are we ready to go?"

They went. On their way out, when they passed Gabriella Roccofino, Rebecca saw her wink at Bobby in spite of having Salvatore Passatempo lined up and six kids waiting to be made.

31

AS THE AMIGOS GET IN THE GENESIS, THEY ENDURE A RECOVERED MEMORY

The first October after Rebecca became one of the amigos, Maple Grove was elaborately decorated for the entire month leading up to the holiday. The streets within the six square blocks that might charitably be called a "downtown" were strung with more than half a million orange and red lights. Every store window displayed a spooky diorama or featured fearsome scenes applied to the glass with water-soluble paint. The eyes and grins and snarls of two thousand jack-o'-lanterns pulsed with demonic candlelight. Inflatable spiders as big as cars quivered menacingly on some rooftops. A bus parked in the town circle was occupied by grisly mannequins made up as the riding dead, their rotting faces leering out of the windows, as if the driver had made a wrong turn and gotten lost and stubbornly refused to admit it until everyone aboard had grown old and died. Scores of others with axes buried in their skulls or with viscera spilling from slashed abdomens or with snake heads protruding from empty eye sockets stood in strategically chosen places so that those strolling through the spectacle would encounter them unexpectedly. Hanged mannequins dangled from the trees in the cemetery, a tip of the hat to Maple Grove's history. Tableaus featuring ghosts, vampires, and space aliens—many motorized—occupied front yards. The grange hall had been transformed into a vast haunted house where paying visitors screamed their way through a long series of horrors too graphic for children ten or under, though infants-in-arm were welcome because it was thought their senses were still so undeveloped that they couldn't be traumatized by what they saw.

Although Maple Grove's Month of Christmas attracted thousands of tourists, the Month of Halloween had become the greater draw. Such was the state of the nation.

On the evening of October 31, when the crowds were at their largest, the four amigos roamed the scene, drinking blood, which was really cherry soda, eating gore cream, which was in fact vanilla ice cream blended with a lot of red food dye, and hot dogs. The hot dog vendor had resisted the urge to trick up his wares to be repulsive. However, he wore a necklace of severed fingers, and the sign at his stand referred to his product as DEAD DOGS. The air was redolent of carnival foods—french fries, nachos, cotton candy, churros.

Because they had a reputation as nerds to uphold, the amigos eschewed baroque costumes. Bobby wore a stage arrow through his head. Spencer, who had yet to acquire his trademark porkpie hat, crowned himself with a propeller beanie. Ernie wore horn-rimmed glasses with trick lenses that made his eyes look googly. Outfitted in her usual shambles of thrift-shop clothes, Rebecca painted her face toad-green instead of white and carried a whisk broom, as if she were a witch with the broomstick equivalent of a compact car.

Eventually they arrived at Liberty Park, at the intersection of Cunningham and Winkler. Across the street at the courthouse, a six-member dance troupe wore black bodysuits and masks on which were printed white, radiant images of skeletons; they performed for a standing audience that laughed and applauded, confirming that it is a deplorable trait of human beings to find death hilarious when it isn't their own.

Pathway lamps dwindled through the trees and toward the center of the park, leading to a large, open pavilion with a latticework skirt; fluted columns supported its scalloped roof. The structure included a bandstand and a dance floor that, on other occasions, glowed with romantic rose-colored light reflecting off motorized, mirrored globes that cast slowly turning diamonds of light and encircling patterns of waltzing shadows. On this night, the light was an eerie yellow-green, and the shadows appeared to caper like entities with malevolent intentions.

The grounds offered event planners numerous locations at which to place startlements along the softly lighted paths. On previous nights, this had been a popular attraction. As the amigos gathered at the Cunningham Avenue entrance, however, the park appeared to be deserted except perhaps for some activity at the pavilion.

"Where is everybody?" Ernie wondered as he stepped through the open gate.

"Something's weird here," Bobby warned as he followed Ernie.

"I don't like this," said Spencer, and Rebecca said, "We should call it a night and go home," as they followed Ernie and Bobby into Liberty Park.

To the left and right, ghouls, ghosts, men with goat skulls for heads, and fiends of many kinds popped up as though spring-loaded or shimmered into existence as holograms or were sitting on benches, holding snow cones full of fake shaved ice.

"That hot dog is totally coming back on me," said Bobby as he kept moving.

"What's happening?"

"This isn't right."

"This is so wrong."

Although they openly expressed their misgiving, they progressed as if they were one organism, pacing one another without hesitancy. In their lives leading to this moment, they had suffered a similar sense of abandonment by the families that should have loved them and held them close. Each had reacted by keeping a certain distance from the social circles of which others their age were a part. After all, if you couldn't trust your parents, if they were so high on their lives that they couldn't find their way down to yours, how could you put your faith in people who weren't even part of your family? So you told yourself that your eccentricities were the things about you that made you unlovable, the very things about yourself over which you had little or no control—your appearance, your intelligence, your natural enthusiasms—and you emphasized those qualities until they were no longer your weakness and became your strength, your armor against the world. If then you discovered others like you—nerds in a world of cool kids—there could be an end to loneliness at last and the birth of a group purpose that was a civilizing force. All of that, however, did not explain why the four amigos continued toward the pavilion like one creature with eight legs. They were individuals, defiant enough to take satisfaction in being outcasts in a world of sheep. Yet they proceeded as if they were lemmings, sleepwalking toward a cliff rather than racing toward it.

They reached a flight of four steps. They climbed them. They were aware that some force compelled them, and they didn't like it. They suspected they could resist whatever magnetism drew them, but they surrendered to it because in this case capitulation

was more interesting. The primary way high intelligence compli-
cates life is that it inspires endless questions and the determination to answer them.

They stepped inside. The raised bandstand was at the far
end of the building. In the center of the dance floor stood a tall
man with a thick neck and broad shoulders, his back to them.
Something lay on the floor in front of him, but his form and
the carousel of revolving lights and shadows made it difficult to
deduce what he was standing over.

Like all of his kind, he possessed an uncanny sense of how
long to wait in order to have the greatest dramatic effect before
turning toward his audience. The fact that he was holding a severed head by its hair and that the head appeared to be real also
contributed to the impact he had on those who'd been drawn
here to him.

Although only Bobby had gone into the parsonage weeks earlier and seen Wayne Louis Hornfly in the library armchair, the
other three amigos knew who this must be, which was a tribute to
Bobby's talent to describe a character and which in part explained
his great success as a novelist.

Even in these kaleidoscopic fragments of swarming light
and shadow, they could clearly see the severed head had chubby
cheeks, kind features, and a look of heartbreaking innocence. The
murdered person who once possessed it had surely been a nice and
harmless individual. The amigos most likely all knew—and certainly Rebecca did—that they would never be able to forget this
face. One day years from now, perhaps at the altar on their wedding day or at Adorno's after a nice lunch, this image would flash
into mind with sickening impact and sort of ruin the moment.

"This is a warning," Hornfly said, shaking the severed head so it dripped more copiously on the dance floor. "You have periodically continued your surveillance of Pastor Larry and been researching his past as best you can. You have asked questions of people who knew nothing, and you should be glad they knew nothing, because if they'd known something, we would cut off all *your* heads after gouging out your eyes. You saw something you were never meant to see, Pastor Larry running through the cemetery at night. You went somewhere you had no right to go, down into the church basement where those poorly constructed men were lying naked, a mistaken creation about which we are much embarrassed. You must stop now or you will be stopped in an exhibition of the most gleeful violence of which we're capable, and we are capable of gleeful violence greater than you can imagine with your limited human brainpower."

Everyone was silent for a moment. The mirrored globes revolved overhead, and beams of light directed at them fractured into lacy patterns that swept around the dark pavilion. Music often enlivened this place, but there was no music now. Ernie Hernishen lamented the lack of music, for a nice tune would help settle everyone's nerves. It is a mystery what inspires us to take the path in life we choose, but it might have been here that Ernie decided to be a songwriter.

Rebecca was the first to speak to Hornfly. "Don't you think this warning of yours is more extreme than it needs to be?"

The monster did not take this criticism well, which monsters seldom do. "You are obstinate mules. Like all mules you will die like dogs if you don't stay in your stable where you belong."

"May I make an observation that might be helpful?" she asked.

"You have nothing of value to give us."

"Just the same, I suggest that before you use similes to make your point, you think them through. Mules die like mules, not like dogs. And generally speaking, neither mules nor dogs are kept in stables."

"I see you shaking," Hornfly retorted. "Don't think I don't see you shaking."

"It's a little chilly tonight," Rebecca said. "Anyway, take the time to think through your similes. We'll wait."

Bobby said, "How do we know that's a real head?"

Although Hornfly had a face that distorted any expression into one that was hard to read, there was astonishment in the killer's voice. "We are not a genotype that makes empty threats."

"Genotype?" Spencer asked. "What's a genotype?"

"He just gave us a clue," Ernie said.

"How do you spell that?" Rebecca asked. "With an *a* or an *o*?"

"What is wrong with you?" Hornfly demanded. He stepped aside, revealing a headless body on the floor. "This will be you if you poke your nose in where noses don't belong. Are you all insane?"

"No, no," Spencer assured him. "We are just some kids who've been kicked around and dumped on pretty much since we came into the world, and we've had enough of it."

Bobby said, "We're not going to take it anymore. We're not going to be called names and laughed at and just keep our heads down. We're not going to find monsters in a church basement and scurry away and do nothing about it."

Rebecca said, "We're not going to be intimidated by some lumpy orange-eyed monster with a wriggling beard and three names like a serial killer, some stupid genotype who rips the heads off innocent people just to make a point." She spoke with passion, although in truth it was not just her stirring speech that caused her three amigos to tremble and to feel that their bladders were full. "We have been the objects of endless mockery and vitriol and plain old meanness, targeted by barbarians who express their feelings for us with their fists, with hair pulling and shin kicking, abandoned by the people whose highest responsibility was to take care of us when we were little and vulnerable. But at last, we have someone. We have each other. We're amigos. We've been through the wringer, nothing more can be wrung out of us. And *you*"—she imbued the pronoun with cold scorn and contempt—"*you* stand there with a severed head, trying to look sooo scary, thinking you can bend us to your will, terrify us so much we'll turn tail and run. Well, that shows how clueless you are, because *we don't even have tails*, you despicable turd."

Ernie shook one fist. "Totally."

Spencer said, "Damn straight."

"I second that emotion," Bobby said.

Ernie stood tall. "Back off, buttercup."

Spencer said, "All for one—"

"—and one for all," Bobby said.

Hornfly turned his fiery stare on Ernie, on Spencer, on Bobby, on Rebecca. After making eye contact with each, during which none of them looked away, he cleared his throat. In spite of his game-show voice, he sounded sincere and profoundly impressed when he said, "Holy crap, what a bunch of losers." He took one step forward, and they took one step backward in unison. "Time for you to come back from Neverland and face reality. This tourist who came to Maple Grove and got himself beheaded," said

Hornfly, "can't just be left here to be found. He must disappear. Do you know how we're going to make him disappear?"

The amigos shook their heads. They had suspicions regarding how Hornfly would make the dead man disappear, but they were reluctant to entertain those suspicions at any length.

The monster said, "We are going to eat him. By 'we' I am not referring to you. We do not need your assistance to eat him. Do you want to know how we are going to eat him?"

"Not really," said Ernie, and his amigos shook their heads again.

"We are going to eat him right here. It won't take more than two minutes, maybe three. You really should watch, because if you dweebs don't back off and mind your own business, we will eat you just the same way."

"Whoa," Spencer said, consulting his wristwatch, "I didn't realize how late it is. They expected me home before this."

"Me too," said Bobby. "I'm out way past curfew."

Ernie and Rebecca made noises of agreement, although no one in any of their lives cared how late they stayed out or whether they ever came home.

Wayne Louis Hornfly said, "We like to start eating from the crown of the head and finish with the toes. Because this man is in two pieces, we would much enjoy having an intermezzo of some kind, something soft and rotten, but as the Rolling Stones have told us, 'You can't always get what you want.' So there will only be a short pause between courses." He bit into the skull as if it were no harder than a peach and began to gobble through the brain.

The amigos bolted from the pavilion.

32

LIBERTY PARK

So then, following a late lunch at Adorno's Ristorante and the mutual recovery of the lost memory involving Wayne Louis Hornfly and Halloween night, Bobby suggested they engage in some brainstorming and that Liberty Park should be the place to do it. When Rebecca and Spencer at once agreed, Bobby felt warmed by a sense of friendship almost as intense as the camaraderie that he had enjoyed so much back in the day.

In the Genesis, on the way to the park, when the three amigos spoke of the Night the Tourist Was Eaten, you could hear that they capitalized those words. This doesn't mean the consumption of the chubby-cheeked individual had been designated as an official holiday in picturesque Maple Grove. It certainly had not. But now that the amigos had been made to remember that long-forgotten episode, the incident possessed such terrible power that Bobby couldn't speak of it entirely in lowercase, and his friends also adopted the subtle vocalization of capital letters. Indeed, standard capitalization did not seem adequate to convey the horror of that murder and devouring. However, while capital letters can be conveyed by the human voice, italics and bold typeface cannot; if we stop to consider the issue for a moment, which is what's being proposed here, we must agree we can hear the capital letters in "Memorial Day" or

"New Year's Day," but we are unable even to imagine how italics or bold typeface would sound.

During the drive, they arrived at the inescapable conclusion that memories of forgotten events were not returning spontaneously. Someone was intentionally unlocking their memory vaults, setting free the experiences of which all recollection had been previously denied. The unknown master of memory must be supernatural or in possession of a technology far more advanced than anything human beings had yet developed.

In the latter case, the amigos didn't feel qualified to reach a conclusion about who the technological wizard might prove to be. If they failed to find clues that led them to the responsible party, they would perhaps consult a scientist—or better yet, a science-fiction writer, if one could be found who was sober.

That thought was not a slam at science-fiction writers. Bobby did not believe they were more likely to be inebriated than authors working in other genres. He'd met a lot of writers of all kinds, and it seemed to him that the stress of their work led them to strong drink more often than occurred with people in other professions. The pressing need to decide whether to use a comma or semicolon; whether to employ a dialogue tag, what that tag should be, and whether it should come before or after the speaker's name; the extent to which the use of adverbs must be limited; whether the best choice for a lead character was a perky brain surgeon or maybe a moody homicide detective or perhaps a perky homicide detective studying to fulfill his or her dream of becoming a moody brain surgeon—several such decisions needed to be made every minute of a workday, without surcease. Any wrong choice could lead to a finished novel that, for the life of copyright, resulted in semiannual royalty payments that never exceeded nine cents.

This might seem to have nothing to do with visiting the scene of the beheading in Liberty Park and brainstorming about what steps to take next. But it's important to understand that, as a writer perpetually seeking material and considering how it might best be developed, Bobby had mundane concerns that crowded into his mind along with all his worries about Hornfly. He was *distracted*. This is important because distraction could cause him to make a mistake and become the only amigo to die horribly. We should prepare for that eventuality.

And so, well fed but with much on their minds, the three amigos stepped onto the dance floor of the pavilion, though not to dance.

The late-summer day was pleasantly warm, with a light breeze out of the west. The leaves of the surrounding maples fluttered prettily, as if the trees were demure Japanese maidens concealing their lovely faces behind geisha fans.

On benches throughout Liberty Park, people were reading books, feeding squirrels, and mesmerized by their smartphones. A few walked dogs, and fewer pushed strollers carrying small children who were in various states of uneasy consideration of the world into which they had recently been thrust.

In the pavilion, Bobby's attention—and that of his friends— was initially focused on the approximate center of the floor, where Wayne Louis Hornfly had stood over a mutilated corpse, holding a severed head by its hair. They half expected to find telltale stains that had been dulled but not worn away by thousands of feet engaged in waltzes, foxtrots, jitterbugs, cha-chas, sambas, and contemporary terpsichorean performances that had no names, prescribed steps, or obvious connections to the word *dance*. But of course, more than once over these twenty-one years, the concrete had been sanded, resealed, and polished to facilitate graceful movement.

Suddenly Rebecca's eyes widened, and she covered her mouth with one hand. This could have meant she had eaten too much garlic, or it could have been an expression signifying that she'd had a surprise realization of such potential importance that she was reluctant to speak without being sure that she remembered correctly. The latter was the case, but she nonetheless at once revealed what had occurred to her.

"Björn Skollborg," she said.

The name electrified Spencer. "Björn Skollborg! That was him. His severed head. His headless corpse. He was the one."

"He and his wife, Karamia, both disappeared," Bobby recalled.

"Their photos were in the newspaper, all over TV. I remember their faces clearly," Spencer said, excited by the montage of images cascading through his mind. Indeed, his excitement was so keen that some might have found it unseemly under the circumstances. "Yeah, yeah, I remember exactly how the newspaper looked as it lay there on the table, in the booth at Adorno's, with a piece of pepperoni that fell off Ernie's slice and landed right on the face of Karamia, so it looked like Björn was married to a sausage. The polished-chrome napkin dispenser. The ceramic salt and pepper shakers, one a figure of a chef, the other a waitress with—"

"They were from upstate," Rebecca interrupted. "They were staying at the Spreading Oaks."

"It was just a motel then," Bobby said.

"It's just a motel now," Rebecca said. "Björn owned a bakery up in the state capital. Karamia was a cupcake specialist."

"The cops never did find their bodies."

"Because they were eaten."

"Never found their car, either."

"At the time, we wondered if Hornfly could have eaten that, too."

"We couldn't go to the police."

"Who would have believed us? A monster who eats people in two minutes, maybe three? Ten half-formed naked men lying in the church basement? Pastor Larry hates humanity and is part of some conspiracy to destroy us all? They would've locked us up in an asylum."

"Enough of this," Bobby said. "We're just telling one another things that all of us already know, the way characters do in lazy books and movies to get information to the audience. We've got to decide what to do next."

They were silent, lost in their thoughts, staring out at the maples and the velvety lawns that surrounded the pavilion, which was when Bobby noticed the person with binoculars. A figure in dark clothes. Standing in tree shadows. Toward the north end of the park. He would not have noticed that someone was con-ducting surveillance if the watcher hadn't shifted position to get a better view, briefly stepping into a shaft of sunlight that flared off the lenses of the binoculars. Then the snoop took several steps for-ward, and Bobby saw something dreadful. Fear gripped him not merely because of the spy's identity but also because he expected an encounter to ensue. As he watched, the dreadful thing hap-pened again. The flare of a black cape. Britta.

33

THE AMIGOS REFUSE TO RUN FOR IT

When Bobby directed his friends' attention to the right place, Spencer Truedove saw Britta Hernishen watching them from a distance, and he was certain she saw him seeing her. He hoped never to know firsthand what war was like, but at that moment in the pavilion, he better understood the chaos and the terror portrayed in Picasso's famous painting, *Guernica*. He felt as the Spanish partisans must have felt when, in furious battle with insurgents, they heard the Nazis approaching in their bombers and knew they were going to die along with many civilians. His leg bones seemed to jellify, and he was overcome by an urge to flee the park even if in an embarrassing and wobbly run.

Had two of his amigos not been there, if the third hadn't been walled behind a foldaway bed and at risk of genuine death, Spencer might have hightailed it out of the pavilion. But "all for one and one for all" meant holding your ground at any price for as long as your amigos held theirs. Besides, running away would make him too much like his father and, come to think of it, also like his mother. Not that he would cohabit with a sweaty stripper or become his own sister. But he would be so mortified of himself that he might never look in a mirror again, thus robbing himself of the pleasure of admiring how he looked in his hat.

He rather hoped that his friends would run for it so he'd be justified in running, too. But that would never happen.

Rebecca was as spirited and stalwart as Whistlejacket, the horse in the painting of the same name by the eighteenth-century artist George Stubbs. She'd trample anyone who meant to harm her amigos.

Neither would Bobby ever back down. He strove never to become as faithless as his inscrutable birth parents, who had abandoned him when he was a month old. He had been left on a church pew with a four-leaf clover taped to his forehead. Pinned to his diaper, a typewritten note declared, WE HAVE LIVES TO LIVE, AND SO DOES HE, BUT NOT TOGETHER. HE'S A BAD-LUCK LEPRE-CHAUN WHO SHOULD BE FED TO THE SNAKES THAT SAINT PATRICK DROVE OUT OF IRELAND, BUT WE DON'T HAVE SNAKES OR KNOW WHERE TO GET ANY. The authorities called him "Baby Shamrock," in reference to the four-leaf clover. He was offered for adoption, but no one wanted a bad-luck leprechaun. Being unwanted and knowing they have narrowly avoided being chopped up and fed to serpents, most babies would have made up their minds, right then and there, never to trust anyone again, but not Bobby. He believed in his amigos and never let them down.

In the distance, Britta Hernishen shrank backward into shadows and stepped to her right, behind a tree. The three friends waited for her to reappear, but she did not do so at once, or after a minute, or after three minutes, as if she had transformed herself into a crow and flown away.

A looming threat as frightening as Britta tended to concentrate the mind. Evidently, Rebecca had been thinking hard and fast while waiting for the caped professor to reappear.

"At breakfast, when I was on the phone with Hornfly, he didn't like the way I talked to him. He said, 'We will not forget. We are not a pussy-willow genotype like another I could name.' A genotype is nothing more than the type of genes possessed by an organism. While Spencer was having fun arm wrestling Fred Sanford, I looked it up with my phone. What did he mean 'a pussy-willow genotype like another I could name'?"

"He means us," Bobby said. "Human beings. Compared to whatever species he might be, we're a milquetoast genotype incapable of all the things he can do, like eat people as if they were bananas."

"No. That's not it. A genotype isn't an entire species. It's the particular genes in each organism. The three of us are human, but each of us has a different group of genes. For instance . . . consider the gene for blond hair. All genes are diploid, meaning pairs of which one is dominant and one is recessive. So there are three possibilities when it comes to, say, blond hair—you either have two dominant genes for blond hair or two recessive genes, or one of each. I evidently have two dominant genes."

"Unless you dye your hair," Spencer said.

She looked askance at him. As a talented actress, looking askance was something she did with maximum impact. "Why would you even say that?"

Spencer was flustered. "I don't know. Sometimes I just say things. I *know* you don't dye your hair. It was this same color when we were kids, from the first time you sat with us in Adorno's. Back then you wouldn't have dyed your hair. You looked like something the cat dragged in, and you didn't care."

Cocking her head to look askance at Spencer from a different perspective, Rebecca said, "Honey, if you ever feel compelled to paint in the high romantic style of Rossetti or Millais, that would be a bad idea."

"Oh, I know that's not my forte. Besides, I can't draw."

"Genotype," Bobby reminded them as he nervously scanned the park for Britta. "If human beings aren't the 'pussy-willow genotype' he was referring to—then what is?"

"I don't know how many genes we have—thousands, I guess—but the possible number of genotypes is almost infinite. They think at least a hundred *billion* people have been born, and no two were alike except for identical twins. Hornfly always says 'we' or 'us,' never 'I' or 'me.' Yet he refers to his kind as a 'genotype.' A genotype isn't a species. It's always and only a unique organism. Human beings are a species, each human being is a unique genotype."

As he listened, Spencer understood why he had become an artist instead of a scientist. "But what does all this mean?"

Rebecca said, "What it *seems* to mean is that Hornfly and those ten naked men in the basement and the creature that was molting in Ernie's house are all part of one organism, one consciousness, that can manifest in different forms, a colony of individuals that act as one. And they—it—lives among us. Or more likely under us, as it seems to move around through drains. When the manifestation calling itself Hornfly says it's not 'a pussy-willow genotype like another I could name,' I think it means there is a second creature similar to it, and they're some kind of rivals."

Bobby was impressed. "You got all this info about genetics from your phone while Spencer was losing at arm wrestling?"

"No, no. As soon as I got a firm definition of 'genotype,' all the rest came together for me. I've just been refining it in my mind before dropping it on you."

"How is that possible? How could you figure that out from just the definition of 'genotype'?"

"I was up for the female lead in a big-budget flick based on something Michael Crichton scribbled on an index card that was found after his death. The idea was on one side of the card, and on the other side he had written 'bigger than *Jurassic Park.*' It was about genetic engineering, so I studied the subject at the time. During a development process that took four years, there were nine writers and three directors who worked on it, but Michael was a very smart man, and no one in the biz seemed to have the brain power to figure out what he meant."

"Wow," said Spencer, "that's a lost opportunity that must have given you some sleepless nights."

"For sure. Especially because I was in for eight percent of the gross from first dollar."

Bobby said, "Yeah, okay, but all this seems to leave us with even more questions than before. And what, if anything, does this tell us about why there's no crime in Maple Grove anymore? Or why Ernie is in a coma or suspended animation or whatever the hell he's in?"

Spencer regarded Rebecca expectantly, apparently assuming that from now on she would be a fountain of unassailable theories, but he was to be disappointed.

She said, "I don't know yet."

"And who locked away our memories, and how did they do that, and why are they now unlocking them?" Bobby asked. "And where is Hornfly? And why didn't he deal with us when we were kids, like he threatened to do that night in the pavilion? In fact, since his goal—their goal, its goal, whatever—is to destroy humankind, why hasn't that war begun? Why hasn't it begun at least here in Maple Grove?"

They stood in a silence of profound befuddlement.

As the world continued to turn, it seemed the pavilion did not turn with it, as if time had stopped inside this fanciful structure, as if the pavilion were the stable core of the universe from which all reality was generated and set in motion. For clarity, a point needs to be made: The pavilion was *not* in fact the stable core of the universe from which all reality was generated. That is only how it *felt* to the three amigos who were befuddled by urgent questions for which they desperately needed answers if they were to survive. You see, their inability to think their way through the maze of questions rendered them mute, left them paralyzed by dread and by recognition of the depth of their ignorance. This, of course, is a condition of brief duration; they will not be standing in the pavilion for the remainder of the story.

So the leaves of the surrounding maple trees fluttered in the summer breeze, and songbirds graced the sky, and people walked their dogs, and the amigos remained frozen in perplexity. One can hardly imagine a circumstance in which they would be more vulnerable to the sudden arrival of Britta Hernishen. However, they were not at the moment subjected to that ordeal. Abruptly, as one, they said, "The hospital!" That exclamation brought an end to their paralysis but did not fully cure their befuddlement.

They looked at one another, expecting someone to say something more definitive about the hospital, but that brief cry was the whole of it.

"What? What about the hospital?" Bobby asked in frustration. "Who put those words in our minds? How did they do that?

Are we supposed to go to the hospital? What do we do when we get there?"

Before Bobby could ask enough questions to cast them into paralytic befuddlement again, Rebecca said, "Something happened there. It was around Thanksgiving that year. No, not 'around.' It was smack-dab on turkey day."

"What year?"

"The year of Hornfly. A few weeks after that Halloween night when he ate Björn Skollborg."

Spencer said, "He probably ate Björn's wife that same night."

"Karamia," said Rebecca. "You think he could eat two people in one evening?"

"The way that geek chewed into Björn's head, he could probably eat as many as he wanted to."

Bobby the Sham was always listening not only to what people said but also to how they said it. He believed that a good novelist needed to be a keen observer of diction and idiom in order to create believable dialogue. Even in the current circumstances, with peril waiting around every corner, he found himself wondering exactly how he would convincingly portray those exchanges between Spencer and Rebecca if this were a novel he was writing.

"It's not possible," he said.

Spencer said, "How do you figure? I mean, if I can easily eat two cheeseburgers at a sitting—and I can—why couldn't a creature like Hornfly eat two people?"

"I wasn't referring to eating people," Bobby said. "I was just thinking about . . . Never mind. Listen, the three of us thought of the hospital at the same time, but the rest of the memory seems to be returning in dribbles, not all at once like before. So maybe we're beginning to remember things on our own."

"Britta doesn't believe in Thanksgiving," Spencer said.

Bobby frowned. "Britta doesn't believe in anything but Britta."

"Yeah, and so Ernie was with us on that Thanksgiving. The four of us were together."

Rebecca recalled, "For the holidays, Grandpa Charlie and Grandma Ruth went to Key West with their friends Jack and Sandy Reamer. They all hate one another and have the time of their lives pretending they don't."

"The Pinchbecks always ate dinner at four o'clock," Bobby said. "Then he worked crossword puzzles and she crocheted until they went to bed at seven. That year, every year, they had their traditional Thanksgiving dinner—fish sticks, boiled potatoes, brussels sprouts, and tapioca. I begged off and met up with you guys at Spencer's place in the late morning. We spent the day making dinner together."

"I hadn't sold the kitchen appliances yet," Spencer said. "Dad was already living at the church with Porifera. There was a holiday orgy that night."

"Yeah, yeah, I remember," Rebecca said. "You showed us the flyer they sent to parishioners. It was an especially naughty orgy."

"They called it Spanksgiving," Spencer said.

They were silent for a moment, although they were not paralyzed by befuddlement.

Then Bobby shuddered. "I don't like to think about how insane we might be now if we'd never teamed up and become amigos."

"So why did we go to the hospital that day? It was in the evening, long after dinner."

"I don't know."

"Me neither," Spencer said.

Face wrenched with frustration and anxiety, Rebecca stood lost in thought. Even with her face thus contorted, she was strikingly beautiful.

Bobby couldn't stop staring at her, and he thought it was a shame that her beauty would always limit the roles for which she would be considered. She could never play a homely woman, let alone an ugly one. Her talent would allow her to do so, but the director would require her to perform under ten pounds of makeup, a fright wig made of oxtail hair, matching eyebrows, with a hunchback prosthesis—and *still* she would be gorgeous.

Over the more than two decades they had known each other, he had regarded her strictly as a friend, not with romantic interest. In this world of loneliness and alienation, true friends were rarer and more desirable than potential lovers. He treasured her as a friend and understood that by pursuing a more intimate arrangement, he would perhaps diminish or destroy what they had now. Only since their return to Maple Grove had he now and then regarded her with romantic longing. It had to stop. He loved her as an amigo, like a sister, and he dared not risk that profoundly valued relationship. Because he wouldn't go so far as to put his eyes out, he had to rely on willpower.

Of course if he died horribly in an encounter with Wayne Louis Hornfly (a possibility for which a warning was previously issued), that would resolve the matter.

Rebecca's wrenched face returned to its usual spectacularness. She said, "Maybe we should go to the hospital now. Maybe just seeing the place or walking into it will jog our memories."

Late-afternoon sunshine slanted through the maples, layering a magical light among the shadows as the amigos exited the pavilion. Squirrels scampered up trees, fearing that one dog or another would pull loose of its leash and savage them, while here and there a dog squatted or hiked a leg to pee. Hidden in a bower, an owl hooted in anticipation of the mice it would snatch off the grass to devour, come night. A new crop of infants in strollers gaped anxiously at the world, innocent of its true nature but intuitively, vaguely cognizant of terrors to come.

The world is a hard place. There are moments of great beauty and peace and plenty. Eventually, however, it was like the Gene Pitney song: sooner or later, you found yourself in a town without pity.

Soon, twenty-four hours would have passed since Ernie Hernishen disappeared from the hospital. By this time tomorrow, the police—who otherwise had nothing meaningful to do—would initiate a search for him, find him, and give him to a coroner or mortician who would make sure he was as dead as Björn Skollborg.

THREE

READER, PREPARE YOURSELF

34

ERNIE PATIENTLY WAITING

Lying behind the foldaway bed, with his five senses shut down and his heart as still as a stone, Ernie was periodically soothed by the kindly male and female voices that came not through his ears but arose within him. He could not understand how it was possible to "hear" them without actually hearing them, but he didn't waste time worrying about that, even though in his current circumstances he had plenty of time to waste. He continued to compose country songs. The exercise of his musical genius was from time to time interrupted by memories on which he dwelled with interest. At the moment, he was thinking about Thanksgiving in the year of Wayne Louis Hornfly. He knew intuitively and beyond doubt that, elsewhere in Maple Grove, his amigos were obsessed with the same long-ago holiday. That, too, was something he could not possibly know, but he didn't worry about how he knew it. After all, if he wasn't worried about being a disembodied consciousness adrift in what seemed to be a lightless vacuum, there wasn't much point in being worried about anything.

Whether on Thanksgiving and other holidays or on ordinary evenings, Britta Hernishen rarely dined with her son. She'd never done so regularly, and she had entirely disengaged from the practice on the night of Ernie's fifth birthday.

Sitting directly across the dining room table from his mother, he had been talking about a battery-powered dump truck that could tilt its bed back to spill its contents. It was red, and it was big for a toy, bigger than the four-slice toaster in the kitchen.

He thought she was riveted by his description of the truck, but she interrupted him to say, "Stop playing with your peas."

"I'm not playing with them."

"Am I to understand that you would have me believe you are not playing with your peas when I can plainly see that you are? Is that your position?"

"I'm just moving them."

"Is it your habit to reposition your vegetables at every meal? Do you reposition them when Ms. Merkwurdig feeds you?"

Ms. Merkwurdig was the nanny who looked after him in Britta's absence, which was most of the time.

"What does 'reposition' mean?" he asked.

Britta put her fork down and patted her lips with her napkin and returned the napkin to her lap, staring at Ernie in disbelief throughout the procedure. "How could it be possible that you have reached the age of five without being able to define 'reposition'? Are you able to explain that to me, Ernest?"

"No, ma'am."

"I thought not. Do you not see that you are still playing with your peas? I expressly asked you to stop."

"I'm just moving them."

"And to where are you moving them?"

"To the other side of my mashed potatoes."

"It is important that we do the things we do in life for clear and rational reasons. Can you explain why you must move your peas to the other side of your mashed potatoes? Can you do that, Ernest?"

"They taste better when they're on that side."

She had begun to pick up her fork. She put it down again. "Are you seriously contending that peas taste better when consumed from the left side of your mashed potatoes than they do when they have been served on the right side?"

"Yeah."

"As I have asked you before, I ask you yet again to refrain from using the word 'yeah.' It is an informal derivative of the proper word 'yes.'"

"Other kids say it."

"Yes, they do. You must understand, however, that children who speak imprecisely—or, worse, descend to the use of slang—will grow up to be ill-spoken adults who are condemned to such menial careers as plumbers and car mechanics."

"Plumbers and car mechanics are cool jobs."

"In the interest of maintaining a cheerful mood on this special occasion, we will not further discuss suitable careers. Are we in agreement that this restriction will apply throughout the remainder of this celebratory dinner?"

"Yes, ma'am."

After a prolonged silence, Britta observed, "You have eaten only half of your filet medallions. Should I not have placed them directly opposite your mashed potatoes?"

"I wanted hamburgers for my birthday."

"What we want and what we should have are not always the same thing. An individual might want to drink vast quantities of sugary cola every day of his life, but as he lies dying of diabetes at the age of thirty-four, he will recognize the folly of having failed to appreciate the consequences of always choosing what he wanted rather than what he should have had. Do you understand, Ernest?"

"I guess so. But most people call me Ernie."

"Those are people I would severely censor if I could. I am the one who named you after Mr. Hemingway. He was a properly proud man. He would never have allowed anyone to call him Ernie. An *Earnest* is a person of importance. An *Ernie* is the kind of person who works twelve hours a day, belowdecks in a commercial fishing trawler, gutting the day's catch. Am I to assume that is the life you yearn for, Ernest, a life standing knee-deep in fish guts?"

"No, ma'am."

After a long silence followed by a longer one, his mother brought him a slice of cake and a small scoop of ice cream.

"It's not a whole cake," Ernest said.

"If I provided an entire cake, you would eat a second slice later, another tomorrow, on and on, until eventually you had eaten the whole thing. One slice is all that is required for an adequate celebration. I am determined you will not become diabetic—or grow into an enormous fat person who would be an embarrassment to me."

"I'm five. There's only one candle."

"One is sufficient, Ernest. Burning candles produce carbon dioxide. We were not born for the purpose of imperiling the planet by contributing to climate change."

She produced a silver snifter with which he was required to extinguish the candle, because blowing it out would be uncouth.

A year later, shortly after Ernie's sixth birthday, Hilda Merkwurdig was fired from her position as his nanny when Britta discovered from whom her son had learned the phrase *crazy bitch*.

Hilda's replacement, Bertha Fettleibig, lasted eight months before she was fired when Britta discovered from whom Ernie had learned the phrase *shit for brains*.

By the time the boy turned seven, his mother decided that he could be left home alone and that it was time for him to make his way through the world unaccompanied. She wanted to ensure that he would not go astray and would grow up to be a manly man like his famous namesake. She also wanted to spare herself from the daily annoyance of conversing with a child of somewhat high but not exceptional intelligence. Therefore, Britta provided a hundred-page notebook filled with rules and expectations. Ernie was required to memorize all entries whether he understood them or not. Over the years that followed, he was regularly quizzed as to his compliance.

When he was fourteen and warmed by the company of his amigos, in the year of Hornfly, there came a four-day Thanksgiving weekend of terror and revelation that had subsequently been expunged from his memory. Now, cosseted in the space behind the foldaway bed but unaware that his body had been stashed in Spencer's empty house in the last block of Harriet Nelson Lane, in the neighborhood of the Nelsoneers, who were even at that moment preparing for a community barbecue with lawn bowling and badminton, Ernie was on the brink of remembering the fateful events of that long-ago turkey day and what followed, but not quite yet.

At this juncture, you might be marveling at how neatly all the disparate elements of this book seem to be knitting together toward a satisfying and convincing ending. Others of you, though perhaps entertained, might find the tale too fantastic to be true, although I have assured you it is as true as anything you will read in the papers or see on the evening news. I take no offense at your doubt. However, I commend to you the quotation from the great novelist Thomas Hardy, which serves as the epigraph at the front of this volume and which, for your convenience, I repeat herewith: *Though a good deal is too strange to be believed, nothing is too strange to have happened.*

35

DRIVING TO THE HOSPITAL, SPENCER RECALLS THE NIGHT REBECCA EMERGED FROM HER UNLOVELY-PERSON COCOON

Following Hornfly's consumption of Björn Skollborg in Liberty Park pavilion on Halloween night, through the first seventeen days of November, the young amigos made no progress in their quest to learn the truth about Maple Grove. They discussed ways they might intimidate Pastor Larry into explaining the ten incompletely formed humans arranged like a chain of paper dolls in the church basement. Also, why did he allow a hulking orange-eyed monster with weird hair to lounge around, reading for pleasure, in the rectory library? Why did the collection of books therein apparently contain so many novels featuring great quantities of blood, pain, mayhem, cruelty, murder, and mass death, which was just the kind of entertainment a human-eating monster would enjoy? And did his sister in fact have serious dental surgery, and did he really travel upstate to look after her for a few days—or was he elsewhere, conniving with malevolent forces to destroy humankind? Whatever the answers might be, one thing was already clear: Pastor Larry was not really a man of God.

On the Sunday evening before Thanksgiving, Spencer and Ernie and Bobby were in the back booth at Adorno's Pizzeria, unaware that it would become a ristorante in less than twenty years; unaware that major cities would literally become cesspools with widespread public defecation and legions of drug addicts dying in the gutters; unaware that an engineered virus would kill millions and that no authorities would care enough to discover its source; unaware that David Letterman would retire from TV and grow a strange Gabby Hayes beard, leaving late-night comedy to die; in short, unaware that the future would fail to be like the world in which the Jetsons had lived and would become a place that alarmed even the Addams family. The amigos drank their cherry Cokes, their vanilla Cokes, their chocolate Cokes, as they anticipated a future without war, without disease, without the annoyance of unsolicited phone sales. They refrained from choosing and ordering pizzas until the fourth amigo arrived, for theirs was an association rooted in democracy; furthermore, Spencer and Bobby and Ernie were not misogynists.

The night was chilly. When the front door opened, a cold draft briefly fanned through the pizzeria, bringing with it a fragrance as pleasantly picturesque as the town through which it had blown to get there. A remarkably pretty girl entered and stood just inside the door as it closed behind her. She wore pink sneakers, fitted jeans, and a tan jacket over a pink sweater and white blouse.

As this marvelous apparition unzipped her jacket, shrugged it off, and unwound a scarf from around her neck, the three amigos in the back booth goggled at her, though only for three seconds, after which they glanced at one another and then turned their attention to their Cokes.

Although they never discussed the protocols of girl watching, the three friends conducted that activity in precisely the same fashion. If an attractive girl appeared within your line of sight, you could look at her for three seconds, maybe four if you happened to be in a bold and reckless mood, and then you must redirect your attention. To stare longer would be to risk that the girl would become aware of your interest and make eye contact with you, which was a thrilling prospect but also one certain to lead to disaster. If she made eye contact, the chances that she would approach and say something became intolerably high. If it was going to be one of the worst days of your life, she would actually speak to you. Then what? THEN WHAT? Then, inevitably, you would stammer incoherently or say something so stupid that you would die a little while you listened to yourself say it. Then a blank look would come into her eyes, as though you had become invisible, so that she wondered whatever had possessed her to speak aloud when no one was there to be spoken to. Your friends—if you had any friends and they were with you—would regard you with abject pity, though they could not have thought of anything better that you could have said, that anyone could have said in the history of the world, under such perilous circumstances.

So after Spencer, Bobby, and Ernie briefly goggled at the girl who came in from the November night, they stared at their Cokes, heads lowered as if they were saying grace for the blessing of cola-flavored sodas. Although they were usually talkative, they were at the moment bludgeoned by beauty into a state of stupefaction. They were not the kind of boys who made crude or even suggestive remarks about girls; as certified nerds, they regarded sex and voodoo as equally mysterious territories, where the wrong words could bring a hideous curse down on them.

When the blonde in the pink sweater crossed the pizzeria to their booth, they did not see her coming even with their peripheral vision. They expected her to take a table as far away from them as the layout of the premises allowed. When she threw her scarf and jacket into the booth, they reacted as if she had lobbed a grenade among them, and when she sat beside Ernie, across from Spencer and Bobby, their collective gasp sucked a significant portion of the air out of the room.

Only when she said "Hey, guys" did they recognize her from her voice. On being struck by the realization that this was Rebecca, they found speech impossible. They stared at her, their expressions like those of frogs gazing in wonder at the moon, until Spencer heard himself say, "What's happened to you?" in a tone of voice and with an emphasis that made it sound as if he were saying, *Dear God, girl, you were once presentable, but now you're a beast. How have you let yourself go?*

On the last word of Spencer's question, Ernie pointed at Rebecca with a trembling finger. "You're moving on!" Heartbreak shivered through his voice. "You're moving on, aren't you?"

Clearly puzzled, Rebecca said, "Moving on from what?"

"From us."

"From you? Why would I?"

"Look at us," Bobby said.

Spencer said, "And look at you."

"I'm dying inside," Ernie said, having always been the most sentimental of them.

"Thanksgiving's coming and nothing to be thankful for," said Spencer, because he was years away from having his special hat to comfort him. "Nothing, nothing."

Bobby asked, "Why? What did we do? We deserve to know why."

Rebecca made eye contact with each of them in turn and then squinted like Clint Eastwood conveying keen impatience. "Listen up, dudes. Are we amigos or are we amigos?"

"I thought we were," Bobby said.

And Spencer said, "I hoped we were."

"But now it comes crashing down," said Ernie.

Gia Adorno arrived at the table. The boys ordered as if they had nothing to live for but food.

To Rebecca, Gia said, "I'm happy to see you stopped with the Bride of Frankenstein act."

The boys at once rebelled at Gia's implied approval of the new Rebecca:

"I *liked* the way you looked before."

"I *loved* the way you looked before."

"I *adored* the way you looked before."

To Rebecca, Gia said, "They're sweet but impossible."

"They're not completely impossible," Rebecca said. "They're works in progress."

With evident admiration, Gia said, "I gotta say, you're a better friend than I could be."

"They're good friends, too," Rebecca replied. "They're the best. They just need a shot of Thorazine from time to time."

As Gia went to the kitchen, Rebecca regarded her amigos with tenderness that they interpreted as pity, as confirmation that she was done with them. Some of them wanted to cry, but to protect their dignity, the names of those who were near tears won't be revealed, though it was all of them.

"Do you remember, I told you I always must be treated as one of the guys?"

They stared at her as if any response they could make would have disastrous consequences.

"Remember how you all agreed to that without hesitation?"

They weren't deer on a highway, and there were no headlights aimed at them, but anyone seeing them at this moment would have thought of that same analogy.

"If you are unable to respond with words," Rebecca said, "just nod in confirmation or shake your heads to disagree."

They all nodded.

"Good. That's great. Well, nothing has changed. I'm still one of the guys."

With apparent reluctance, they shook their heads.

"Oh, yes I am. Nothing has changed. What has happened is that, in little more than two months of friendship, you have given me the courage to be who I am. I'm no longer afraid of dealing with those boys who used to come on to me as if I should fall on my back and let them do what they wanted."

The deer in that analogy were suddenly red-faced as no real deer ever could be.

"Through your friendship, you've given me confidence. Because of the weird things we've experienced together, my spine has gone from jelly to steel. If I can stand up to Hornfly when he's holding a severed head by the hair, I can stand up to anyone— especially with you at my side. And I give you strength, too. I know I do. Okay, I look different from how I did yesterday, but I'm still me. We all need to grow up, but we don't need to grow apart. We're amigos, and we always will be."

Ernie was the first to find his voice. "But you're not a nerd anymore. You're not a nerd like we are."

"Honey, don't say such a hurtful thing. I am too a nerd. I'm a total nerd. Nerds come in all shapes and appearances. Nerdism is a state of mind, internal rather than external. Some people are nerds, but you'd never know it by just looking at them. They have to start talking first and trying to share their interests with you, their opinions, their hopes. *Then* you know."

Spencer was doubtful. "Appearance is part of it. Just look at Ernie and Bobby and me, and anyone will right away think *nerds*."

"It's not the way you look," Rebecca insisted. "It's the way you dress, the way you comb or don't comb your hair, the things you like and don't like, the things you say. Nerdism is about wanting the right things—love, friendship, family, hope, peace, justice, happiness—*but being clueless about how to get them*." Again, she made eye contact with her amigos, one at a time. "*Being clueless about how to get them.* But together we're *learning* how. We can't do it alone. You can't do it without me. I can't do it without you. Together, and only together, we'll get where we need to go. We'll become the people we want to become."

Unnoticed, Gia Adorno had arrived with four different flavors of fountain Cokes on a tray. She stood staring at Rebecca for a long moment. Then as she transferred the drinks from tray to table, she said, "This round is on the house."

The amigos thanked her effusively if inarticulately. Although four free Cokes was a small thing, they were moved by the gesture.

Gia said, "In fact, tonight only, all drinks from this point are free." Then she gently admonished, "But you'll still have to pay for pizzas and everything else."

When the waitress departed to attend to other customers, Bobby said, "Maybe we can do this."

Rebecca waited for a moment and then pressed him. "Do what?"

"Still think of you as one of the guys."

"And a nerd," Spencer said.

"An amigo," Ernie added.

Bobby consolidated it all. "A nerd amigo guy."

Rebecca wasn't satisfied. "'Maybe'?"

"We can do it," Ernie said.

Spencer agreed. "We already are doing it."

Rebecca smiled. "I love you guys."

They flinched as one organism, and Bobby said, "Guys don't say they love one another."

"My mistake," she acknowledged. "Forget I ever said it. Rewind your memories, and over-record that with this: You're the best damn bunch of screwup losers in the world, and I'm proud to hang with you."

They high-fived one another across the table.

36

A MISUNDERSTANDING

Let's refresh: Having made some progress in their brainstorming session in the Liberty Park pavilion, having caught sight of Britta watching them through binoculars, the three amigos had heard a voice telling them the next clue would be found at the hospital. A sense of urgency overcame them, a compelling need to recall what happened at County Memorial on Thanksgiving Day, twenty-one years earlier.

So now, on this warm summer day, Spencer piloted his Genesis SUV toward the hospital while remembering the Sunday before that Thanksgiving when Rebecca, looking like a goddess, walked out of the chilly night and into Adorno's. Meanwhile, the movie star and the novelist were in the back seat, trying to recall where they had gone once inside the hospital on that long-ago holiday. By the time they arrived at County Memorial, they were certain only that the place they sought was somewhere on the third floor.

Three people, prowling a hospital for they knew not what, were sure to draw unwanted attention, especially when one of them was a famous movie star. Spencer suggested a plausible cover story. To equip themselves for it, the amigos ventured first to the gift shop. A tall cooler with a glass door displayed a limited selection of small flower arrangements; Rebecca chose one with red roses, white chrysanthemums, and fern fronds. A collection of helium-inflated foil balloons did not include any that were personalized, but Spencer took one emblazoned with the words THE LORD LIFTETH ME, which seemed to be the kind of thing that would be carried by the most innocent of visitors with no intention of snooping around. Bobby the Sham chose a balloon without words; it bore just the smiling face of Kermit the Frog, the most endearing of the Muppets.

The sixtysomething woman at the cash register had white hair in tight curls, a cherubic face, rosy cheeks, and the bubbly manner of a Welcome Wagon lady who had been sitting in her kitchen, sipping sherry, waiting for the new neighbors to show up so that she could greet them with a gift basket in the name of everyone on the block and induce them to become part of her gossip network. "Well, just look at you three darlings. The very sight of you would make any poor, sick person feel better. Would you like a talking get-well card to go with all of this?"

"No, thank you," Bobby said. "I think we can do without a card."

"Nothing encourages wellness like a talking card," the clerk said. "We have some with the most heartwarming messages. Your loved one will listen to it over and over again until the little battery fails."

Holding the flower arrangement, Rebecca said, "Our loved one isn't the sentimental type. He would mock a greeting card."

"I know the type you mean, dear. They respond to humor, not to compassionate sentiments. In that case, we have another line of cards sure to get a laugh. Everyone needs a laugh, especially those poor souls who are ailing. Our most popular number of that kind, one that amuses everybody—when you read the front and then open it, the card makes vomiting sounds."

"No card," Spencer said.

The clerk looked at his hat, and it seemed she was intimidated by it when she relented on the card. "What about a box of candy? We have Russell Stovers, of course, but also sophisticated chocolates made in France."

"That would be wonderful," Rebecca said, "but our friend is diabetic."

"In that case, we have sugar-free chocolates containing only unsaturated fats."

"We'll take a box," said Bobby, just to get their purchases moving along expeditiously.

The clerk turned to a wall of shelves behind her, plucked one of the boxes stacked there, and placed it on the counter. She winked at Bobby. "This is just the thing to lift his spirits." She patted a stack of small hardcover gift books beside the register. Before any of the amigos could claim their loved one was illiterate, the clerk continued, "A joke book about bodily functions, perfect hospital reading. Statistics show that if you laugh a lot while in hospital, you're able to be discharged one point six days sooner. If you laugh about your symptoms and your prospects for recovery, they're less depressing. The chapters on constipation and diarrhea are especially hilarious."

Before visiting hours could come to an end, Bobby said, "Sounds like fun. Give us one."

Thus laden and then some, they departed the gift shop. In the lobby, Michael Z, the guard with whom they'd shared an elevator the previous day, was interrogating a boy of about ten. The child stood with his back pressed to a column and his hands in the air. Neither Bobby nor his amigos suggested an intervention.

They rode the elevator to the third floor, where nurses were busy with carts from which they were serving dinner trays. It was only 5:30, but dinner was served early in hospitals, perhaps out of consideration for people who were going to die later and miss their last chance at more pudding.

Confident that they appeared no more suspicious than others who were visiting sick friends and relatives, the amigos walked boldly along the main hall and, without hesitation, into room 315. Spencer could almost believe that they had traveled back in time twenty-four hours, because Butch was sitting up in the nearer bed, glowering at his dinner, as personalized helium-filled foil balloons tied to the bedrail bobbled above him.

Referencing the patient's head, Rebecca said to Spencer, "You were right—just like a mortar round."

Looking up from his dinner, scowling at the balloons and the flower arrangement, Butch said, "He bit the big one."

Without context, none of the amigos could make sense of that statement. In the interest of acquiring additional information that might lead to comprehension, Bobby said, "Why?"

Butch regarded him with an incredulous frown. "*Why?* You don't have any choice, pal. When the big one comes, you bite it or you bite it, and that's all there is."

"Big one?" Rebecca asked.

Apparently agitated that he'd been interrupted while glowering at his meal, Butch said, "Yeah, yeah, yeah, big one. What's bigger? Nothing's bigger than the big one."

Realizing he had used the wrong interrogative, Bobby switched to a pronoun. "Who?"

"*Who?*" Butch asked, frustrated by their thick-headedness. "You want to know who?"

"Yes, please."

"You come here with all that shit, even a balloon says 'The lord lifteth me,' and you don't know who?"

To Bobby, Rebecca said, "I'll try another one." She smiled at Butch, favoring him with that special smile she had practiced for years, in case she ever got a chance to play a nun. "What? What is the big one?"

Butch was now red-faced. "Don't give me that smutty smile, lady. I'm not that kind of guy. I'm not talking about anyone's pecker. What's *wrong* with you people?"

Spencer stepped into the fray. "All we want to know is who bit the big one, what the big one is, and why he bit it."

"Are you a smart-ass?" Butch demanded. "If I could get out of this bed, I'd kick the hell out of your smart ass."

In spite of humankind's enduring difficulty understanding one another, a confusion like this will come to an end sooner or later. In this instance, the end hove into sight when Spencer looked at the empty bed that stood beyond Butch and said, "What happened to your roomie?"

"HE BIT THE BIG ONE!" Butch roared. "He doesn't need your fancy flowers. He had terminal cancer. You know what 'terminal' means, you jackass? It means a lot more than where you get a bus."

"Ahhh," the three amigos responded, and then Bobby said, "Sorry about the confusion. We didn't come to visit him, whoever he was. We came to visit you."

Butch's face accommodated a look of perplexity while still half-possessed by anger, which made him look like an enormous pouting baby. A dangerous baby. "Me? You came to visit me?"

"You," Bobby repeated.

"I don't even know you two. I don't really know this jackass in the hat, either. He came in here yesterday to take my wheelchair."

"Borrow your wheelchair," Spencer said.

"You said 'borrow,' but you never brought it back."

"I'm sorry about that."

"They had to get another wheelchair to take me to treatment this morning. They gave me the stink eye."

"The what?"

"The stink eye. Like I must have stolen the damn wheelchair myself."

Rebecca said, "How could you have stolen it when you need assistance to get out of bed?"

"You'd think the idiots would figure that out, wouldn't you?" Butch complained.

Recognizing an opportunity for reconciliation, Rebecca tried the nun smile again. "That's why we came to visit. To say we're sorry about the wheelchair."

"You brought me balloons, flowers, and candy because you stole the hospital's wheelchair?"

"Borrowed," said Spencer. "We left it in the parking lot."

If Butch was quick to take offense, he was equally quick to forgive and forget. "Gee, that's sweet. I mean, who does something like that these days?"

"We do," Bobby said. "It's just who we are."

Butch smiled at the flower arrangement Rebecca had put on the nightstand. "They're real pretty."

"I hope you like roses," she said.

"I love roses." He turned his attention to his dinner tray and grimaced. "Will you look at this stuff."

"I'd rather not," Bobby said. The food tray was on a wheeled table. At Butch's request, he rolled it away from the bed. "I'm Bobby, this is Rebecca, and the man in the hat is Spencer."

Rebecca said, "Butch, you've got to eat, keep your strength up."

"I'm not eating that slop."

"Do you like pizza?"

"Who doesn't?"

"What about Adorno's pizza?"

"It's the best."

"Would you be allowed to have it?"

"I'm not on a special diet. I'm here for my toe."

"I'll call Adorno's and have them deliver whatever pizza you like. Plus they can sneak you a couple of beers, if you want."

"They'd deliver to a hospital room?"

"They will for me."

"That would be fantastic. You must he somebody important."

She shrugged, and he told her what he would like, and she made the phone call.

As planned, now that they had ingratiated themselves with Butch and established themselves as visitors, Spencer went on a tour of all three wings of the third floor, as though looking for another friend to visit. If he found something that jarred his memory as to what had happened here on Thanksgiving many years earlier, he would return with that news and then sit with Butch while Bobby or Rebecca continued the investigation.

37

THE TOE

Before the Keppelwhite Institute financed and constructed County Memorial thirty-five years earlier, area residents had taken their critical illnesses to Fassbinder Hospital, which was located in a less esteemed neighborhood. That facility had been built in 1922 and named after Otto Fassbinder, who served as a medic in World War I. For his exceptional bravery, Otto received numerous military honors that were bestowed on him by General Klaus von Fassbinder, who was said to be no relative whatsoever of Otto. Over the decades, in spite of several investigations conducted by hotheads in Congress and partisan journalists hellbent on uncovering a scandal, no one could prove the scurrilous rumor that General Klaus von Fassbinder, himself a hero of the United States Army, had in fact been in the service of Kaiser Wilhelm and Germany. Likewise, no tad of evidence was ever found that Senator Adolph Klanghoffer, who steered the bill of appropriation for the hospital through Congress, ever benefited by even as much as one dime from the project. Construction costs had turned out to be four times the original estimate, but this occurred in the Roaring Twenties, when the nation was awash in new money and inflation was bubbling. Soon after General Fassbinder retired from the army, he was worth twelve million dollars, an immense fortune in those days. However, he had acquired his wealth legitimately, for he proved to be a shrewd investor, a genius at stock-market analysis, whose marvelous success could be attributed to his frugality and his uncanny ability to make only the right investments. The fieriest of his critics in the press and elsewhere eventually were revealed as mentally unstable individuals when they either committed suicide or killed each other. Fassbinder Hospital had collapsed in a hailstorm the very year and month that Keppelwhite Institute completed construction of the new hospital and opened the doors to serve the residents of the county.

County Memorial was a U-shaped building with a long wing that lay east to west and two shorter wings that ran from north to south. The immense—some would say megamonolithic— Keppelwhite Institute backed up to the hospital, and in fact connected to the short wings of that health-care facility to form a courtyard. In the center of the courtyard, a massive fountain featured thirty arcing jets of water. In the center of the fountain, on a granite plinth, stood a twenty-foot-tall bronze statue of Gustoff Keppelwhite, the founder of the family empire, who began his working life as an assistant copyboy at the *New York Times*. In 1891, the year that he married Hilda Fassbinder, Gustoff claimed to have invented the modern hinge and filed for patent protection. The press, even the *Times*, mocked the young inventor and entrepreneur. However, the prestigious law firm of Klanghoffer, Knacker, Hisscus, and Nork—with lavish offices in New York, Chicago, and Washington—agreed to represent Gustoff Keppelwhite on a contingency basis, whereupon the mockery stopped as abruptly as a capering clown would stop if a piano were dropped on his head from the tenth floor of a high-rise. In just four months, Gustoff's patent was granted. Thereafter, he received a royalty on every door that was hung, on every pair of eyeglasses manufactured, every breadbox, and thousands of other items.

As Spencer Truedove roamed the third-floor hallways, striving to look like a relative of several patients abed in different wings of the establishment, he couldn't help but think about the history of the Keppelwhite family, which had been taught from grade school through high school in Maple Grove since the year construction had begun on the institute. As a troubled child, he'd wanted to be a Keppelwhite. As an artist, he'd yearned to see a painting of his installed one day in the home of James Alistair Keppelwhite and Wilamina "Willy" Keppelwhite, the doyen and doyenne of the current generation of the family.

Therefore, he was dismayed as well as unsettled by the effect their hospital exerted on him. As he walked the hallways, stepping into a room here and there and looking it over, wherever intuition led him, he became convinced that a malevolent, unseen presence was aware of him. Cameras were limited to stairwells and public spaces. He knew that, if indeed he was being watched, the watcher was not anything as benign as the security personnel.

Each time that he entered a room where the patients were not sleeping or preoccupied, he asked if either of them was Jim James, who of course was nonexistent, merely an excuse for violating their privacy. In room 344, two middle-aged men were sitting up in their beds. The nearer man was reading a hardcover novel, while the fellow in the second bed agitatedly twisted the segments of a Rubik's Cube. The book reader looked up and asked, "Can I help you?"

Scanning the room for an anomaly that might be a clue as to why he and his amigos were drawn to the hospital, Spencer said,

"I think this is the wrong room. I'm looking for a patient named Jim James."

"I'm Jim James," said the man with the book.

"You're shitting me," said Spencer.

The guy frowned. "Excuse me?"

"You're not really Jim James."

"I've been Jim James all my life."

A medical chart hung by a chain from the footrail of the bed. Spencer lifted it, read it. "Jim Jamie James."

"My mother was a poet. She liked alliteration."

"A poet. Would I have heard of her?"

"She was a bad poet," said Jim Jamie James. "She was never published. But she was a sweet, dear soul."

"My mother abandoned me," Spencer said, surprised to have made such a personal revelation to a stranger. There was something about Jim Jamie James that made Spencer want to open his heart to the guy and perhaps become lifelong friends. "She went off to New Orleans to relive a past life."

"How did you feel about that?"

"I was devastated."

"Did you get counseling?"

"No. I wish I had."

"My father was a sweet, dear soul. We can always count on our dads to get us through anything."

In the second bed, the man with the Rubik's Cube began to curse it in the most explicit terms.

"*My* father was gone," Spencer said.

An expression of profound sympathy drew Jim James's face into a longer geometry. "I'm so sorry. How old were you when he died?"

"Oh, he's still alive. He abandoned me, too."

"How extraordinary. Why would he do such a thing?"

"He opened a church for sexual degenerates and took a hooker for his common-law wife."

"Well, that's unusual. How did you feel about that?"

"I got through it, thanks to my amigos."

"Friends are treasures," Jim James said. "Has your father explained himself to you? Is he regretful?"

"We don't really talk that much. He's in prison for sticking up armored cars. What about you? What're you in hospital for?"

"My toe."

"What's the matter with your toe?"

"I'd rather not talk about it. I'm a positive person. I don't like to dwell on the horrors of the world."

A nurse appeared with a dinner tray, put it on a wheeled table, and maneuvered it in front of Jim James.

To Spencer, Jim said, "Don't go just because my dinner is here. Keep me company. Chat a little while."

In the far bed, the guy with the Rubik's Cube was red-faced, sweating rivers, and still cursing.

With a smile, indicating his roommate with a hitchhiker's gesture of the thumb, Jim James said, "Harry is a nice man, a good God-fearing man, but intense. At the moment, he's not the best company."

"I've got some work to do," Spencer said. "But I'll come back to visit tomorrow if you think you'll still be here."

"Oh, I'll be here. I'll be here a long time. I'll be here a heck of a lot longer than tomorrow, with this toe."

The nurse brought a second dinner tray from the cart in the hall and carried it toward the wheeled table that was associated with Harry's bed.

Jim James said, "Pudding for dessert again. I despise pudding."

On hearing that, Spencer marveled that fate had brought him to this room.

"I hate to waste things," Jim James said. "Would you like my pudding?"

"I despise pudding, too," said Spencer.

Jim James said, "The only pudding I'll eat is crème brûlée."

"Me too! But nobody calls it pudding."

"Nobody does," Jim James agreed, "but, darn it, crème brûlée *is* pudding."

As the nurse tried to maneuver the wheeled table in front of Harry, he cursed the Rubik's Cube, threw it at a wall, cursed the nurse, and began to spasm in the strangest way.

The nurse pressed the call button on Harry's bed and alerted the physician on duty. "Heart attack in three forty-four. I need help stat."

"Well, this is a downer," said Jim James. "But I'm sure he'll be okay. They provide excellent care here."

Spencer said, "I better be going, get out of their way."

"You'll come back tomorrow?"

"I'll certainly try," Spencer assured Jim James. He stepped out of the room as a doctor and a bevy of nurses arrived on the run.

The scene was powerful, dramatic. Spencer wished he were the kind of artist who could draw so that he could produce a painting that would convey the emotion of the moment, but he wasn't that kind of artist.

Two minutes later, at the south end of the southeast wing of County Memorial, he came to a fire-rated metal door that was closed. A sign declared NO ADMITTANCE / CREDENTIALED PERSONNEL ONLY.

The short wings of the hospital connected with the Keppelwhite Institute. He wondered what part of the institute might be found beyond this door.

He looked behind him. The hallway was deserted at the moment, perhaps because the staff in the immediate area had been summoned to Jim and Harry's room.

When he tried the lever handle, he was not surprised to find the door locked. What *did* surprise him was the chill that shivered through him and the sense of dread that made his heart race and his knees quiver as if they would fail him.

Here. Here is where they'd gone on that long-ago Thanksgiving. They had seen something beyond this door that they had been made to forget—something they needed to remember if they were to save Ernie and themselves.

38

THE OTHER TOE

In room 315, the additional two balloons had been tied to the headrail of the bed. The book of jokes about bodily functions was within Butch's reach, on the nightstand with the flower arrangement.

Although the pizza and beer had yet to be delivered, he was eating the candy, guided by the diagram on the inner face of the box lid, which identified the flavor of each piece.

For some reason she couldn't understand, Rebecca felt a need to mother Butch, perhaps because of his unfortunate head or because he looked somewhat like a huge baby, except for being so exceptionally hairy. Perched on a stool provided to lift a sitting visitor to eye level with the patient, she said, "Don't eat so many that you spoil your dinner when it gets here."

"Angel, don't you worry about me. I never have taken my meals in any particular order. Sometimes, I'll start with the potatoes, follow them with the dessert, then move on to the meat. Sometimes I make a peanut butter and jelly sandwich by eating the peanut butter out of its jar, then eating the jelly out of another jar, and then eating the bread with nothing on it. I've always been an independent thinker about many, many things. If someone tells me I can't have mud pie and chicken wings and coleslaw on the same plate—by God, I will, with gravy. Anyhow, this is diabetic candy. It doesn't have calories."

"It has calories," Rebecca said. "It just doesn't have sugar."

"Whatever," Butch said. "It's not filling, and I have a big appetite. I've been in this place for three days. Considering how bland the food is, it's a wonder I haven't shrunk away to nothing."

"You said you're here because of your toe."

"That's right."

"What's wrong with your toe?"

"If you don't mind, I'd rather not go there."

"I didn't mean to pry," Rebecca said.

"It shames me even to let the doctor look at it."

"Then we'll talk about something else."

"I will tell you it's the big toe, and it's the one on my right foot. But that's all I'm saying, so don't ask to look at it."

"What you've said is more than enough to satisfy my curiosity," Rebecca lied. "That was very sharing of you." The look she shot Bobby was meant to say, *Help me with conversation here.*

The Sham stood with his back to the window, leaning against the sill, backlighted by the dazzling orange radiance of the late-day sun. "I've been wondering how many of those helium balloons would have to be tied to Butch to lift him off the bed."

Butch beamed. "So happens I have the calculations. A friend did research. One balloon lifts three ounces. I weigh two hundred fifty pounds. That's four thousand ounces. Assuming every balloon lifts the same, you need one thousand three hundred thirty-three balloons. It would be kind of fun, but I don't think it's worth the cost."

To Rebecca, Bobby said, "That's all I've got."

She was spared from having to pick up the conversational ball when Spencer threw open the door. He bounded into the room and declared, "I found it! It's at the end of the southeast wing."

Bobby put a finger to his lips, and Rebecca covered her mouth with one hand, and Butch said, "Found what?"

"Uh," Spencer said. "Well. Found. You know. The bathroom. The public restroom."

"There's a bathroom right here," Butch said, indicating a door at the far end of the room.

"Well, but that's your bathroom."

"They don't want me on my toe, so I have to use a bed potty."

"Well, but it's still your roommate's bathroom."

"He's dead," said Butch.

Determined not to give up his looking-for-a-restroom alibi, Spencer said, "It's still his bathroom."

"What's a dead guy need a bathroom for?"

Looking as if he had walked into a tar pit, Spencer stood in silence, and everyone watched him expectantly, and at last he said, "It's a religious thing with me. During the month the person died, I'm forbidden to use the bathroom where the death occurred."

"He died in that bed," Butch said.

"Then I'm forbidden to use that bed during this month or any bathroom within seventy feet of it."

Rebecca waited for Butch to ask the name of this religion, but the big guy had a soft spot for people of faith. "Everybody's got a right to believe what he thinks God wants him to believe."

Bobby appeared to be disappointed that the issue had been resolved while it still had a lot of potential entertainment value. He said, "I'm going downstairs to meet the Adorno guy, make sure he doesn't deliver the pizza to the wrong room."

❦

Bobby had lied about going downstairs to look for the pizza-delivery guy. It wasn't such a significant lie that he feared being condemned to Hell for it, but he was about to engage in even further deception. From end to end, Maple Grove seemed to be a terrible lie that concealed a sinister purpose. He regretted participating in that dissimulation even by telling little falsehoods in order to find and expose the truth. Some of you might feel his sensitivity in this matter is excessive. However, when it comes to abhorrence of lies and a profound desire always to tell the truth, that's just how novelists are.

With an anxious expression, Bobby paced back and forth at the end of the southeast wing, as if a loved one somewhere here on the third floor must be in critical condition. When none of the staff was in sight, he drew from his jacket the lock-release gun that he had used at the church the previous night. He stepped to the fire-rated extra-wide door, slipped the automatic pick into the keyway, and pulled the trigger four times until the deadbolt disengaged. He opened the door. An empty room.

He crossed the threshold and closed the door behind him. He had the curious feeling that this room was a machine of some kind, that it currently wasn't turned on, that it might be a security vestibule where visitors were held until their identity could be verified, and that it would be a very different and frightening space if someone threw the switch to activate it. He could only suppose that his uneasiness arose from an experience he'd endured here years earlier.

He opened another door and crossed the threshold. The chamber in which he stood was large, windowless, and white. Maybe forty feet on a side. The glossy white-tile floor featured four drains, each six inches in diameter, placed like four dots on dice. White tile wainscoting to a height of about four feet. White plasterboard above. Light panels inlaid in the white ceiling. In the far wall, another extra-wide closed door stood directly opposite the one by which he'd entered. As bland a chamber as could be imagined, the place appeared to be a surgery not yet equipped.

He stepped to the nearest drain. Instead of a standard grid strainer, a solid plate covered the mouth of the opening. Yet he knew these four holes must be drains, because he clearly recalled that no coverings like this one had capped them twenty-one years earlier. There had not been grid strainers, either. On that long-forgotten night, they were just openings to . . .

Openings to what?

For several minutes, Bobby stood in the center of the room, each hole equidistant from him. He turned slowly, staring at one drain and then at the next—if they *were* drains. He strained to recall more of what he had seen back in the day. He was deeply frustrated, as are we all, that his memory remained locked tight. The far door offered further penetration of the institute but also the chance that he would disappear into its depths, never to be seen again. The longer he lingered, the greater the risk. He stepped out of the chamber and let the door close behind him.

Rebecca watched with interest as Spencer avoided going near the bed where a man had died, which he'd claimed that his faith required of him. He perched on the second stool, however, which was intended for a visitor to Butch's former roommate. He and Rebecca were at eye level with Butch, but on different sides of his bed. She wondered what Spencer would say if Butch asked why he was permitted to sit on the dead man's stool but not on the edge of the dead man's bed.

Spencer said, "There seems to be at least a mini epidemic of toe disease. I just met a fellow in your condition."

Butch took mild offense. "I don't have a disease. What I have is a condition."

"A toe condition," Spencer said.

"That's right."

"What did you do?"

"There's nothing you do that causes such a condition. It just happens to you. Like a meteor slams into you or a python falls onto you from out of a tree and strangles you. You didn't go asking for it to happen to you."

"What are the symptoms?" Spencer asked.

"You'll know what the symptoms are if it happens to you. God forbid. I don't want to talk about it."

"Of course. Thoughtless of me. What shall we talk about?"

He looked at Rebecca, but she only shrugged.

Butch said, "What if you're where there's only one bathroom, they hauled a dead guy out an hour ago, and you've got to pee bad?"

"I'd leave that place and go somewhere else."

"What if you couldn't hold it, you had to go *right now*?"

"Well . . . I guess I'd pee out the window."

"We're on the third floor. What if there were a lot of people below, having dinner?"

"Why would there be people having dinner?"

"Maybe it's a restaurant patio."

"Then I'd pee in a bottle."

"Where are you gonna get a bottle so quick?"

"There are bottles everywhere."

"There's not one in this room," Butch observed.

"There's the water carafe on your nightstand."

"What're you going to do with the water in it?"

"I guess I'd have to pour it on the folks having dinner below."

"They'll be happy it wasn't pee."

"Exactly."

To Rebecca, Butch said, "Do you go to the same church he does?"

"No."

Butch nodded with what seemed like approval. "I keep thinking I know you from someplace."

Bobby was taking forever. An eternity.

"Where might I know you from?" Butch asked.

Rebecca smiled. "Maybe I look like someone on TV."

"No, that's not it."

The pizza-delivery guy entered room 315, followed by Bobby. Rebecca and Spencer spun off their stools. The three amigos sprang into action. In no time, the wheeled table projected over the bed railing, and the aromatic pizza was on the table, and one beer was open. The second bottle waited within reach of Butch, safe in the insulated delivery bag. Rebecca had paid the check with cash. Goodbyes were said. An invitation to visit again was extended. No one was crying, though Butch appeared to be close to tears.

In the corridor, a new shift of third-floor nurses, in white uniforms with pale-blue trim, were making their way east toward the nurse's station, virtually radiating compassion and dedication to the work ahead.

The amigos moved westward against the tide. When they reached the elevator alcove, all the cabs were descending to the lobby. As they waited for an elevator, they could not help but overhear two nurses who stood nearby in conversation, one from the departing shift and the other newly arrived.

"How's Travis dealing with you being on nights?"

"He likes it too much."

"Dipping his willy in some tart?"

"He would if he wasn't too tired to tomcat."

"Losin' his pep, is he?"

"He eats my dinners and sleeps from six o'clock till dawn."

"He doesn't wonder why he sleeps like an old dog?"

"It's Travis, remember. Not a lot of wondering in him."

"You got to protect the man from himself."

"Exactly. So what's the news of the day?"

"We lost Mr. Blomhoff in isolation."

"Well, it was way beyond the toe with him."

The amigos turned to the nurses. Rebecca said, "I didn't mean to eavesdrop. But did you say Mr. Blomhoff died, Aldous Blomhoff. Was he still the head of the institute after all these years?"

Everyone in town knew Blomhoff. He spoke at high school graduation most years and supported numerous Maple Grove charities.

"That's him," said the wife of Travis. "His brother, Pastor Turnbuckle, came to see him at last, but it was too late."

"Pastor Larry was his brother?"

"Half brother. They were estranged for a long time."

The nurse who wasn't married to Travis said, "We shouldn't say anything more. We shouldn't even have said that much."

"Patient privacy," said the wife of Travis.

They turned from the amigos, exited the alcove, and disappeared around the corner into the main corridor.

Bobby quoted Travis's wife. "'It was way beyond the toe with him.'"

The doors opened on one of the six elevators. From within came a recorded voice: "Going down."

The amigos stared into the empty cab. The cab was patient, but not infinitely so. A tone sounded—*boing*—and the doors closed.

Rebecca, Bobby, and Spencer hurried back to room 315.

39

TOE TO TOE

When the three amigos bustled into room 315, Butch had not yet touched his pizza and beer. He was scowling into the open get-well card as it made vomiting noises.

As the amigos gathered at his bed railing, Butch said, "What the hell is this?"

Rebecca said, "A talking card."

"In what language?"

"That one doesn't say anything."

"It just makes vomiting noises," Spencer said.

Bobby said, "It's the funniest talking card they had."

"It's not funny," Butch disagreed.

"It's at least amusing."

"No." He closed the card. "Did you buy this in the gift shop? Did the clerk have curly white hair, rosy cheeks? Were her glasses hanging around her neck on a beaded chain?"

"That's her," said Spencer. "She was very helpful."

"That's Miriam. She's a hustler. Nobody wants to work in a hospital gift shop, always around sick people. They could get her to take the job only by paying a commission. That woman could sell you your own shoes."

"Now that we're talking about jobs," said Bobby, "we never asked where you work."

Putting the card aside, Butch said, "I'm chief of security at Keppelwhite Institute. Why?"

To avoid answering the question, Rebecca said, "You haven't touched your pizza. It'll get cold."

"I like it cold. You came back just to ask where I work?"

"Your beer is getting warm."

"I like pizza cold and beer warm. I'm an independent thinker. What's it matter where I work?"

"It doesn't," Bobby said. "It doesn't matter at all."

Spencer said, "We had a bet, that's all."

"A bet?"

"About what kind of work you do."

"What is that a thing to bet on?" Butch asked.

Rebecca said, "Your pizza is getting warm." As Butch frowned in consideration of what she said, Rebecca took hold of her amigos' hands. "Come on, guys, we gotta scoot. Ernie is waiting."

She didn't want to be there when Butch asked more questions that they would not answer, which was sure to make him suspicious. More urgently, she didn't want to be there when he picked up the joke book.

In room 344, Harry was still dead from Rubik's Cube, and his bed remained empty, while Jim Jamie James sat in the first bed, gazing dispiritedly at his untouched pudding.

"Hey, Jim," Spencer said brightly, "I have a couple of friends I want you to meet."

Jim smiled broadly and sat up straighter as Rebecca reached across the bed railing to shake his hand. "I'm Rebecca."

"Oh, gosh almighty, I know who *you* are. Everybody in the world knows who *you* are."

"I'm an actress," she said, and the Sham at once offered his hand, provided his first name, and said, "I'm a writer."

Spencer said, "And I never told you, I'm a painter, an artist."

Dazzling Jim by taking his hand again and holding it in both of her hands, Rebecca said, "So, what are you?"

"What am I?"

"What work do you do?"

"I'm head of human resources."

"That's a big job, Jim."

"There's a lot of responsibility, but it's not that big a job."

She squeezed his hand. "I like it when an important man is also humble. I'm very attracted to that. What company, Jim?"

"Company?"

"What company is lucky enough to have you as head of human resources?"

"It's not a company exactly. It's more of a nonprofit research facility. Darn if you aren't even more beautiful in real life than you are on TV and in the movies."

"That's so sweet. I'm never going to forget how sweet you are, Jim. We just—"

He interrupted. "You can call me Jamie. 'Jim' is for business, 'Jamie' for friends. Your eyes are amazing."

Nodding, smiling, she said, "Listen to me, Jamie. I want you to focus. Can you focus for me, Jamie? No? Okay, don't look at my eyes, Jamie. Look at my nose. Can you look at my nose? Good. All right. Now focus for me. What is the name of this nonprofit research facility where you're head of human resources?"

"The Keppelwhite Institute. Dear God, I could just look at you all day."

"No you can't, Jamie. Not possible. You take care of yourself and have a good life."

She let go of his hand. With her amigos close behind, she split the scene.

40

LET'S NOT FORGET ERNIE

Ernie Hernishen decided he would never become accustomed to being without a heartbeat, without the need to breathe, without a need to ingest or excrete—and still be able to think and not go crazy. This had to come to an end soon. Without sight, smell, touch, taste, and hearing (except for the internal voices that comforted him), he was a creature of pure thought, limited to writing country songs, pondering the larger questions of existence, and vividly reliving key moments of his past. Furthermore, these long-forgotten rekindled memories were often strange because they were experiences recorded as perceived by an innocent child and interpreted now by a worldly adult.

Currently, the memory that returned to him was one of events he didn't even know had occurred, a dramatic conflict and resolution that he couldn't have understood at the time. However, having been recorded in some deep convolution of his brain, all the details of the incident came back to him, almost as unpleasant as a jalapeño-rich Mexican dinner revisiting in the form of acid reflux.

He was one month short of his third birthday. He could wash and dry his own hands and dress without help. He could prepare a bowl of cereal by himself. The only cereal Mother would allow him to have was a gritty Swedish brand, whatever "Swedish" meant. It smelled like straw and tasted like dusty wood; he knew what dusty wood tasted like because he still sometimes liked to chew on furniture, and Hilda Merkwurdig—the nanny and housekeeper—often neglected the dusting. He could speak and be understood half the time, and he was able to carry on a conversation of three or four sentences. He had been potty trained for almost a year and had stopped wetting the bed three months ago. He no longer sucked his thumb, because doing so resulted in his mother sitting down with him to engage in long conversations in which she described the grisly things that would happen to him if he didn't start acting more like an adult. He was really coming along in the world.

On the evening that now rose out of his memory, it was Hilda Merkwurdig's day off. Ernie was sitting alone at the kitchen table, applying crayons to the pages of a drawing tablet, producing images that looked to him like dogs and cows and trains and farmers growing tastier cereal grains, though to everyone else they were meaningless scribbles. The doorbell rang. He was not interested in visitors; they were always professors from the college, people who made him wish he were able to change into a dog and run far away. Besides, he had no idea what a professor did, though from what he had seen so far in his short life, they didn't do interesting things like drive tractors and trains. More than a few smelled funny, too. Mother said the smell was "weed," but Ernie thought it smelled like his Swedish breakfast cereal as it had smelled that time when the milk he poured on it turned out to be sour.

After a few minutes, a strange man entered the kitchen, closely followed by Mother. The man was interesting because he didn't look like a professor; he was tall and looked like the stars of shows on the TV that Hilda Merkwurdig watched. He smelled good, too. The man stood looking down at Ernie and smiling, but there were tears in his eyes that didn't match the smile. The man said, "Look at you, just look at you," so Ernie tried as best he could to look at various parts of himself, although he couldn't see much of his own face.

Mother was not happy. She was never happy the way some other people were happy, and now she looked as if the tall man had pounded her toes with a hammer and as if she intended to do the same to him only harder. She said some things to the man that Ernie couldn't understand, and the man said something about sticks and stones. Gradually, Mother's angry expression went away, and she got that scarier look that came over her whenever she sat Ernie down for a long talk, as if she were gazing at a bug and deciding how to deal with it.

The man said something about "my sun." Mother said, the sun was hers—"my sun, only mine." The words *"my"* and *"mine"* were critical to Ernie because, when spoken, they established limits regarding what could be taken from him or done to him. The crayons were "my crayons," and the stuff in the mug next to the drawing tablet was "my hot chocolate." The bed he slept in was "my bed," which was important because the space under the bed belonged to the monster that lived there; as long as Ernie didn't violate this arrangement by crawling under the bed, the monster was obliged not to climb on top of the bed with him. Hearing the word *"my"* repeatedly coupled with the word *"sun"* confused Ernie because he had thought the sun belonged to everyone. If his mother owned the sun, as she claimed, then the day must belong to her. If the day belonged to her, who owned the night? You would think the person who owned the night would be a lot scarier than the person who owned the day. So if Mother owned the day, Ernie hoped that he would never meet whoever owned the night. When Mother and the man got loud with each other, Ernie bent closer to the big tablet and drew harder than before, so hard he broke some crayons. He selected other colors and drew with them; when they broke, too, he made pictures with the fragments.

Mother and the man left the kitchen and went to her study so that she could give him a "payoff," whatever that was. He promised that when he had the payoff, he would "never come back into your life." They were in the study only a few minutes when the man cried out—not loudly, but different from how anyone had ever cried out in Ernie's experience. Following his cry came a solid thud simultaneous with a clatter, as if someone had fallen into something and knocked it down.

Although he was tired of drawing, Ernie continued to draw because he didn't know what else to do. He was afraid to leave the kitchen and go elsewhere in the house, though he didn't quite know why he was afraid. He couldn't go outside at twilight with darkness coming, not alone, not until he knew who owned the night. His mother returned and said it was bedtime. It didn't feel like bedtime; there was still some light at the windows, and he was not at all sleepy. However, he rarely disobeyed his mother—that she knew about. *Have you forgotten what the punishment is for disobedient boys, Ernest? Must I refresh your memory, young man? Is that your position, Ernest—that you need to have your memory refreshed?* Ernie didn't need to have his memory refreshed. She didn't even need to ask that question on this occasion. He followed the hall, passed the closed door of her study, and climbed the stairs to his room. He changed from his day clothes into pajamas and used the potty and washed his hands and brushed his teeth and climbed into bed, but he didn't turn down the nightstand lamp. Unable to sleep in full darkness, he always set the three-way lamp at its dimmest level. Tonight, he left it bright.

His mother came to his room and stood looking down at him. She said that no man had been to the house earlier. When Ernie said he had seen the man, Mother repeated that no such person had been to the house. He must never say that anyone had come to the house this night. She explained that if Ernest didn't obey her on this point, the punishment would be far greater than any he had earned before, worse than anything the monster under his bed had ever thought of doing to him. *When I'm done punishing you, Ernest, you'll be crying like a baby. You'll cry for hours and hours, and when you finally cease crying, I will bind your wrists and ankles and shove you under your bed, to see what pieces of you a monster finds foul-tasting and spits out. Have I made myself clear, Ernest? Do you have a clear picture in your mind of what will happen to you if you disobey me on this most important issue? Are we, as they say, on the same page?*

Yes. He understood. He would never disobey. He thought he better say he loved her and ask her to kiss him goodnight. *Of course you love your mother, Ernest. Stating the obvious is tedious. People are animals, and even many lesser animals exhibit affection between the offspring and their parents.* Without kissing him, she turned off the lamp and crossed the room by the hall light that came through the open door. She pulled the door shut behind her.

Lying in the dark, shivering uncontrollably, Ernie listened to his mother as she set about some labor downstairs. The muffled howl of a vacuum cleaner rose from the study. Quiet. After a while, the door that slammed seemed to be the one between the house and garage. Quiet. Again the door slammed. The rattling noise was familiar, but he didn't identify it until it stopped; then he realized it had been the erratic wheels on the flatbed gardening cart that Mother used to move bags of fertilizer, new plants, and tools around her half acre of flowering gardens. Quiet again. Later, the cart was on the move once more. The door between the house and garage slammed again. In time, the garage door rumbled up on its tracks. The car started. She pulled outside. The garage door rumbled down. She drove away.

For the first time ever, Ernie was home alone.

He sat up and switched on the lamp. He could hear the monster breathing under the bed. Ernie held his own breath to hear better, and the monster held its breath, too. The monster was very sneaky. Ernie thought he should go downstairs and look around, but Mother would know what he had done. Mother knew everything. She knew for sure that she didn't want to be called "mama" or "mom." Using those words was big trouble. He remained in bed.

The nightstand didn't hold a clock. Clocks had no significance for him. As yet, minutes and hours were the same, just words. He had recently grasped the concept of "today" and "yesterday," although "tomorrow" was a fuzzy notion. When referring to anything that had happened in the past, he always said it had happened "last night." Last night was a busy place, especially considering what had just happened last night. He wished Hilda Merkwurdig were here, but when she had a day off, it was the whole day and the night, too. He was determined not to fall asleep while alone in the house. He fell asleep.

When he woke—or half woke—with lamplight close but shadows all around, his mother was standing over the bed. She looked tired. Darkness beyond the windows. The house very quiet. *Do you remember what happened last night, Ernest?* Because his entire life was "last night," he told her that everything, just everything, had happened last night. Mother sat on the edge of the bed. She said, *This is what happened last night. I made macaroni and cheese for dinner. There were vegetables and you didn't want to eat them, but I made you or you wouldn't get dessert. Dessert was a scoop of vanilla ice cream with sliced, fresh peaches on top. After that I read you a story about a boy who could fly, but his dog couldn't fly, so the boy gave up flying. You very much liked the story, but I said it was stupid. Then you went to bed.* Ernie almost reminded her that she hadn't made dinner of any kind and that he'd gone to bed hungry. However, although he couldn't yet tell time, he knew how long his punishment would last for mentioning such a thing. Very long.

She told him the lie about last night, and then she made him tell it over and over, in one mangled version or another. Each time he fell asleep, she shook him awake and forced him to go through it again. At last, Mother got up from the edge of the bed and turned off the light and told him to go to sleep. He woke once, and though the room was pitch dark, he felt her standing there, heard her soft breathing, and he knew she was staring down at him, as if she were able to see without light. He wondered what she was thinking, and then he decided he didn't want to know. He went back to sleep and dreamed that his mother was under the bed and breathing softly so that he wouldn't hear her.

In the days that followed, no one came around to ask about the man who claimed to own the sun. Ernie gradually forgot that such a person had really been there. Instead, he remembered him as the father in the story about the boy who could fly. Long before Ernie could read a clock and tell time, he had entirely forgotten the tall man and the flying boy and the earthbound dog.

Now, lying in the dead space behind the foldaway bed, he wished this memory had never returned to him. Once you recalled that your mother murdered your father and got away with it, you didn't have many choices about the direction your life would take after the acquisition of such knowledge. He knew that he had not recovered the memory on his own, that whoever placed him in suspended animation had dredged it out of his subconscious or from even deeper realms. And now the interior voices—male and female, which came to him from other than his ears—acknowledged responsibility. They apologized in sincere, soothing voices. The project, they explained, required that they know everything there was to know about the attitudes and fears and joys of every subject they studied. It was unfortunate that Ernie had to remember such things as this for the project to succeed, but that's how it had to be. Some of the wisest human beings often said of unpleasant developments, "It is what it is." Even if they said that so often you wanted to smack them, it was nonetheless true.

Ernie will certainly learn the identity of the entity that placed him in suspended animation and why, but it is most unlikely that he—or any of us—will understand by what mechanism or strange power his memory could be stimulated and ransacked in the fashion that we have just witnessed. We should not be disappointed if that one element remains unexplained. There are many, many things in life of which we have no understanding, such as why the universe goes on forever and why time does not occasionally run backward; it just is what it is. Apologies are herewith extended to the reader for the way in which this chapter interrupted the general narrative flow with long paragraphs of dense prose, but it seemed essential that this dismaying information be conveyed in

307

order for you to better understand Ernie and his mother, Britta. A separate and heartfelt apology is herewith offered for the inevitable sadness inspired by the discovery that Ernie's father was murdered long ago and that Ernie therefore will never have a chance to know him. Until this chapter, the story has been intended to be highly amusing—and is likewise structured for that purpose in what follows—but for this one interlude, deep melancholy could not be avoided. It just is what it is.

41

THE PLAGUE BY ALBERT CAMUS

The three amigos did not depart County Memorial at a run, but neither did they simply amble out of the building as if they had nowhere to go and weeks to get there. Spencer could feel things coming to a head.

As they clambered into the Genesis, Bobby in back and Rebecca riding shotgun, they were afraid, as they had been since arriving in Maple Grove the previous day. However, the primary cause of their fear had changed. Initially, their biggest fear was that Ernie was dying and a piece of their hearts with him, but when they realized he was not dying, their greatest fear was that, by embalming him, a mortician would kill him. Once they had stashed precious Ernie in a window seat, where no mortician might find him, their greatest fear became that Wayne Louis Hornfly would behead and eat them. In the interims between those big fears, there were many causes for lesser terror: the half-formed naked men in the church basement, the living molts that had been shed by some slime monster they had never seen, Britta Hernishen, the Nelsoneers, and more. Now, though all those things bubbled in their minds, a witch's stew of frights, the terror that preoccupied Spencer and also his friends was the possibility that they would die from a mysterious and disgusting disease.

From the back seat, Bobby declared, "What's happening to Butch and Jim James and Pastor Larry's brother, this terrible thing—it's maybe like Camus."

"What's camus?" Spencer asked as he drove out of the parking lot, for he was a man of images rather than words.

"Not what. Who. He was a famous French writer."

Rebecca said, "He wrote a classic novel titled *The Plague*."

"What kind of plague starts on the big toe?" Spencer wondered.

"It might sound absurd," Bobby said, "but Aldous Blomhoff is dead from it."

"Butch and Jim Jamie James might not be the only people in town who're infected," Rebecca suggested. "Remember how each of them was ashamed of the way his big toe looked? They didn't want us to see their toes."

Bobby got her point at once. "There could be people all over town, hobbling around in the privacy of their homes, embarrassed for a doctor to see their toes, hoping they'll heal on their own or with maybe this or that ointment."

"Meanwhile, they're rotting from the toe up."

"Or something worse than rotting."

"What could be worse than rotting?"

"Dissolving," Bobby said.

Rebecca shook her head. "Rotting is worse."

"Now that I think about it, I agree."

"The smell," she said.

Their minds were racing along such parallel tracks that they began to finish each other's sentences.

He said, "Oh my God, what if—"

"—what if they're becoming—"

"—becoming molting—"

"—slime creatures. Is that—"

"—crazy? It's no crazier than—"

"—than everything else that's happened."

"You know what Thomas Hardy said. 'Though a good deal is—'"

"'—is too strange to be believed—'"

"'—nothing is too strange to have happened,'" Bobby finished.

Spencer was driving a random route through town as his amigos strove to analyze their situation and arrive at a consensus as to the degree of the peril they faced. As he listened, he knew that the development Bobby and Rebecca had been resisting was inevitable. Their love for each other as friends would never fade, but they were layering another kind of affection on top of it. That progression didn't disappoint Spencer. He didn't feel marginalized as a friend, and he wasn't jealous that Bobby was going to win the heart of such a gorgeous and smart woman. He was happy for Bobby and Rebecca, even if they hadn't quite realized how far along the path of romance they had traveled. Come what may, they would always be amigos, their bonds too strong ever to be weakened. The three of them and Ernie were amigos now and forever—unless one of them died.

If one of them died in Maple Grove, he hoped it would be him. *But what if three of them died, and he was the sole survivor?* Such a terror of loss thrilled through Spencer that in an instant his palms became sweaty, and the steering wheel slipped through his hands, and he almost lost control of the Genesis. Although they lived separate lives, in places distant from one another, the fact that they were out there, that they stayed in touch, that they cared intensely for one another was the only thing that kept his anxiety at bay. He'd had no friends before them, and the friends he'd made since leaving Maple Grove were, face it, no more than valued acquaintances of whom he was at best fond.

The prospect of being the lone amigo proved so intolerable that he fled his thoughts, rushed into the conversation between Rebecca and Bobby, and heard himself say, "Hey, nobody's turning into a slime creature from the toe up. They said the disease—infection, virus, whatever—killed Aldous Blomhoff. If that wasn't true and he became a monster, they would have had to take him away somewhere and hide him, lock him up, maybe study him later. That's what they do with monsters. But then the nurses, three shifts of them and lots of other people, would be aware of what really happened to him. With that many people in the know, you can't keep a secret. Besides, the moment they saw Aldous changing, they would've taken Jim James and Butch and hid them away, too. Until Aldous died today, they thought it was a weird infection, something that could be treated with antibiotics and standard procedures. Maybe they continue to believe this. The molting slime creature was its own thing, not some guy who woke up one morning with a strange toe and went werewolf."

When Spencer finished, his passengers sat in amazed silence, and then Bobby said, "That makes perfect sense. But how did you picture it all together so fast?"

Spencer had surprised himself. "I didn't. It came out of me in words like . . . like the way words just spill out of other people."

"We're all under a lot of stress," Rebecca said.

"You can say that again," Spencer agreed. "I'm sweating here."

After a mutual thoughtful silence, Bobby said to Rebecca, "You didn't go to college."

"Thank God, no. I still have common sense."

"But you read *The Plague*. People only read it if it's required for a course or they want to torment themselves."

"I read a summary. You didn't go to college, either."

"Thank God, no," he said. "I read it because I was in a bad mood and wanted to torment myself. Why would you read a summary?"

Rebecca sighed. "I was offered the lead in a film adaptation. The studio changed it so it wasn't fleas, carried by rats, that spread the black plague. It was a plot by alien invaders living secretly in England in 1665. My role was a time traveler going back to London of that era to foil the aliens. There were problems with the script, the director was arrested for keeping llamas for sexual purposes, and they deep-sixed the project."

Spencer thought he was turning from street to street without purpose, going nowhere with conscious intention, but perhaps his unconscious knew better. A block ahead, Saint Mark's rose fundament to spire. It looked like a thousand other churches, a noble tribute to the sacred. No dark cloud hung over the place, nor did the stained-glass windows glimmer with demonic light.

The rectory, on the other hand, appeared no less ominous than an outpost in the coldest region of Hell, a place where those who slaughtered innocents were tortured for eternity with everything from red-hot branding irons to episodes of the 1960s TV sitcom *My Mother the Car*. To Spencer, the bricks looked like blocks of frozen meat. The windows might have been the blank eyes of demons that were blind to the existence of Goodness. He could well imagine that the basement was filled with blood to a depth of ten thousand feet and that, in December, the hallways were hung with entrails to mock Christmas holly. If the hateful house radiated evil—and it did—then it must surely be Pastor Larry who emitted particles of dark energy as deadly as those flowing out of the fissile element known as plutonium, saturating the walls and spraying into Maple Grove, mutating all with which it came into contact. Because Spencer could not draw, were he to risk painting this residence on a large canvas, he would have to do so by getting into a fugue state and rendering it in symbolic shapes and colors, which he feared doing out of concern that every patron ever to lay eyes on it would die. Perhaps because of the sudden and colorful collapse of his family when he was fourteen, Spencer often exhibited a tendency to overdramatize events.

As they sat in the Genesis SUV, in the public parking lot next to the courthouse, across the street from the rectory, Bobby and Rebecca found the residence far less ominous than did Spencer. To them, it appeared to be an ordinary brick house with a slate roof and white trim. In light of what they knew about Pastor Larry, the very ordinariness of the place is what chilled them.

Rebecca said, "More than twenty years ago, Hornfly said Pastor Larry hates humanity and thinks the Earth can be saved only when no people are left in the world. Now we know his brother, Aldous, was the CEO and chief research scientist at the institute. Why the heck are we still sitting here? Why aren't we over there, in that house, having tea with the reverend, tea and tea and more tea, and more damn tea, until he can't take any more tea, until the very idea of more tea terrifies him and he tells us everything he knows."

Spencer was pretty sure that by the word *"tea,"* Rebecca was not talking about tea. She looked very much like Heather

Ashmont at the end of *Shriek Hard, Shriek Harder*, when at last, after three movies, she managed to kill Judyface with his own pickax, industrial nail gun, acetylene torch, and box of dynamite. For the first time since they had become amigos, Spencer was a little bit afraid of Rebecca.

42

AS THEY PREPARE TO VISIT PASTOR LARRY, THE AMIGOS RECALL A THANKSGIVING HORROR

Part 1

So there they were, fourteen years old, none with a supportive family to which they could turn for help.

Often when a bad thing has happened and perhaps something worse is expected, people say they are waiting for the other shoe to drop. During the two uneventful weeks following the Liberty Park encounter with Wayne Louis Hornfly, when he had eaten the head and surely then the body of Björn Skollborg, the amigos waited for the other shoe to drop. Hornfly warned them that Skollborg's fate would be theirs if they didn't cease conducting surveillance of Pastor Larry and looking into his background, that they would be safe if they obeyed. They had respected that warning at least for the time being, but they did not believe that a creature like Hornfly, who could somehow devour a head in less than a minute, could be relied upon to keep his word. Sooner than later, a big shoe would drop.

Trusting Hornfly would be as stupid as accepting an invitation to Dracula's castle after being assured that your host has such an allergy to your blood type that he will go into anaphylactic shock and die again if he consumes so much as a drop. It would be as stupid as including the Frankenstein monster in a state dinner at the White House under the assumption that he possesses perfect table manners and is a witty conversationalist. During those two weeks when the amigos felt constrained from further investigation, they came up with scores of as-stupid-as comparisons. They had to do *something* or go mad. They also spent hours speculating on what kind of creature could do what Hornfly had done. What was his biology? What were his origins? Where did he dwell when he wasn't reading stories about blood, pain, mayhem, cruelty, murder, and mass death in Pastor Larry's library? Why did he refer to himself as "we" and "us" instead of "I" and "me"? What did he mean by "Beta is smart. Alpha is stupid," and what *were* Alpha and Beta?

By Thanksgiving Day, they had exhausted themselves in fruitless speculation and were frustrated by being afraid to act. Sometimes they sat together in weary silence, as if all the brainstorming had washed everything out of their skulls.

Their mood improved by the time they got together at Spencer's house on Thanksgiving morning. The previous afternoon, they had gone grocery shopping. They intended to prepare a holiday feast together.

Bobby's foster parents, the Pinchbecks, were indifferent as to whether he stayed home for the traditional fish sticks and boiled potatoes.

Ernie's mother found Thanksgiving such an offensive idea that she chose to fast on the day and had no intention of cooking for her son. "There are numerous frozen comestibles at the supermarket. I will provide you with funds to purchase whatever indigestible items young people of your age are foolish enough to consume. If you must give thanks for something, thank the food-processing conglomerates who keep the market freezers full of insalubrious edibles that will in time destroy your heart while in the short term providing just sufficient calories and nutrients to sustain life. Is that a plan that you feel comfortable with? Shall I fund this endeavor?"

Rebecca's grandparents were on vacation in Key West with the friends they loved to hate, a hatred revealed only in shrewd and subtle ways when face-to-face but expressed with withering viciousness when not in their company.

And of course it was Spanksgiving at the Church of the Sacred Erogenous Revelation.

The amigos had psychologically processed all of that and were comfortable with the plan for the day. Because they had been pretty much looking after themselves for years, each had experience with kitchen chores and some culinary skills. The preparation for a feast, which took hours, was never tedious, never seemed like labor. They were together. They liked one another. They were having fun.

You might be saying to yourself or shouting at the page, *How can they be having fun when there's a monster threatening them?* That is one of the most admirable things about human beings. Even in the dire circumstances of war, people tell jokes; they laugh at their folly and at the idiocy of their enemies, even at their leaders. Laughter inspires hope, which is essential if we are to have any chance of survival. Only in movies is everything mercilessly grim once the monster arrives on the scene. In life, one of our best weapons against fear, therefore against monsters, is to mock them. After all, Rebecca called Wayne Louis Hornfly a "despicable turd," yet she and her friends were still alive.

So the amigos sat down to Thanksgiving dinner, shared stories from their lives, and laughed. The food was abundant and delicious. However, in keeping with a previous narrative decision, it will not be described. Suffice it to say they were stuffed and happy.

As they cleared the table and washed the dishes, they discussed Hornfly, a subject they had been avoiding. The conversation evolved until Bobby remembered something from the encounter with the monster in Pastor Larry's library back in September, an odd detail in Hornfly's rambling so incomprehensible that he had forgotten it.

"*The third floor . . . comatose people . . .*"

"There's no third floor on the rectory," Rebecca said.

"That's what I told Hornfly. He said Alphas did things to people on the third floor."

"What things?" Ernie asked.

Bobby strove to remember. "He didn't say. He told me I was too stupid to live. He was even more rude than scary. He said if . . . if I were comatose, they would find nothing in my tiny brain."

"Who wouldn't?"

"The Alphas, I guess."

"Back to square one. Who or what are the Alphas?"

Handing a washed plate to Ernie so that he could dry it, Rebecca said, "Did he mean these Alphas would cut open your head to examine your brain?"

"I don't know. It didn't make sense. A third floor where there wasn't one. Alphas are stupid. Betas are smart. It was gibberish. At the same time he said he would crush me like a grape or else burst upon me and destroy me from the inside out with his filaments and felts. I was more focused on the threats than on the rest of it."

As Ernie finished drying the plate, he said, "For two months, I've been trying to figure out that business about bursting on you and filling you with filaments and felts. It still sounds like nonsense. Can a monster be wacko?"

"They're all wacko," Rebecca said. She had not rewashed any dinnerware or flatware. She didn't consider wiping out the sink with hand-sanitizing gel. She was unaware of the obsession that would one day grip her. "Being wacko is part of being a monster. Leatherface in *Texas Chainsaw Massacre* wasn't just a homicidal psychopath. He was as delusional as a rabid monkey."

"Can monkeys get rabies?" Ernie asked as he put the plate away.

Bobby said, "Why couldn't they?"

"I just never heard of a rabid monkey."

Rebecca said, "If they can send a monkey into space, then why couldn't a monkey get rabies?"

That non sequitur caused Ernie to look at her askance, which he could do pretty well even though he had no intention of becoming an actor. "Who sent a monkey into space?"

"We did, the US, years and years ago. Sent it up before we sent up astronauts, just to be sure that weightlessness wouldn't maybe cause a stroke or something."

"That must have been one pissed-off monkey."

Bobby said, "I wonder if a grizzly bear could get rabies. Or what about an elephant?"

"I wouldn't want to be locked in a room with them when they were foaming at the mouth," Ernie declared.

Since Bobby first mentioned the third floor and the comatose people, Spencer had been staring at a plate of pumpkin cookies with chocolate chips, as if he didn't know what they were and was trying to puzzle out their purpose. In fact, a series of images were falling together in his mind, and he was converting them into words.

Now he said, "Where do you find comatose people? You find them in a hospital. How many floors does County General have? Three. How do you study a human brain? One way is scan it. Where do you find MRI machines and CAT scanners? In a hospital. County General is connected to the Keppelwhite Institute. Among Keppelwhite companies, some develop pharmaceuticals and medical devices. Then there's Keppelwhite Neotech. I'm pretty sure Alpha and Beta are terms often used in medical research, including in the names of experiments."

He looked up. Everyone was staring at him as though he had announced that he was not born on this planet.

"What I think we need to do," Spencer said, "is I think we need to go to the hospital for a look around."

"When?" Ernie asked.

"Now," Spencer said.

"Isn't that a little rash?"

"We can't play this game according to Hornfly's rules, on his—their—timetable. We have to show some initiative."

"We don't have to show it tonight," Rebecca said. "We just had a heavy meal."

"We're all bloated and groggy," Ernie said. "It was flavorful, but it was heavy. I won't describe dinner. We all know what we ate. But already I feel like a nap."

"Spencer's right," Bobby said. "We have to get our butts in gear. Those who nap die. If we don't act, I expect Hornfly to kill me, if not necessarily tonight or tomorrow night, then a year from now or twenty-one years from now. We need to find him—them—and destroy him if we can."

"Well," said Ernie, "I guess if we've got to go to County General and poke around, looking for something weird on the third floor, this is a good time for it. Visiting hours will be over by the time we get there. The staff will probably be smaller on a major holiday, maybe not fewer nurses, but fewer everybody else."

"If you're all going," Rebecca said, "then I'm going even though I'm bloated and gaseous and feel like my face is melting."

"You still look really good," Spencer said.

Bobby said, "Not that we pay any attention to how you look."

"You better not. I'm just one of the guys."

"What I meant," said Spencer, "is that for someone bloated and gaseous and as haggard as you are, you look alert and healthy."

Departing the kitchen to fetch the coats they had been wearing on this nippy November day, Bobby raised an issue that might seem peculiar but only reveals that even then he had a career in mind. "If this were a story instead of just real life, would it be better to break the chapter here or all the way after we find whatever there is to find at the hospital?"

"That's a weird question," said Ernie. "This *is* real life."

"It's just a thing I wonder about—how life sometimes goes by in long, slower passages and at other times moves ahead more like a series of shorter, quicker chapters. Wouldn't it be more fun if life was all shorter, quicker episodes? Or when I'm older, will I want it slow?"

As they shrugged into their coats, Spencer said, "I don't need to go philosophical. Being a nerd takes all the energy I have."

43

AS THEY PREPARE TO VISIT PASTOR LARRY, THE AMIGOS RECALL A THANKSGIVING HORROR

Part 2

As the three amigos sat in the Genesis, across the street from Saint Mark's rectory, they remained as still as mannequins, although only for three minutes. As will soon be discovered, events of that fateful, distant Thanksgiving were being spooled into them in a remarkably condensed fashion by a mind of immense power that was almost beyond human comprehension. In three minutes, they vividly recalled the entire holiday when they were fourteen.

So twenty-one years earlier, the four amigos were all together, bloated and gaseous, on a night of wondrous beauty.

They came out of Spencer's house into a cold stillness through which the first snow of the season fell in skeins as plumb as rain falls on a windless day. Rebecca marveled at the ermine blanket that softened the hard edges of everything on a horizontal plane. Without wind to paste the flakes to the sides of things, nearly all vertical planes remained dark and dry, in stark contrast to the horizontal planes. When she brought this to the attention of the guys, Rebecca further remarked on the fact that tree bark and other rough vertical surfaces captured and held a small percentage of the snow directly proportional to the depth of the texture. Being nerds, they had all noticed this detail, but sharing it aloud filled them with a warm sense of camaraderie.

They could almost believe that, in truth, they were the cool kids in town. They were too honest with themselves to entertain that delusion, and it quickly passed.

The hospital was within walking distance of Spencer's house. Everything in Maple Grove was within walking distance of everything else. No passing traffic disturbed the stillness; the town seemed deserted. When you strolled by the river in the thrall of such a stillness, the sight of white snow falling upon dark water inspired a sense of peace and produced a whisper almost as quiet as a loving spirit sending you blessings through the veil between the living and the dead. On this occasion, the amigos weren't walking by the river, but it was out there, waiting for them, if they changed directions.

However, they stayed faithful to the route they had chosen, and soon they arrived at the hospital. Although vehicles were acquiring a coat of snow in the staff parking lot, the visitor lot was empty at that hour.

The lobby door might well have been unlocked, but the amigos took direction from a sign that guided those who were making deliveries to the hospital kitchen located in the southeast wing. Large flanking dumpsters indicated the entrance they sought. In addition, the extra-wide door was boldly labeled KITCHEN and well illuminated by an overhead lamp.

The chilly air outside the entrance smelled of tobacco smoke, suggesting someone had recently stepped from the kitchen to have a cigarette. At 10:10, patients' dinners had long ago been served. Edible items had been eaten, trays returned, banks of industrial dishwashers loaded, and clean trays removed. All the cooks and other food-prep staff had surely departed. Breakfast would consist of something like orange juice, toast, commercial prescrambled eggs reheated in microwaves, and solid blocks of home fries produced in Poland and shipped to the US on a refrigerated freighter. It would be served at seven o'clock. The culinary staff wouldn't arrive for maybe six hours.

During the months since he'd used a glass cutter and blue painter's tape to gain entrance to Saint Mark's rectory, Bobby the Sham had indulged his writerly curiosity and talent for dogged research to find a source for a set of lockpicks, acquire them, and learn the techniques with which to make the best use of them. As noted when previously he engaged in an illegal entry, we should not think less of Bobby for what is technically a crime, because in fact he had no criminal or malicious intent. If we must take offense at—and place severe blame on—someone, let us look no further than Mr. Werner von Grappenfokker, a retired locksmith, who was bitter about both the meager nature of his pension and the fact that his wife, Theda, had twice attempted to poison him. Bobby had paid von Grappenfokker for the picks and instructions with fees earned from writing why-I-want-to-go-to-Harvard and equivalent essays for college-bound seniors. If it seems to you that a misdemeanor or even more serious offense was committed by Bobby when he paid for the burglary tools and knowledge of how to use them with money received for defrauding Harvard and other similar institutions, then it is suggested that you try to imagine it had been *you* fostered by the Pinchbecks and required to live in that House of Tedium with Mr. and Mrs. Zero Personality, where the loudest sound was the drip-drip-drip of a leaky faucet. Without a source of income, your adolescence would have been bleak, and you would probably have engaged in every nefarious activity from beating up smaller kids for their lunch money to carjacking. So get off your high horse, and for God's sake let's get on with what happened on that Thanksgiving night.

Using the Grappenfokker tool set (which sounds like the title of a novel by the late Robert Ludlum), Bobby expertly picked the lock of the door to the hospital kitchen. The four amigos boldly entered a large, chilled chamber that served as a receiving center for perishable foods but also as long-term storage for canned and bottled goods. The lights were off. However, Ernie had brought a small flashlight. The beam traveled over many hundreds of linear feet of shelving that contained large cans of stewed prunes, fruit cocktail, artificially flavored chicken soup, fat-free lard, boxes and boxes of Jell-O, enormous eighty-ounce cans of pudding, and other delectables.

The one other door in the chamber proved to be unlocked. With caution, they passed through it, into the vast kitchen. Half the room was revealed by overhead light panels, although not every panel glowed as they would during working hours. The second half of the room lay in shadows. Rows of worktables, ovens, microwave ovens, refrigerators, cooktops, industrial mixers, and other equipment of arcane and suspicious purpose divided the space into a maze.

Somewhere in the lighted area, out of sight, two men conversed as they worked. Because their voices waxed and waned, they could not be clearly heard; although they seemed to be talking about football or soccer, the words *bitch* and *bastard* were spoken several times with such hatred and volume that perhaps they were discussing their unfaithful wives and how best to murder the men who poached their women.

The conversation was continually punctuated by a disturbing crisp metallic sound that might have been produced by a saw blade carving through the bones of a murdered womanizer, rendering the corpse into pieces that could be disposed of more easily than an intact body. The amigos listened intently, nervously, not sure if they should venture farther. Then Bobby whispered, "They're opening lots of pull-tab cans with enormous lids." This revelation relaxed everyone, because there was nothing to fear about angry foulmouthed men if they were merely opening five-pound cans of pudding.

The amigos wended single-file through the shadow-swathed half of the kitchen, in search of an exit. As they moved, they peered between the ranks of equipment that partitioned one aisle from the next, expecting to glimpse the duo they could hear, but the men remained unseen, as if they were haunting spirits of workers who died here in a tragic can-opening incident. The air wasn't woven through with cooking odors; even if it had been, they would not be described. The place smelled like a pine-scented disinfectant, and that's that.

They came to a pair of swinging doors, each with a porthole, and proceeded into the ground-floor corridor of the southeast wing, which was as quiet and deserted as a passageway in a pharaoh's pyramid that remained undiscovered beneath Egyptian sands. According to the designations on the doors, here were offices of second-tier executives, a records center, and other rooms where no one worked at night.

At the northeast and southeast corners, lighted signs announced EXIT. With their snow-wet sneakers squeaking on the vinyl-tile floor, the amigos went to the southeast end of the corridor. Rebecca opened the fire door below the exit sign. Beyond lay a vestibule. Directly ahead of her was another fire door under a glowing exit sign. To the right, stairs led to the higher floors.

For a group that sometimes seemed to talk incessantly, the four friends remained admirably disciplined as they ascended the stairs in silence. At the third floor, Rebecca eased open the door and peered into the corridor. No one. She led her amigos out of the stairwell.

At this hour, most of the patients were asleep. Others no doubt were lying awake, worrying about the future or wishing they had been able to go to church to participate in the Spanksgiving orgy. The hallway lights were dimmed. The quiet felt eerie. For most of this shift, the nurses would be at the central station for this floor, except to check on those few patients who needed late-night meds or other attention.

Hornfly had informed Bobby that Alpha, whatever it might be, was doing "absurd things to people" here. Logic supported the conclusion that the nurses of County Memorial were not involved in conducting experiments on their charges. If absurdities were being perpetrated, they were occurring at the Keppelwhite Institute.

The three floors of the hospital joined the institute at the southeast and southwest wings, a total of six connections beyond which strange things might be happening. Hornfly had specified the third floor of this wing, and though monsters were seldom helpful and trustworthy, the amigos could see no reason why their colorful acquaintance and would-be executioner would lie to them in this matter. He seemed capable of showing up anywhere without notice, eating them from the head down, and getting away with it, which suggested that he had no need to set a trap for them.

At the south end of the hallway, a formidable-looking metal door advised NO ADMITTANCE / CREDENTIALED PERSONNEL ONLY. Even if the amigos had not been induced to come here, on seeing that stern advisory emblazoned on a mysterious door, they would have been motivated to breach it. Indeed, there wasn't a nerd in the world who wouldn't scheme to find a way to get past that barrier; more than mundane people, nerds were quick to imagine—and be overtaken by a fierce certainty—that beyond any forbidden door must be the bodies of extraterrestrials recovered from a crashed starship or the first android that could pass for human, or proof of Bigfoot's existence, or a genetically engineered golden retriever possessing human-level intelligence, or compelling evidence that JFK had been assassinated by a robot terminator from the future and that the historic events in Dallas had been fabricated, or all of the above. Nerds were nerds because they were very intelligent, but we must also understand that, in spite of their intelligence, they were willing to believe in an array of the most fantastic things because they didn't much believe in themselves. A void will always be filled.

Now, in the southeast corridor, with the lights dimmed to the graveyard-shift level, with patients dreaming of miracle cures or inescapable doom, Bobby used his set of picks, acquired from the unscrupulous and bitter Werner von Grappenfokker. (The naive amigos were unaware that Grappenfokker was the cousin of Adolph Klanghoffer IV, whose great-great grandfather was Senator Adolph Klanghoffer, that the senator had been the brother of Reinhard Klanghoffer of the law firm Klanghoffer, Knacker, Hisscus, and Nork. Nor did the amigos have a clue that, in 1891, Reinhard Klanghoffer represented Gustoff Keppelwhite in the latter's successful attempt to get a patent on the hinge, which was the basis on which the Keppelwhite fortune became the largest in America. All of that might have nothing to do with the events of this narrative or the fix in which the amigos found themselves, but you must admit it's interesting and perhaps even suspicious.) So as the witching hour fast approached on Thanksgiving night, Bobby picked the lock on the door that riffraff like him and his pals were forbidden to open, and he opened it.

Beyond lay a vestibule so featureless that it almost seemed not to exist. The palest-of-blue walls were so smooth that corners were not discernible, yet the friends had no sense of being in a circular chamber. Of a blue precisely matching the walls, the floor made no sound underfoot and conveyed no impression of support, as if they were standing in midair, at risk of a mortal fall. The eye failed to perceive a ceiling. No source of light could be seen; it seemed to issue from every surface. As a seed of panic began to sprout in each of the amigos, they turned to discover that the door by which they entered had vanished. If it waited to be opened, it couldn't be because it had transitioned seamlessly to the walls and floor, without a visible knob or handle. Worse than pitch darkness, this soft but omnipresent light exposed no smallest detail of the space, and the sense of standing in a void suggested that the next step would plunge them into a blue abyss.

Ernie spoke for everyone when he said, "I don't know what lies beyond death, but maybe it's this."

Their tension built toward a scream, but at least a minute before the first of the amigos could go mad, a door irised open in front of them. Beyond the aperture lay light of a different quality from that around them; however, a haze obscured what might wait there. They felt like Richard Dreyfuss in *Close Encounters of the Third Kind*, when he stood at the foot of the starship ramp, gazing up into the bright mystery of that vessel, but they also felt like Richard Dreyfuss in *Jaws*, when he was leaning over the stern of the fishing boat when a great white as big as a whale rose toward him out of the sea, while simultaneously they felt like Richard Dreyfuss in *The Goodbye Girl*, when he realized that he loved Marsha Mason and her adorable little girl more than he loved the idea of being a star on Broadway. In these circumstances, remembering the first two films made sense, but why the third should come to mind was inexplicable, although in addition to being much beloved by general audiences of successive generations, Mr. Dreyfuss had always been a particular favorite of nerds.

Even as brave as they were, the four amigos nonetheless wanted to turn back, feel the nearly invisible wall until they located the door, and return to the hospital. Of course, anyone who is familiar with situations such as this knows that retreat is never possible. There is always and only one option—to go forward into terror, horror, and enduring psychological damage. They had never seen the *Shriek* films, because the first *Shriek* had not yet been filmed, let alone the sequels, but those of us who have seen those movies can feel pretty sure that what awaited them could not be as frightening as Judyface.

It was worse.

They passed through the aperture and obscuring haze, into a windowless white room perhaps forty by forty feet, with four evenly spaced six-inch-diameter holes in the floor. The holes apparently designated positions for four gurneys, but at the moment, only two were present, one bearing a man, the other a woman. Both patients wore hospital gowns and were draped with lightweight blankets. They appeared to be unconscious or even comatose. The scene itself was odd, although no more frightening than an uneventful teeth cleaning or a visit from a door-to-door team of pamphlet-laden folks who are certain they know more about Jesus than you do and are determined to prove it.

What was *happening* to the patients was the terrifying thing, the horrifying thing, the disgusting and repellent thing. From out of each hole in the floor next to the gurneys had risen something like a boa constrictor but not a snake, like a dark worm but not a worm. Although they were coherent forms, the substance seemed to be constantly churning, with the amorphous potential to reshape itself into anything it wished. Judging by the appearance of the forms, you would suppose their tissue was thicker than mere slime but thinner than typical sludge. Each dreadful apparition rose above its patient—or victim—and divided into six tentacles; four were the diameter of soda straws; the fifth and sixth were approximately twice the width of a garden hose. Of the thinner extensions, two had inserted themselves into the patient's ears, two into the nostrils. The fifth and thickest had forced its way into the patient's mouth and no doubt down the throat. The sixth rose above the others, swaying back and forth as though waiting in case the need arose to probe into the patient by any remaining opening. Pulsations traveled the length of every tentacle and into the comatose pair. It was not possible to be deluded into the conclusion that these two abominations were merely machines; they were organic and more loathsome than any creature that had existed in the history of Earth. Perhaps they were not two distinct monstrous individuals but mere appendages of something far below and more grotesque than anyone other than certified lunatics would be able to imagine. So unless you're a lunatic, don't even try.

The four amigos stood tightly grouped in an arc, immobilized and silenced not by terror, but because they were controlled by a power unknown. A soothing voice arose within them, assuring them that they must not be afraid, that they would not be harmed, that all would be well, that their favorite beverage, Coca-Cola, would continue to be produced for decades to come. Although they didn't believe a word of what was said, their fear faded.

Dressed in white like orderlies, two young men entered through a door that could lead nowhere but farther into the Keppelwhite Institute. The men smiled. They looked nice. They wanted only the best for everyone. Of that the amigos were in agreement, although they were unable to express their relief and confidence to one another.

The abhorrent tentacles withdrew from the man and woman. They retreated through the holes in the floor.

In retrospect, they didn't seem disgusting or fearsome. In fact, they had been graceful and almost beautiful.

The nice young men wheeled the gurneys and their occupants out of the white room.

In minutes, they returned with two other gurneys, and then they brought two more.

The amigos each had a gurney to lie upon. It was very nice to be there, resting together.

They closed their eyes.

Something cool parted their lips, like a spoon of ice cream. It felt refreshing going down the throat.

Time passed.

Although they were not aware that they all woke at 3:10 a.m., they did indeed, each in his or her own home, own bed. Snow streamed through the darkness, past the windows.

On waking, each smiled, remembering the Thanksgiving together. Rebecca, Ernie, Bobby, and Spencer—friends forever. Family.

For months after that, Rebecca dreamed of being filthy and somehow contaminated. One night, she was slogging through a muddy river, muddy fields. The next night, she was in a rat- and roach-infested hotel where everything was soiled, grimy. No matter what the dream, she was always desperate to find her way home and get clean, but she couldn't escape where she was, and there was no home to get to.

Ernie dreamed that someone was trying to control him and take his life in strange directions that he didn't want to go. Sometimes it was the man who sold hot dogs called "dead dogs" downtown during the Month of Halloween, at other times Pastor Larry. Often he was in the Liberty Park pavilion on a summer night, when the swing band was performing. The bandleader, Björn something, had Britta's head instead of his own and wanted to dance with him. Ernie loved swing, but the music of Björn's big band was discordant and scary, so Ernie needed to write new music; in some dreams Garth Brooks taught him how, but in other dreams it was Johnny Cash.

Spencer dreamed of strange, disturbing shapes; behind his back, they were crawling around and up to no good. Night after night, he attempted to describe them to everyone from Venus Porifera to the president of the United States, but everyone said that he was making no sense, that he should draw them, but he couldn't draw. He dreamed of taking lessons in drawing, but they were dreams of anxiety and frustration in which he always flunked the class.

Bobby dreamed of writing term papers and then novels while eating boiled potatoes with the Pinchbecks. He also dreamed someone was after him, a person who frequently had no head, but when the guy did have a head, he had tentacles instead of arms; the only way to avoid this creature was to keep on the move—city to city, state to state, country to country.

In time, those dreams faded away for all of them, and sleep was filled with other adventures.

They became fifteen years old and sophomores. Then sixteen and juniors. Seventeen and seniors. Year by year, grade by grade, the four of them grew closer, until it seemed as though they had always been together.

When their desires and careers took Spencer, Bobby, and Rebecca to far-flung places, they remained in touch with one another and with Ernie back in Maple Grove. They called one another frequently, visited one another, planned vacations during which they gathered at this resort or that resort, but always together. Eventually they enjoyed video contact through Zoom.

The poet Coleridge wrote, "Friendship is a sheltering tree," and Charles Dickens wrote, "The wing of friendship never moults a feather," and neither of those wise gentlemen was full of shit.

44

A VISIT WITH THE PASTOR

As the three amigos sat in the Genesis that was parked in the courthouse lot, the revelation of events they had experienced on that long-ago Thanksgiving seemed to take hours to recount. Though as noted earlier, a mysterious mind of immense power transmitted it to the amigos in just three minutes. More precisely, it required two minutes and fifty-four seconds.

Spencer, Rebecca, and Bobby needed twice that long to recover from the impact of what they had been made to remember and to share their reactions to it. Then they needed another three minutes—more precisely two minutes and forty-nine seconds—to steel themselves for a visit with Pastor Larry.

So much had happened on this second day of their return to Maple Grove that it seemed night should have fallen again. However, night had not fallen, and it would *not* fall until remaining events needed it to do so. The sun backlighted scattered clouds in the west, transforming them into golden galleons sailing on a cobalt sea—not literally, but metaphorically.

However, if the five-hour ordeal on Harriet Nelson Lane had not sapped their energy to the point of exhaustion, nothing would. They exited the SUV and gathered in front of it and stared south, toward the rectory, dramatically sunlit from their right, shadows falling to the left, Rebecca looking as determined as Heather Ashmont, Bobby looking stalwart, Spencer with his hat. They fearlessly crossed the street, not bothering to use the crosswalk at the end of the block.

After arriving alive on the south side of Winkler Street, they ascended the steps of the rectory, crossed the front porch, and considered the doorbell. The time had passed for using the lock-release gun, for breaking and entering, for a stealthy room-to-room search for evidence. In their crusade to recover their lost past and discover how to save Ernie from eternal suspended animation or worse, they now needed to take bold action, and quickly. Because they were not comfortable with interrogation techniques that drew blood and caused extreme pain, they would have to torture Pastor Larry with spoons, get him drunk on sacramental wine, tickle him mercilessly, or find some other way to make him talk.

The most formidable obstacle to the successful achievement of their goal was, of course, Hornfly. They could not be certain that the creature would disrupt their plan, though the likelihood of it was high. Should the beast appear, determined to fulfill the promise to destroy them, their only hope seemed to be somehow to induce the monster to eat Pastor Larry first, giving them time to escape the house.

With considerable courage, Bobby rang the doorbell. This does not mean that his courage was greater than that of either Rebecca or Spencer. Not a minim of difference would be found in the measurement and comparison of their courage. Bobby was the one to press the bell push only because he was nearest to it, and he beat the others when they all reached simultaneously.

Smiling his dreamy smile, the good reverend opened the door at once, as if he had been standing at it with his hand on the knob. "Come in, come in. All are welcome here."

This smelled like a trap, but the amigos could neither say *Sorry, wrong address* as they beat it off the porch nor claim to know a lot more about Jesus than he did, not when they lacked supporting pamphlets.

They stepped into the foyer, and Pastor Larry closed the door, which seemed to make a sound like a three-thousand-pound bank-vault door slamming shut against its architrave. "Why don't you young people come with me to the parlor?"

The parlor was stuffed full of heavy Victorian sofas and armchairs with crocheted antimacassars on the arms and backs. The lamps featured silk shades with tassels; the tables that held them were covered in tasseled and embroidered cloths. Flowered wallpaper. Draperies as heavy as theater curtains. Displayed throughout were fine porcelains of animals and prominent figures from the Bible. In a house with a parlor of this kind, it seemed the doorbell should have been answered by an elderly woman in orthopedic shoes, a granny dress, and shawl.

To be able to sit on a William Morris sofa covered in midnight-blue mohair, Rebecca and Bobby rearranged a collection of decorative pillows, while Spencer selected an armchair.

"Would anyone like a refreshment?" Pastor Larry asked. "Coffee, tea, hot chocolate? They're always having hot chocolate in movies on the Hallmark Channel. I so enjoy the Hallmark Channel."

The amigos politely declined a refreshment.

The reverend settled in an armchair. He smiled at them, and they found themselves smiling in return. Events were not proceeding in any fashion they had imagined.

Having played a prosecuting attorney in a story about a factory owner whose operation emitted a poisonous cloud that killed every resident of a small town with a population of 543, having destroyed him in cross-examination and shredded his claim that satanists had done it, Rebecca knew what demeanor to adopt and the right tone to strike, so she began the interrogation.

"Pastor Turnbuckle—"

"Larry. Call me Larry or Pastor Larry. I do not believe in clerical formalism."

"Yes, I see. All right then. Pastor Larry, late on a summer night twenty-one years ago, my friends and I happened to see you running pell-mell through the graveyard, in a panic."

"Oh, dear woman, it could not have been me. Running would be undignified for one in my line of work, and I have never owned a pair of Nikes or other shoes manufactured for that activity."

"Pastor, I'm not saying you were running for exercise. You were in a panic, late at night, evidently running *from* something and—"

"Furthermore, I am sorry to say that my constitution does not allow me to run."

"Constitution?"

"I have an enlarged heart, mitral valve prolapse, moderate stenosis of the pulmonary valve, angina, and a strange symptom the cause of which no cardiologist has yet been able to determine. In addition, I have chronic obstructive pulmonary disease, periodic bouts of pleurisy, and a rare condition that can cause a dangerous overproduction of phlegm if I exert myself too much."

"How terrible for you," Rebecca said with a subtle note of scorn. "It's a wonder you're still alive."

"It is indeed. But the love of the Lord sustains even when it doesn't cure."

"Can I assume you have a doctor who can confirm that you suffer from these conditions?"

The reverend's dreamy smile acquired a sly edge. He failed to answer her question. "Oh, I refuse to suffer. I embrace my pain and limitations, because it is the journey that God wishes me to take."

Bobby and Spencer were gaping at the reverend. During two days in Maple Grove, they had had an extraordinary number of occasions requiring them to gape.

Drilling forward, Rebecca said, "On that summer night, you made your way to the church and went down to the basement. When you came out of there, you seemed even more greatly distressed than when you had been running through the graveyard. What caused that distress, Pastor Larry?"

"But that couldn't have been me running, as weak as I am. And if ever I exited the basement in distress, it was because in those days the heating system included an unstable boiler. I was always concerned that it would blow up."

"Did it ever blow up?"

"Thank the Lord, no."

"Larry, what were those half-formed men in the basement, ten creatures connected like paper dolls?"

"I have no idea what you mean. What a strange question. You seem troubled, child. Have you consulted a therapist?"

Bobby said, "We all saw them that night."

Pastor Larry had a diagnosis. "Mass psychosis. Will you pray with me right now for your mutual recovery?"

Scowling and scooting forward on the sofa, Rebecca said, "That isn't going to happen, Larry. One way or another, we're going to dig the truth out of you."

The reverend's fey smile became beseeching as he turned his attention to Spencer and changed the subject. "Forgive me, son, but I can't help being dismayed that you're wearing a hat here in the rectory. I regret to say I find it disrespectful. Would you please remove your hat?"

"No," said Spencer.

"I would be most grateful."

"No."

"In your heart, son, you know it's the right thing to do."

"No."

"The Lord himself wants you to remove your hat."

"NO! NO, NO, NO! I don't hear the Lord asking for any such thing."

"Your anger is sorrowful, son. I will pray for your soul."

Defensively, Spencer said, "It's *my* hat." When he repeated those words, his emphasis shifted. "It's my *hat.*"

Sensing some deep psychological need, Pastor Larry tried to upend the situation, seize the advantage. "In the end, son, when your time comes, everything belongs to the Lord."

"The Lord admires my hat? The Lord God wants my *hat?*"

"He doesn't want it, son. He can't want what is already His. All things are His. He already owns your hat."

The color of Spencer Truedove's face was approximately like that of a Delicious apple. More precisely, it was nearly the color of a luscious but not overripe tomato. "I paid for this hat, *me,* not anyone else. It was *my* idea to make it part of my image. I've bought a *dozen* hats like it. *A dozen!* I take care of them. Nobody takes care of my hats but me. I have a cleaning kit I take everywhere I take my hat, *which is everywhere.* God gave me life, and that's a big deal, but no one's ever *given* me anything else, not even the people who had a responsibility to take care of me when I was a child. I was left to live alone without resources. I had to sell off the furniture, the appliances, the dishes, *the draperies!* I felt like such a thief, but there was nothing else. I sure would like to sell the furniture here. This is prime stuff. This stuff would bring in some real cash."

From the mohair sofa, Bobby gaped at Spencer as, earlier, he had gaped at Pastor Larry.

The reverend's dreamy half smile had become a smug full smile. "Son, my best advice to you—the thing you most need to do to find comfort—is honor thy father and mother."

Rebecca erupted from the sofa. Her eyes were the searing blue of natural-gas flames, and her hands were curled into fists, and her face was set in an expression that even dull-witted people should at once see meant *stand back if you value your life.*

Looming over Pastor Larry's armchair, staring down at him with venomous contempt, she said, "You little worm, you cockroach, you snake, you liar, you pathetic excuse for a human being, you're going to tell us the whole truth, everything you know, you reeking lump of animated sewage. I once killed a man, planted the blade of a pickax in his shoulder, shot him with a dozen two-inch steel spikes from an industrial nail gun, set him on fire with an acetylene torch, and while his face burned like candle wax—*like candle wax*—I blew him up with an entire boxful of dynamite. There was nothing left of him but bloody sludge and one intact ear. If you screw with us anymore, you piece of shit, I'll start with you by pulling down your pants and tearing off your tiny little testicles and feeding them to you with one of your eyes."

Such withering fury expressed by anyone would be intimidating; for whatever reason, when coming from a beautiful woman, it was flat-out terrifying, especially when she had won two Emmys and knew how to deliver her lines.

During Rebecca's tirade, Pastor Larry shrank in his armchair until he could shrink no further, whereupon he began to cry. Sobs racked him. Tears flooded down his cheeks. His face was pasty white and looked as soft as bread dough. He bawled, blubbered, ululated, begged for mercy, until strings of snot hung from his nostrils.

As Pastor Turnbuckle subsided to mere weeping and soft pleading noises, another voice arose in the house. Somewhere upstairs a woman began to sing a pleasing melody but not the words that went with it. She lah-lah-lahed and nah-nah-nahed and otherwise hummed through John Lennon's "Imagine." The singer seemed to be descending the stairs. While the tune was recognizable, it was performed in a voice so eerie that the three amigos turned to stare at the parlor archway beyond which lay the ground-floor hall, their expressions suggesting that they expected a ghost to manifest.

45

MOTHER

She came into the parlor, tall and willowy, weirdly seductive in a sapphire-blue silk robe, wearing high heels but perhaps nothing under the softly shimmering robe. She regarded Pastor Larry with a pained expression signaling frustration, disgust, and contempt, as one would regard an abject coward who had responded to a challenge by soiling his pants. Pastor Larry might well have soiled his pants, but as yet there was no olfactory evidence of it.

When she was done fixing the reverend with a desiccating stare that should have left him as dry and crisp as an autumn leaf, Britta Hernishen turned her attention to Rebecca. "Quite a performance. Are you sure you didn't leave out a few proofs of your savage rage that occurred before the dynamite? Perhaps you broke the villain's feet with a sledgehammer, pulled his hair, gave him a wedgie, forced him to eat scorpions."

"I'd like to force *you* to eat scorpions," Rebecca said, "but the venom in your blood suggests you already eat them every day for breakfast."

Bobby knew better than to insert himself into a confrontation between Hannibal Lecter and Clarice Starling, yet he stepped forward and said, "What are you doing here? No, don't tell me. But please tell me this sorry pile of human debris"—he indicated the reverend—"isn't Ernie's father."

Ignoring him, Britta tapped the venom in her heart to respond to Rebecca. "You are a naive little girl who has foolishly gone to war with a power greater than you can comprehend."

"It worked for Joan of Arc. But I will admit you're more of a man than I could ever be."

"Is it your habit to respond to unpleasant truths with juvenile insults? Perhaps that could be a consequence of reading nothing but summaries of summaries of illiterate screenplays. What do you think? Is that a credible hypothesis?"

Bobby said, "Please tell me Larry isn't Ernie's father."

"What I think," Rebecca said, "is you're a phony intellectual. If they revoked the degrees you faked and cheated your way through, you'd be on the dole or making a living by scavenging discarded soda cans from dumpsters."

"If I were you," Britta said, "I would not blithely challenge the academic achievements of others when your only education has been acquired while lying on your back for a series of producers."

"Please tell me Larry isn't Ernie's father," Bobby pleaded.

Spencer said, "Tell him. Please. Please tell him."

No more bowed than George Washington was in the dark days at Valley Forge, Rebecca declared, "You browbeat people, bully them, so they won't dare call you out on all the mean, stupid things you say and do. Is that an assessment we can agree on? What is your position on the matter?"

"My position, Ms. Movie Star," said Britta, "is that you are an empty vessel who makes her way through life by playing roles. For example—"

"Me? Your entire life is pretense," Rebecca countered. "The wise and confident professor has no wisdom."

"I will generously forgive your interruption," said Britta. "Your kind cannot help being rude. It is as congenital as any *physical* birth defect."

"Please. Tell us," Bobby urged. "Ernie's dad. Not Larry."

"I can't take this," Spencer said. "Not knowing. I can't."

Britta continued, "To my Larry, you promoted the absurd claim that you killed a man. That was mere acting, and of a low quality. You haven't the spine and calculation to kill a man. I know what it requires to succeed at homicide. I killed Ernie's father. I was not caught and never will be."

The silence in the parlor was preternatural until Bobby said, "Well, that's different."

"It wasn't me," Pastor Larry said. "I'm not the boy's father. My affair with Britta started long after Ernest was born. And it's the best sex of my life. Her lust is—"

"No!" Bobby commanded just as Spencer shouted, "Shut up, shut up, shut up!"

Words alone might not have stopped Pastor Larry from revealing something that would have caused the amigos grievous psychological damage that no therapist ever born could ameliorate. However, when Bobby and Spencer made threatening moves toward him, the reverend quieted and covered his face with his hands.

"Who *was* Ernie's dad?" Rebecca asked.

"That does not matter," Britta replied. "He was a person of no consequence. You are all persons of no consequence—I am surrounded by your kind—but he was of even less consequence than you, if you can imagine such a thing. He returned when Ernest was three years old and expected to be in my son's life. He learned otherwise."

"Wow," said Rebecca.

"You will cease to take that impertinent tone with me," Britta said. "I will not tolerate it. You are in no position to behave as you have been behaving, and you will cease. Do you understand what you have been told? Have you the intelligence to recognize the predicament you're in and respond to it rationally?"

Rebecca shook her head. "You're bug-shit crazy."

"I am saner than any of you. I have been wise enough to align myself with Beta."

"Praise Beta," said Pastor Larry.

Britta smiled. "You will all die here shortly. Beta will see to that."

"Praise Beta," Larry repeated.

46

ALPHA

The amigos had much to think about, and in spite of what Britta said, they were intelligent enough to know the following: (1) the professor was as insane as she was arrogant; (2) Pastor Larry was a pig; (3) they would never align with Beta because Ernie's mother was hooked up with it and because Hornfly was as well; (4) whatever else Beta might be, it was evil; (5) they were going to have to endure one of those tiresome talking-head scenes in order to learn what Alpha and Beta were; (6) the talking head would be Britta; (7) they were in deep doo-doo.

So when the murderous, lusting professor told them to sit down and pay attention, the three perched side by side on the mohair sofa as a statement of solidarity.

Knowing that she had a captive audience and relishing her hold on their attention, Britta swanned around the room as she made her revelations, forcing the amigos to turn their heads and crane their necks to follow her.

Pastor Larry also kept his eyes on her, smiling that creepy smile. Because he was likely to be thinking about his paramour's "charms," none of the amigos could stand to look at him without being overcome by nausea, acid reflux, and a death wish.

"Most people know nothing about anything worth knowing about," said the professor. "These ignorant bores resemble cud-chewing cows more than they do people, and I would vote to have them put out to pasture, by which I do not mean 'pasture' or merely 'put out.' Of the people who know something, at least half the information they possess is incorrect, and they are just a different kind of fool from the ignorant bores."

Pastor Larry said, "Which is one good reason to exterminate ninety percent of humanity."

Britta continued, "Ignorant scientists of numerous disciplines believe they have identified the world's largest organism and its location. They claim it is a fungus called *Armillaria ostoyae*, in the Malheur National Forest of Oregon. It produces amber-colored honey mushrooms in the autumn, but that is all it reveals of itself aboveground. It covers over twenty-four hundred acres, might weigh thirty-five thousand tons, and is said by some to be as much as eight thousand years old. By comparison to *our* fungus in Maple Grove, the *Armillaria* in Oregon is pindling."

"Pindling?" Bobby asked.

The professor fixed him with her Medusa stare. "It means 'tiny.' It is a colloquial word, yes, and of older use, but it remains a legitimate descriptive."

"I like it. I'll use it in one of my novels."

"One of the laborious works you insist on *calling* novels. Now, Mr. Sham—"

"Shamrock."

"—I will thank you not to interrupt me again."

"Thank you," he said.

Britta's eyes narrowed to slits. "Why are you thanking me?"

"*You* thanked *me*, which is something I never thought I'd hear from you, so I'm thanking you for thanking me."

"I didn't thank you. I never would," she said acidly.

"I distinctly heard you."

"My clear implication was that if you could shut up, I might at some future date be of a mind to thank you. But you are a talkative moron, so I will never be required to thank you for your silence or anything else."

Bobby shrugged. The professor was incapable of believing that anyone would mock her. The effort to do so was fun but unproductive.

"Now attend me carefully," she said, "while I explain to you what you have thrust yourselves into and what will happen to you. *Our* fungus is of a species never found anywhere but here. It has not been properly named—they simply call it Alpha—and its existence has not been revealed to any scientists except those who are employed by the Keppelwhite Institute. They are so highly paid that they will keep secrets—although in one sense or another, the institute also has them by the scrotum and will make them cry like babies if they even *think* about betraying the project. And what they're thinking is at all times known."

The joyful, rebellious spirit that had animated the amigos when they were fourteen now returned like a tide. Spencer raised a hand.

Britta glared at him, wordlessly demanding silence. However, when he waved his hand vigorously, she relented. "Yes, yes. What is it?"

"Are there no female scientists on the project?"

"Of course there are. Perhaps a quarter of them are women."

"Women don't have scrotums," Spencer said, "so what part of the female anatomy does the institute have them by?"

"That is a ridiculous question."

"Ah, so you don't have an answer."

"Mr. Truelove—"

"It's dove. Truedove."

Approaching the sofa, Britta said, "I have a different name for you, and it's not as stupid and syrupy as your real one. Now, if you do not remain quiet, I will summon Wayne Louis Hornfly and have him eat you alive, starting with your hands."

The threat alarmed the amigos. They shrank back on the sofa.

Their alarm amused Pastor Larry. Something that was apparently laughter issued from him, a sound like a chicken being strangled. "We'll exterminate *all* the artists, not just ninety percent of them. Painters, writers, actors, people who do origami. All of them, every last one. We will save the planet by greatly diminishing the plague of humanity and completely eradicating the disease of the arts."

Britta began to stalk through the parlor once more, her silk robe swirling around her. "The fungus we call Alpha is the largest organism in the world. It extends under forty-two-hundred acres, almost twice as much as the *pindling Armillaria* in Oregon. It weighs in the neighborhood of sixty thousand tons."

"Obese," said Bobby.

"And it is eleven thousand years old. This mass lies beneath a large part of Maple Grove and surrounding land. It was discovered thirty-seven years ago by researchers from Keppelwhite Algae and Fungi, which later merged with Keppelwhite Essential Substances."

"A division of Keppelwhite Urine and Feces," said Rebecca.

Britta would not dignify their interjections by admitting she had heard them. "It was at once recognized that there existed an immense potential for a new generation of powerful antibiotics and other drugs in the secretions of Alpha. Soon something more exciting was discovered."

"A way to make you shut up?" Bobby asked.

"In any other species of fungi, every cell is identical to every other cell. The individual grows larger by a kind of cloning. In Alpha, however, there are many profoundly integrated smaller structures within the greater mass, and in every substructure, the genotype is unique, with far more genes and more complex proteins than in any other known fungus. Yet, amazingly, these individuals that make up Alpha operate as a single organism."

At that moment, Britta was behind Pastor Larry. She reached over the back of his armchair and pulled at his shoulders. "Don't slump." Larry sat up straighter, but not straight enough to please her. She took hold of his ears. "Up, up. Stiffen your spine." The reverend's expression suggested that this pulling-on-the-ears business did not in the least embarrass or annoy him. In fact, he appeared to take pleasure in it, as if it were related to some more stimulating practice in which they engaged when alone.

Like substructures of an Alpha fungus, the amigos responded in perfect harmony; they kept their mouths shut, avoided looking at one another, and decided never to speak—or even think about—what ears might have to do with the couple's lusty relationship.

Now that Larry was smiling like a degenerate in a schoolyard and sitting up in the chair as stiff-spined as any prisoner in an electric chair anticipating the *thrill* of the current, his demon lover once more slinked around the parlor, expounding on the many wonders of Alpha.

"Some scientists on the Keppelwhite team feel Alpha shouldn't be called a fungus, that an entire new genus should be founded if it's to be properly categorized. However, to accomplish that, the existence of it would have to be made public. Given the astonishing truth of Alpha—which I've yet to reveal—the whistleblower would most likely not be believed. In any case, his intentions would be known before he could act, whereupon his life expectancy would be eleven minutes. The relationship between Alpha and the Keppelwhite family is the most valuable relationship in the history of the world, and they will do *anything* to protect it."

"Relationship?" Bobby asked.

Rebecca said, "This doesn't sound much like the family history of the altruistic Keppelwhites that every kid in Maple Grove is taught from first grade through twelfth."

Britta's sneer, expressing her intellectual contempt, would have made Einstein so doubt his theory of relativity that he might have hung himself in mortification. "Ms. Crane, do not play naive with me. You are not a bright bulb, but after a fifteen-year career in TV and film, you are not *so* stupid as to have any illusions left. Who do you think *runs* this country? The family's vaunted charitable work is accomplished through the Keppelwhite Foundation. The board of directors includes nine hundred and sixty-five men and women, all relatives of politicians or major media figures, each paid a six-figure salary to show up once a year for a meeting. Keppelwhite Financial holds the mortgages on the homes of seven hundred key bureaucrats and provides under-the-table rebates of half of each monthly mortgage payment. Keppelwhite this and Keppelwhite that—they're more ubiquitous than McDonald's. And by the way, they have gained total control of the pickle market and are trying to become the sole source in the world for ketchup."

Spencer shook his head in amazement. "I had no idea of their reach and power."

"Mr. Truelove, for a visual artist of your talent, I have no expectation you would know anything significant about anything."

"All this from an 1891 patent on the hinge," Bobby marveled. "Does a patent last forever?"

"That one does," Britta said. "In 1920, Senator Guenther Ohlendorf and Congressman Gottfried Himmelfurter—affectionately known to their constituents as 'Gunny' and 'Frank'— shepherded through the legislature a bill making that patent eternal and expanding it to include the piano hinge and the whisk broom."

"I guess maybe all of this puts Alpha in some useful context," Rebecca admitted. "But you told us the truth of the fungus was astonishing. Can we get back to that? What truth?"

Britta sat on the arm of Pastor Larry's chair and stroked his head as if he were a beloved cat. Both looked smug, as if they knew something earthshaking. Then she said, "Alpha has a brain."

"Whose brain?" Spencer asked.

"Its own brain, of course. Keppelwhite scientists estimate that of its sixty thousand tons, its brain accounts for two point five tons."

"Quite a large brain," said Larry. "It's very smart. Smarter than you, of course. Smarter than all of you combined. Far smarter than any artificial intelligence ever likely to be developed in this century."

This news did not sit well with the amigos. They looked at one another as if they had just heard how the world would end.

"Alpha supplies the Keppelwhites with concepts, designs, and formulae that make them ever richer," said Britta. "Larry and I don't care about that. We are not envious. We know who we are and like who we are, for we are at the very top of the evolutionary ladder. But . . ."

As Britta seemed about to choke on what she needed to say next, Pastor Larry picked up the narrative. "Alpha—the damn thing's noble intentions are what infuriate us. The Keppelwhites found the damn thing thirty-seven years ago. They needed a year to figure out what the damn thing was they found. They built the Keppelwhite Institute, and it took them three more years to establish contact with the damn thing. Then two more years to convince the damn thing to use its big brain for more than just dreaming and philosophizing, as it had been doing ever since it became self-aware nine thousand years ago. With some coaxing, the damn thing eventually helped the Keppelwhites in ways that also helped humanity—cures for diseases, technological break-throughs. Over the years, the crazy damn thing decided it loved humanity and would dedicate itself to the slow improvement of the human condition."

Britta rose from the arm of the chair and clenched her fists and shook them at the heavens or at least at the ceiling. "It does not understand humanity at all. The potential of that huge brain wasted. Wasted! Two point five tons of stupidity. It has the power to devise a thousand ways to wipe humanity off the Earth, but it wants to *serve* humanity. For millennia, it was indifferent to—in fact oblivious of—humanity. Then in a few short years, it mor-phed into a sanctimonious do-gooder sixty-thousand-ton pile of shit."

"The damn thing. The damn, damn thing," Pastor Larry raged, no longer sitting up straight, shrinking back in his chair, becoming a black hole of bitterness and hatred.

"Alpha possesses a form of telepathy," Britta revealed. "It is able to radiate thought waves that can make people happier if they happen to be receptive, and most of the idiots in this town are receptive. Happy and happier—that is all they want. They are, the lot of them, perpetual infants sucking at the tit of happiness. And Alpha also can produce thought waves that make people feel guilt and remorse about doing something wrong or even *thinking* about doing the wrong thing. It doesn't control them—I'll grant you that—but it *encourages* what it believes to be the right behavior. Now Maple Grove has become virtually crime-free. We can only hope that this despicable condition never takes hold beyond Maple Grove. What kind of world would it be if no one ever committed a crime? It wouldn't be a world where a sane person would want to live. Without contempt and hatred and violence and murderous envy, life would have no *flavor*."

"The damn, damn, damn thing!" roared Pastor Larry. He struggled to get up from his armchair, but his hatred and rage were so intense that they robbed him of all physical coordination. He floundered and slapped at the leather arms, at the cushion, until he collapsed once more into what now seemed less like a chair than like a huge Venus flytrap determined to swallow him.

Much more needed to be explained and understood, but before Britta Hernishen could launch into another of her stupefying performances, Rebecca asked, "Larry, I understand your late half brother, Aldous Blomhoff, was a high executive at the institute."

At the mention of his brother, Pastor Larry twitched, and his empurpled face emptied of color as if a drain plug had been pulled open in his neck. Even before the reverend spoke, any observer alert to the emotions of others would have known that his sudden pallor had nothing to do with grief. "*That* sonofabitch," said Larry. "That preening, people-loving, Pollyanna phony. If you counted all the time he spent virtue signaling and polishing his image, there was maybe one hour in the day when he wasn't thinking about himself and how wonderful he was. Maybe forty minutes. Oh, how I despised that insufferable bastard. But I hid it well. He never knew. He was the head of the Alpha Project, and he brought me into the inner circle as adviser on the ethical and spiritual issues related to Alpha and the exploitation of its abilities, which is why I know everything about their research."

Spencer held his hat on his head as if they were in such a pit of evil that someone would snatch it from him.

Britta felt it necessary to add, "Fungi, Alpha, and the hope that the creature would commit genocide and wipe out humanity—for months, that was our pillow talk."

Favoring her with a lecherous smile, Pastor Larry said, "That was such an exciting time."

"Such a fulfilling time," Britta agreed.

"So tender."

"So passionate."

Rebecca said, "I wish I had that talking card." Before either the reverend or the professor could ask what she meant, she posed another question. "Is what I heard correct—that your brother died earlier today of toe fungus?"

The reverend's ashen face acquired the soft pink radiance of unseemly delight. "It began on the big toe of the right foot. Then it spread to the other four. Across the foot, up the leg, across the abdomen, down the other leg, then back up into the chest, the heart, and all the way to the top of the head. The best part was that it kept him alive and cognizant until it had thoroughly infected him. Only when he was paralyzed head to foot and unable to speak, only when he realized he had no hope of a cure, only then did it slowly collapse his lungs and suffocate him."

Britta took his hand. He stared longingly at her. Obviously, they wanted to fly up the stairs on wings of love.

"What a horrible way to die," Rebecca said.

"Yesss," Pastor Larry replied with enthusiasm.

"I thought this was a benign fungus, if it's a fungus at all."

Britta said, "Alpha is everything you would expect of a benign intelligent fungus, if you have the wit to expect anything at all. It is optimistic, caring, understanding, forgiving, reassuring, and disgustingly sentimental. Alpha is exactly the kind of intelligent fungus that the hoi polloi would hope for if they were hoping for a fungus. The all-too-common men and women who live dull lives of no importance would open their hearts to a fungus like Alpha and feel their relationship with it gave meaning to their existence at last, and Alpha would love them in return. As a movie that you starred in, it would be intolerably middlebrow and sweet enough to kill every diabetic in the country. It was not Alpha that murdered the fatuous, people-loving Mr. Blomhoff. It was Beta."

"Praise Beta," said Pastor Larry.

47

TO MORE QUICKLY IMPART VITAL AND FEARSOME INFORMATION

In a novel of deep mystery and strangeness, informational conversations between the good guys and the bad guys nearly always come near the end of the story. They must be written in such a way that they don't bring the narrative to a stop, have entertainment value of their own, and avoid just shoveling revelations at the reader. This is often achieved by disclosing surprising and yet logical new facets to the characters (as with Britta's lustful nature), by maintaining an atmosphere of imminent violence, by dialogue that alarms or amuses, and by additional techniques that will not be revealed here, where no one is paying to learn them. However, there comes a point at which our desire to know how the hell it all ends becomes paramount. Who lives, who dies, and what kind of mess do they leave behind? This can be especially true when the author has used foreshadowing to warn that at least one of the good guys (Bobby) is very likely to perish. Consequently, a change in tactics of narration becomes essential. Remaining revelations must be made, but succinctly, dwelling less on atmosphere, trimming descriptions of characters' actions, and thus thrusting us on toward the terror, violence, and destruction that we all enjoy so much. Let's see if this works:

To Rebecca, in the parlor of the rectory, Britta and Larry appeared arrogant and self-assured, as if this confrontation must be a matter of life and death and as if the amigos were already doomed. "Beta killed Aldous Blomhoff? What is Beta?"

"Another intelligent fungus," said Britta.

Pastor Larry said, "Praise Beta."

"It's only nine thousand years old," Britta continued, "not eleven like Alpha. It weighs about forty-eight thousand tons, not sixty thousand. It lives under the portion of Maple Grove that Alpha doesn't occupy, and in acreage north of town."

Nervously adjusting his hat, Spencer said, "Two immense intelligent funguses in the same small town. Is there something special about the soil, something in the water? Do you have any theories about this?"

"The current theory," Britta said, "is that twelve thousand years ago or so, a large meteor impacted here, shattering its way deep into the earth, bearing the spores of two intelligent fungi from elsewhere in the galaxy. One developed faster than the other."

"Or," said Larry, "it was one fungus. Some spores went to the light and some to the darkness, figuratively speaking."

"So Alpha is good, and Beta is evil," Rebecca said.

Pastor Larry's glare was venomous. "You will wish you'd never said that."

Britta's expression was merely smug. "Alpha loves humanity. Beta hates it. From our perspective, *Alpha* is the evil one. Beta wants to eradicate ninety percent of humankind to save the Earth. It loves the planet. So do Larry and I. Genocide is noble in the right cause."

"It's because of the bigotry of people like you," Larry said, "that Beta won't cooperate with the institute like Alpha does."

Bobby gave Rebecca a look that said, *They're about to spring a trap on us. They wouldn't be revealing all this if they thought there was any chance of us getting out of here alive. Stay alert!*

That was a lot to convey in just a look, but so tight with one another were the amigos that she understood and nodded once.

Larry said, "Beta dared to try infecting the top officials at the institute and destroy the Alpha Project. It almost worked. It taught my hateful half brother a thing or two. Unfortunately, Alpha has already come up with a cure. Jim James and Butch Fossbocker will be well and out of the hospital tomorrow, the bastards."

Spencer said, "Sixty thousand tons, forty-eight thousand tons—what do they feed on?"

"The *Armillaria* in Oregon feeds on trees," said Britta. "It destroys forests. That doesn't happen here. Maybe Alpha and Beta draw nutrients from the soil. They won't say what they feed on."

"Why not?"

"We think they might be embarrassed."

"Embarrassed funguses?"

"Embarrassed *intelligent* funguses. Maybe part of what they feed on is worms, termites, other insects, rotting roots, bodies in the graveyard, and mole shit. If that's part of what you ate, would you want to talk about it?"

"No," Spencer admitted.

"Who wiped from our memories all that weird stuff that happened when we were fourteen?" Bobby asked.

"Alpha," said Pastor Larry. "You'd seen things you were never meant to see, including Hornfly in my library. Beta would not have allowed you to go on living. Alpha went to all that trouble to save you, an effort certainly not worth its time and energy."

Britta said, "As I've been trying to convey to you, Alpha is a sentimental Goody Two-Shoes. But as usual you have proved slow on the uptake."

"And I guess Alpha restored our memories. But why?"

"I suspect," said Britta, "it wanted you to come back to Maple Grove and take Ernest away. It's just the kind of nosy do-gooder who would think I've been a bad mother. Which is a scurrilous lie."

"That night we were lying on the gurneys in the institute," Rebecca said. "Those . . . tentacles."

"Alpha can semi-liquefy its tissue, creating appendages to manipulate and study things."

Pastor Larry managed to rise from his armchair and throw back his shoulders to brag about Beta with ideological passion. "Our Beta is a brilliant sculptor of avatars. Hornfly is a manifestation made of fungus. When the day comes that Beta can fashion creations that are perfectly realistic, it will form an army that can pass among you without notice—until suddenly they attack and eat billions of human beings alive. That'll be the day." He shivered with delight, as though the day, if it came, would be an orgasmic experience. "I'm not going to tell you when that day will be upon you. Just know that it's soon, very soon, with most people gone and the planet saved."

Being a writer with a deep understanding of human psychology, which some writers have but not others, Bobby the Sham taunted the reverend with a cunning purpose. "It's nine thousand years old, and it still hasn't learned how to create truly convincing replicas of people? What—is it an intelligent fungus with a low IQ?"

Pastor Larry was incensed. "Funguses are nearly immortal. Their sense of time isn't like yours. A thousand years is but a month to them. Beta is smarter than ten thousand of you, but it will work to its own timetable. It won't be told how or when to act. You and your friends are as impertinent as you are foolish."

"Yeah? Well, I bet Alpha can make replicas that don't have wriggling hair, orange eyes, green teeth. I bet it can make replicas whose heads aren't weirdly shaped like Hornfly's stupid head."

Pastor Larry was shaking with anger. He probably would have thrown a few punches if he had known how. "Alpha is two thousand years older. Give Beta a month, and it'll be able to do everything better than Alpha."

"Ha! A month. You mean a thousand years. As I thought—Alpha can already make perfect replicas."

Britta shoved Pastor Larry back into his armchair and came face-to-face with Bobby. "Have you any inkling what is about to happen to you, Mr. Sham? Can we agree that indeed you have no inkling? Or is it your position that you aren't a fool? What do you say? Are you confident enough to take the position that you aren't a fool? It would be interesting to hear you defend that position in a debate. It would be most instructive."

Rebecca said, "Before whatever happens that is going to happen, I have a few more questions."

"'Before whatever happens that is going to happen.' I wonder, Ms. Crane, when filming a scene written even in puerile English, how many takes are required for you to deliver the needed words in any coherent fashion? How often do your despairing director and fellow thespians have to be persuaded not to commit suicide on the set?"

Ignoring the insult, Rebecca said, "What are all the comatose people about?"

"I will answer your question, Ms. Crane, in the compassionate spirit of—and for the same reason as—a guard in a prison would bring you a meal shortly before escorting you to a room containing nothing more than a single metal chair and a long electric cord. The fungus known as Alpha inexplicably loves humanity so much that it wants to know everything it can possibly learn about our ridiculous and tedious species. Because everyone's experiences and perceptions of events are different, Alpha regards each of us as an enthralling novel, and it feels the need to 'read' as many of us as possible. When it puts a person into suspended animation, it can leaf through our millions of memories as easily as we turn the pages of a book. In one to four days, even the most complex and richly experienced of lives can be read in detail, whereupon the subject is released from suspended animation. Why Alpha wishes to read the petty lives of individuals such as yourselves, lives as shallow and clichéd and poorly written as the average novel created as a movie tie-in, I cannot explain. Not when an elegant life, a life rich in stirring drama and accomplishment, a life of passion and keen perception, such as mine, remains on the shelf."

"The damn, damn thing," Pastor Larry cursed from the depths of the chair into which he had been shoved.

Exhibiting the dogged analytic curiosity with which an actress seeks to understand a character—in this case a fungus—Rebecca said, "But *how*? How does Alpha put people into suspended animation? How does it read memories as if they're pages in a book?"

Britta Hernishen sighed wearily and covered her ears with her hands, as though she lacked the patience to continue talking to zoo animals with the hope they would understand what she told them in response to their gibbering and hooting. With another sigh, this one of the long-suffering variety, she lowered her hands and said, "Ms. Crane, I'm sure you saw a pair of pretty shoes in a shop window and can't stop thinking about them, saw some ripped dude on the street who tickled your excitable libido, but I would be most grateful if you would put aside all such distractions and try your very best to think about what I tell you. Is that a possibility? Do you sincerely believe you can summon the concentration and possess the potential for comprehension to do such a thing?"

"I'll try," Rebecca said.

"You precious child, that's all I ask of you—that you try. I am aware that the effort alone will exhaust you. If it develops that you are unable to grasp the implications of what I tell you, I will not be angry or even impatient. I will simply extend my best wishes to you and get on with my life."

"Okay."

"Very well. Here it is. I do not know how Alpha puts people in suspended animation or how it reads their memories. No one possesses an answer to those questions. No one. This is a world of mysteries. There are many things about the world that no one understands. You must accept the existence of the unknown— and even the unknowable—and just get on with wasting your life in foolish pursuits. As I have already told you, Alpha's brain weighs as much as two and a half tons. It is therefore forty thousand times larger than *your* brain. Over thousands of years, a brain that large will have evolved powers beyond our ability to imagine.

And now that I have patiently endured questioning alike to the incessant badgering of a three-year-old, I have only one question of my own. *What have you done with my son?*"

To Rebecca, Spencer said, "She just implied that your brain weighs only two ounces."

Britta said, "I am amazed and astonished—the first a condition of the mind, the latter of the heart—that any of you possesses the math skills just demonstrated. *Now what have you done with my son?*"

Even if there had been time to take offense, Rebecca wouldn't have done so. What was the point? Anyhow, time had run out. Heavy footsteps sounded from the rear of the house, hobnail boots crashing against the floor. There could be no doubt who had arrived either through the back door or out of the kitchen-sink drain.

Bobby glanced at Rebecca. The look he gave her said, *If I die here in the next few minutes or even an hour from now, maybe two hours, whenever, I want you to know that I love you like a friend, always have and always will, but recently I've realized that I also love you in the most profound romantic sense that a man can love a woman, and I will die for you if it comes to that.*

This was considerably more information than the earlier glance had been meant to impart, but the amigos were so simpatico that Rebecca understood everything Bobby meant to convey, not just in a broad sense, but in every particular and nuance. Because the feeling was mutual, she almost teared up. However, when a monster is coming, the last thing one ought to do is tear up, for the creature might take satisfaction in the mistaken apprehension that you're shedding tears of dread. By a nod and a small smile and a wink, Rebecca let Bobby know she felt toward him the very thing he felt toward her.

Hornfly hove into sight with all the drama of a sea monster suddenly rising out of the waves to tower over a ship. He appeared to be bigger, stronger, uglier, and even more fierce than he had been while holding a severed head in the Liberty Park pavilion. He seemed to fill the archway between the hall and the parlor. Clearly, he had taken time to refine and practice his entrance.

"Praise Beta," declared Pastor Larry, thrusting out of the armchair. "Praise Hornfly."

"Isn't he a handsome boy?" Britta said. "Isn't he the most handsome boy you've ever seen?"

"Hail Beta!" the reverend cried. "Hail Hornfly!"

The amigos were chilled head to foot and back to front.

If Hornfly had not been standing there, if he'd been lying in a huge black bassinet that was skirted with black taffeta, hooded and flounced with black organza, this moment would have been like the end of the last chapter of *Rosemary's Baby*, except absurd.

"Hail Beta! Hail Hornfly!"

At least from this side of the publishing process, it seems to have worked well to minimize the number of words devoted to setting, atmosphere, and the thoughts of the characters in order to provide answers to the many remaining questions without losing momentum, as would have been the case if the bones of the chapter had been fully fleshed with another four thousand words. One hopes it worked well from *your* side of the publishing process.

"Hail Beta! Hail Hornfly!"

48

WAYNE LOUIS HORNFLY

So there they were, the three amigos, still in the parlor with Britta and Pastor Larry and Hornfly, where it seemed that nothing good could happen. Although Saint Mark's Ladies of Compassion and Saint Mark's Gentlemen for Jesus still gathered here twice a month, as they had done twenty-one years earlier, this wasn't an evening when either group had scheduled a meeting. Considering that the reverend and his lady friend had set these hours aside for the satisfaction of their lust, it was unlikely that they were expecting anyone to visit—unless they were even more degenerate than yet revealed.

Getting past Hornfly would be next to impossible. Even if the amigos could somehow distract the eater of people and slip away, they were not likely to get out of this place alive. Surely slime monsters molting gobs of fungus, like the one that removed Ernie from the window seat, would be waiting elsewhere in the house to block their escape. Beta had condemned them to death, and although it weighed only forty-eight thousand tons and was only nine thousand years old, it was nonetheless a formidable enemy.

Stepping out of the archway and into the parlor, Hornfly spoke in that game-show-host voice that was scarier than it should have been. "Spencer Truedove of Chicago, Robert Shamrock of all points on the compass, and Rebecca Crane of Malibu, welcome to your execution. Twenty-one years ago, on Halloween night, we laid down the rules, and you broke them by Thanksgiving. You were saved by the despicable squish they call Alpha, a disgusting human-loving sentimentalist, when it repressed your memories regarding the truth of Maple Grove and became your guardian. By returning from afar, where we couldn't get to you, you have brought about your own destruction."

Pastor Larry thrilled to the monster's threat. "Hail Beta! Hail Hornfly!"

Addressing the amigos, Hornfly said, "Which of you losers would rather be devoured first, sparing yourself the horror and terror of watching your friends be eaten? Do we have a volunteer?"

"Before we get into all of that," Rebecca said, "I have a few questions."

"Questions? You have no right to ask questions of us. You have a right to die and nothing more."

Britta regarded Rebecca much as the Red Queen in Wonderland regarded an annoying child like Alice. "You had your chance to ask questions. No one denied you the chance. You had a thousand stupid questions. Now you die, and my son will no longer fall under your malign influence, which he has since he was fourteen."

Raising her chin defiantly, Rebecca said, "I have not posed questions to Mr. Hornfly, only to you. You were tedious. In whatever form it takes, Beta is far more interesting than you."

"Bite off her head," Britta told Hornfly.

"We don't like this Rebecca person," Hornfly said, "but we also don't like being told what to do. We will bite her head off, but only when we're ready. Besides, she has called us 'interesting.'"

"More interesting than Alpha," Rebecca said.

Spencer and Bobby were gaping at Rebecca, and their gape was not intended to convey as much as a glance conveyed, only this: *What the hell are you doing?*

Rebecca was fearful but not flat-out terrified, which surprised her. It also concerned her, because controlled terror, rather than merely fear, made the mind sharper and inspired greater caution in a lethal confrontation. Terror didn't cancel courage. Heather Ashmont had been more terrified of Judyface than anyone in the cast, yet she was the hero who stood against him effectively, the only survivor.

"What I want to know, what I *need* to know," she told Hornfly, "is how you ate Björn Skollborg's head so fast. So far as I could see at the time, no major teeth were involved."

Hornfly was such a hideous beast that it was difficult to interpret his facial expressions, but he appeared to swell with pride. "We produce an acid so intense it dissolves bone and flesh instantly. Even as the substance of Skollborg dissolved, we sucked it into ourselves. Not a drop lost. A construct like Hornfly is for the purpose of destroying humanity on the Day of Fun. It's designed to be as lethal as possible. Thus the acid thing."

"Fascinating," Rebecca said. "I would never have thought that a fungus could develop such biological-engineering skills."

"Well, we are an immense colony of integrated funguses with an enormous brain and millennia with nothing to do but prepare to kill ninety percent of humanity."

Rebecca began to understand that terror failed to overcome her because she sensed a powerful ally nearby. This was a convincing psychic perception, a supernatural awareness, not just a hunch, and certainly not just a wish such as that unicorns were real and would come prancing into the room. Of course the presence of Bobby and Spencer gave her courage—dear friends always did that—however, they weren't the ally that she could *feel* close and then rushing closer, a building pressure.

Stalling for time, she said, "Why the name Wayne Louis Hornfly for your avatar, or what you call a 'construct'?"

"We thought it sounded cute," said Hornfly. "Don't you think it sounds cute?"

"I hate this," said Britta. "The master of Armageddon shouldn't be saying it wants to be cute."

"'Hornfly,'" said Rebecca, "sounds scary, but Wayne and Louis might be the names of nice boys who live next door. Altogether, combining scary and nice, it's an effective name, catchy."

"Thank you," said Hornfly. "Now, no more questions. We have not bided our time for nine thousand years just to answer questions from a TV-sitcom personality."

"I'm not a 'personality.' I'm an actor."

To Hornfly, Britta said, "That is her position, by which I mean her contention. She has taken that position in the past, but I have yet to hear her defend it credibly."

"Besides," Rebecca said, "I also make feature films."

"We are aware of feature films," Hornfly assured her. "They are religious services attended by worshippers of nonexistent demigods such as Superman, Aquaman, Batman, and Ant-Man. Have you portrayed such a demigod?"

"No."

With a sneer so sharp and fixed that it was likely to become a permanent feature of her face, Britta told Hornfly, "The bitch has appeared on *Dancing with the Stars*."

"That is a damnable lie," Rebecca said, and it was a lie.

"She's a true star," said Bobby, "not just a celebrity."

Spencer said, "She's a fine, fine actress. She can act the pants off anyone in the business."

"*There* is a true statement," said Britta.

"We have never before eaten a fine actress. We will eat one now." Hornfly moved boldly into the room, full of supercaustic digestive acid and ready to deploy it.

Bobby stepped into the monster's way. "Hey, hey, hey! You leave her alone," he shouted.

Although Bobby was a novelist who avoided clichés and tiresome moments to be found in countless novels written by others, he did not have the time, in this situation, to sit down at a computer and craft a line of clever dialogue or to conceive a credible attack on the monster. This was real life, where clichés and stupid actions were the coin of the realm, so to speak. Hornfly knocked him aside with such violence that he was lifted off his feet and slammed into the sofa, tipping that mohair marvel onto its hind legs and falling over it as it was upended, crashing to the parlor floor in a shudder of humiliation as a cascade of decorative pillows spilled over him and, with their tassels, tickled him into a fit of sneezing.

"Hail Beta!" Pastor Larry exclaimed. "Hail Hornfly!"

As Hornfly loomed over Rebecca, she said, "I have one more question."

"As we told you," the monster told her, "no more questions are permitted. Your time is up. The buzzer has sounded. You have lost. It's dinnertime."

"That's so unfair. You're big and scary and all that, but I never thought of you as unfair. Until now. You are so unfair."

Hornfly's orange eyes dimmed. His face squinched with what might have been puzzlement and hurt feelings. "We are not unfair."

"*You* asked me a question. I was nice enough to answer you. So it seems to me that it's only fair I be allowed one more question."

Scratching his head of wriggling hair, Hornfly said, "What question did we ask you?"

"You wanted to know if I'd ever played a nonexistent demigod like Superman. I told you I hadn't, and that was true."

He stared down at her, into her eyes, and she stared boldly up into his.

A terrible and expectant silence pooled in the parlor until Britta said, "Damn it all, bite her head off."

The impatient pastor shouted, "Heil Beta! Heil Hornfly! Bite her head off!"

To Rebecca, Hornfly said, "One more. Don't try to trick us into two or three."

"Thank you," Rebecca said. "I'm so sorry I called you unfair, but you seemed to deserve it at the time. Here's what I'm curious about. When the Day of Fun comes, which will actually last for a year or more, you'll kill ninety percent of humanity to save the planet but leave ten percent to enjoy life in a less populated world. That ten percent will obviously include Pastor Larry and Professor Hernishen. Now, I know you aren't a liar. An intelligent forty-eight-thousand-ton fungus who is immortal and who possesses awesome powers has no need to lie. I have no doubt you'll tell me the truth. Once the Day of Fun has ended, however long that might prove to be, how much longer will the ten percent be allowed to live, and what will you do with them?"

"You've just posed a two-part question," Hornfly said, "but that's fair. We will not devour you until we respond to both parts. At this point, we imagine that the ten percent will be kept alive for three months, although we hope to be able to accomplish what needs to be done in two. You must understand that nothing of this scale has ever been attempted before, so our schedule is necessarily approximate rather than precise. From the ten percent, we intend to select perhaps a thousand of the most interesting specimens. We will then devour the rest."

"That is so very and entirely wrong," said Pastor Larry. "That, that, that is amoral, outrageous."

Perhaps for the first time in her life, Britta was speechless.

Hornfly continued, "The thousand will be put into suspended animation or perhaps placed into large jars of preservatives to be displayed in a museum so that we never forget how disgusting and repellent your species was. There. We believe we have answered your question as fully as it can be answered at this time."

The presence of an ally, which Rebecca had perceived in part as an increasing pressure, like that of an impending thunderstorm exerted as it built toward the first flash of lightning, was stronger by the second, but no anti-fungus SWAT team appeared. Her mind was spinning at top speed for her, which was as fast as anyone's mind could race, but she could not see any way she—or even Heather Ashmont—could thwart the monster's murderous intent.

Hornfly had placed his hands on her shoulders and by some strange power had rendered her unable to pull away from him. He lowered his hateful face toward hers, and his mouth stretched wide, stretched wider, until it was almost as wide as his head. At the back of that greedy orifice, a bulbous gland rose out of the throat, no doubt the sac containing the acid that could instantly dissolve bone and flesh.

Rebecca regretted that she would never have an opportunity to play a dedicated epidemiologist who saved the world from a plague or an idiot savant barely able to speak but gifted with the ability to write great symphonies (which was the kind of role for which she would likely receive an Oscar). Because her mind worked so quickly, she also had time to regret that she'd never see her amigos again or rescue Ernie, or marry Bobby, or have children, or persuade Spencer that he would be handsome and personable and successful without the porkpie hat.

Perhaps four seconds before the acid sac would have burst and seven seconds before her dissolving head would have been sucked into Hornfly's maw, two heating-vent grilles, set high in opposite walls, exploded off their mountings. From the ductwork erupted tentacles formed—as far as we understand—of fungus sludge. They were whip-quick, elongating until they reached the center of the parlor and wrapped around Hornfly without touching Rebecca. They ripped him away from her.

Because of fear or shock or merely consternation, the Beta avatar was not able to hold the shape that had been Wayne Louis Hornfly. It morphed into a vaguely humanoid entity which probably resembled the molting slime monster that had taken Ernie out of the window seat. In an instant, the furious tentacles tore the disgusting creature apart; pieces were flung hither and yon. Like the molts in Ernie's basement, these lumps of muck began to crawl and hump and slither, not with the intention of rejoining a mother mass this time, but frantic to escape the wrath of Alpha. They tried to hide under chairs and tables, behind a plant stand, in the knee space of a small corner desk. They were faster than the molts had been, but not fast enough. The two thick tentacles split into a dozen slender appendages and rapidly probed here and there throughout the room. They found, clutched, and absorbed every desperately fleeing scrap of Hornfly and then retreated into the ductwork.

Bobby came to Rebecca and took her into his arms, and she held fast to him for a moment. She went to Spencer, and they held fast to each other. Spencer and Bobby held fast to each other, and then they were done with that.

The amigos stood in silence together, staring at Pastor Larry and Britta Hernishen. The reverend and the professor stared back at them; the wicked pair looked as if they had learned nothing from what they had just seen and been told.

Rebecca said, "You are very bad people."

"You deserve each other," Bobby said.

Spencer said, "We'll show ourselves out," which they did.

49

WHITE HORSE, BLACK HAT

When they came out of Saint Mark's rectory, the sun still bathed Maple Grove in the golden light of late afternoon because the amigos preferred to return to the last block of Harriet Nelson Lane when they could see the Nelsoneers coming.

At the house where Spencer had lived alone during his teens, on the second floor, Bobby pulled the foldaway bed out of the wall.

Ernie was tucked in there, wearing the clothes in which they had dressed him at the hospital two days ago. He was awake and patiently waiting to be released. As he clambered out, he said, "Hi, guys! Alpha finished reading my memory a little while ago, woke me, and told me everything that's happened since you came back. It's wild, huh? Totally nuts. I'm sorry Mother wanted you all dead, but you know how she is."

Rebecca hugged him, and Bobby hugged him, and Spencer hugged him, and they all engaged in a group hug, and then they got out of there before the doorbell rang and neighbors showed up with food.

Night had *still* not fallen when they arrived at Ernie's house. He had not bathed since before being admitted to the hospital, and he felt unclean.

While Ernie took a quick shower and changed into fresh clothes, the other three amigos gathered in the kitchen. Rebecca tried to resist wiping down everything with an antiseptic solution—and found that she could control the urge.

When Ernie reappeared, he said, "I'm starved. What about dinner at Adorno's?"

That sounded good to all of them, but just then an ear-pleasing voice spoke to them from the sink drain. "Hey up there, it's only me, Alpha. Fear not." A mass of fungus sludge erupted from the sink drain, spilled over the counter, and piled up on the floor.

Initially it seemed like an unnecessary volume of material, but then it shaped itself into a white horse, and the volume proved to be required. From the horse's mouth came the voice that first spoke from the drain. "As you know, I find it morally objectionable ever to deceive human beings by passing for one of them. I respect your species. I love you guys. So I thought . . . well, a horse. Horses are so beautiful. It's not a real horse. It's not going to take a dump here in the kitchen. Is a horse okay with you?"

The four amigos agreed that a horse was okay.

"Here's the thing," said the horse. "When I started reading Ernie's memories, I was deeply moved. Deeply, deeply moved. He has suffered so much, but he remains an optimist in love with life. He holds no grudge regarding anything that happened to him. Ernie is incapable of resentment, even toward his mother, which in my book makes him a saint. Through Ernie's memories, I became familiar with all of you, deeply familiar and deeply moved. Are you with me?"

The amigos said they were with him. After their experiences of the past two days, they found nothing at all strange about engaging in a conversation with a horse.

"I fell in love with all of you," the horse said. "I don't mean romantic love. I'm a fungus, after all. Platonic love. But very deep platonic love. You are special people. If I could cry real tears right now, I would, but I can only cry fake tears, and that wouldn't be right. That would be disrespectful, especially because the tears would be coming from a horse. Please don't feel awkward about my expression of affection. I'm an old softie, a *very* old softie, and that's just the way I am."

The amigos assured him that they did not feel awkward and that in fact they were touched. It was always a blessing to hear that someone cared about you, even if the someone wasn't human.

"I made a mistake years ago," the horse admitted, "when I took the liberty of repressing the memories of what you saw in the church basement and of your encounters with Hornfly. I wasn't trying to protect Beta. Who would? I was only trying to protect myself from being discovered by others than the folks at the institute. I am basically a shy individual. I abhor the prospect of fame. I love people, adore people, but the idea of great crowds of them tramping over these four thousand acres, hoping to talk to me . . . I would be mortified. But because your memories were repressed, you became neurotic. Are you at all aware that you are neurotic?"

"We've had an inkling," Rebecca admitted.

The horse said, "Bobby, you travel the world incessantly, never settling down. You're fleeing from something, but you don't know what."

"I know now," Bobby said. "From Hornfly. From Beta. I can put that behind me now."

"You, Rebecca, always scrubbing things because what happened left you feeling unclean. Not because you *should* feel unclean, but because you couldn't remember and therefore imagined worse things than what really happened. Spencer, why do you wear that black hat twenty-four hours a day, seven days a week?"

With something akin to affection, Spencer patted the crown of his hat with one hand. "It's part of my image, makes me memorable. Without it, I'm the kind of person who fades into the furniture."

"Okay, then," the horse said, "that had nothing to do with me repressing your memories. It's because your father endlessly told you that you were as plain as white bread, with a personality less interesting than that of a squash. I'm not to blame for that. I feel much better about myself. But please get rid of the hat. Your dad was a jackass. He still is—a jackass in prison."

Ernie said, "What about me? What are my neuroses?"

"You don't have any. You're the sweetest, most uncomplicated soul. Your memories are not colored by negative emotions. But you have allowed yourself to become a mama's boy—and she's one really bad mama. You need to get away from her and stay away. Sell your house, leave Maple Grove, live near your amigos, and write your wonderful songs."

"Will you come visit?" Ernie asked. "Maybe not as a horse, at least not such a big horse. That would be awkward. Maybe a bird?"

"Neither I nor Beta has any power to control our avatars beyond this place where we have grown," the horse said regretfully. "But if from time to time you get an emoji that is a smiling fungus, you'll know who sent it."

Rebecca stepped closer to the horse and smoothed a hand along its magnificent neck. "Why is it that you speak of yourself as 'I' and 'me,' while Beta says 'we' and 'us'?"

"Beta is a fascist-communist fungus that favors collectivism. I am a fungus with a great respect for freedom. We will be contesting over Maple Grove for a long time—another reason you don't want to be here. Beta will be destructive. Although I will do my best to be *con*structive, I will no doubt make mistakes. My brain does not weigh two and a half tons, as the institute estimates, but two and a third tons. We grow slowly. I am embarrassed to say it will be two hundred sixty years until my brain weighs two and a half tons. I believe I have thus far done the right thing by making this town crime-free, but because my brain is not yet as big as it should be, I suspect I have inspired too intense a feeling of community among the residents in the last block of Harriet Nelson Lane."

"You might be right about that," Bobby said.

"However," Rebecca assured Alpha, "in general you've done a great job."

"A spectacular job," said Spencer and Bobby simultaneously.

"No one could have done better," said Ernie.

The horse lowered its head, humbled by praise. "Ah, shucks."

From a bowl of fruit on the kitchen island, Rebecca plucked an apple and offered it.

Whatever Alpha fed on, it didn't feed on apples, and it didn't feed itself through an avatar. However, the amigos and the fungus understood this was a gesture that symbolized many things, in fact too many to start listing them all at this late point in the story. Suffice it to say the horse that wasn't a horse ate the apple that definitely was an apple. Rebecca didn't take further fruit from the bowl, because one symbolic apple was enough to make her point.

s seen   ) be the   moment for the   igos to hank the horse and hug it goodbye, whereupon it would become fungus sludge once more and return to Alpha by way of the sink drain.

Evidently it was not the ideal moment, after all, because the horse had something more to say. "My dear friends, if you remain in town beyond tomorrow, Beta might find a way to harm you. It's always scheming. Beta turned evil eight thousand years ago, and it's not likely to join an evil-fungus redemption program. Besides, there isn't any evil-fungus redemption program. I'll keep you safe for twenty-four hours, which is all I can be sure of. Have a wonderful dinner at Adorno's and a good night's sleep at Spreading Oaks Motor Hotel, but hightail it out of here by tomorrow afternoon. I have already given the institute a cure for the lethal toe fungus with which Beta afflicted them, but you never know what will come next."

Now the amigos flanked the horse and hugged it. The magnificent equine avatar became fungus sludge once more and returned to Alpha by way of the sink drain, leaving the friends emotionally exhausted.

Ernie suggested that they sleep here rather than at the motel. He had enough bedrooms to accommodate them.

That invitation allowed them to walk to Adorno's as they had often walked the picturesque streets of Maple Grove when they had been young and nerds. So that they could fully enjoy the beauty of the town, it *still* remained afternoon, with everything bathed in golden light, the Victorian architecture of the houses conveying a comforting sense of stability and timelessness.

50

AMIGOS

Sixteen months later, in Southern California, the sun rose and set as the tables of rotation and revolution of the Earth predicted it would. By that Thanksgiving, all was normal in the lives of the amigos. In the late morning, Ernie and Spencer drove to Rebecca and Bobby's house, where they intended to spend the day preparing a feast for their dinner. The four lived within ten minutes of one another.

On this occasion, no one who has followed their story should be expecting monsters of any variety or any degree whatsoever of life-and-death drama. That is of no interest to them now, for they are among the fortunate who have gotten past the monsters of childhood and arrived at a place where they can be themselves without having to explain themselves, where they can know themselves without being discouraged by what they know.

The great novelist Thomas Hardy (cited earlier) would not have found much material in this simple gathering, although he had possessed a generous, kind heart that allowed him to appreciate the value of friendship and the joy to be found in common things. Thomas Hardy's ashes were placed in the Poets' Corner of Westminster Abbey, but his heart was buried in Dorsetshire, in that landscape and among those people he had celebrated in his writing.

Robert Shamrock—Bobby the Sham—would one day be interred in just one place. It would not be Maple Grove. The amigos expected to live for decades yet, but they had taken inspiration from some of the residents who lived at the end of Harriet Nelson Lane; they purchased enough grave plots to accommodate them and however many loved ones they were likely to build lives with in years to come.

Throughout their childhood and adolescence, they dreaded going home in the dark to houses where no one lived with them or where those who lived with them were no less strangers than would be any nameless and solitary figure met on a windswept plain or on a dock at night in some port on the far side of the Earth. Friendship is a kind of love, and even on nights when one of the amigos is alone, they live in the light of their friendship. At the end of our days in this world, each of us goes home in the dark, to what we cannot know. The prospect of that journey is fearsome, but if we have loved and been loved, we do not go alone. We go with the memory of light and those who shared it with us, and if our hope is not misplaced, we go from light into light. See, no monsters.

ABOUT THE AUTHOR

International bestselling author Dean Koontz was a senior in college when he won an *Atlantic Monthly* fiction competition. He has never stopped writing. Koontz is the author of *The Bad Weather Friend, After Death, The House at the End of the World, The Big Dark Sky*, and seventy-nine *New York Times* bestsellers, fourteen of which were #1: *One Door Away from Heaven, From the Corner of His Eye, Midnight, Cold Fire, The Bad Place, Hideaway, Dragon Tears, Intensity, Sole Survivor, The Husband, Odd Hours, Relentless, What the Night Knows*, and *77 Shadow Street*. Hailed by *Rolling Stone* as "America's most popular suspense novelist," Koontz has published books in thirty-eight languages and sold more than five hundred million copies worldwide. Born and raised in Pennsylvania, he now lives in Southern California with his wife, Gerda, their golden retriever, Elsa, and the enduring spirits of their goldens Trixie and Anna. For more information, visit his website at www.deankoontz.com.